Fourteen master criminal minds create a killing
collection of shocking deception and ingenious
acts of evil!

FELONIOUS ASSAULTS

Other Mystery Anthologies
Edited by Bill Pronzini and Martin H. Greenberg

Published by Ivy Books:

FELONIOUS ASSAULTS

EDITED BY BILL PRONZINI AND MARTIN H. GREENBERG

IVY BOOKS • NEW YORK

Ivy Books
Published by Ballantine Books
Copyright © 1989 by Bill Pronzini and Martin H. Greenberg

Library of Congress Catalog Card Number: 89-91132

ISBN 0-8041-0295-3

Manufactured in the United States of America

First Edition: July 1989

Acknowledgments

"Great-Aunt Allie's Flypapers," by P. D. James. Copyright © 1979 by P. D. James. First published in *Verdict of Thirteen*. Reprinted by permission of Roberta Pryor Inc. and Elaine Greene Ltd. (England).

"A Reason to Die," by Michael Collins. Copyright © 1985 by Dennis Lynds. First published in *New Black Mask #2*. Reprinted by permission of the author.

"Little Lamb," by Bill Pronzini. Copyright © 1988 by Bill Pronzini. First published in *Small Felonies*. Reprinted by permission of the author.

"Chee's Witch," by Tony Hillerman. Copyright © 1986 by Tony Hillerman. First published in *New Black Mask #7*. Reprinted by permission of the author.

"Collecting Ackermans," by Lawrence Block. Copyright © 1977 by Lawrence Block. First published in *Alfred Hitchcock's Mystery Magazine*. Reprinted by permission of the author.

"The Man Who Shot Lewis Vance," by Stuart M. Kaminsky. Copyright © 1984 by Stuart M. Kaminsky. First published in *The Eyes Have It*. Reprinted by permission of the author.

"The Granny Woman," by Dorothy B. Hughes. Copyright © 1963 by Dorothy B. Hughes. First published in *Gamma*. Reprinted by permission of the author.

"The Siren and the Shill," by John Jakes. Copyright © 1956 by Atlantis Publishing Co., Inc.; copyright renewed 1984 by John Jakes. First published in *Accused*. Reprinted by permission of the author.

Acknowledgments

Contents

Introduction

The crime story has undergone numerous refinements and updatings during the twentieth century. It reflects its time perhaps better than any other form of popular writing, and therefore has not only flourished but has taken its rightful place as a major facet of world literature. Today the popularity of the crime story is at such an all-time high that this may be termed the "New Golden Age of Crime Fiction," owing in no small part to the growing number of innovative writers working to stretch the once-confining limits of the genre.

Felonious Assaults is the fifth in a series of anthologies designed to bring the modern reader some of the most unusual, finely crafted, and entertaining stories by today's crime fiction specialists, as well as by important figures in other areas of popular and mainstream fiction. The first four volumes in the series—*Prime Suspects, Suspicious Characters, Criminal Elements,* and *Homicidal Acts*—contain the work of such luminaries as Stephen King, Ruth Rendell, Loren D. Estleman, Donald E. Westlake, John Jakes, P. D. James, John D. MacDonald, Lawrence Block, Ed McBain, Isaac Asimov, Robert Bloch, Marcia Muller, Brian Garfield, Jonathan Gash, Simon Brett, Edward D. Hoch, William Campbell Gault, Sara Paretsky, John Lutz, Sue Grafton, Tony Hillerman, Richard S. Prather, Joseph Hansen, Edward Gorman, Norman Mailer, Leslie Charteris, Ray Bradbury, Margaret Millar, Arthur C. Clarke, Stephen Greenleaf, and Jesse Hill Ford. This volume features wholly different stories by some of the above, plus first-rate efforts by Stuart M. Kaminsky, Harry Kemelman, Michael Collins, Dorothy B. Hughes, Clark Howard, and Jack Adrian.

Future entries in the series will showcase different works by many of these writers, and by such others as Eric Ambler, Hugh Pentecost, Jack Finney, Dorothy Salisbury Davis, and Robert J. Randisi—most if not all the best writers producing contemporary mystery and suspense fiction.

Good reading.

—Bill Pronzini and
Martin H. Greenberg

Great-Aunt Allie's Flypapers

•

P. D. James

Before turning to mainstream suspense novels in 1980 with her best-selling Innocent Blood, *P. D. James published six well-received mysteries about Chief Superintendent Adam Dalgliesh. These include* Cover Her Face *(1962),* Unnatural Causes *(1967),* Shroud for a Nightingale *(1971), and* Death of an Expert Witness *(1977). Dalgliesh's appearance in a short story is quite rare—and he is in rare form in this unconventional tale of the solving of a sixty-year-old crime.*

"**Y**ou see, my dear Adam," explained the Canon gently as he walked with Chief Superintendent Dalgliesh under the vicarage elms, "useful as the legacy would be to us, I wouldn't feel happy in accepting it if Great-Aunt Allie came by her money in the first place by wrongful means."

What the Canon meant was that he and his wife wouldn't be happy to inherit Great-Aunt Allie's fifty thousand pounds or so if, sixty-seven years earlier, she had poisoned her elderly husband with arsenic in order to get it. As Great-Aunt Allie had been accused and acquitted of just that charge in a 1902 trial, which for her Hampshire neighbors had rivaled the Coronation as a public spectacle, the Canon's scruples were not altogether irrelevant. Admittedly, thought Dalgliesh, most people faced with the prospect of fifty thousand pounds would be happy to subscribe to the commonly accepted convention that once an English court has pronounced its verdict, the final truth of the matter has been established once and for all. There may possibly be a higher judicature in the next world, but hardly in this. And so Hubert Boxdale might normally have been happy to believe. But faced with the prospect of an unexpected fortune, his scrupulous conscience was troubled. The gentle but obstinate voice went on.

2

"Apart from the moral principle of accepting tainted money, it wouldn't bring us happiness. I often think of the poor woman driven restlessly around Europe in her search for peace, of that lonely life and unhappy death."

Dalgliesh recalled that Great-Aunt Allie had moved in a predictable progress with her retinue of servants, current lover, and general hangers-on from one luxury Riviera hotel to the next, with stays in Paris or Rome as the mood suited her. He was not sure that this orderly program of comfort and entertainment could be described as being restlessly driven around Europe or that the old lady had been primarily in search of peace. She had died, he recalled, by falling overboard from a millionaire's yacht during a rather wild party given by him to celebrate her eighty-eighth birthday. It was perhaps not an edifying death by the Canon's standards, but he doubted whether she had, in fact, been unhappy at the time. Great-Aunt Allie (it was impossible to think of her by any other name), if she had been capable of coherent thought, would probably have pronounced it a very good way to go. But this was hardly a point of view he could put to his companion.

Canon Hubert Boxdale was Superintendent Adam Dalgliesh's godfather. Dalgliesh's father had been his Oxford contemporary and lifelong friend. He had been an admirable godfather, affectionate, uncensorious, genuinely concerned. In Dalgliesh's childhood he had been mindful of birthdays and imaginative about a small boy's preoccupations and desires. Dalgliesh was very fond of him and privately thought him one of the few really good men he had known. It was only surprising that the Canon had managed to live to seventy-one in a carnivorous world in which gentleness, humility, and unworldliness are hardly conducive to survival, let alone success. But his goodness had in some sense protected him. Faced with such manifest innocence, even those who exploited him, and they were not a few, extended some of the protection and compassion they might show to the slightly subnormal.

"Poor old darling," his daily woman would say, pocketing pay for six hours when she had worked five and helping herself to a couple of eggs from his refrigerator. "He's really not fit to be let out alone." It had surprised the then young and slightly priggish Detective Constable Dalgliesh to realize that the Canon knew perfectly well about the hours and the eggs, but thought that Mrs. Copthorne with five children and an indolent husband needed both more than he did. He also knew that if he started paying for five hours, she would promptly work only four and extract another two eggs and that this small and only dishonesty was somehow necessary to her self-esteem. He was good. But he was not a fool.

He and his wife were, of course, poor. But they were not unhappy; indeed, it was a word impossible to associate with the Canon. The death of his two sons in the 1939 war had saddened but not destroyed him. But he had anxieties. His wife was suffering from disseminated sclerosis and was finding it increasingly hard to manage. There were comforts and appliances that she would need. He was now, belatedly, about to retire and his pension would be small. The legacy would enable them both to live in comfort for the rest of their lives and would also, Dalgliesh had no doubt, give them the pleasure of doing more for their various lame dogs. Really, he thought, the Canon was an almost embarrassingly deserving candidate for a modest fortune. Why couldn't the dear silly old noodle take the cash and stop worrying? He said cunningly: "She was found not guilty, you know, by an English jury, and it all happened nearly seventy years ago. Couldn't you bring yourself to accept their verdict?"

But the Canon's scrupulous mind was impervious to such sly innuendos. Dalgliesh told himself that he should have remembered what, as a small boy, he had discovered about Uncle Hubert's conscience; that it operated as a warning bell and that, unlike most people, he never pretended that it hadn't sounded or that he hadn't heard it or that, having heard it, something must be wrong with the mechanism.

"Oh, I did accept it while she was alive. We never met, you know. I didn't wish to force myself on her. After all, she was a wealthy woman. Our ways of life were very different. But I usually wrote briefly at Christmas and she sent a card in reply. I wanted to keep some contact in case, one day, she might want someone to turn to and would remember that I am a priest."

And why should she want a priest? thought Dalgliesh. To clear her conscience? Was that what the dear old boy had in mind? So he must have had doubts from the beginning. But of course he had! Dalgliesh knew something of the story, and the general feeling of the family and friends was that Great-Aunt Allie had been extremely lucky to escape the gallows. His own father's view, expressed with reticence, reluctance, and compassion, had not in essentials differed from that given by a local reporter at the time.

"How on earth did she expect to get away with it? Damn lucky to escape topping, if you ask me."

"The news of the legacy came as a complete surprise?" asked Dalgliesh.

"Indeed, yes. We never met except at that first and only Christmas six weeks after her marriage, when my grandfather died. We always talk of her as Great-Aunt Allie, but in fact, as you know, she married my grandfather. But it seemed impossible to think of her as a step-grandmother. There was the usual family gathering at Colebrook Croft at the time and I was there with my parents and my twin sisters. I was only four and the twins were barely eight months old. I can remember nothing of my grandfather or of his wife. After the murder—if one has to use that dreadful word—my mother returned home with us children, leaving my father to cope with the police, the solicitors, and the newsmen. It was a terrible time for him. I don't think I was even told that Grandfather was dead until about a year later. My old nurse, who had been given Christmas as a holiday to visit her own family, told me that soon after my return home. I asked her if Grandfather was now young and beautiful for always. She, poor woman, took it as a sign of infant prognostication and piety. Poor Neillie was sadly superstitious and sentimental, I'm afraid. But I knew nothing of Grandfather's death at the time and certainly can recall nothing of the visit or of my new step-grandmother. Mercifully, I was little more than a baby when the murder was done."

"She was a music hall artiste, wasn't she?" asked Dalgliesh.

"Yes, and a very talented one. My grandfather met her when she was working with a partner in a hall in Cannes. He had gone to the south of France with a manservant for his health. I understand that she extracted a gold watch from his chain and when he claimed it, told him that he was English, had recently suffered from a stomach ailment, had two sons and a daughter, and was about to have a wonderful surprise. It was all correct except that his only daughter had died in childbirth, leaving him a granddaughter, Marguerite Goddard."

"And all easily guessable from his voice and appearance," said Dalgliesh. "I suppose the surprise was the marriage?"

"It was certainly a surprise, and a most unpleasant one, for the family. It is easy to deplore the snobbishness and the conventions of another age, and indeed there was much in Edwardian England to deplore. But it was not a propitious marriage. I think of the difference in background, education and way of life, the lack of common interest. And there was this great disparity of age. My grandfather had married a girl just three months younger than his own granddaughter. I cannot wonder that the family were concerned; that they felt that the union could not in the end contribute to the contentment or happiness of either party.''

And that was putting it charitably, thought Dalgliesh. The marriage certainly hadn't contributed to their happiness. From the point of view of the family, it had been a disaster. He recalled hearing of an incident when the local vicar and his wife, a couple who had actually dined at Colebrook Croft on the night of the murder, first called on the bride. Apparently old Augustus Boxdale had introduced her by saying:

"Meet the prettiest little variety artiste in the business. Took a gold watch and notecase off me without any trouble. Would have had the elastic out of my pants if I hadn't watched out. Anyway, she stole my heart, didn't you, sweetheart?'' All this accompanied by a hearty slap on the rump and a squeal of delight from the lady, who had promptly demonstrated her skill by extracting the Reverend Venables's bunch of keys from his left ear.

Dalgliesh thought it tactful not to remind the Canon of this story.

"What do you wish me to do, sir?'' he inquired.

"It's asking a great deal, I know, when you're so busy at the Yard. But if I had your assurance that you believed in Aunt Allie's innocence, I should feel happy about accepting the bequest. I wondered if it would be possible for you to see the records of the trial. Perhaps it would give you a clue. You're so clever at this sort of thing.''

He spoke with no intention to flatter but with an innocent wonder at the peculiar avocations of men. Dalgliesh was, indeed, very clever at this sort of thing. A dozen or so men at present occupying security wings in Her Majesty's prisons could testify to Chief Superintendent Dalgliesh's cleverness, as indeed could a handful of others walking free whose defending counsel had been in their way as clever as Chief Superintendent Dalgliesh. But to re-examine a case over sixty years old seemed to require clairvoyance rather than cleverness. The trial judge and both learned counsel had been dead

6

for over fifty years. Two world wars had taken their toll. Four reigns had passed. It was probable that of those who had slept under the roof of Colebrook Croft on that fateful Boxing Day night of 1901, only the Canon still survived.

But the old man was troubled and had sought his help. And Dalgliesh, with nearly a week's leave due to him, had the time to give it.

"I'll see what I can do," he promised.

The transcript of a trial that had taken place sixty-seven years ago took time and trouble to obtain even for a chief superintendent of the Metropolitan Police. It provided little potential comfort for the Canon. Mr. Justice Medlock had summed up with that avuncular simplicity with which he was wont to address juries, regarding them, apparently, as a panel of well-intentioned but cretinous children. But the salient facts could have been comprehended by any intelligent child. Part of the summing up set them out with admirable lucidity:

And so, gentlemen of the jury, we come to the evening of 26 December. Mr. Augustus Boxdale, who had perhaps indulged a little unwisely on Christmas Day and at luncheon, had retired to rest in his dressing room at three o'clock, suffering from a slight recurrence of the digestive trouble which had afflicted him for most of his life. You have heard that he had taken luncheon with members of his family and ate nothing which they, too, did not eat. You may feel that you can acquit that luncheon of anything worse than over-richness. Mr. Boxdale, as was his habit, did not take afternoon tea.

Dinner was served at 8 P.M. promptly, as was the custom at Colebrook Croft. Members of the jury, you must be very clear who was present at that meal. There was the accused, Mrs. Augustus Boxdale; there was her husband's elder son, Captain Maurice Boxdale, with his wife; the younger son, the Reverend Edward Boxdale, with his wife; the deceased's granddaughter, Miss Marguerite Goddard, and there were two neighbors, the Reverend and Mrs. Henry Venables.

You have heard how the accused took only the first course at dinner, which was ragout of beef, and then left the dining room, saying that she wished to sit with her husband. That was about eight-twenty. Shortly after nine o'clock, she rang for the parlormaid, Mary Huddy, and ordered a basin of gruel to be brought up to Mr. Boxdale. You have heard that the deceased was fond of gruel, and indeed, as prepared by Mrs. Muncie, the cook, it sounds a most nourishing and comforting dish for an elderly gentleman of weak digestion.

You have heard Mrs. Muncie describe how she prepared the gruel, according to Mrs. Beeton's admirable recipe, in the presence of Mary Huddy, in case, as she said, "The master should take a fancy to it when I'm not at hand and you have to make it." After the gruel had been prepared, Mrs. Muncie tasted it with a spoon and Mary Huddy carried it upstairs to the main bedroom, together with a small jug of water in case it should be too strong. As she reached the door, Mrs. Boxdale came out, her hands full of stockings and underclothes. She has told you that she was on her way to the bathroom to wash them through. She asked the girl to put the basin of gruel on the washstand to cool and Mary Huddy did so in her presence. Miss Huddy has told you that, at the time, she noticed the bowl of flypapers soaking in water and she knew that this solution was one used by Mrs. Boxdale as a cosmetic wash. Indeed, all the women who spent that evening in the house, with the exception of Mrs. Venables, have told you that they knew that it was Mrs. Boxdale's practice to prepare this solution of flypapers.

Mary Huddy and the accused left the bedroom together and you have heard the evidence of Mrs. Muncie that Miss Huddy returned to the kitchen after an absence of only a few minutes. Shortly after nine o'clock, the ladies left the dining room and entered the drawing room to take coffee. At nine-fifteen, Miss Goddard excused herself to the company and said that she would go to see if her grandfather needed anything. The time is established precisely because the clock struck the quarter hour as she left and Mrs. Venables commented on the sweetness of its chime. You have also heard Mrs. Venables's evidence and the evidence of Mrs. Maurice Boxdale and Mrs. Edward Boxdale that none of the ladies left the drawing room during the evening, and Mr. Venables has testified that the three gentlemen remained together until Miss Goddard appeared about three quarters of an hour later to inform them that her grandfather had become very ill and to request that the doctor be sent for immediately.

Miss Goddard has told you that when she entered her

grandfather's room, he was just beginning his gruel and was grumbling about its taste. She got the impression that this was merely a protest at being deprived of his dinner rather than that he genuinely considered that there was something wrong with the gruel. At any rate, he finished most of it and appeared to enjoy it despite his grumbles.

You have heard Miss Goddard describe how, after her grandfather had had as much as he wanted of the gruel, she took the bowl next door and left it on the washstand. She then returned to her grandfather's bedroom and Mr. Boxdale, his wife, and his granddaughter played three-handed whist for about three quarters of an hour.

At ten o'clock, Mr. Augustus Boxdale complained of feeling very ill. He suffered from griping pains in the stomach, from sickness, and from looseness of the bowel. As soon as the symptoms began, Miss Goddard went downstairs to let her uncles know that her grandfather was worse and to ask that Dr. Eversley should be sent for urgently. Dr. Eversley has given you his evidence. He arrived at Colebrook Croft at 10:30 P.M., when he found his patient very distressed and weak. He treated the symptoms and gave what relief he could, but Mr. Augustus Boxdale died shortly before midnight.

Gentlemen of the jury, you have heard Marguerite Goddard describe how, as her grandfather's paroxysms increased in intensity, she remembered the gruel and wondered whether it could have disagreed with him in some way. She mentioned this possibility to her elder uncle, Captain Maurice Boxdale. Captain Boxdale has told you how at once he handed the bowl with its residue of gruel to Dr. Eversley with the request that the doctor should lock it in a cupboard in the library, seal the lock, and himself keep the key. You have heard how the contents of the bowl were later analyzed and with what result.

An extraordinary precaution for the gallant captain to have taken, thought Dalgliesh, and a most perspicacious young woman. Was it by chance or by design that the bowl hadn't been taken down to be washed as soon as the old man had finished with it? Why was it, he wondered, that Marguerite Goddard hadn't rung for the parlormaid and requested her to remove it? Miss Goddard appeared the only other suspect. He wished that he knew more about her.

But except for the main protagonists, the characters in the drama did not emerge very clearly from the trial report. Why, indeed, should they? The accusatorial legal system is designed to answer one question. Is the accused guilty beyond reasonable doubt of the crime charged? Exploration of the nuances of personality, interesting speculation, and common gossip have not place in the witness box. Was it really possible after nearly seventy years that these dry bones could live?

The two Boxdale brothers came out as very dull fellows indeed. They and their estimable and respectable sloping-bosomed wives had sat at dinner in full view of each other from eight until nearly nine o'clock (a substantial meal, that dinner) and had said so in the witness box in more or less identical words. The bosoms of the ladies might have been heaving with far from estimable emotions of dislike, envy, embarrassment, or resentment of the interloper. If so, they didn't choose to tell the court. But the two brothers and their wives were clearly innocent, even if it had been possible to conceive of the guilt of gentlefolk so respected, so eminently respectable. Even their impeccable alibis for the period after dinner had a nice touch of social and sexual distinction. The Reverend Henry Venables had vouched for the gentlemen; his good wife for the ladies.

Besides, what motive had they? They could no longer gain financially by the old man's death. If anything, it was in their interests to keep him alive in the hope that disillusionment with his marriage or a return to relative sanity might occur to cause him to change his will.

And the rest of the witnesses gave no help. Dalgliesh read all their testimony carefully. The pathologist's evidence. The doctor's evidence. The evidence of Allegra Boxdale's visit to the village store, where, from among the clutter of pots and pans, ointments and liniments, it had been possible to find a dozen flypapers for a customer even in the depth of an English winter. The evidence of the cook. The evidence of the parlormaid. The remarkably lucid and confident evidence of the granddaughter. There was nothing in any of it which could cause him to give the Canon the assurance for which he hoped.

It was then that he remembered Aubrey Glatt. Glatt was a wealthy amateur criminologist who had made a study of all the notable Victorian and Edwardian poison cases. He was not interested in anything earlier or later, being as obsessively wedded to his period

10

as any serious historian, which indeed he had some claim to call himself. He lived in a Georgian house in Winchester—his affection for the Victorian and Edwardian age did not extend to its architecture—and was only three miles from Colebrook Croft. A visit to the London Library disclosed that he hadn't written a book on the case, but it was improbable that he had totally neglected a crime so close at hand and so in period. Dalgliesh had occasionally helped him with technical details of police procedure. Glatt, in response to a telephone call, was happy to return the favor with the offer of afternoon tea and information.

Tea was served in his elegant drawing room by a parlormaid in goffered cap with streamers. Dalgliesh wondered what wage Glatt paid her to persuade her to wear it. She looked as if she could have played a role in any of his favorite Victorian dramas, and Dalgliesh had an uncomfortable thought that arsenic might be dispensed with the cucumber sandwiches.

Glatt nibbled away and was expansive.

"It's interesting that you should have taken this sudden and, if I may say so, somewhat inexplicable interest in the Boxdale murder. I got out my notebook on the case only yesterday. Colebrook Croft is being demolished to make way for a new housing estate and I thought I might visit it for the last time. The family, of course, hasn't lived there since the 1914–18 war. Architecturally it's completely undistinguished, but one hates to see it go. We might motor over after tea if you are agreeable.

"I never completed my book on the case, you know. I planned a work entitled *The Colebrook Croft Mystery, or Who Killed Augustus Boxdale?* But alas, the answer was all too obvious."

"No real mystery?" suggested Dalgliesh.

"Who else could it have been but the bride? She was born Allegra Porter, incidentally. Allegra. An extraordinary name. Do you suppose her mother could have been thinking of Byron? I imagine not. There's a picture of Allie on page two of the notebook, by the way, taken in Cannes on her wedding day. I call it 'Beauty and the Beast.' "

The photograph had scarcely faded and Great-Aunt Allie smiled plainly at Dalgliesh across nearly seventy years. Her broad face with its wide mouth and rather snub nose was framed by two wings of dark hair swept high and topped, in the fashion of the day, by an immense flowered hat. The features were too coarse for real beauty, but the eyes were magnificent, deep-set and well-spaced; the chin

11

was round and determined. Beside this vital young Amazon poor Augustus Boxdale, smiling fatuously at the camera and clutching his bride's arm as if for support, was but a frail and pathetic beast. Their pose was unfortunate. She looked as if she were about to fling him over her shoulder.

Glatt shrugged. "The face of a murderess? I've known less likely ones. Her counsel suggested, of course, that the old man had poisoned his own gruel during the short time she left it on the washstand to cool while she visited the bathroom. But why should he? All the evidence suggests that he was in a state of postnuptial euphoria, poor senile old booby. Our Augustus was in no hurry to leave this world, particularly by such an agonizing means. Besides, I doubt whether he even knew the gruel was there. He was in bed next door in his dressing room, remember."

Dalgliesh asked, "What about Marguerite Goddard? There's no evidence about the exact time when she entered the bedroom."

"I thought you'd get on to that. She could have arrived while her step-grandmother was in the bathroom, poisoned the gruel, hidden herself either in the main bedroom or elsewhere until it had been taken in to Augustus, then joined her grandfather and his bride as if she had just come upstairs. It's possible, I admit. But is it likely? She was less inconvenienced than any of the family by her grandfather's second marriage. Her mother was Augustus Boxdale's eldest child and married, very young, a wealthy patent medicine manufacturer. She died in childbirth and the husband only survived her by a year. Marguerite Goddard was an heiress. She was also most advantageously engaged to Captain the Honorable John Brize-Lacey. It was quite a catch for a Boxdale—or a Goddard. Marguerite Goddard, young, beautiful, secure in the possession of the Goddard fortune, not to mention the Goddard emeralds and the eldest son of a lord, was hardly a serious suspect. In my view, defense counsel—that was Roland Gort Lloyd—was wise to leave her strictly alone."

"It was a memorable defense, I believe."

"Magnificent. There's no doubt Allegra Boxdale owed her life to Gort Lloyd. I know that concluding speech by heart.

" 'Gentlemen of the jury, I beseech you in the sacred name of justice to consider what you are at. It is your responsibility and yours alone to decide the fate of this young woman. She stands before you now, young, vibrant, glowing with health, the years stretching before her with their promise and their hopes. It is in your power to cut off all this as you might top a nettle with one swish of your cane. To condemn her to the slow torture of those last waiting weeks; to that last dreadful walk; to heap calumny on her name; to desecrate those few happy weeks of marriage with the man who loved her so greatly; to cast her into the final darkness of an ignominious grave.'

"Pause for dramatic effect. Then the crescendo in that magnificient voice. 'And on what evidence, gentlemen? I ask you.' Another pause. Then the thunder. 'On what evidence?' "

"A powerful defense," said Dalgliesh. "But I wonder how it would go down with a modern judge and jury."

"Well, it went down very effectively with that 1902 jury. Of course, the abolition of capital punishment has rather cramped the more histrionic style. I'm not sure that the reference to topping nettles was in the best of taste. But the jury got the message. They decided that, on the whole, they preferred not to have the responsibility of sending the accused to the gallows. They were out six hours reaching their verdict and it was greeted with some applause. If any of those worthy citizens had been asked to wager five pounds of their own good money on her innocence, I suspect that it would have been a different matter. Allegra Boxdale had helped him, of course. The Criminal Evidence Act, passed three years earlier, enabled him to put her in the witness box. She wasn't an actress of a kind for nothing. Somehow she managed to persuade the jury that she had genuinely loved the old man."

"Perhaps she had," suggested Dalgliesh. "I don't suppose there had been much kindness in her life. And he was kind."

"No doubt. No doubt. But love!" Glatt was impatient. "My dear Dalgliesh! He was a singularly ugly old man of sixty-nine. She was an attractive girl of twenty-one!"

Dalgliesh doubted whether love, that iconoclastic passion, was susceptible to this kind of simple arithmetic, but he didn't argue. Glatt went on.

"And the prosecution couldn't suggest any other romantic attachment. The police got in touch with her previous partner, of course. He was discovered to be a bald, undersized little man, sharp as a weasel, with a buxom uxorious wife and five children. He had moved down the coast after the partnership broke up and was now working with a new girl. He said regretfully that she was coming along nicely, thank you, gentlemen, but would never be a patch on Allie, and that if Allie got her neck out of the noose and ever wanted a job, she knew where to come. It was obvious even to the most suspicious policeman that his interest was purely professional. As he said, what was a grain or two of arsenic between friends?

"The Boxdales had no luck after the trial. Captain Maurice Boxdale was killed in 1916, leaving no children, and the Reverend Edward lost his wife and their twin daughters in the 1918 influenza epidemic. He survived until 1932. The boy Hubert may still be alive, but I doubt it. That family were a sickly lot.

"My greatest achievement, incidentally, was in tracing Marguerite Goddard. I hadn't realized that she was still alive. She never married Brize-Lacey or, indeed, anyone else. He distinguished himself in the 1914–18 war, came successfully through, and eventually married an eminently suitable young woman, the sister of a brother officer. He inherited the title in 1925 and died in 1953. But Marguerite Goddard may be alive now, for all I know. She may even be living in the same modest Bournemouth hotel where I found her. Not that my efforts in tracing her were rewarded. She absolutely refused to see me. That's the note that she sent out to me, by the way."

It was meticulously pasted into the notebook in its chronological order and carefully annotated. Aubrey Glatt was a natural researcher; Dalgliesh couldn't help wondering whether this passion for accuracy might not have been more rewardingly spent than in the careful documentation of murder.

The note was written in an elegant upright hand, the strokes black and very thin but unwavering.

Miss Goddard presents her compliments to Mr. Aubrey Glatt. She did not murder her grandfather and has neither the time nor the inclination to gratify his curiosity by discussing the person who did.

Aubrey Glatt said, "After that extremely disobliging note I felt there was really no point in going on with the book."

Glatt's passion for Edwardian England extended to more than its murders and they drove to Colebrook Croft, high above the green Hampshire lanes, in an elegant 1910 Daimler. Aubrey wore a thin tweed coat and deerstalker hat and looked, Dalgliesh thought, rather like a Sherlock Holmes, with himself as attendant Watson.

"We are only just in time, my dear Dalgliesh," he said when they arrived. "The engines of destruction are assembled. That ball on a chain looks like the eyeball of God, ready to strike. Let us make our number with the attendant artisans. You as a guardian of the law will have no wish to trespass."

The work of demolition had not yet begun, but the inside of the house had been stripped and plundered. The great rooms echoed to their footsteps like gaunt and deserted barracks after the final retreat. They moved from room to room, Glatt mourning the forgotten glories of an age he had been born thirty years too late to enjoy, Dalgliesh with his mind on more immediate and practical concerns.

The design of the house was simple and formalized. The second floor, on which were most of the main bedrooms, had a long corridor running the whole length of the facade. The master bedroom was at the southern end, with two large windows giving a distant view of Winchester Cathedral tower. A communicating door led to a small dressing room.

The main corridor had a row of four identical large windows. The curtain rods and rings had been removed, but the ornate carved pelmets were still in place. Here must have hung pairs of heavy curtains giving cover to anyone who wished to slip out of view. And Dalgliesh noted with interest that one of the windows was exactly opposite the door of the main bedroom. By the time they had left Colebrook Croft and Glatt had dropped him at Winchester station, Dalgliesh was beginning to formulate a theory.

His next move was to trace Marguerite Goddard if she was still alive. It took him nearly a week of weary searching, a frustrating trail along the south coast from hotel to hotel. Almost everywhere his inquiries were met with defensive hostility. It was the usual story of a very old lady who had become more demanding, arrogant, and eccentric as her health and fortune had waned; an unwelcome embarrassment to manager and fellow guests alike. The hotels were all modest, a few almost sordid. What, he wondered, had become of the Goddard fortune? From the last landlady he learned that Miss Goddard had become ill, really very sick indeed, and had been removed six months previously to the local district general hospital. And it was there that he found her.

The ward sister was surprisingly young, a petite dark-haired girl with a tired face and challenging eyes.

"Miss Goddard is very ill. We've put her in one of the side wards. Are you a relative? If so, you're the first one who has bothered to call and you're lucky to be in time. When she is delirious she seems to expect a Captain Brize-Lacey to call. You're not he, by any chance?"

"Captain Brize-Lacey will not be calling. No, I'm not a relative. She doesn't even know me. But I would like to visit her if she's well enough and is willing to see me. Could you please give her this note?"

He couldn't force himself on a defenseless and dying woman. She still had the right to say no. He was afraid she would refuse him. And if she did, he might never learn the truth. He thought for a second and then wrote four words on the back page of his diary, signed them, tore out the page, folded it, and handed it to the sister.

She was back very shortly.

"She'll see you. She's weak, of course, and very old, but she's perfectly lucid now. Only please don't tire her."

"I'll try not to stay too long."

The girl laughed. "Don't worry. She'll throw you out soon enough if she gets bored. The chaplain and the Red Cross librarian have a terrible time with her. Third door on the left. There's a stool to sit on under the bed. We ring a bell at the end of visiting time."

She bustled off, leaving him to find his own way. The corridor was very quiet. At the far end he could glimpse through the open door of the main ward the regimented rows of beds, each with its pale-blue coverlet; the bright glow of flowers on the over-bed tables; and the laden visitors making their way in pairs to each bedside. There was a faint buzz of welcome, the hum of conversation. But no one was visiting the side wards. Here in the silence of the aseptic corridor Dalgliesh could smell death.

The woman propped high against the pillows in the third room on the left no longer looked human. She lay rigidly, her long arms disposed like sticks on the coverlet. This was a skeleton clothed with a thin membrane of flesh, beneath whose yellow transparency the tendons and veins were plainly visible as if in an anatomist's model. She was nearly bald, and the high-domed skull under its spare down of hair was as brittle and vulnerable as a child's. Only the eyes still held life, burning in their deep sockets with an animal vitality. And when she spoke her voice was distinctive and unwavering, evoking as her appearance never could the memory of imperious youth.

She took up his note and read aloud four words: " 'It was the child.' You are right, of course. The four-year-old Hubert Boxdale killed his grandfather. You sign this note 'Adam Dalgliesh.' There was no Dalgliesh connected with the case."

"I am a detective of the Metropolitan Police. But I'm not here in any official capacity. I have known about this case for a number of years from a dear friend. I have a natural curiosity to learn the truth. And I have formed a theory."

"And now, like that Aubrey Glatt, you want to write a book?"

"No. I shall tell no one. You have my promise."

Her voice was ironic. "Thank you. I am a dying woman, Mr. Dalgliesh. I tell you that not to invite your sympathy, which it would be an impertinence for you to offer and which I neither want nor require, but to explain why it no longer matters to me what you say or do. But I, too, have a natural curiosity. Your note, cleverly, was intended to provoke it. I should like to know how you discovered the truth."

Dalgliesh drew the visitor's stool from under the bed and sat down beside her. She did not look at him. The skeleton hands, still holding his note, did not move.

"Everyone in Colebrook Croft who could have killed Augustus Boxdale was accounted for, except the one person whom nobody considered, the small boy. He was an intelligent, articulate, and lonely child. He was almost certainly left to his own devices. His nurse did not accompany the family to Colebrook Croft and the servants who were there had the extra work of Christmas and the care of the delicate twin girls. The boy spent much time with his grandfather and the new bride. She, too, was lonely and disregarded. He could have watched her making her arsenical face wash and when he asked, as a child will, what it was for, could have been told: 'To make me young and beautiful.' He loved his grandfather, but he must have known that the old man was neither young nor beautiful. Suppose he woke up on that Boxing Day night overfed and excited after the Christmas festivities. Suppose he went to Allegra Boxdale's room in search of comfort and companionship and saw there the basin of gruel and the arsenical mixture together on the washstand. Suppose he decided that here was something he could do for his grandfather."

17

The voice from the bed said quietly: "And suppose someone stood unnoticed in the doorway and watched him."

"So you were behind the window curtains on the landing, looking through the open door?"

"Of course. He knelt on the chair, two chubby hands clasping the bowl of poison, pouring it with infinite care into his grandfather's gruel. I watched while he replaced the linen cloth over the basin, got down from his chair, replaced it with careful art against the wall, and trotted out into the corridor back to the nursery. About three seconds later Allegra came out of the bathroom and I watched while she carried the gruel in to my grandfather. A second later I went into the main bedroom. The bowl of poison had been a little heavy for Hubert's small hands to manage and I saw that a small pool had been spilt on the polished top of the washstand. I mopped it up with my handkerchief. Then I poured some of the water from the jug into the poison bowl to bring up the level. It only took a couple of seconds and I was ready to join Allegra and my grandfather in the bedroom and sit with him while he ate his gruel.

"I watched him die without pity and without remorse. I think I hated them both equally. The grandfather who had adored, petted, and indulged me all through my childhood had deteriorated into this disgusting old lecher, unable to keep his hands off his woman even when I was in the room. He had rejected his family, jeopardized my engagement, made our name a laughingstock in the county, and for a woman my grandmother wouldn't have employed as a kitchen maid. I wanted them both dead. And they were both going to die. But it would be by other hands than mine. I could deceive myself that it wasn't my doing."

Dalgliesh asked, "When did she find out?"

"She guessed that evening. When my grandfather's agony began, she went outside for the jug of water. She wanted a cool cloth for his head. It was then that she noticed that the level of water in the jug had fallen and that a small pool of liquid on the washstand had been mopped up. I should have realized then that she would have seen the pool. She had been trained to register every detail; it was almost subconscious with her. She thought at the time that Mary Huddy had spilt some of the water when she set down the tray and the gruel. But who but I could have mopped it up? And why?"

"And when did she face you with the truth?"

"Not until after the trial. Allegra had magnificent courage. She

18

knew what was at stake. But she also knew what she stood to gain. She gambled with her life for a fortune.''

And then Dalgliesh understood what had happened to the Goddard inheritance.

"So she made you pay."

"Of course. Every penny. The Goddard fortune, the Goddard emeralds. She lived in luxury for sixty-seven years on my money. When she moved with her lovers from hotel to hotel, it was on my money. She paid them with my money. And if she has left anything, which I doubt, it is my money. My grandfather left very little. He had been senile for years. Money ran through his fingers like sand.''

"And your engagement?''

"It was broken, you could say by mutual consent. A marriage, Mr. Dalgliesh, is like any other legal contract. It is most successful when both parties are convinced they have a bargain. Captain Brize-Lacey was sufficiently discouraged by the scandal of a murder in the family. He was a proud and highly conventional man. But that alone might have been accepted with the Goddard fortune and the Goddard emeralds to deodorize the bad smell. But the marriage couldn't have succeeded if he had discovered that he had married socially beneath him, into a family with a major scandal and no compensating fortune.''

Dalgliesh said, "Once you had begun to pay, you had no choice but to go on. I see that. But why did you pay? She could have hardly told her story. It would have meant involving the child.''

"Oh, no! That wasn't her plan at all. She never meant to involve the child. She was a sentimental woman and she was fond of Hubert. She intended to accuse me of murder outright. Then, if I decided to tell the truth, how would it help me? How could I admit that I had watched Hubert, actually watched a child barely four years old preparing an agonizing death for his grandfather without speaking a word to stop him? I could hardly claim that I hadn't understood the implication of what I had seen. After all, I wiped up the spilt liquid, I topped up the bowl. She had nothing to lose, remember, neither life nor reputation. They couldn't try her twice. That's why she waited until after the trial. It made her secure forever. But what of me? In the circles in which I moved, reputation was everything. She needed only to breathe the story in the ears of a few servants and I was finished. The truth can be remarkably tenacious. But it wasn't only reputation. I paid because I was in dread of the gallows.''

Dalgliesh asked, "But could she ever prove it?"

Suddenly she looked at him and gave an eerie screech of laughter. It tore at her throat until he thought the taut tendons would snap.

"Of course she could! You fool! Don't you understand? She took my handkerchief, the one I used to mop up the arsenic mixture. That was her profession, remember? Sometime during that evening, perhaps when we were all crowding around the bed, two soft plump fingers insinuated themselves between the satin of my evening dress and my flesh and extracted that stained and damning piece of linen."

She stretched out feebly toward the bedside locker. Dalgliesh saw what she wanted and pulled open the drawer. There on the top was a small square of very fine linen with a border of handstitched lace. He took it up. In the corner was her monogram, delicately embroidered. And half of the handkerchief was still stiff and stained with brown.

She said, "She left instructions with her solicitors that this was to be returned to me after her death. She always knew where I was. She made it her business to know. You see, it could be said that she had a life interest in me. But now she's dead. And I shall soon follow. You may have the handkerchief, Mr. Dalgliesh. It can be of no further use to either of us now."

Dalgliesh put it in his pocket without speaking. As soon as possible he would see that it was burned. But there was something else he had to say. "Is there anything you would wish me to do? Is there anyone you want told, or to tell? Would you care to see a priest?"

Again there was that uncanny screech of laughter, but it was softer now.

"There's nothing I can say to the priest. I only regret what I did because it wasn't successful. That is hardly the proper frame of mind for a good confession. But I bear her no ill will. No envy, malice, or uncharitableness. She won; I lost. One should be a good loser. But I don't want any priest telling me about penance. I've paid, Mr. Dalgliesh. For sixty-seven years I've paid. Great-Aunt Allie and her flypapers! She had me caught by the wings all the rest of my life."

She lay back as if suddenly exhausted. There was silence for a moment. Then she said with sudden vigor: "I believe your visit has done me good. I would be obliged if you would make it convenient to return each afternoon for the next three days. I shan't trouble you after that.''

Dalgliesh extended his leave with some difficulty and stayed at a local inn. He saw her each afternoon. They never spoke again of the murder. And when he came punctually at 2 P.M. on the fourth day, it was to be told that Miss Goddard had died peacefully in the night, with apparently no trouble to anyone. She was, as she had said, a good loser.

A week later, Dalgliesh reported to the Canon.

''I was able to see a man who has made a detailed study of the case. He had already done most of the work for me. I have read the transcript of the trial and visited Colebrook Croft. And I have seen one other person closely connected with the case but who is now dead. I know you will want me to respect confidences and to say no more than I need.''

It sounded pompous and minatory, but he couldn't help that. The Canon murmured his quiet assurance. Thank God he wasn't a man to question. Where he trusted, he trusted absolutely. If Dalgliesh gave his word, there would be no more questioning. But he was anxious. Suspense hung around them. Dalgliesh went on quickly: ''As a result, I can give you my word that the verdict was a just verdict and that not one penny of your grandfather's fortune is coming to you through anyone's wrongdoing.''

He turned his face away and gazed out the vicarage window at the sweet green coolness of the summer's day so that he did not have to watch the Canon's happiness and relief. There was silence. The old man was probably giving thanks in his own way. Then he was aware that his godfather was speaking. Something was being said about gratitude, about the time he had given up to the investigation.

''Please don't misunderstand me, Adam. But when the formalities have been completed, I should like to donate something to a charity named by you, one close to your heart.''

Dalgliesh smiled. His contributions to charity were impersonal; a quarterly obligation discharged by banker's order. The Canon obviously regarded charities as so many old clothes; all were friends, but some fitted better and were more affectionately regarded than others.

Then inspiration came.

''It's good of you to suggest it, sir. I rather liked what I learned about Great-Aunt Allie. It would be pleasant to give something in her name. Isn't there a society for the assistance of retired and indigent vaudeville artistes, conjurers, and so on?''

The Canon, predictably, knew that there was and could name it.

Dalgliesh said, ''Then I think, Canon, that Great-Aunt Allie would agree that a donation to them would be entirely appropriate.''

A Reason to Die

•

Michael Collins

Michael Collins is one of five pseudonyms (the other four are Mark Sadler, John Crowe, William Arden, and Carl Dekker) used by Dennis Lynds, one of today's most incisive suspense novelists. Act of Fear, the first of his novels under the name of Collins to feature one-armed New York private detective Dan Fortune, won an MWA Edgar for Best First Novel of 1967. Equally accomplished are the dozen that have followed, among them Walk a Black Wind (1971), The Nightrunners (1978), Freak, (1983), and Minnesota Strip (1987). "A Reason to Die," about the murder of a high-steel worker's wife—and much more—is typically probing and multileveled Collins/Fortune fare.

There are many kinds of courage. Maybe the hardest is doing what you have to do. No matter how it looks to other people or what happens in the end.

Irish Johnny's Tavern is a gray frame house near the railroad tracks in Syracuse, New York. A beacon of red and blue neon through the mounded old snow in the dusk of another cold winter day too far from Chelsea. My missing left arm hurt in the cold, and one of the people I was meeting was a killer.

I'd been in Irish Johnny's before, on my first day in Syracuse looking for why Alma Jean Brant was dead. Her mother had sent me.

"You go to Irish Johnny's, Mr. Fortune," Sada Patterson said. "They'll tell you about my Alma Jean."

"What can they tell me, Mrs. Patterson?" I said. I'd read the Syracuse Police Department's report, made my voice as gentle as I could in the winter light of my office-apartment loft above Eighth Avenue.

23

"They can tell you my girl wasn't walkin' streets without she got a reason, and whatever that there reason was it got to be what killed her."

"Every girl on the streets has a reason, Mrs. Patterson," I said.

"I don't mean no reason everyone got. I means a special reason. Somethin' made her do what she never would do," Sada Patterson said.

"Mrs. Patterson, listen—"

"No! You listen here to me." She held her old black plastic handbag in both hands on the lap of her starched print dress and fixed me across the desk with unflinching eyes. "I did my time hookin' when I was a girl. My man he couldn't get no work, so one day he ain't there no more, and I got two kids, and I hooked. A man got no work, he goes. A woman got no man, she hooks. But a woman got a man at home, she don't go on no streets. Not a good woman like my Alma Jean. She been married to that Indian ten years, and she don't turn no tricks 'less she got a powerful reason."

"What do you want me to do, Mrs. Patterson?"

Ramrod straight, as thin and rock hard as any Yankee farmer, Sada Patterson studied me with her black eyes as if she could see every thought I'd ever had. She probably could. The ravages of sixty years of North Carolina dirt farms, the Syracuse ghetto, and New York sweatshops had left her nothing but bones and tendon, the flesh fossilized over the endless years.

"You go on up there 'n' find out who killed my Alma Jean. I can pay. I got the money. You go to Irish Johnny's and ask 'bout my Alma Jean. She ain't been inside the place in ten years, or any place like it. You tell 'em Sada sent you and they talk to you even if you is a honkie."

"It's a police job, Mrs. Patterson. Save your money."

"No cop's gonna worry hard 'bout the killin' of no black hooker. You go up there, Fortune. You find out." She stood up, the worn plastic handbag in both hands out in front of her like a shield. A grandmother in a print dress. Until you looked at her eyes. "She was my last—Alma Jean. She come when we had some money, lived in a house up there. She almos' got to finish grade school. I always dressed her so good. Like a real doll, you know? A little doll."

Inside, Irish Johnny's is a single large room with a bandstand at the far end. The bar is along the left wall, backed by bottles and fronted by red plastic stools. Tables fill the room around a small dance floor. Behind the bar and the rows of bottles is a long mirror. The rear wall over the bandstand is bare, except when it is hung with a banner proclaiming the band or *artiste* to perform that night.

On the remaining two walls there is a large mural in the manner of Orozco or maybe Rivera. Full of violent, struggling ghetto figures, it was painted long ago by some forgotten radical student from the university on the hill above the tavern.

The crowd had not yet arrived, only a few tables occupied as I came in. The professor and his wife sat at a table close to the dance floor. I crossed the empty room under the lost eyes of the red, blue, and yellow people in the mural.

I knew who the killer was, but I didn't know how I was going to prove it. Someone was going to have to help me before I made the call to the police.

The police are always the first stop in a new town. Lieutenant Derrida of the Syracuse Police Department was an older man. He remembered Sada Patterson.

"Best-looking hooker ever walked a street in Syracuse." His thin eyes were bright and sad at the same time, as if he wished he and Sada Patterson could be back there when she had been the best-looking hooker in Syracuse, but knew it was too late for both of them.

"What made Alma Jean go to the streets, Lieutenant?"

He shrugged. "What makes any of 'em?"

"What does?" I said.

"Don't shit me, Fortune. A new car or a fur coat. Suburbs to Saskatchewan. It just happens more in the slums where the bucks ain't so big or easy."

"Sada says no way unless the girl had a large reason," I said. "She didn't mean a fur coat or a watch."

"Sada Patterson's a mother," Derrida said.

"She's also a client. Can I earn my fee?"

He opened a desk drawer, took out a skinny file. "Alma Jean was found a week ago below a street bridge over the tracks. Some kids going to school spotted her. The fall killed her. She died somewhere between midnight and four A.M., the snow and cold made it hard to be sure. It stopped snowing about two A.M., there was no snow on top of her, so she died after that."

Derrida swiveled in his chair, looked out his single window at the gray sky and grayer city. "She could have fallen, jumped, or been pushed. There was no sign of a struggle, but she was a small woman; one push would have knocked her over that low parapet. M.E. says a bruise on her jaw could have come from a blow or from hitting a rock. No suicide note, but the snow showed someone had climbed up on the parapet. Only whoever it was didn't get near the edge, held to a light pole, jumped off the other way back onto the street."

"What's her pimp say?"

"Looks like she was trying to work independent."

I must have stared. Derrida nodded.

"I know," he said, "we sweated the pimp in the neighborhood. Black as my captain, but tells everyone he's a Polack. He says he didn't even know Alma Jean, and we can't prove he did or place him around her."

"Who do you place around her?"

"That night, no one. She was out in the snow all by herself. No one saw her, heard her, or smelled her. If she turned any tricks that night, she used doorways; no johns are talking. No cash in her handbag. A bad night."

"What about other nights?"

"The husband, Joey Brant. He's a Mohawk, works high steel like most Indians. They married ten years ago, no kids and lived good. High steel pays. With her hooking he was *numero uno* suspect, only he was drinking in Cherry Valley Tavern from nine till closing with fifty witnesses. Later, the bartender, him, and ten others sobered up in a sweat lodge until dawn."

"Anyone else?"

"*Mister* Walter Ellis. Owns the numbers, runs a big book. He was an old boyfriend of Sada's, seems to have had eyes for the daughter. She was seen visiting him a couple of times recently. Just friendly calls, he says, but he got no alibi."

"That's it?"

Derrida swiveled. "No, we got a college professor named Margon and his wife. Margon was doing 'research' with Alma Jean. Maybe the wrong kind of research. Maybe the wife got mad."

I took a chair at the table with the Margons. In Irish Johnny's anyone who opened a book in the university above the ghetto was a "professor." Fred Margon was a thin, dark-haired young man in his midtwenties. His wife, Dorothy, was a beauty-contest blonde with restless eyes.

"A temple," Fred Margon said as I sat down. "The bartenders are the priests, that mural is the holy icon painted by a wandering disciple, the liquor is God."

"I think I'll scream," Dorothy Margon said. "Or is that too undignified for the wife of a scholar, a pure artist?"

Fred Margon drank his beer, looked unhappy.

"Booze is their god," Dorothy Margon said. "That's very good. Isn't that good, Mr. Fortune? You really are bright, Fred. I wonder what you ever saw in me? Just the bod, right? You like female bods at least. You like them a lot when you've got time."

"You want to leave?" Fred said.

"No, tell us why drink is their god. Go on, tell us."

"No other god ever helped them."

"Clever," Dorothy said. "Isn't he clever, Mr. Fortune? Going to do great scholarly research, teach three classes, and finish his novel all at the same time. Then there's the female bods. When he has time. Or maybe he makes time for that."

"We'll leave," Fred said.

"All day every day: scholar, teacher, novelist. For twenty whole thousand dollars a year!"

"We manage," Fred Margon said.

"Never mind," Dorothy said. "Just never mind."

I met him in a coffee shop on South Crouse after a class. He looked tired. We had coffee, and he told me about Alma Jean.

"I found her in an Indian bar six months ago. I like to walk through the city, meet the real people." He drank his coffee. "She had a way of speaking full of metaphors. I wrote my doctoral dissertation on the poetry of totally untrained people, got a grant to continue the research. I met her as often as I could. In the bars and in her home. To listen and record her speech. She was highly intelligent. Her insights were remarkable for someone without an education, and her way of expressing her thoughts was pure uneducated poetry."

"You liked her?"

He nodded. "She was real, alive."

"How much did you like her, professor?"

"Make it Fred, okay? I'm only a bottom-step assistant professor, and sometimes I want to drop the whole thing, live a real life, make some money." He drank his coffee, looked out the cafe window. He knew what I was asking. "My wife isn't happy, Mr. Fortune. When she's unhappy, she has the classic female method of showing it. Perhaps in time I would have tried with Alma Jean, but I didn't. She really wasn't interested, you know? In me or any other man. Only her husband."

"You know her husband?"

"I've met him. Mostly at her house, sometimes in a bar. He seems to drink a lot. I asked her about that. She said it was part of being an Indian, a 'brave.' Work hard and drink hard. He always seemed angry. At her, at his bosses, at everything. He didn't like me, or my being there, as if it were an insult to him, but he just sat in the living room, drinking and looking out a window at the tall buildings downtown. Sometimes he talked about working on those buildings. He was proud of that. Alma Jean said that was the culture; a 'man' did brave work, daring."

"When was the last time you saw her?"

"The day she died." He shrugged as he drank his coffee. "The police know. I had a session with her early in the day at her house. Her husband wasn't there, and she seemed tired, worried. She'd been unhappy for months, I think, but it was always hard to tell with her. Always cheerful and determined. I told her there was a book in her life, but she only scorned the idea. Life was to be lived, not written about. When there were troubles, you did something."

"What troubles sent her out on the streets?"

He shook his head. "She never told me. A few weeks ago she asked me to pay her for making the tapes. She needed money. I couldn't pay her much on my grant, but I gave her what I could. I know it wasn't anywhere near enough. I heard her talking on the telephone, asking about the cost of something."

"You don't know what?"

"No." He drank coffee. "But whoever she was talking to offered to pay for whatever it was. She turned him down."

"You're sure it was a him?"

"No, I'm not sure."

"Who killed her, professor?"

Outside, the students crunched through the snow in the gray light. He watched them as if he wished he were still one of them, his future unknown. "I don't know who killed her, Mr. Fortune. I know she didn't commit suicide, and I doubt that she fell off that bridge. I never saw her drunk. When her husband drank, she never did, as if she had to be sober to take care of him."

"Where were you that night?"

"At home," he said, looked up at me. "But I couldn't sleep, another argument with my wife. So I went out walking in the snow. Didn't get back until two A.M. or so."

"Was it still snowing?"

"It had just stopped when I got home."

"Did you see anyone while you were out?"

"Not Alma Jean, if that's what you want to know. I did see that older friend of hers. What's his name? Walter Ellis?"

"Where?"

"Just driving around. That pink Caddy of his is easy to remember. Especially in the snow, so few cars driving."

"And all you were doing with her was recording her speech?"

He finished his coffee. "That's all, Mr. Fortune."

After he left, I paid for the coffee. He was an unhappy man, and not just about money or work.

The scar-faced man stood just inside the door. Snow dripped from his dirty raincoat into a pool around his black boots. A broad, powerfully built man with a fresh bandage on his face. Dark stains covered the front of his raincoat. The raincoat and his black shirt were open at the throat. He wore a large silver cross bedded in the hair of his chest.

"Now there's something you can write about," Dorothy Margon said. "Real local color. Who is he? What is he? Why don't you make notes. You didn't forget your notebook, did you, Fred?"

"His name is Duke," Fred Margon said. "He's a pimp, and this is his territory. A small-time pimp, only three girls on the street now. He takes eighty percent of what they make to protect them, lets them support him with most of the rest. But the competition is fierce, and business is bad this season. He gives students a cut rate; professors pay full price."

"Of course," Dorothy said. "Part of your 'research' into 'ordinary' people. All for art and scholarship." She looked at the man at the entrance. "I wonder what his girls are like. Are they young or old? Do they admire him? I suppose they all love him. Of course they do. All three of them in love with him."

"In love with him and afraid of him," I said.

"Love and fear," Fred Margon said. "Their world."

"Do I hear a story?" Dorothy said. "Is everything a story? Nothing real? With results? Change? A future?"

I watched him come across the dance floor toward our table. Duke Wiltkowski, the pimp in the streets where Alma Jean had been found dead.

The pimp's office was a cellar room with a single bare bulb, a table for a desk, some battered armchairs, a kerosene heater, and water from melted snow pooled in a dark corner. Times had been better for Duke Wiltkowski.

"You sayin' I killed her? You sayin' that, man?" His black face almost hidden in the shadows of the cellar room, the light of the bare bulb barely reaching where he sat behind the table.

"Someone did," I said. "You had a motive."

"You say I kill that chippie, you got trouble, man. I got me a good lawyer. He sue you for everthin' you got!"

"The police say she was in your territory."

"The police is lyin'! The police say I kill that chippie, they lyin'!" His voice was high and thin, almost hysterical. It's a narrow world of fear, his world. On the edge. Death on one side, prison on the other, hunger and pain in between.

"She was free-lance in your territory. You can't let her do that. Not and survive. Let her do that, and you're out of business."

He sat in the gloom of the cold basement room, unmoving in the half shadows. The sweat shone on his face like polished ebony. The face of a rat with his back to the wall, cornered. Protesting.

"I never see that chippie. Not me. How I know she was working my turf? You tell the cops that, okay? You tell the cops Duke Wiltkowski never nowhere near that chippie."

He sweated in the cold cellar room. A depth in his wide eyes almost of pleading. Go away, leave him alone. Go away before he told what he couldn't tell. Wanted to tell but couldn't. Not yet.

"Where were you that night?"

"Right here. An' with one o' my pigs. All night. Milly-O. Me 'n' Milly-O we was makin' it most all night. You asks her."

One of his prostitutes who would say anything he told her to say, to the police or to God himself. That desperate. An alibi he knew was no alibi. Sweated. Licked his lips.

"That Injun husband she got, maybe he done it. Hey, they all crazy, them Injuns! That there professor hangs in Irish Johnny's. Hey, he got to of been playin' pussy with her. I mean, a big-shot white guy down there. Hey, that there professor he got a wife. Maybe she don't like that chippie, right?''

"How about Walter Ellis? He was out in the snow that night."

The fear on his face became sheer terror. "I don' know nothin' 'bout Mr. Ellis! You hears, Fortune! Nothin'!"

Now he walked into Irish Johnny's with the exaggerated swing and lightness of a dancer. Out in public, the big man. His face in the light a mass of crisscross scars. The new bandage dark with dried blood. He smiled a mouthful of broken yellow teeth.

"Saw it was you, professor. That your lady?" He clicked his heels, bowed to Dorothy Margon. A Prussian officer. "Duke Wilt-kowski. My old man was Polack." He nodded to me, cool and casual, expansive. An image to keep up and no immediate fear in sight. "Hey, Fortune. How's the snoopin'?"

"Slow," I said, smiled. "But getting there."

"Yeh." The quick lick of the lips, and he sat down at the table, legs out in his Prussian boots. The silver cross at his throat reflected the bright tavern light. He surveyed the room with a cool, imperious eye. Looked at Dorothy Margon. "You been holdin' out on the Duke, professor. You could do real business with that one."

The Duke admired Dorothy's long blonde hair, the low-cut black velvet dress that looked too expensive for an assistant professor's wife, her breasts rising out of the velvet.

"It's not what I do," Fred Margon said.

Dorothy Margon tore a cardboard coaster into small pieces, dropped the pieces onto the table. She began to build the debris into a pyramid. She worked on her pyramid, watched the Duke.

The people were filling the tavern now. I watched them come out of the silence and cold of the winter night into the light and noise of the tavern. They shed old coats and worn jackets, wool hats and muddy galoshes, to emerge in suits and dresses the colors of the rainbow. Saturday night.

The Duke sneered. "Works their asses a whole motherin' year for the rags they got on their backs." He waved imperiously to a waiter. "Set 'em up for my man the professor 'n' his frau. Fortune there, too. Rye for me."

Dorothy Margon built her pyramid of torn pieces of coaster. "What happened to your face?"

31

"Injuns." The Duke touched the bandage on his face, his eyes fierce. "The fuckers ganged me. I get 'em."

"Alma Jean's husband?" I said. "The Cherry Valley bar?"

The Cherry Valley Tavern was a low-ceilinged room with posts and tables and a long bar with high stools. As full of dark Iroquois faces as the massacre that had given it its name. All turned to look at me as I entered. I ordered a beer.

The bartender brought me the beer. "Maybe you'd like it better downtown, mister. Nothing personal."

"I'm looking for Joey Brant."

He mopped the bar. "You're not a cop."

"Private. Hired by his mother-in-law."

He went on mopping the bar.

"She wants to know who killed her daughter."

"Brant was in here all night."

"They told me. What time do you close?"

"Two."

"When the snow stopped," I said.

"We went to the sweat lodge. Brant, too."

"Good way to sober up on a cold night. Maybe Brant has some ideas about who did kill her."

"Down the end of the bar."

He was a small man alone on the last bar stool. He sat hunched, a glass in both hands. An empty glass. Brooding into the glass or staring up at himself in the bar mirror. I stood behind him. He didn't notice, waved at the bartender, violent and arrogant.

"You had enough, Joey."

"I says when I got enough." He scowled at the bartender. The bartender did nothing. Brant looked down at his empty glass. "I got no woman, Crow. She's dead, Crow. My woman. How I'm gonna live my woman's dead?"

"You get another woman," the bartender, Crow, said.

Brant stared at his empty glass, remembered what he wanted. "C'mon, Crow."

"You ain't got two paychecks now."

Brant swung his head from side to side as if caught in the mesh of a net, thrashing in the net. "Lemme see the stuff."

The bartender opened a drawer behind the bar, took out a napkin, opened it on the bar. Various pieces of silver and turquoise Indian jewelry lay on the towel. There were small red circles of paper attached to most pieces. Rings, bracelets, pendants, pins, a silver cross. Joey Brant picked up a narrow turquoise ring. It was one of the last pieces without a red tag.

"Two bottles," Crow said.

"It's real stuff, Crow. Four?"

"Two."

I thought Brant was going to cry, but he only nodded. Crow took an unopened bottle of cheap rye blend from under the bar, wrote on it. Close, Brant's shoulders were thickly muscled, his arms powerful, his neck like a bull. A flyweight bodybuilder. Aware of his body, his image. I sat on the stool beside him. He stared at my empty sleeve. Crow put a shot glass and a small beer on the bar, opened the marked bottle of rye.

"On me," I said. "Both of us."

Crow stared at me, then closed the marked bottle, poured from a bar bottle. He brought my beer and a chaser beer, walked away. The small, muscular Indian looked at the whisky, at me.

"Why was Alma Jean on the street, Joey?" I said.

He looked down at the whisky. His hand seemed to wait an inch from the shot glass. Then he touched it, moved it next to the beer chaser.

"How the hell I know? The bitch."

"Her mother says she had to have a big reason."

"Fuck her mother." He glared at my missing arm. "You no cop. Cops don't hire no cripples."

"Dan Fortune. Private detective. Sada Patterson hired me to find out who murdered Alma Jean. Any ideas?"

He stared into the shot glass of cheap rye as if it held all the beauty of the universe. "She think I don' know? Stupid bitch an' her black whoremaster! I knows he give her stuff. I get him, you watch. Make him talk. Black bastard, he done it sure. I get him." He drank, went on staring into the bottom of the glass as if it were a crystal ball. "Fuckin' around with that white damn professor. Think she fool Joey Brant? Him an' that hot-bitch wife he got. Business, she says; old friends, she says. Joey knows, yessir. Joey knows."

"You knew," I said, "so you killed her."

There was a low rumble through the room. The bartender, Crow, stopped pouring to watch me. They didn't love Brant, but he was one of them, and they would defend him against the white man. Any white man, black or white.

Brant shook his head. "With my friends. Not worth killin'. Nossir. Joey Brant takes care of hisself." He drained the shot, finished the beer chaser, and laid his head on the bar.

The bartender came and removed the glasses, watched me finish my beer. When I did, he made no move to serve another.

"He was in here all night; fifty guys saw him. We went to the reservation and sweated. Me and ten other guys and Brant."

"Sure," I said.

I felt their eyes all the way out. They didn't like him, even despised him, but they would all defend him, lie for him.

The band burst into sound. Dancers packed into a mass on the floor. A thick mass of bodies that moved as one, the colors and shapes of the mural on the wall, a single beast with a hundred legs and arms. Shrill tenor sax, electronic guitar, keyboard, and trumpet blaring. Drums.

"Or did Brant find you?" I said.

The Duke scowled at the dancers on the floor. "Heard he was lookin' to talk to the Duke, so I goes to the Cherry Valley. He all shit and bad booze. He never know me, 'n' I never knows him. I tells him I hear he talkin' 'bout me 'n' from now on all I wants to hear is sweet nothin'."

"You're a tough man," I said. "I'll bet you scared him."

He licked his lips. I watched the sweat on his brow, the violent swinging of his booted foot. He was hiding *something*.

"I tell him I never even heard o' his broad. What I know about no Injun's broad? I tell him iffen she goes out on the tricks, it got to be he put her out. Happens all the time. Some ol' man he needs the scratch, so he puts the ol' woman out on the hustle." The swinging foot in its black boot seemed to grow more agitated. His eyes searched restlessly around the packed room, the crowded dance floor. "I seen it all times, all ways. They comes out on the streets, nice chicks should oughta be home watchin' the kids, puttin' the groceries on the table. I seen 'em, scared 'n' no way knows what they s'posed to do. All 'cause some dude he ain't got what it takes."

Restless, he sweated. The silver cross reflected the tavern light where it lay on his thick chest hair above the black shirt. Talked. But what was he telling me?

"Is that when he jumped you? Pulled a knife?"

The Duke sneered. "Not him. He too drunk. All of 'em, they ganged me. He pull his blade, sure, but he ain't sober 'nuff he can cut cheese. It was them others ganged me. I got some of 'em, got out o' there.''

''Did you see him out on the street that night, Duke? Is that what you really told him? Why they ganged on you?''

He jerked back as if snakebitten. ''I ain't seen no one that there night! I ain't on the street that there night. I—''

He stared toward the door. As if he saw a demon.

Joey Brant stood inside the tavern entrance blinking at the noise and crowd. Walter Ellis stood beside Brant. Which one was the Duke's demon?

It was a big house by Syracuse-ghetto standards. A two-story, three-bedroom, cinder-block box painted yellow and green, with a spiked wrought-iron fence, a swimming pool that took up most of the postage-stamp side yard. Concrete paths wound among bird-baths and fountains and the American flag on a pole and naked plaster copies of the Venus de Milo and Michelangelo's David.

Walter Ellis met me on his front steps. ''The cops send you to me, Fortune?''

He was a tall, slim man with snow-white hair and a young face. He looked dangerous. Quick eyes that smiled now. Simple gray flannel slacks, a white shirt open at the throat, and a red cashmere sweater that gave a vigorous tint to his face. Only the rings on both pinkies and both index fingers, diamonds and rubies and gold, showed his money and his power.

''They said you knew Alma Jean Brant,'' I said.

''Her and her mother. Come on in. Drink?''

''Beer if you have it.''

He laughed. ''Now you know I got beer. What kind of rackets boss wouldn't have a extra refrigerator full of beer? Beck's? Stroh's? Bud?''

''Beck's, thanks.''

''Sure. A New York loner.''

We were in a small, cluttered, overstuffed living room all lace and velvet and cushions. Ellis pressed a button somewhere. A tall, handsome black man in full suit and tie materialized, not the hint of a bulge anywhere under the suit, was told to bring two Beck's.

''Not that I'm much of a racket boss like in the movies, eh? A small-town gambler. Maybe a little border stuff if the price is right.'' He laughed again, sat down in what had to be his private easy chair, worn and comfortable with a footstool, waved me to an overstuffed couch. I sank into it. He lit a cigar, eyed me over it. "But you didn't come about my business, right? Sada sent you up to find out what happened to Alma Jean."

"What did happen to her?"

"I wish I knew."

The immaculate black returned with two Beck's and two glasses on an ornate silver tray. A silver bowl of bar peanuts. Ellis raised his glass. We drank. He ate peanuts and smoked.

"You liked her?" I said. "Alma Jean?"

He savored the cigar. "I liked her. She was married. That's all. Not my age or anything else. She didn't cheat on her husband. A wife supports her husband."

"But she went on the streets."

"Prostitution isn't cheating, Fortune. Not in the ghetto, not down here where it hurts. It's the only way a woman has of making money when she got no education or skills. It's what our women do to help in a crisis."

"And the men accept that?"

He smoked, drank, fingered peanuts. "Some do, some don't."

"Which are you?"

"I never cottoned to white slaving."

"You were out that night. In your car. On the streets down near Irish Johnny's.

He drank, licked foam from his lips. "Who says?"

"Professor Fred Margon saw you. I think Duke Wiltkowski did, too. He's scared, sweating, and hiding something."

His eyes were steady over the glass, the peanuts he ate one by one. "I like a drive, a nice walk in the snow. I saw the Duke and Margon. I didn't see no one else. But a couple of times I saw that wife of Margon's tailing Alma Jean."

"Was it snowing when you got home?"

He smiled.

I watched Walter Ellis steer Joey Brant to a table on the far side of the dance floor. Brant was already drunk, but his startled eyes were wary, almost alert. This wasn't one of his taverns. The Duke watched Walter Ellis.

I said, "It's okay; we know he was out that night. He saw you, knows you saw him, and it's okay. Who else did you see?"

The Duke licked his lips, looked at Fred Margon.

"You writes, yeh, professor?"

He looked back across the dance floor to Ellis and Joey Brant.

"I means," the Duke said, "like stories 'n' books 'n' all that there?"

"God, does he write!" Dorothy Margon said. "Writes, studies, teaches. All day, every day. Tell the Duke about your art, Fred. Tell the Duke what you *do*. All day, every damn day."

"Like," the Duke said, "poetry stuff?" He watched only Fred Margon now. "Words they got the same sound 'n' all?"

"I write poetry," Fred said. "Sometimes it rhymes."

"You likes poetry, yeh?"

"Yes, I like poetry. I read it."

"Oh, but it's so hard!" Dorothy said. "Tell the Duke how hard poetry is, Fred. Tell him how hard all *real* writing is. Tell him how you can learn most careers in a few years, but it takes a lifetime to learn to write well."

"We better go," Fred said.

I watched the people packed body to body on the dance floor, flushed and excited, desperate for Saturday night. On the far side Walter Ellis ordered drinks. Joey Brant saw us: the Duke, me, Fred, and Dorothy Margon. I watched him turn on Ellis. The racket boss only smiled, shook his head.

Dorothy smiled at the Duke. "I'm a bitch, right? I wasn't once. Do your women talk to you like that, Duke? No, they wouldn't, would they? They wouldn't dare. They wouldn't want to. Tell me about the Indians? How many were there? Did they all have knives? Do they still wear feathers? How many did you knock out? Kill?"

The Duke watched Fred Margon. "You writes good, professor?"

"You see," Dorothy said, "we're going to stay at the university three more years. We may even stay forever. Isn't that grand news? I can stay here and do nothing forever."

The Duke said to Fred, "They puts what you writes in books?"

Dorothy said, "Did you ever want something, wait for something, think you have it at last, and then suddenly it's so far away again you can't even see it anymore?"

"I'm a writer," Fred said. "A writer and a teacher. I can't go to New York and write lies for money."

Dorothy stood up. "Dance with me, Duke. I want to dance. I want to dance right now."

* * *

She opened the apartment door my second day in Syracuse, looked at my duffel coat, beret, and missing arm.

"He's out. Go find him in one of your literary bars!"

"Mrs. Margon?" I said.

She cocked her head, suspicious yet coy, blonde, and flirtatious. "You want me?"

"Would it do me any good?"

She laughed. "Do we know each other, Mr.—?"

"Fortune," I said. "No."

She eyed me. "Then what do you want to talk to me about?"

"Alma Jean Brant," I said.

She started to close the door. "Go and find my husband."

I held the door with my foot. "No, I want you. Both ways."

She laughed again, neither flirtatious nor amused this time. Self-mocking, a little bitter. "You can probably have me. Both ways." But stepped back, held the door open. "Come in."

It was a small apartment: a main room, bedroom, kitchenette, and bathroom. All small, cramped. The furniture had to have been rented with the apartment. They don't pay assistant professors too well, and the future of a writer is at best a gamble, so without children they saved their money, scrimped, did without. She lit a cigarette, didn't offer me one.

"What about that Alma Jean woman?"

"What can you tell me about her?"

"Nothing. That's Fred's territory. Ask him."

"About her murder?"

She smoked. "I thought it was an accident. Or suicide. Drunk and fell over that bridge wall, or jumped. Isn't that what the police think?"

"The police don't think anything one way or the other. I think it was murder."

"What do you want, Mr. Fortune? A confession?"

"Do you want to make one?"

"Yes, that I'm a nasty bitch who wants more than she's got. Just more. You understand that, Mr. Fortune."

"It's a modern disease," I said, "but what's it got to do with Alma Jean Brant?"

She smoked. "You wouldn't be here if someone hadn't seen me around her."

"Her husband," I said. "And Walter Ellis."

The couch creaked under her as if it had rusty springs. "I was

38

jealous. Or maybe just suspicious. He's so involved in his work, I'm so bored, our sex life is about zero. We never do anything! We talk, read, think, discuss, but we never *do*! I make his life miserable, I admit it. But he promised we would stay here only five years or until he published a novel. We would go down to New York, he'd make money, we'd have some life! I counted on that. Now he wants to get tenure, stay here!"

"So he can teach and write?" I said. "That's all? No other reason for wanting to stay here?"

She nodded. "When he started going out all the time, I wondered, too. Research for his work, he said, but I heard about Alma Jean. So I followed him and found where she lived. Then I followed her to see if she'd meet him somewhere else. That's all. I just watched her house, followed her a few times. I never saw him do a damn thing that could be close to cheating. At her house that husband of hers was around all the time. He must work nights."

"Did you see her do anything?"

She smoked. "I saw her visit the same house three or four times. I got real suspicious then. I hadn't seen Fred go in, but after she left the last time, I went up and rang the bell. A guy answered, but it wasn't Fred, so I made some excuse and got out of there. She was meeting someone all right, but not Fred."

"Any idea who?"

She shook her head. "He wasn't an Indian, I can say that."

"What was he?"

"Black, Mr. Fortune. One big black man."

Through the mass of sound and movement, bodies and faces that glistened with sweat and gaudy color and melted into the bright colors and tortured figures of the mural on the walls, I watched Joey Brant across the dance floor drinking and talking to Walter Ellis, who only listened.

I watched Dorothy Margon move lightly through the shuffle of the massed dancers. Her slender body loose and supple, her eyes closed, her lips parted, her face turned up to the Duke. I could see a man she denied turn to someone else. A man who could not give her what she wanted turning to someone who wanted less.

Her hips moved a beat behind the band; her long blonde hair swung free against the black velvet of her dress and the scarred face of the Duke. I could see her, restless and rejecting, but still not wanting her man to go anywhere else.

"I can't tell the dancers from the people in the mural," Fred Margon said. "I can't be sure which woman is my wife with the Duke and which is the woman chained in the mural."

He was talking about himself: a man who could not tell which was real and which was only an image. He could not decide, be certain, which was real to him, image or reality.

"Which man is the Duke on the dance floor with my wife," Fred Margon said, "and which is the blue man with the bare chest and hammer in the mural? Am I the man at the ringside table with a glass of beer in a pale, indoor hand watching the Duke dance with his wife, or the thin scarecrow in the mural with his wrists chained and his starving face turned up to an empty sky?"

He was trying to understand something, and across the dance floor Joey Brant was talking and talking to Walter Ellis. Ellis only listened and watched the Duke and Dorothy Margon on the dance floor. The Duke sweated, and Dorothy Margon danced with her eyes closed, her body moving as if by itself.

Walter Ellis sat alone in the back of his pink Cadillac. I leaned in the window.

"A black man, she said. A big black man Alma Jean visited in a house in the ghetto."

"A lot of big black men in the ghetto, Fortune."

"What was the crisis?" I said. "You said going on the streets was what ghetto women did in a crisis."

"I don't know."

"You offered to pay for whatever she needed money for."

"She only told me she needed something that cost a lot of money."

"Needed what?"

"A psychiatrist. I sent her to the best."

"A black? Big? Lives near here? Expensive?"

"All that."

"Can we go and talk to him?"

"Anytime."

"And you didn't give her the money to pay him?"

"She wouldn't take it. Said she would know what it was really for even if it was only in my mind."

The Duke said, "There was this here chippie. I mean, she's workin' my streets 'n' I don' work her, see? I mean, it's snowin'

40

bad 'n' there ain't no action goin' down, my three pigs're holed up warmin' their pussy, but this chippie she's out workin' on my turf. Hey, that don't go down, you know? I mean, that's no scene, right? So I moves in to tell her to fly her pussy off'n my streets or sign up with the Duke.''

I said, "The last time it snowed was the night Alma Jean died."

Dorothy Margon built another pyramid of torn coasters on the tavern table and watched the Saturday night dancers. Fred Margon and I watched the Duke. The Duke mopped his face with a dirty handkerchief, a kind of desperation in his voice that rose higher, faster, as if he could not stop himself, had to talk while Fred Margon was there.

"I *knows* that there fox. I mean, I gets up close to tell her do a fade and I remembers that chippie in the snow."

I said, "It was Alma Jean."

He sweated in that hot room with its pounding music and packed bodies swirling and rubbing. It was what he had been hiding, holding back. What he had wanted to tell from the start. What he had to tell.

"Back when I was jus' a punk kid stealin' dogs, my ol' man beatin' my ass to go to school, that there chippie out in the snow was in that school. I remembers. Smart 'n' clean 'n' got a momma dresses her up real good. I remembers, you know? Like, I had eyes for that pretty little kid back then."

The band stopped. The dancers drifted off the floor, sat down. A silence like a blow from a hammer in the hands of the big blue man in the mural.

"I walks off. I mean, when I remembers that little girl, I walks me away from that there chippie. I remembers how good her momma fixes her up, so I walks off 'n' lets her work, 'n' I got the blues, you know. I got the blues then, 'n' I got 'em now."

"Everybody got the blues," Dorothy said. "We should write a song. Fred should write a poem."

"It was Alma Jean, Duke," I said.

Walter Ellis stopped to say a few low words to the tall, handsome doctor, while I walked down the steps of his modest house and out to the ghetto street. The numbers boss caught up with me before I reached his Cadillac.

"Does that tell you who killed her?" Ellis said.

"I think so. All I have to do is find a way to prove it."

He nodded. We both got into the back of the pink car. It purred away from the curb. The silent driver in the immaculate suit drove slowly, sedately, parading Ellis through his domain where the people could see him.

"Any ideas?" Ellis said.

"Watch and hope for a break. They've all got something on their minds; maybe it'll get too heavy."

He watched the street ahead. "That include me?"

"It includes you," I said. "You were out that night."

"You know what I've got on my mind?"

"I've got a hunch," I said. "I'm going to meet the Margons in Irish Johnny's tonight. Why don't you come around and bring Brant, friend of the family."

We drove on to my motel.

"The Duke hangs out in Irish Johnny's," Ellis said.

"I know," I said.

"I writes me a poem," the Duke said. " 'Bout that there chippie. I go home 'n' write me a poem."

The scarred black face of the Duke seemed to watch the empty dance floor as he told about the poem he had written. Fred Margon looked at him. All through the long room the Saturday night people waited for the music to begin again. Across the floor Walter Ellis talked to those who came to him one by one to pay their respects. Joey Brant drank, stared into his glass, looked toward me and the Margons and the Duke.

"Do you have it with you?" Fred said.

The Duke's eyes flickered above the scars on his face and the new bandage. Looked right and left.

"Did you bring it to show me?" Fred Margon said.

The Duke sweated in the hot room. Nodded.

"All right," Fred said. "But don't just show it to me, read it. Out loud. Poetry should be read aloud. While the band is still off, get up and read your poem. This is your tavern; they all know you in here. Tell them why you wrote it, how it came to you, and read it to them."

The Duke stared. "You fuckin' with me, man?"

"Fred?" Dorothy Margon said.

"You wrote it, didn't you? You felt it. If you feel something and write it, you have to believe in it. You have to show it to the world, make the world hear."

"You a crazy man," the Duke said.

Dorothy tore another coaster. Across the room Joey Brant and Walter Ellis watched our table. I waited.

"Give it to me," Fred said.

The Duke sat there for some time, the sweat beaded on his face, his booted foot swinging, while the people all through the room waited for Saturday night to return.

"What happened to Alma Jean, Duke?" I said.

Fred Margon said, "You wrote it; give it to me."

The Duke reached into his filthy raincoat and handed a torn piece of lined notebook paper to Fred Margon. Fred stood up. On the other side of the dance floor Joey Brant held his glass without drinking as Fred Margon walked to the bandstand, jumped up to the microphone.

"Ladies and gentlemen!"

In the long room, ice loud in the glasses and voices in the rumble of conversation, the people who waited only for the music to begin again, Saturday night to return, turned toward the bandstand. Fred Margon told them about the Duke and the chippie working his territory without his permission. The Duke alone in the night with the snow and the chippie.

"The Duke remembered that girl. He let her work, went home, and wrote a poem. I'm going to read that poem."

There were some snickers, a murmur of protest or two, the steady clink of indifferent glasses. Fred called for silence. Waited. Until the room silenced. Then he read the poem.

> *Once I was pure*
> *as a snow but I fell,*
> *fell like a snowflake*
> *from heaven to hell.*
>
> *Fell to be scuffed,*
> *to be spit on and beat,*
> *fell to be like*
> *the filth in the street.*
>
> *Pleading and cursing*
> *and dreading to die*
> *to the fellow I know*
> *up there in the sky.*

The fellow his cross
I got on this chain
I give it to her
she gets clean again.

Dear God up there,
have I fell so low,
and yet to be once
like the beautiful snow.

Through the smoke haze of the crowded tavern room they shifted their feet. They stirred their drinks. The musicians, ready to return, stood in the wings. A woman giggled. The bartenders hid grins. Some men suddenly laughed. A murmur of laughter rippled through the room. The Duke stood up, stepped toward the bandstand. Fred came across the empty dance floor.

"I like it," Fred Margon said. "It's not a good poem; you're not a poet. But it's real and I like it. I like anything that says what you really feel, says it openly and honestly. It's what you had to do."

The Duke's eyes were black above the scars and the bandage. The Duke watched only Fred, his fists clenched, his eyes wide.

"It's you," Fred said. "Go up and read it yourself. Make them see what you saw out there in the snow when you remembered Alma Jean, the girl whose mother dressed her so well. To hell with anyone who laughs. They're laughing at themselves. The way they would have laughed if Alma Jean had told them what she was going to do. They're afraid, so they laugh. They're afraid to know what they feel. They're afraid to feel. Help them face themselves. Read your poem again. And again."

The Duke stood in Irish Johnny's Tavern, five new stitches in his scarred face under the bandage, and read his poem to the people who only wanted Saturday night to start again with the loud blare of the music and the heavy mass of the dancing and a kind of oblivion. He read without stumbling over the words, not reading but hearing it in the smoke of the gaudy tavern room. Hearing it as it had come to him when he stood in the snow and remembered the girl whose mother had always dressed her so well.

There was no laughter now. The Duke was doing what he had

44

to do. Fred and Dorothy Margon were listening, and no one wanted to look stupid. Walter Ellis and Joey Brant were listening, and no one wanted to offend Mr. Ellis. So they sat, and the band waited to come back and start Saturday night again, and I went to the telephone and called Lieutenant Derrida.

Walter Ellis moved his chair, and I faced Joey Brant across the tavern table. "High steel pays good money, but you haven't been making good money in a long time. You were home whenever Professor Margon went to talk to Alma Jean. You were home when Dorothy Margon watched Alma Jean. You haven't been working high steel for over a year. That's why she went out on the streets. You even had to sell Alma Jean's jewelry to buy whisky at Cherry Valley Tavern. One of those pieces wasn't hers, though, and that was a mistake. It was the cross the Duke gave her the night she was killed, the one he wrote about in his poem. You knew someone else had given it to her, but you didn't know the Duke had given it to her that night, and it proves you killed her. You grabbed it from her neck before you knocked her off that bridge."

Lieutenant Derrida stood over the table. The room was watching now. The Duke with his poem in his hand, Walter Ellis sad, Fred and Dorothy Margon holding hands but not looking at each other. Derrida said, "It's the cross the Duke gave her that night, has his initials inside. Your boss says you haven't worked high steel in over a year, just low-pay ground jobs when you show up at all. When the bartender, Crow, saw we had proof and motive, he talked. You left the tavern when it closed, didn't get to the sweat lodge until pushing 3:30 A.M. You brought the jewelry to Crow after she was dead."

Joey Brant drained his whiskey, looked at us all with rage in his dark eyes. "She didn't got to go on no streets. We was makin' it all right. She got no cause playin' with white guys, sellin' it to old men, working for black whoremasters. I cut him good, that black bastard, 'n' I knocked her off that there bridge when she was out selling her ass so she could live high and rich with her white friends and her gamblers and her black pimps! Sure, I hit her. I never meant to kill her, but I saw that cross on her neck 'n' I never give her no cross 'n' I hit her and she went on over."

I said, "Her mother said she would only go on the streets for a big reason. You know what that was, Brant? You know why she went back on the streets?"

45

"I know, mister. Money, that's why! 'Cause I ain't bringing home the big bucks like the gambler 'n' the professor 'n' the black pimp!"

"She wanted to hire a psychiatrist," I said. "You know what that is, Joey. A man who makes a sick mind get better."

"Psychiatrist?" Joey Brant said.

"A healer, Joey. For a scared man who sat at home all day and drank too much. An expensive healer, so she had to go out on the streets to make the money she couldn't make any other way."

"Shut up, you hear? Shut up!" His dark face almost white.

I shook my head. "We know, Joey. We talked to the psychiatrist and your boss. You're afraid of heights, Joey. You couldn't even go to the edge of that bridge parapet and see where she had fallen. You can't go up high on the steel anymore, where the big money is. Where a brave goes. Up there with the real men. You became afraid and it was killing you and that was killing her and she had to try to help you, save you, so she wanted money to take you to a psychiatrist who would cure you, help you go up on the steel again where you could feel like a man!"

"Psychiatrist?" Joey Brant said.

"That's right, Joey. Her big, special reason to make big money the only way she knew how."

Joey Brant sat there for a long time looking at all of us, at the floor, at his hands, at his empty whisky glass. Just sat while Lieutenant Derrida waited and everyone drifted away, and at last he put his head down on the table and began to cry.

Derrida had taken Joey Brant away. The Duke had stopped reading his poem to anyone who would listen. I sat at the floor-side table with Fred and Dorothy Margon. Out on the floor the Saturday night people clung and twined and held each other in their fine shimmering clothes, while in the mural the silent yellow women and bent blue men frozen in the red and yellow sky watched and waited.

"Dance with me, Fred," Dorothy Margon said.

"I'm a bad dancer," Fred Margon said. "I always have been a bad dancer. I always will be a bad dancer."

"I know," Dorothy said. "Just dance with me now."

They danced among the faceless crowd, two more bodies that would soon go their separate ways. I knew that and so did they. Fred would teach and write and go on examining life for what he must write about. Dorothy would go to New York or Los Angeles to find more out of life than an assistant professor, a would-be writer. What they had to do.

The Duke has one kind of courage and Fred Margon has another. Joey Brant lost his. Fred Margon's kind will cost him his wife. Alma Jean's courage killed her. The courage to do what she had to do to help her man, even though she knew he would not understand. He would hate her, but she had to do it anyway. Courage has its risks, and we don't always win.

In my New York office-apartment Sada Patterson listened in silence, her worn plastic handbag on her skinny lap, the ramrod back so straight it barely touched my chair.

"I knew she had a big reason," she said. "That was my Alma Jean. To help her man find hisself again." She nodded, almost satisfied, "I'm sorry for him. He's a little man." She stood up. "I gonna miss her—Alma Jean. She was my last: I always dressed her real good."

She paid me. I took the money. She had her courage, too. And her pride. She'd go on living, fierce and independent, even if she couldn't really tell herself why.

Little Lamb

•

Bill Pronzini

Beginning with The Stalker *in 1971, Bill Pronzini has published more than forty novels in a variety of fields. Sixteen feature his San Francisco-based "Nameless Detective," the most recent of which is* Shackles *(1988). When writing short fiction he often chooses the vignette form because of its challenging nature; "Little Lamb," the tale of an unhappy married woman who finally decides to take a lover, is one example of his work of this type. Others can be found in* Small Felonies *(1988), a collection of his fifty best criminous short-shorts.*

The place where they met for dinner was a Neapolitan restaurant on the edge of North Beach, not far from Don's apartment. The decor was very old-fashioned—red-and-white checked tablecloths, Chianti bottles with candle drippings down the necks and sides— but then Don was old-fashioned, too, at least in some ways, so she wasn't surprised when he said it was his favorite restaurant. Meg had never been there before. It wasn't the kind of place Gene would ever have taken her, not in a million years.

They sat at a little table in one corner, away from the windows that overlooked the street, and Don ordered a bottle of wine, something called Valpolicella. He was nervous, probably as nervous and tense as she was, but with him it was close to the surface, not pushed down deep inside. Poor Don. He must suspect why she'd called him, why she'd coaxed him into meeting her for dinner. How could he not suspect? He felt the same about her as she felt about him, she was sure of that. She'd noticed how he looked at her at the Currys' party that night three years ago, felt the mutual attraction then and every time they'd run into each other since. But he'd never done anything about it—never called her or tried to see her alone somewhere. And of course she'd never done anything about it, either. Until tonight.

But I should have, she thought. I shouldn't have waited so long—all those bad, empty months and years with Gene. I should have arranged to see Don right away after that party at the Currys. If I had . . .

But she hadn't. She was such a little lamb. That was what Gene said, anyway, what he always called her in private. His little lamb. He hadn't meant it affectionately, as her being cute and cuddly and soft. No, he'd meant she was placid, no mind of her own, lost without someone to guide her. Just a poor little lost lamb.

Not any more, though. Not tonight.

The waiter came with the wine and to take their orders. She'd asked Don to order for both of them, because he'd come here so often and knew what was especially good. She wanted the dinner, like everything else about this night, to be perfect. He must have wanted that, too, in his own way; he was very deliberate, asking the waiter several questions before he made up his mind. What he finally ordered was zuppa di vongole, green salad, breadsticks, and fusili alla Vesuviana.

"What is fusili alla Vesuviana?" she asked after the waiter went away.

"Noodles with tomato and cheese. Vesuvius style."

"Vesuvius? It won't erupt while we're eating, will it?"

He laughed, but it was a small laugh—forced, brittle. "You don't have to worry about that."

"I guess I'm not very good at making jokes . . ."

"No, no, it was a good joke."

There was an uncomfortable little silence. The only thing she could think to say was, "Don, aren't you glad you came?"

". . . Yes, I'm glad."

"You're not acting like it."

"It's just that . . . well."

"Well what?"

"I don't think Gene would like it if he knew."

"He's not going to know. I told you, he's away."

"I know you did, but—"

"Until tomorrow," she said. "Sometime tomorrow."

Don seemed about to say something, changed his mind, and took a too-quick drink from his glass and spilled a dribble of wine down his chin. She had an impulse to reach over and wipe it away, touch him, but she didn't let herself do it. Not just yet.

She tasted her own wine. It was heavy, faintly sweet, not at all the kind of wine she usually liked. Tonight, though, it went with the ambiance here, with this special occasion. She drank a little more, watching Don drain his glass and pour another. She mustn't have too much herself before the food came. She had no tolerance for alcohol and she mustn't get tipsy, mustn't do anything to spoil things for either of them. When she got tipsy she would giggle or have an attack of the hiccups or knock over her glass—something silly and embarrassing like that. So she must be very careful. One glass of wine, no more.

It was just the opposite with Don. He drank two full glasses of Valpolicella and part of a third before he began to relax. Then she was able to draw him out a bit, get him to talk about his job—he was an editor with one of San Francisco's regional publishing firms—and about people they both knew. When she told him about Marian Cobb's latest trip to a fat farm, and he laughed a genuine laugh, she felt both relieved and reassured.

It's going to be all right, she told herself. It really is. Tonight is going to be just fine.

The zuppa di vongole came. She wasn't at all hungry, she had been sure she would only pick at her food, but she finished all of the soup, and all of the green salad that followed, and then most of the fusili alla Vesuviana. It amazed her just how much of an appetite she had. And all the while they continued to talk, not about anything personal, just small talk, but there was an intimacy in it of the sort that she and Gene had never shared over a meal. Don felt it, too. She could see him gradually give in to it, let the warmth of it enfold him as it was enfolding her.

Afterward they had espresso and a funny licorice-tasting liqueur—Zambucca?—that was served with a coffee bean floating in it. Over their second cup of espresso, she caught him looking at her, an unmistakably hungry look that he quickly covered up. It made her tingle, made her wet down below. She had never responded sexually when Gene looked at her that way. Oh, maybe in the beginning she had, a little. But not like this. She had never felt about Gene as she did about Don.

Why didn't I do this a long time ago? she asked herself again. Why, why, why didn't I?

The waiter came with the check. Don paid in cash, and when

they were alone again she said, "What I'd like to do now is walk a bit. It's such a nice night."

"Good idea."

"Then what I want to do is go to your apartment."

She said it so casually, so boldly, it surprised her almost as much as it surprised Don. She hadn't meant to be so brazen; the words had just come out. He blinked in a way that was almost comical, like a startled owl. "Meg," he said, and then didn't go on.

"Wouldn't you like to?" she asked.

"I . . . don't think it would be a good idea."

"Why not?"

"You know why, for God's sake."

"Well, I think it's a wonderful idea," she said. "It's what I want and I think it's what you want, too. Isn't it?"

He gave her a long searching look. Then he let his gaze slide away and said abruptly, almost painfully. "Yes, damn it. Yes."

"You mustn't be ashamed. I'm not."

"It isn't that I'm ashamed . . ."

She touched him then, touched his hand with the tips of her fingers. It made him jump as if with an electrical shock. "It's all right," she said. "Don—it's all right."

"It's not all right."

"But it is."

"You're a married woman . . ."

"I don't love Gene. I'm not sure I ever did."

"That isn't the point."

"It is the point. It *is*," she said. "Please, let's leave now. I'd like to walk."

She got to her feet and stood waiting for him to do the same. It wasn't a long wait, only a few seconds. They went outside together, along the crowded sidewalks of upper Grant. Somewhere she could hear music playing, guitar music—flamenco guitar? She smiled. It was such a nice night.

Beside her, Don said, "Meg, I don't understand this. Why? Tell me why."

"You know why," she said. "I've known all along how you felt about me. And I've felt the same about you, from the very first."

"Then why did you wait three years? That's what I don't understand. Why tonight, all of a sudden?"

"It was time," she said. "Past time. I couldn't wait any longer."

He was silent, walking.

"Don? You do want to be with me tonight, don't you? Alone together, the whole night?"

"You know I do. I won't deny it."

"Then that's all that matters, darling. Us together, tonight."

She heard him sigh softly. And then she heard him say, "God help us both."

Yes, she thought, God help us both.

She took his arm and moved close to him, as if they were already lovers. And for the first time, she thought about the bruises and wondered if the most recent ones still showed. Well, it didn't matter so much if they did. She would ask Don to turn the lights down low or shut them off altogether. That way, he would not notice tonight. Tomorrow . . . well, tomorrow was tomorrow. He would find out then, in any case, not so very long after he found out about Gene.

She thought about Gene, but only briefly. Only briefly did she picture him lying there in the bedroom they had shared, the bedroom where time and again he had beaten his poor little lamb, the bedroom where she had shot him to death at four o'clock this afternoon. *Yes, officer, I emptied the gun into him. He was coming at me, he was drunk and ready to beat me again, and I took the gun and I shot him and then I ran out and drove around and around—and then I called Don Murdock and arranged to have dinner with him and later spent the night with him for the first and last time. Do you think that's awful? Do you believe I'm some kind of monster?*

No, she mustn't think that way. All of that was tomorrow. First, there was tonight. And no matter what anyone believed, tonight was very important—very, very important. Like the last night before the end of the world.

She hugged Don's arm and smiled up at him, thinking about tonight.

Chee's Witch

•

Tony Hillerman

There have been relatively few American Indian detectives in crime fiction, and none more believable than Tony Hillerman's two Navajo tribal policemen, Joe Leaphorn and Jim Chee. Hillerman, who numbers many Navajos among his friends, knows the Navajo culture, and his evocations of it and the New Mexico landscape are flawless, as "Chee's Witch" convincingly attests. Jim Chee has appeared in several novels to date, among them The People of Darkness *(1980) and* A Thief of Time *(1988). One of the Joe Leaphorn novels,* Dance Hall of the Dead, *received a Mystery Writers of America Edgar for Best Novel of 1973.*

Snow is so important to the Eskimos they have nine nouns to describe its variations. Corporal Jimmy Chee of the Navajo Tribal Police had heard that as an anthropology student at the University of New Mexico. He remembered it now because he was thinking of all the words you need in Navajo to account for the many forms of witchcraft. The word Old Woman Tso had used was "anti'l," which is the ultimate sort, the absolute worst. And so, in fact, was the deed that seemed to have been done. Murder, apparently. Mutilation, certainly, if Old Woman Tso had her facts right. And then, if one believed all the mythology of witchery told among the fifty clans who comprised The People, there must also be cannibalism, incest, even necrophilia.

On the radio in Chee's pickup truck, the voice of the young Navajo reading a Gallup used-car commercial was replaced by Willie Nelson singing of trouble and a worried mind. The ballad fit Chee's mood. He was tired. He was thirsty. He was sticky with sweat. He was worried. His pickup jolted along the ruts in a windless heat, leaving a white fog of dust to mark its winding passage across the Rainbow Plateau. The truck was gray with it. So was

Jimmy Chee. Since sunrise he had covered maybe 200 miles of half-graded gravel and unmarked wagon tracks of the Arizona-Utah-New Mexico border country. Routine at first—a check into a witch story at the Tsossie hogan north of Teec Nos Pos to stop trouble before it started. Routine and logical. A bitter winter, a sandstorm spring, a summer of rainless, desiccating heat. Hopes dying, things going wrong, anger growing, and then the witch gossip. The logical. A bitter winter, a sandstorm spring, a summer awry. The trouble at the summer hogan of the Tsossies was a sick child and a water well that had turned alkaline—nothing unexpected. But you didn't expect such a specific witch. The skinwalker, the Tsossies agreed, was The City Navajo, the man who had come to live in one of the government houses at Kayenta. Why the City Navajo? Because everybody knew he was a witch. Where had they heard that, the first time? The People who came to the trading post at Mexican Water said it. And so Chee had driven westward over Tohache Wash, past Red Mesa and Rabbit Ears to Mexican Water. He had spent hours on the shady porch giving those who came to buy, and to fill their water barrels, and to visit, a chance to know who he was until finally they might risk talking about witchcraft to a stranger. They were Mud Clan, and Many Goats People, and Standing Rock Clan—foreign to Chee's own Slow Talking People—but finally some of them talked a little.

A witch was at work on the Rainbow Plateau. Adeline Etcitty's mare had foaled a two-headed colt. Hosteen Musket had seen the witch. He'd seen a man walk into a grove of cottonwoods, but when he got there an owl flew away. Rudolph Bisti's boys lost three rams while driving their flocks up into the Chuska high pastures, and when they found the bodies, the huge tracks of a werewolf were all around them. The daughter of Rosemary Nashibitti had seen a big dog bothering her horses and had shot at it with her .22 and the dog had turned into a man wearing a wolfskin and had fled, half running, half flying. The old man they called Afraid of His Horses had heard the sound of the witch on the roof of his winter hogan, and saw the dirt falling through the smoke hole as the skinwalker tried to throw in his corpse powder. The next morning the old man had followed the tracks of the Navajo Wolf for a mile, hoping to kill him. But the tracks had faded away. There was nothing very unusual in the stories, except their number and the recurring hints that City Navajo was the witch. But then came what Chee hadn't expected. The witch had killed a man.

The police dispatcher at Window Rock had been interrupting Willie Nelson with an occasional blurted message. Now she spoke directly to Chee. He acknowledged. She asked his location.

"About fifteen miles south of Dennehotso," Chee said. "Homeward bound for Tuba City. Dirty, thirsty, hungry, and tired."

"I have a message."

"Tuba City," Chee repeated, "which I hope to reach in about two hours, just in time to avoid running up a lot of overtime for which I never get paid."

"The message is FBI Agent Wells needs to contact you. Can you make a meeting at Kayenta Holiday Inn at eight P.M.?"

"What's it about?" Chee asked. The dispatcher's name was Virgie Endecheenie, and she had a very pretty voice and the first time Chee had met her at the Window Rock headquarters of the Navajo Tribal Police he had been instantly smitten. Unfortunately, Virgie was a born-into Salt Cedar Clan, which was the clan of Chee's father, which put an instant end to that. Even thinking about it would violate the complex incest taboo of the Navajos.

"Nothing on what it's about," Virgie said, her voice strictly business. "It just says confirm meeting time and place with Chee or obtain alternate time."

"Any first name on Wells?" Chee asked. The only FBI Wells he knew was Jake Wells. He hoped it wouldn't be Jake.

"Negative on the first name," Virgie said.

"All right," Chee said. "I'll be there."

The road tilted downward now into the vast barrens of erosion that the Navajos call Beautiful Valley. Far to the west, the edge of the sun dipped behind a cloud—one of the line of thunderheads forming in the evening heat over the San Francisco Peaks and the Coconino Rim. The Hopis had been holding their Niman Kachina dances, calling the clouds to come and bless them.

Chee reached Kayenta just a little late. It was early twilight and the clouds had risen black against the sunset. The breeze brought the faint smells that rising humidity carry across desert country—the perfume of sage, creosote brush, and dust. The desk clerk said that Wells was in room 284 and the first name was Jake. Chee no longer cared. Jake Wells was abrasive, but he was also smart. He had the best record in the special FBI Academy class Chee had attended, a quick, tough intelligence. Chee could tolerate the man's

55

personality for a while to learn what Wells could make of his witchcraft puzzle.

"It's unlocked," Wells said. "Come on in." He was propped against the padded headboard of the bed, shirt off, shoes on, glass in hand. He glanced at Chee and then back at the television set. He was as tall as Chee remembered, and the eyes were just as blue. He waved the glass at Chee without looking away from the set. "Mix yourself one," he said, nodding toward a bottle beside the sink in the dressing alcove.

"How you doing, Jake?" Chee asked.

Now the blue eyes re-examined Chee. The question in them abruptly went away. "Yeah," Wells said. "You were the one at the Academy." He eased himself on his left elbow and extended a hand. "Jake Wells," he said.

Chee shook the hand. "Chee," he said.

Wells shifted his weight again and handed Chee his glass. "Pour me a little more while you're at it," he said, "and turn down the sound."

Chee turned down the sound.

"About thirty percent booze," Wells demonstrated the proportion with his hands. "This is your district then. You're in charge around Kayenta? Window Rock said I should talk to you. They said you were out chasing around in the desert today. What are you working on?"

"Nothing much," Chee said. He ran a glass of water, drinking it thirstily. His face in the mirror was dirty—the lines around mouth and eyes whitish with dust. The sticker on the glass reminded guests that the laws of the Navajo Tribal Council prohibited possession of alcoholic beverages on the reservation. He refilled his own glass with water and mixed Wells's drink. "As a matter of fact, I'm working on a witchcraft case."

"Witchcraft?" Wells laughed. "Really?" He took the drink from Chee and examined it. "How does it work? Spells and like that?"

"Not exactly," Chee said. "It depends. A few years ago a little girl got sick down near Burnt Water. Her dad killed three people with a shotgun. He said they blew corpse powder on his daughter and made her sick."

Wells was watching him. "The kind of crime where you have the insanity plea."

"Sometimes," Chee said. "Whatever you have, witch talk makes you nervous. It happens more when you have a bad year like this. You hear it and you try to find out what's starting it before things get worse.''

"So you're not really expecting to find a witch?"

"Usually not," Chee said.

"Usually?"

"Judge for yourself," Chee said. "I'll tell you what I've picked up today. You tell me what to make of it. Have time?''

Wells shrugged. "What I really want to talk about is a guy named Simon Begay." He looked quizzically at Chee. "You heard the name?''

"Yes," Chee said.

"Well, shit," Wells said. "You shouldn't have. What do you know about him?''

"Showed up maybe three months ago. Moved into one of those U.S. Public Health Service houses over by the Kayenta clinic. Stranger. Keeps to himself. From off the reservation somewhere. I figured you federals put him here to keep him out of sight.''

Wells frowned. "How long you known about him?''

"Quite a while," Chee said. He'd known about Begay within a week after his arrival.

"He's a witness," Wells said. "They broke a car-theft operation in Los Angeles. Big deal. National connections. One of those where they have hired hands picking up expensive models and they drive 'em right on the ship and off-load in South America. This Begay is one of the hired hands. Nobody much. Criminal record going all the way back to juvenile, but all nickel-and-dime stuff. I gather he saw some things that help tie some big boys into the crime, so Justice made a deal with him.''

"And they hide him out here until the trial?''

Something apparently showed in the tone of the question. "If you want to hide an apple, you drop it in with the other apples," Wells said. "What better place?''

Chee had been looking at Wells's shoes, which were glossy with polish. Now he examined his own boots, which were not. But he was thinking of Justice Department stupidity. The appearance of any new human in a country as empty as the Navajo Reservation provoked instant interest. If the stranger was a Navajo, there were instant questions. What was his clan? Who was his mother? What was his father's clan? Who were his relatives? The City Navajo had no answers to any of these crucial questions. He was (as Chee had been repeatedly told) unfriendly. It was quickly guessed that he was a "relocation Navajo," born to one of those hundreds of Navajo families that the federal government had tried to re-establish forty years ago in Chicago, Los Angeles, and other urban centers. He was a stranger. In a year of witches, he would certainly be suspected. Chee sat looking at his boots, wondering if that was the only basis for the charge that City Navajo was a skinwalker. Or had someone seen something? Had someone seen the murder?

"The thing about apples is they don't gossip," Chee said.

"You hear gossip about Begay?" Wells was sitting up now, his feet on the floor.

"Sure," Chee said. "I hear he's a witch."

Wells produced a pro-forma chuckle. "Tell me about it," he said.

Chee knew exactly how he wanted to tell it. Wells would have to wait a while before he came to the part about Begay. "The Eskimos have nine nouns for snow," Chee began. He told Wells about the variety of witchcraft on the reservations and its environs: about frenzy witchcraft, used for sexual conquests, of witchery distortions, of curing ceremonials, of the exotic two-heart witchcraft of the Hopi Fog Clan, of the Zuni Sorcery Fraternity, of the Navajo "chindi," which is more like a ghost than a witch, and finally of the Navajo Wolf, the anti'l witchcraft, the werewolves who pervert every taboo of the Navajo Way and use corpse powder to kill their victims.

Wells rattled the ice in his glass and glanced at his watch.

"To get to the part about your Begay," Chee said, "about two months ago we started picking up witch gossip. Nothing much, and you expect it during a drought. Lately it got to be more than usual." He described some of the tales and how uneasiness and dread had spread across the plateau. He described what he had learned today, the Tsossie's naming City Navajo as the witch, his trip to Mexican Water, of learning there that the witch had killed a man.

"They said it happened in the spring—couple of months ago. They told me the ones who knew about it were the Tso outfit." The talk of murder, Chee noticed, had revived Wells's interest. "I went up there," he continued, "and found the old woman who runs the outfit. Emma Tso. She told me her son-in-law had been out looking for some sheep, and smelled something, and found the body under some chamiso brush in a dry wash. A witch had killed him."

"How—"

Chee cut off the question. "I asked her how he knew it was a witch killing. She said the hands were stretched out like this." Chee extended his hands, palms up. "They were flayed. The skin was cut off the palms and fingers."

Wells raised his eyebrows.

"That's what the witch uses to make corpse powder," Chee explained. "They take the skin that has the whorls and ridges of the individual personality—the skin from the palms and the finger pads, and the soles of the feet. They take that, and the skin from the glans of the penis, and the small bones where the neck joins the skull, and they dry it, and pulverize it, and use it as poison."

"You're going to get to Begay any minute now," Wells said. "That right?"

"We got to him," Chee said. "He's the one they think is the witch. He's the City Navajo."

"I thought you were going to say that," Wells said. He rubbed the back of his hand across one blue eye. "City Navajo. Is it that obvious?"

"Yes," Chee said. "And then he's a stranger. People suspect strangers."

"Were they coming around him? Accusing him? Any threats? Anything like that, you think?"

"It wouldn't work that way—not unless somebody had someone in their family killed. The way you deal with a witch is hire a singer and hold a special kind of curing ceremony. That turns the witch-craft around and kills the witch."

Wells made an impatient gesture. "Whatever," he said. "I think something has made this Begay spooky." He stared into his glass, communing with the bourbon. "I don't know."

"Something unusual about the way he's acting?"

"Hell of it is I don't know how he usually acts. This wasn't my case. The agent who worked him retired or some damn thing, so I got stuck with being the delivery man." He shifted his eyes from glass to Chee. "But if it was me, and I was holed up here waiting, and the guy came along who was going to take me home again, then I'd be glad to see him. Happy to have it over with. All that."

"He wasn't?"

Wells shook his head. "Seemed edgy. Maybe that's natural, though. He's going to make trouble for some hard people."

"I'd be nervous," Chee said.

"I guess it doesn't matter much anyway," Wells said. "He's small potatoes. The guy who's handling it now in the U.S. Attorney's Office said it must have been a toss-up whether to fool with him at all. He said the assistant who handled it decided to hide him out just to be on the safe side.''

"Begay doesn't know much?"

"I guess not. That, and they've got better witnesses."

"So why worry?"

Wells laughed. "I bring this sucker back and they put him on the witness stand and he answers all the questions with I don't know and it makes the USDA look like a horse's ass. When a U.S. attorney looks like that, he finds an FBI agent to blame it on." He yawned. "Therefore," he said through the yawn, "I want to ask you what you think. This is your territory. You are the officer in charge. Is it your opinion that someone got to my witness?"

Chee let the question hang. He spent a fraction of a second reaching the answer, which was they could have if they wanted to try. Then he thought about the real reason Wells had kept him working late without a meal or a shower. Two sentences in Wells's report. One would note that the possibility the witness had been approached had been checked with local Navajo Police. The next would report whatever Chee said next. Wells would have followed Federal Rule One—Protect Your Ass.

Chee shrugged. "You want to hear the rest of my witchcraft business?"

Wells put his drink on the lamp table and untied his shoe. "Does it bear on this?"

"Who knows? Anyway there's not much left. I'll let you decide. The point is we had already picked up this corpse Emma Tso's son-in-law found. Somebody had reported it weeks ago. It had been collected, and taken in for an autopsy. The word we got on the body was Navajo male in his thirties probably. No identification on him."

"How was this bird killed?"

"No sign of foul play," Chee said. "By the time the body was brought in, decay and the scavengers hadn't left a lot. Mostly bone and gristle, I guess. This was a long time after Emma Tso's son-in-law saw him."

"So why do they think Begay killed him?" Wells removed his second shoe and headed for the bathroom.

Chee picked up the telephone and dialed the Kayenta clinic. He got the night supervisor and waited while the supervisor dug out the file. Wells came out of the bathroom with his toothbrush. Chee covered the mouthpiece. "I'm having them read me the autopsy report," Chee explained. Wilson began brushing his teeth at the sink in the dressing alcove. The voice of the night supervisor droned into Chee's ear.

"That all?" Chee asked. "Nothing added on? No identity yet? Still no cause?"

"That's him," the voice said.

"How about shoes?" Chee asked. "He have shoes on?"

"Just a sec," the voice said. "Yep. Size 10D. And a hat, and . . ."

"No mention of the neck or skull, right? I didn't miss that? No bones missing?"

Silence. "Nothing about neck or skull bones."

"Ah," Chee said. "Fine. I thank you." He felt great. He felt wonderful. Finally things had clicked into place. The witch was exorcised. "Jake," he said. "Let me tell you a little more about my witch case."

Wells was rinsing his mouth. He spit out the water and looked at Chee, amused. "I didn't think of this before," Wells said, "but you really don't have a witch problem. If you leave that corpse a death by natural causes, there's no case to work. If you decide it's a homicide, you don't have jurisdiction anyway. Homicide on an Indian reservation, FBI has jurisdiction." Wells grinned. "We'll come in and find your witch for you."

Chee looked at his boots, which were still dusty. His appetite had left him, as it usually did an hour or so after he missed a meal. He still hungered for a bath. He picked up his hat and pushed himself to his feet.

"I'll go home now," he said. "The only thing you don't know about the witch case is what I just got from the autopsy report. The corpse had his shoes on and no bones were missing from the base of the skull."

Chee opened the door and stood in it, looking back. Wells was taking his pajamas out of his suitcase. "So what advice do you have for me? What can you tell me about my witch case?"

"To tell the absolute truth, Chee, I'm not into witches," Wells said. "Haven't been since I was a boy."

"But we don't really have a witch case now," Chee said. He spoke earnestly. "The shoes were still on, so the skin wasn't taken from the soles of his feet. No bones missing from the neck. You need those to make corpse powder."

Wells was pulling his undershirt over his head. Chee hurried.

"What we have now is another little puzzle," Chee said. "If you're not collecting stuff for corpse powder, why cut the skin off this guy's hands?"

"I'm going to take a shower," Wells said. "Got to get my Begay back to LA tomorrow."

Outside the temperature had dropped. The air moved softly from the west, carrying the smell of rain. Over the Utah border, over the Coconino Rim, over the Rainbow Plateau, lightning flickered and glowed. The storm had formed. The storm was moving. The sky was black with it. Chee stood in the darkness, listening to the mutter of thunder, inhaling the perfume, exulting in it.

He climbed into the truck and started it. How had they set it up, and why? Perhaps the FBI agent who knew Begay had been ready to retire. Perhaps an accident had been arranged. Getting rid of the assistant prosecutor who knew the witness would have been even simpler—a matter of hiring him away from the government job. That left no one who knew this minor witness was not Simon Begay. And who was he? Probably they had other Navajos from the Los Angeles community stealing cars for them. Perhaps that's what had suggested the scheme. To most white men all Navajos looked pretty much alike, just as in his first years at college all Chee had seen in white men was pink skin, freckles, and light-colored eyes. And what would the impostor say? Chee grinned. He'd say whatever was necessary to cast doubt on the prosecution, to cast the fatal "reasonable doubt," to make—as Wells had put it—the U.S. District Attorney look like a horse's ass.

Chee drove into the rain twenty miles west of Kayenta. Huge, cold drops drummed on the pickup roof and turned the highway into a ribbon of water. Tomorrow the backcountry roads would be impassable. As soon as they dried and the washouts had been repaired, he'd go back to the Tsossie hogan, and the Tso place, and to all the other places from which the word would quickly spread. He'd tell the people that the witch was in custody of the FBI and was gone forever from the Rainbow Plateau.

Collecting Ackermans

•

Lawrence Block

Winner of an MWA Best Short Story Edgar (for his 1985 Matt Scudder novelette, "By the Dawn's Early Light") and a 1982 Private Eye Writers of America Best Novel Shamus (for his Scudder novel, Eight Million Ways to Die), *Lawrence Block is proficient in different types of crime fiction, from the private eye tale to the spy story to the political thriller to the exercise in mordant suspense. "Collecting Ackermans" is an example of his ability with the last-named type, featuring as it does a most bizarre and chilling motive for murder. Other of his fine short stories can be found in his two collections,* Sometimes They Bite *(1983) and* Like a Lamb to the Slaughter *(1984).*

On an otherwise unremarkable October afternoon, Florence Ackerman's doorbell sounded. Miss Ackerman, who had been watching a game show on television and clucking at the mental lethargy of the panelists, walked over to the intercom control and demanded to know who was there.

"Western Union," a male voice announced.

Miss Ackerman repeated the clucking sound she had most recently aimed at Charles Nelson Reilly. She clucked this time at people who lost their keys and rang other tenants' bells in order to gain admittance to the building. She clucked at would-be muggers and rapists who might pass themselves off as messengers or deliverymen for an opportunity to lurk in the hallways and stairwell. In years past this building had had a doorman, but the new landlord had curtailed services, aiming to reduce his overhead and antagonize longstanding tenants at the same time.

"Telegram for Miz Ackerman," the voice added.

And was it indeed a telegram? It was possible, Miss Ackerman acknowledged. People were forever dying and other people were apt to communicate such data by means of a telegram. It was easier to buzz whoever it was inside than to brood about it. The door to her own apartment would remain locked, needless to say, and the other tenants could look out for themselves. Florence Ackerman had been looking out for her own self for her whole life and the rest of the planet could go and do the same.

She pressed the buzzer, then went to the door and put her eye to the peephole. She was a small birdlike woman and she had to come up onto her toes to see through the peephole, but she stayed on her toes until her caller came into view. He was a youngish man and he wore a large pair of mirrored sunglasses. Besides obscuring much of his face, the sunglasses kept Miss Ackerman from noticing much about the rest of his appearance. Her attention was inescapably drawn to the twin images of her own peephole reflected in the lenses.

The young man, unaware that he was being watched, rapped on the door with his knuckles. "Telegram," he said.

"Slide it under the door."

"You have to sign for it."

"That's ridiculous," Miss Ackerman said. "One never has to sign for a telegram. As a matter of fact they're generally phoned in nowadays."

"This one you got to sign for."

Miss Ackerman's face, by no means dull to begin with, sharpened. She who had been the scourge of several generations of fourth-grade pupils was not to be intimidated by a pair of mirrored sunglasses. "Slide it under the door," she demanded. "Then I'll open the door and sign your book." If there was indeed anything to be slid beneath the door, she thought, and she rather doubted that there was.

"I can't."

"Oh?"

"It's a singin' telegram. Singin' telegram for Miz Ackerman, what it says here."

"And you're to sing it to me?"

"Yeah."

"Then sing it."

"Lady, are you kiddin'? I'm gonna sing a telegram through a closed door? Like forget it."

Miss Ackerman made the clucking noise again. "I don't believe you have a telegram for me," she said. "Western Union suspended their singing telegram service some time ago. I remember reading an article to that effect in the *Times*.'' She did not bother to add that the likelihood of anyone's ever sending a singing telegram to her was several degrees short of infinitesimal.

''All I know is I'm supposed to sing this, but if you don't want to open the door—''

''I wouldn't dream of opening my door.''

''—then the hell with you, Miz Ackerman. No disrespect intended, but I'll just tell 'em I sang it to you and who cares what you say.''

''You're not even a good liar, young man. I'm calling the police now. I advise you to be well out of the neighborhood by the time they arrive.''

''You know what you can do,'' the young man said, but in apparent contradiction to his words he went on to tell Miss Ackerman what she could do. While we needn't concern ourselves with his suggestion, let it be noted that Miss Ackerman could not possibly have followed it, nor, given her character and temperament, would she have been likely at all to make the attempt.

Neither did she call the police. People who say ''I am calling the police now'' hardly ever do. Miss Ackerman did think of calling her local precinct but decided it would be a waste of time. In all likelihood the young man, whatever his game, was already on his way, never to return. And Miss Ackerman recalled a time two years previously, just a few months after her retirement, when she returned from an afternoon chamber music concert to find her apartment burglarized and several hundred dollars worth of articles missing. She had called the police, naively assuming there was a point to such a course of action, and she'd only managed to spend several hours of her time making out reports and listing serial numbers, and a sympathetic detective had as much as told her nothing would come of the effort.

Actually, calling the police wouldn't really have done her any good this time, either.

Miss Ackerman returned to her chair and, without too much difficulty, picked up the threads of the game show. She did not for a moment wonder who might have sent her a singing telegram, knowing with cool certainty that no one had done so, that there had been no telegram, that the young man had intended rape or robbery or some other unpleasantness that would have made her life substantially worse than it already was. That robbers and rapists and such abounded was no news to Miss Ackerman. She had lived all her life in New York and took in her stride the possibility of such mistreatment, even as residents of California take in their stride the possibility of an earthquake, even as farmers on the Vesuvian slopes acknowledge that it is in the nature of volcanoes periodically to erupt. Miss Ackerman sat in her chair, leaving it to make a cup of tea, returning to it teacup in hand, and concentrated on her television program.

The following afternoon, as she wheeled her little cart of groceries around the corner, a pair of wiry hands seized her without ceremony and yanked her into the narrow passageway between a pair of brick buildings. A gloved hand covered her mouth, the fingers digging into her cheek.

She heard a voice at her ear: "Happy birthday to you, you old hairbag, happy birthday to you." Then she felt a sharp pain in her chest, and then she felt nothing, ever.

"Retired schoolteacher," Freitag said. "On her way home with groceries. Hell of a thing, huh? Knifed for what she had in her purse, and what could she have, anyway? Livin' on Social Security and a pension and the way inflation eats you up nowadays she wouldn't of had much on her. Why stick a knife in a little old lady like her, huh? He didn't have to kill her."

"Maybe she screamed," Ken Poolings suggested. "And he got panicky."

"Nobody heard a scream. Not that it proves anything either way." They were back at the stationhouse and Jack Freitag was drinking lukewarm coffee out of a styrofoam container. But for the styrofoam the beverage would have been utterly tasteless. "Ackerman, Ackerman, Ackerman. It's hell the way these parasites prey on old folks. It's the judges who have to answer for it. They put the creeps back on the street. What they ought to do is kill the little bastards, but that's not humane. Sticking a knife in a little old lady, *that's* humane. Ackerman, Ackerman. Why does that name do something to me?"

"She was a teacher. Maybe you were in one of her classes."

Freitag shook his head. "I grew up in Chelsea. West Twenty-fourth Street. Miss Ackerman taught all her life here in Washington Heights just three blocks from the place where she lived. And she didn't even have to leave the neighborhood to get herself killed. Ackerman. Oh, I know what it was. Remember three or maybe it was four days ago, this faggot in the West Village? Brought some other faggot home with him and got hisself killed for his troubles? They found him all tied up with things carved in him. It was all over page three of the *Daily News*. Ritual murder, sadist cult, sex perversion, blah blah blah. His name was Ackerman.''

"Which one?''

"The dead one. They didn't pick up the guy who did it yet. I don't know if they got a make or not.''

"Does it make any difference?''

"Not to me it don't.'' Freitag finished his coffee, threw his empty container at the green metal wastebasket, then watched as it circled the rim and fell on the floor. "The Knicks stink this year,'' he said. "But you don't care about basketball, do you?''

"Hockey's my game.''

"Hockey,'' Freitag said. "Well, the Rangers stink, too. Only they stink on ice.'' He leaned back in his chair and laughed at his own wit and stopped thinking of two murder victims who both happened to be named Ackerman.

Mildred Ackerman lay on her back. Her skin was slick with perspiration, her limbs heavy with spent passion. The man who was lying beside her stirred, placed a hand upon her flesh and began to stroke her. "Oh, Bill,'' she said. "That feels so nice. I love the way you touch me.''

The man went on stroking her.

"You have the nicest touch. Firm but gentle. I sensed that about you when I saw you.'' She opened her eyes, turned to face him. "Do you believe in intuition, Bill? I do. I think it's possible to know a great deal about someone just on the basis of your intuitive feelings.''

"And what did you sense about me?''

"That you would be strong but gentle. That we'd be very good together. It was good for you, wasn't it?''

"Couldn't you tell?''

Millie giggled.

"So you're divorced,'' he said.

"Uh-huh. You? I'll bet your married, aren't you? It doesn't bother me if you are.''

"I'm not. How long ago were you divorced?''

"It's almost five years now. It'll be exactly five years in January.

That's since we split, but then it was another six months before the divorce went through. Why?''

"And Ackerman was your husband's name?''

"Yeah. Wallace Ackerman.''

"No kids?''

"No, I wanted to but he didn't.''

"A lot of women take their maiden names back after a divorce.''

She laughed aloud. "They don't have a maiden name like I did. You wouldn't believe the name I was born with.''

"Try me.''

"Plonk. Millie Plonk. I think I married Wally just to get rid of it. I mean Mildred's bad enough, but Plonk? Like forget it. I don't think you even told me *your* last name.''

"Didn't I?'' The hand moved distractingly over Millie's abdomen. "So you decided to go on being an Ackerman, huh?''

"Sure. Why not?''

"Why not indeed.''

"It's not a bad name.''

"Mmmm,'' the man said. "This is a nice place you got here, incidentially. Been living here long?''

"Ever since the divorce. It's a little small. Just a studio.''

"But it's a good-sized studio, and you must have a terrific view. Your window looks out on the river, doesn't it?''

"Oh, sure. And you know, eighteen flights up, it's gotta be a pretty decent view.''

"It bothers some people to live that high up in the air.''

"Never bothered me.''

"Eighteen floors,'' the man said. "If a person went out that window there wouldn't be much left of her, would there?''

"Jeez, don't even talk like that.''

"You couldn't have an autopsy, could you? Couldn't determine whether she was alive or dead when she went out the window.''

"Come on, Bill. That's creepy.''

"Your ex-husband living in New York?''

"Wally? I think I heard something about him moving out to the West Coast, but to be honest I don't know if he's alive or dead.''

"Hmmm.''

"And who cares? You ask the damnedest questions, Bill.''

"Do I?''

"Uh-huh. But you got the nicest hands in the world, I swear to

God. You touch me so nice. And your eyes, you've got beautiful eyes. I guess you've heard that before?''

"Not really."

"Well, how could anybody tell? Those crazy glasses you wear, a person tries to look into your eyes and she's looking into a couple of mirrors. It's a sin having such beautiful eyes and hiding them."

"Eighteen floors, that's quite a drop."

"Huh?"

"Nothing," he said, and smiled. "Just thinking out loud."

Freitag looked up when his partner entered the room. "You look a little green in the face," he said. "Something the matter?"

"Oh, I was just looking at the *Post* and there's this story that's enough to make you sick. This guy out in Sheepshead Bay, and he's a policeman, too."

"What are you talking about?"

Poolings shrugged. "It's nothing that doesn't happen every couple of months. This policeman, he was depressed or he had a fight with his wife or something, I don't know what. So he shot her dead, and then he had two kids, a boy and a girl, and he shot them to death in their sleep and then he went and ate his gun. Blew his brains out."

"Jesus."

"You just wonder what goes through a guy's mind that he does something like that. Does he just go completely crazy or what? I can't understand a person who does something like that."

"I can't understand people, period. Was this somebody you knew?"

"No, he lives in Sheepshead Bay. *Lived* in Sheepshead Bay. Anyway, he wasn't with the department. He was a Transit Authority cop."

"Anybody spends all his time in the subways, it's got to take its toll. Has to drive you crazy sooner or later."

"I guess."

Freitag plucked a cigarette from the pack in his shirt pocket, tapped it on the top of his desk, held it between his thumb and forefinger, frowned at it, and returned it to the pack. He was trying to cut back to a pack a day and was not having much success. "Maybe he was trying to quit smoking," he suggested. "Maybe it was making him nervous and he just couldn't stand it any more."

"That seems a little farfetched, doesn't it?"

69

"Does it? Does it really?" Freitag got the cigarette out again, put it in his mouth, lit it. "It don't sound all that farfetched to me. What was this guy's name, anyway?"

"The TA cop? Hell, I don't know. Why?"

"I might know him. I know a lot of transit cops."

"It's in the *Post*. Bluestein's reading it."

"I don't suppose it matters, anyway. There's a ton of transit cops and I don't know that many of them. Anyway, the ones I know aren't crazy."

"I didn't even notice his name," Poolings said. "Let me just go take a look. Maybe *I* know him, as far as that goes."

Poolings went out, returning moments later with a troubled look on his face. Freitag looked questioningly at him.

"Rudy Ackerman," he said.

"Nobody I know. Hey."

"Yeah, right. Another Ackerman."

"That's three Ackermans, Ken."

"It's six Ackermans if you count the wife and kids."

"Yeah, but three incidents. I mean it's no coincidence that this TA cop and his wife and kids all had the same last name, but when you add in the schoolteacher and the faggot, then you got a coincidence."

"It's a common name."

"Is it? How common, Ken?" Freitag leaned forward, stubbed out his cigarette, picked up a Manhattan telephone directory and flipped it open. "Ackerman, Ackerman," he said, turning pages. "Here we are. Yeah, it's common. There's close to two columns of Ackermans in Manhattan alone. And then there's some that spell it with two *n*'s. I wonder."

"You wonder what?"

"If there's a connection."

Poolings sat on the edge of Freitag's desk. "How could there be a connection?"

"Damned if I know."

"There couldn't, Jack."

"An old schoolteacher gets stabbed by a mugger in Washington Heights. A faggot picks up the wrong kind of rough trade and gets tied up and tortured to death. And a TA cop goes berserk and kills his wife and kids and himself. No connection."

"Except for them all having the same last name."

"Yeah. And the two of us just happened to notice that because we investigated the one killing and read about the other two."

"Right."

"So maybe nobody else even knows that there were three homicides involving Ackermans. Maybe you and me are the only people in the city who happened to notice this little coincidence."

"So?"

"So maybe there's something we didn't notice," Freitag said. He got to his feet. "Maybe there have been more than three. Maybe if we pull a printout of deaths over the past few weeks we're going to find Ackermans scattered all over it."

"Are you serious, Jack?"

"Sounds crazy, don't it?"

"Yeah, that's how it sounds, all right."

"If there's just the three it don't prove a thing, right? I mean, it's a common name and you got lots of people dying violently in New York City. When you have eight million people in a city it's no big surprise that you average three or four murders a day. The rate's not even so high compared to other cities. With three or four homicides a day, well, when you got three Ackermans over a couple of weeks, that's not too crazy all by itself to be pure coincidence, right?"

"Right."

"Suppose it turns out there's more than the three."

"You've got a hunch, Jack. Haven't you?"

Freitag nodded. "That's what I got, all right. A hunch. Let's just see if I'm nuts or not. Let's find out."

"A fifth of Courvoisier, V.S.O.P." Mel Ackerman used a stepladder to reach the bottle. "Here we are, sir. Now will there be anything else?"

"All the money in the register," the man said.

Ackerman's heart turned over. He saw the gun in the man's hand and his own hands trembled so violently that he almost dropped the bottle of cognac. "Jesus," he said. "Could you point that somewhere else? I get very nervous."

"The money," the man said.

"Yeah, right. I wish you guys would pick on somebody else once in a while. This makes the fourth time I been held up in the past two years. You'd think I'd be used to it by now, wouldn't you? Listen, I'm insured, I don't care about the money, just be careful

71

with the gun, huh? There's not much money in the register, but you're welcome to every penny I got." He punched the No Sale key and scooped up bills, emptying all of the compartments. Beneath the removable tray he had several hundred dollars in large bills, but he didn't intend to call them to the robber's attention. Sometimes a gunman made you take out the tray and hand over everything. Other times the man would take what you gave him and be anxious to get the hell out. Mel Ackerman didn't much care either way. Just so he got out of this alive, just so the maniac would take the money and leave without firing his gun.

"Four times in two years," Ackerman said, talking as he emptied the register, taking note of the holdup man's physical appearance as he did so. Tall but not too tall, young, probably still in his twenties. White. Good build. No beard, no moustache. Big mirrored sunglasses that hid a lot of his face.

"Here we go," Ackerman said, handing over the bills, "No muss, no fuss. You want me to lie down behind the counter while you go on your way?"

"What for?"

"Beats me. The last guy that held me up, he told me so I did it. Maybe he got the idea from a television program or something. Don't forget the brandy."

"I don't drink."

"You just come to liquor stores to rob 'em, huh?" Mel was beginning to relax now. "This is the only way we get your business, is that right?"

"I've never held up a liquor store before."

"So you had to start with me? To what do I owe the honor?"

"Your name."

"My name?"

"You're Melvin Ackerman, aren't you?"

"So?"

"So this is what you get," the man said, and shot Mel Ackerman three times in the chest.

"It's crazy," Freitag said. "What it is is crazy. Twenty-two people named Ackerman died in the past month. Listen to this. Arnold Ackerman, fifty-six years of age, lived in Flushing. Jumped or fell in front of the E train."

"Or was pushed."

"Or was pushed," Freitag agreed. "Wilma Ackerman, sixty-two years old, lived in Flatbush. Heart attack. Mildred Ackerman, thirty-six, East Eighty-seventh Street, fell from an eighteen-story window. Rudolph Ackerman, that's the Transit Authority cop, killed his wife and kids and shot himself. Florence Ackerman was stabbed, Samuel Ackerman fell down a flight of stairs, Lucy Ackerman took an overdose of sleeping pills, Walter P. Ackerman was electrocuted when a radio fell in the bathtub with him, Melvin Ackerman's the one who just got shot in a holdup—'' Freitag spread his hands. "It's unbelievable. And it's completely crazy."

"Some of the deaths must be natural," Poolings said. "Here's one. Sarah Ackerman, seventy-eight years old, spent two months as a terminal cancer patient at St. Vincent's and finally died last week. Now that has to be coincidental."

"Uh-huh. Unless somebody slipped onto the ward and held a pillow over her face because he didn't happen to like her last name."

"That seems pretty farfetched, Jack."

"Farfetched? Is it any more farfetched than the rest of it? Is it any crazier than the way all these other Ackermans got it? Some nut case is running around killing people who have nothing in common but their last names. There's no way they're related, you know. Some of these Ackermans are Jewish and some are gentiles. It's one of those names that can be either. Hell, this guy Wilson Ackerman was black. So it's not somebody with a grudge against a particular family. It's somebody who has a thing about the name, but why?"

"Maybe somebody's collecting Ambroses," Poolings suggested.

"Huh? Where'd you get Ambrose?"

"Oh, it's something I read once," Poolings said. "This writer Charles Fort used to write about freaky things that happen, and one thing he wrote was that a guy named Ambrose had walked around the corner and disappeared, and the writer Ambrose Bierce had disappeared in Mexico, and he said maybe somebody was collecting Ambroses."

"That's ridiculous."

"Yeah. But what I meant—"

"Maybe somebody's collecting Ackermans."

"Right."

"Killing them. Killing everybody with that last name and doing it differently each time. Every mass murderer I ever heard of had a murder method he was nuts about and used it over and over, but this guy never does it the same way twice. We got—what is it, twenty-two deaths here? Even if some of them just happened, there's no question that at least fifteen out of twenty-two have to be the work of this nut, whoever he is. He's going to a lot of trouble to keep this operation of his from looking like what it is. Most of these killings look like suicide or accidental death, and the others were set up to look like isolated homicides in the course of a robbery or whatever. That's how he managed to knock off this many Ackermans before anybody suspected anything. Ken, what gets me is the question of why. Why is he doing this?''

"He must be crazy."

"Of course he's crazy, but being crazy don't mean you don't have reasons for what you do. It's just that they're crazy reasons. What kind of reasons could he have?''

"Revenge."

"Against all the Ackermans in the world?''

Poolings shrugged. "What else? Maybe somebody named Ackerman did him dirty once upon a time and he wants to get even with all the Ackermans in the world. I don't see what difference it makes as far as catching him is concerned, and once we catch him the easiest way to find out the reason is to ask him.''

"*If* we catch him."

"Sooner or later we'll catch him, Jack.''

"Either that or the city'll run out of Ackermans. Maybe *his* name is Ackerman.''

"How do you figure that?''

"Getting even with his father, hating himself, *I* don't know. You want to start looking somewhere, it's gotta be easier to start with people named Ackerman than with people not named Ackerman.''

"Even so there's a hell of a lot of Ackermans. It's going to be some job checking them all out. There's got to be a few hundred in the five boroughs, plus God knows how many who don't have telephones. And if the guy we're looking for is a drifter living in a dump of a hotel somewhere, there's no way to find him, and that's if he's even using his name in the first place, which he probably isn't, considering the way he feels about the name.''

Freitag lit a cigarette. "Maybe he *likes* the name," he said. "Maybe he wants to be the only one left with it.''

"You really think we should check all the Ackermans?''

"Well, the job gets easier every day, Ken. 'Cause every day there's fewer Ackermans to check on.''

"God."

"Yeah."

"Do we just do this ourselves, Jack?"

"I don't see how we can. We better take it upstairs and let the brass figure out what to do with it. You know what's gonna happen."

"What?"

"It's gonna get in the papers."

"Oh, God."

"Yeah." Freitag drew on his cigarette, coughed, cursed and took another drag anyway. "The newspapers. At which point all the Ackermans left in the city start panicking, and so does everybody else, and don't ask me what our crazy does because I don't have any idea. Well, it'll be somebody else's worry." He got to his feet. "And that's what we need—for it to be somebody else's worry. Let's take this to the lieutenant right now and let him figure out what to do with it."

The pink rubber ball came bouncing crazily down the driveway toward the street. The street was a quiet suburban cul-de-sac in a recently developed neighborhood on Staten Island. The house was a three-bedroom expandable colonial ranchette. The driveway was concrete, with the footprints of a largish dog evident in two of its squares. The small boy who came bouncing crazily after the rubber ball was towheaded and azure-eyed and, when a rangy young man emerged from behind the barberry hedge and speared the ball one-handed, seemed suitably amazed.

"Gotcha," the man said, and flipped the ball underhand to the small boy, who missed it, but picked it up on the second bounce.

"Hi," the boy said.

"Hi yourself."

"Thanks," the boy said, and looked at the pink rubber ball in his hand. "It was gonna go in the street."

"Sure looked that way."

"I'm not supposed to go in the street. On account of the cars."

"Makes sense."

"But sometimes the dumb ball goes in the street anyhow, and then what am I supposed to do?"

"It's a problem," the man agreed, reaching over to rumple the boy's straw-colored hair. "How old are you, my good young man?"

"Five and a half."

75

"That's a good age."

"Goin' on six."

"A logical assumption."

"Those are funny glasses you got on."

"These?" The man took them off, looked at them for a moment, then put them on. "Mirrors," he said.

"Yeah, I know. They're funny."

"They are indeed. What's your name?"

"Mark."

"I bet I know your last name."

"Oh, yeah?"

"I bet it's Ackerman."

"How'd you know?" The boy wrinkled up his face in a frown. "Aw, I bet you know my daddy."

"We're old friends. Is he home?"

"You silly. He's workin'."

"I should have guessed as much. What else would Hale Ackerman be doing on such a beautiful sunshiny day, hmmmm? How about your mommy? She home?"

"Yeah. She's watchin' the teevee."

"And you're playing in the driveway."

"Yeah."

The man rumpled the boy's hair again. Pitching his voice theatrically low, he said, "It's a tough business, son, but that doesn't mean it's a *heartless* business. Keep that in mind."

"Huh?"

"Nothing. A pleasure meeting you, Mark, me lad. Tell your parents they're lucky to have you. Luckier than they'll ever have to know."

"Whatcha mean?"

"Nothing," the man said agreeably. "Now I have to walk all the way back to the ferry slip and take the dumb old boat all the way back to Manhattan and then I have to go to . . ." he consulted a slip of paper from his pocket ". . . to Seaman Avenue way the hell up in Washington Heights. Pardon me. Way the *heck* up in Washington Heights. Let's just hope *they* don't turn out to have a charming kid."

"You're funny."

"You bet," the man said.

* * *

"Police protection," the lieutenant was saying. He was a beefy man with an abundance of jaw. He had not been born looking particularly happy, and years of police work had drawn deep lines of disappointment around his eyes and mouth. "That's the first step, but how do you even go about offering it? There's a couple of hundred people named Ackerman in the five boroughs and one's as likely to be a target as the next one. And we don't know who the hell we're protecting 'em *from*. We don't know if this is one maniac or a platoon of them. Meaning we have to take every dead Ackerman on this list and backtrack, looking for some common element, which since we haven't been looking for it all along we're about as likely to find it as a virgin on Eighth Avenue. Twenty-two years ago I coulda gone with the police or the fire department and I couldn't make up my mind. You know what I did? I tossed a goddamn coin. It hadda come up heads."

"As far as protecting these people—"

"As far as protecting 'em, how do you do that without you let out the story? And when the story gets out it's all over the papers, and suppose you're a guy named Ackerman and you find out some moron just declared war on your last name?"

"I suppose you get out of town."

"Maybe you get out of town, and maybe you have a heart attack, and maybe you call the mayor's office and yell a lot, and maybe you sit in your apartment with a loaded gun and shoot the mailman when he does something you figure is suspicious. And maybe if you're some *other* lunatic you read the story and it's like tellin' a kid don't put beans up your nose, so you go out and join in the Ackerman hunt yourself. Or if you're another kind of lunatic which we're all of us familiar with you call up the police and confess. Just to give the nice cops something to do."

A cop groaned.

"Yeah," the lieutenant said. "That about sums it up. So the one thing you don't want is for this to get in the papers, but—"

"But it's too late for that," said a voice from the doorway. And a uniformed patrolman entered the office holding a fresh copy of the New York *Post*. "Either somebody told them or they went and put two and two together."

"I coulda been a fireman," the lieutenant said. "I woulda got to slide down the pole and wear one of those hats and everything, but instead the goddamn coin had to come up heads."

* * *

The young man paid the cashier and carried his tray of food across the lunchroom to a long table at the rear. A half dozen people were already sitting there. The young man joined them, ate his macaroni and cheese, sipped his coffee, and listened as they discussed the Ackerman murders.

"I think it's a cult thing," one girl was saying. "They have this sort of thing all the time out in California, like surfing and est and all those West Coast trips. In order to be a member you have to kill somebody named Ackerman."

"That's a theory," a bearded young man said. "Personally, I'd guess the whole business is more logically motivated than that. It looks to me like a chain murder."

Someone wanted to know what that was.

"A chain murder," the bearded man said. "Our murderer has a strong motive to kill a certain individual whose name happens to be Ackerman. Only problem is his motive is so strong that he'd be suspected immediately. So instead he kills a whole slew of Ackermans and the one particular victim he has a reason to kill is no more than one face in a crowd. So his motive gets lost in the shuffle." The speaker smiled. "Happens all the time in mystery stories. Now it's happening in real life. Not the first time life imitates art."

"Too logical," a young woman objected. "Besides, all these murders had different methods and a lot of them were disguised so as not to look like murders at all. A chain murderer wouldn't want to operate that way, would he?"

"He might. If he was very, very clever—"

"But he'd be too clever for his own good, don't you think? No, I think he had a grudge against one Ackerman and decided to exterminate the whole tribe. Like Hitler and the Jews."

The conversation went on in this fashion, with the young man who was eating macaroni and cheese contributing nothing at all to it. Gradually the talk trailed off and so indeed did the people at the table, until only the young man and the girl next to whom he'd seated himself remained. She took a sip of coffee, drew on her cigarette, and smiled at him. "You didn't say anything," she said. "About the Ackerman murders."

"No," he agreed. "People certainly had some interesting ideas."

"And what did you think?"

"I think I'm happy my name isn't Ackerman."

"What is it?"

"Bill. Bill Trenholme."

"I'm Emily Kuystendahl."

"Emily," he said. "Pretty name."

"Thank you. What *do* you think? Really?"

"Really?"

"Uh-huh."

"Well," he said, "I don't think much of the theories everybody was coming up with. Chain murders and cult homicide and all the rest of it. I have a theory of my own, but of course that's all it is. Just a theory."

"I'd really like to hear it."

"You would?"

"Definitely."

Their eyes met and wordless messages were exchanged. He smiled and she smiled in reply. "Well," he said, after a moment. "First of all, I think it was just one guy. Not a group of killers. From the way it was timed. And because he keeps changing the murder method I think he wanted to keep what he was doing undiscovered as long as possible."

"That makes sense. But why?"

"I think it was a source of fun for him."

"A source of fun?"

The man nodded. "This is just hypothesis," he said, "but let's suppose he just killed a person once for the sheer hell of it. To find out what it felt like, say. To enlarge his area of personal experience."

"God."

"Can you accept that hypothetically?"

"I guess so. Sure."

"Okay. Now we can suppose further that he liked it, got some kind of a kick out of it. Otherwise he wouldn't have wanted to continue. There's certainly precedent for it. Not all the homicidal maniacs down through history have been driven men. Some of them have just gotten a kick out of it so they kept right on doing it."

"That gives me the shivers."

"It's a frightening concept," he agreed. "But let's suppose that the first person this clown killed was named Ackerman, and that he wanted to go on killing people and he wanted to make a game out of it. So he—"

"A game!"

"Sure, why not? He could just keep on with it, having his weird

79

jollies and seeing how long it would take for the police and the press to figure out what was going on. There are a lot of Ackermans. It's a common name, but not so common that a pattern wouldn't begin to emerge sooner or later. Think how many Smiths there are in the city, for instance. I don't suppose police in the different boroughs coordinate their activities so closely, and I guess the Bureau of Vital Statistics doesn't bother to note if a lot of fatalities have the same last name, so it's a question of how long it takes for the pattern to emerge in and of itself. Well, it's done so now, and what does the score stand at now? Twenty-seven?''

"That's what the paper said, I think."

"It's quite a total when you stop to think of it. And there may have been a few Ackermans not accounted for. A body or two in the river, for instance.''

"You make it sound—"

"Yes?"

"I don't know. It gives me the willies to think about it. Will he just keep on now? Until they catch him?''

"You think they'll catch him?''

"Well, sooner or later, won't they? The Ackermans know to be careful now and the police will have stakeouts. Is that what they call it? Stakeouts?''

"That's what they call it on television."

"Don't you think they'll catch him?''

The young man thought it over. "I'm sure they'll catch him," he said, "*if* he keeps it up."

"You mean he might stop?''

"I would. If I were him."

"If you were him. What a thought!''

"Just projecting a little. But to continue with it, if I were this creep, I'd leave the rest of the world's Ackermans alone from here on in.''

"Because it would be too dangerous?''

"Because it wouldn't be any fun for me."

"Fun!"

"Oh, come on," he said, smiling. "Once you get past the evilness of it, which I grant you is overwhelming, can't you see how it would be fun for a demented mind? But try not to think of him as fundamentally cruel. Think of him as someone responding to a challenge. Well, now the police and the newspapers and the Ackermans themselves know what's going on, so at this point it's not a game anymore. The game's over and if he were to go on with it he'd just be conducting a personal war of extermination. And if he doesn't really have any genuine grudge against Ackermans, well, I say he'd let them alone.''

She looked at him and her eyes were thoughtful. "Then he might just stop altogether.''

"Sure.''

"And get away with it?''

"I suppose. Unless they pick him up for killing somebody else.'' Her eyes widened and he grinned. "Oh, really, Emily, you can't expect him to stop this new hobby of his entirely, can you? Not if he's been having so much fun at it? I don't think killers like that ever stop, not once it gets in their blood. They don't stop until the long arm of the law catches up with them.''

"The way you said that.''

"Pardon me?''

" 'The long arm of the law.' As if it's sort of a joke.''

"Well, when you see how this character operated, he does make the law look like something of a joke, doesn't he?''

"I guess he does.''

He smiled, got to his feet. "Getting close in here. Which way are you headed? I'll walk you home.''

"Well, I have to go uptown—''

"Then that's the way I'm headed.''

"And if I had to go downtown?''

"Then I'd have urgent business in that direction, Emily.''

On the street she said, "But what do you suppose he'll do? Assuming you're right that he'll stop killing Ackermans, but he'll go on killing. Will he just pick out innocent victims at random?''

"Not if he's a compulsive type, and he certainly looks like one to me. No, I guess he'd just pick out another whole category of people.''

"Another last name? Just sifting through the telephone directory and seeing what strikes his fancy? God, that's a terrifying idea. I'll tell you something, I'm glad my name's not such a common one. There aren't enough Kuystendahls in the world to make it very interesting for him.''

"Or Trenholmes. But there are plenty of Emilys, aren't there?''

"Huh?''

"Well, he doesn't have to pick his next victim by last name. In fact, he'd probably avoid that because the police would pick up on something like that in a minute after this business with the Acker-mans. He could establish some other kind of category. Men with beards, say. Oldsmobile owners."

"Oh, my God."

"People wearing brown shoes. Bourbon drinkers. Or, uh, girls named Emily."

"That's not funny, Bill."

"Well, no reason why it would have to be Emily. *Any* first name—that's the whole point, the random nature of it. He could pick guys named Bill, as far as that goes. Either way it would probably take the police a while to tip to it, don't you think?"

"I don't know."

"You upset, Emily?"

"Not upset, exactly."

"You certainly don't have anything to worry about," he said, and slipped an arm protectively around her waist. "I'll take good care of you, baby."

"Oh, will you?"

"Count on it."

They walked together in silence for awhile and after a few moments she relaxed in his embrace. As they waited for a light to change he said, "Collecting Emilys."

"Pardon?"

"Just talking to myself," he said. "Nothing important."

The Man Who Shot Lewis Vance

•

Stuart M. Kaminsky

An historian and critic of films, Stuart Kaminsky makes good use of his Hollywood expertise in his novels about private eye Toby Peters, who operates in the movie world of the thirties and forties. Each of the dozen Peters adventures—among them, Bullet for a Star *(1977),* Never Cross a Vampire *(1980),* He Done Her Wrong *(1983), and* Think Fast, Mr. Peters *(1987)—features such legendary figures as Humphrey Bogart, Mae West, Bela Lugosi, Howard Hughes, and Peter Lorre, and is loaded with film lore. In "The Man Who Shot Lewis Vance," set in the winter of 1942, his client is none other than John Wayne. Kaminsky also writes nonseries suspense novels such as* When the Dark Man Calls *(1983), and a series of police procedurals set in Moscow and featuring Porfiry Petrovich.*

When I opened my eyes, I saw John Wayne pointing a .38 at my chest. It was my .38. I closed my eyes.

The inside of my head seemed to be filled with strawberry cotton candy with little unnamed things crawling through its sickly melting strands. Nausea forced my eyes open again. John Wayne was still there. He was wearing trousers, a white shirt and a lightweight tan windbreaker. He was lean, dark, and puzzled.

"Don't close your eyes again, Pilgrim," he said.

I didn't close them. He was standing over me and I slumped in a badly sprung cheap understuffed hotel chair. I tried to sit up and speak, but my tongue was an inflated, dry, pebbly football. There was a flat, half full glass of brown Pepsi on the stained yellow table in front of me, but I didn't reach for it. That glass, and what had been in it, had put me out.

I wasn't sure of the day and the time. When I took that last few gulps of Pepsi, it had been a Sunday night in the winter of 1942. I

83

had been sitting in a cheap Los Angeles hotel room with a guy who had identified himself as Lewis Vance.

Lewis Vance had left a message for me at my office, but I had been out of town filling in for a gate guard at an old people's home in Goleta. It had netted me $20 minus gas. The message on my desk, left in the uncertain hand of Sheldon Minck, the dentist I rent space from, had said I should call Lewis Vance in Room 303 of the Alhambra Arms over on Broadway. I'd called and Vance had told me to come right over. I didn't even have to drive. My office was on Hoover a few blocks away and I ambled over knowing I needed a shave and worrying about which island the Japanese had taken while I was in Goleta.

My gray seersucker was crumpled but reasonably clean if you ignored the remnants of mustard stain on the sleeve. It was the best suit I had. The sky threatened rain, but no one on the street seemed concerned. Soldiers, sailors, overly painted women laughing too hard to make a buck and sour-faced visitors flowed with me. Before the war, the crowds had been thick on Broadway on a Sunday, but tourists didn't make their way to Los Angeles after the first threats of an invasion by the Japanese.

Now Broadway was kids in uniform, waiting women and girls, and people who couldn't afford to or were too stubborn to leave. I was one of the latter.

Vance had said he had a job for me. Since I am a private investigator, I assumed it had something to do with my profession. At forty-six with a bad back, pushed-in nose, and black graying hair, I was a reasonably formidable sight as a bodyguard. If I were over five foot-nine, I'd probably be busy nine or ten months a year with celebrities who wanted to show they could afford protection they usually didn't need. But there were plenty of muscle builders from the beaches—Santa Monica, Venice—who could be bought cheap and look bigger and meaner than I did. They weren't meaner, but they were fine for show as almost everything was and is in Los Angeles.

The people who hire me usually get my name from someone who has used me in the past. They really want protection or a grandmother found or a stern word or two to a former friend who owes them a few hundred bucks. Vance hadn't said what he wanted me for.

The lobby of the Alhambra Arms was wilting badly, had been since long before the war. There were four big wooden pots in the lobby that had once held small palm trees. The palms had sagged to the floor years before and now the chipped green pots were used as ash trays and garbage bins. It didn't look too bad because you couldn't see much of anything in the Alhambra lobby. There was a strict policy of not replacing light bulbs as they died. The ceiling was a cemetery of darkened bulbs with a few dusty die-hards still glowing away. Considering the way I looked, I didn't mind the shadows of the Alhambra. I had filled in as hotel detective here twice in the last two years, both times on weekends. There had been no detecting involved, no thefts. The job was to keep the uniformed kids and ununiformed prostitutes from destroying the place and each other. It had kept me busy. The last time I had held down the duty I had done almost as much damage to the Allies as the Japanese fleet. Two sailors in diapers had taken umbrage at my telling them to refrain from destroying the lobby. Had they been sober I might have had a problem. They walked away from our discussion with a concussion, broken thumb, badly lacerated thigh, and a black eye. The damage was divided rather evenly between them.

The guy behind the desk when I walked into the Alhambra lobby on Sunday was named Theodore Longretti, better known on the streets as Teddy Spaghetti. Teddy is about fifty, long, lean, and faintly yellow from whatever it is cheap hotel clerks put into themselves to make the world think they are awake and relatively sane. Teddy's once white hair was even turning yellow again, not the yellow it might have been when and if he was a kid, but the yellow of white yarn dipped in cheap bourbon.

"Teddy," I said walking across the empty morning lobby and listening to my shoes clap the worn linoleum made to look like Spanish tiles.

"Toby?" he said, squinting through the darkness in my direction.

A desk lamp stood on the counter next to Teddy. Lights bounced off of the center making the welcoming clerk look like the skeleton of Woodrow Wilson.

"You've got a Lewis Vance, 303?" I said coming near the desk but not too close. A little of Teddy Spaghetti can go a long way. Besides he thought we were buddies.

"I've got a Lewis Vance," he admitted looking down at his open book, "and a half dozen Browns, a sprinkling of Andersons, a

Kelly or two, but no Smiths. It's a fallacy that people use the name Smith when they go to a hotel. You know what I mean?''

"I know," I said.

"Even people named Smith avoid saying they're Smith. It looks too suspicious," Teddy said seriously, finally looking up from his book. "So what can I do for you?"

"Vance look kosher?"

Teddy shrugged, his yellow face moving into a thoughtful pout. "Never saw him before, but looks like a straight arrow," he said. "But I ask you, if he's so straight, what's he checking in here for?"

Teddy looked around, into the dark corners, past the chipped green former palm holders. I had to admit he had a point.

"Thanks," I said and headed for the stairway.

"No trouble, Toby," he stage whispered. "I see you're packing heat. I'm in for two shifts and I don't want to identify the remains of former guests. You know what I mean?"

"I know, Teddy," I said whispering back. "The gun's just for show, to impress the client. You know what I mean?"

I patted the holster under my seersucker jacket and winked at Teddy though I doubted if he could see me.

"I know what you mean," he said and I jogged up the stairs.

The holster thumped against my chest as I went up and my back told me not to be so athletic. I slowed down and followed the trail of dimly lit landings to the third floor. Room 303 was next to Room 301 where what sounded like a child soprano was singing "Praise the Lord and Pass the Ammunition" with frequent stops for giggling. I knocked on the door of 303, adjusted my jacket, ran a hand through my hair, and tried to look as if I wasn't afraid of anything less than a Panzer attack.

The guy who opened the door looked familiar, at least his outline did against the back light. He was tall, good shoulders, a full size nose, and a good head of dark hair.

"Peters?" he said.

"Right," I answered. He opened the door and I walked in.

When I turned to face him, he didn't look quite so much like John Wayne as I had thought, but the resemblance was there.

Vance had a glass of amber liquid in his hand. He was wearing a weary smile and a lightweight brown suit with a white shirt and no tie. It wasn't Beverly Hills, but it beat what I was wearing and he was the client.

"How about a drink?" he said holding up the glass.

"Nothing hard," I said looking around the small room, seeing nothing but shabby furniture, an open unmade Murphy bed, and a dirty window.

"Coke?" he asked.

"Pepsi if you've got it," I answered sinking into the worn chair next to the splintery yellow coffee table.

"I've got it," he said moving to the dresser where a group of bottles huddled together. One, indeed, was a Pepsi. "Even got some ice."

His back was to me as he poured and started to talk. He kept talking as he turned and handed me the glass.

"Job is simple," he said. "I'm John Wayne's stand-in. Maybe you can see the resemblance."

"I can see it," I said.

"I'm doing Duke a little favor here." He went on swirling his glass and sitting across from me on a wooden chair pulled away from the spindly-legged desk in the corner. "He owes some people and they want to collect. Word's out that the Duke is registered at a downtown hotel as Lewis Vance. Meanwhile, the Duke is out calling in some loans to pay these guys off. My job, our job, is to keep them busy and away from Duke till he collects and pays them off. Don't worry about your money. We're talking big bills here. He can pay you with pocket money. No offense."

"None taken" I said, picking up the Pepsi. I wasn't offended by the money insult. It was true. It was the story that offended me. It had more holes than the U.S. Navy ships in Pearl Harbor. There were lots of possibilities here, I thought as I took a sip of the Pepsi. First, the story is true and John Wayne is doing one of the most stupid things imaginable. Second, Lewis Vance, who sat across from me watching for a reaction through dancing brown eyes, was a first-class nut who had thought this up for ends I couldn't imagine. Three, I was being set up for something though I couldn't begin to figure what that something might be. I took a deep drink of the slightly bitter Pepsi and pretended to weigh the offer. What I really wanted to do was get the hell out of this room before I found out what was going on.

I finished the Pepsi, put the glass down, and stood up. Vance was bigger than me, younger too, but I was used to getting past people or keeping them from getting past me. He didn't look as if he had too much experience with either. I didn't see anything on him that looked like a gun bulge.

"I think I'll pass on this one, Mr. Vance," I said.

He stood up quickly not loosening his grip on the glass.

"Wait," he said with real panic. "I can pay whatever your fee is. Duke authorized me to pay. Cash. Just one day's work. He'll really be grateful."

"Sorry," I said. "Truth is, Mr. Vance, you don't smell right to me."

Something went dull inside my head and should have been a warning, but I've taken so many blows over the years that I tend to regard occasional aches, pains, and ringing bells as natural.

"I'll prove it," Vance said holding out his free hand to get me to wait. "We'll call Duke. He'll tell you."

Maybe John Wayne had gone mush-headed. My head certainly wasn't feeling too good. Maybe the forty-eight hours straight in Goleta and the drive back was getting to me.

"Make the call," I said. Hell, I needed the money.

"Fine," he said with a smile, his hand still out. "Just sit down again and I'll get him."

I sat down again. Actually, I fell backwards.

"Fine," I repeated.

Vance walked slowly to the phone on the desk, his eyes on me all the time as if to keep me from moving. My upper lip felt numb and my eyes didn't want to stay open, but I forced them to as Vance slowly, very slowly made his call or pretended to. I was rapidly losing my grip on the room and the situation.

"Right," Vance said. He kept looking at me and nodding his head. "Right. Mr. Peters is right here and he wants to talk to you."

Vance was looking at me now with a triumphant and mean little grin. He held out the phone.

"It's the Duke," he said. "He wants to talk to you. All you have to do is walk over here and take the phone."

I tried to get up, but it couldn't be done. It was at that point, long after a lobotomized chimp would have figured it out, that I knew I had been slipped something in my Pepsi. I could but hope that it wasn't lethal as I gave up, sank back, and closed my eyes.

It rained while I was asleep. I don't know how I knew it while clowns danced before me, but I knew it and it was confirmed when I woke up with John Wayne, the real John Wayne, holding my gun on me. I looked at the single window and watched the downpour splatter and ask to come in.

"Water," I said.

"That it is, Pilgrim," he agreed, the gun steady and level.

"No, need water," I said pointing to my tongue.

He nodded, understanding, and pointed to the sink in the corner. I made three tries at getting up and succeeded on the fourth. I staggered to the sink, turned on the tap, and looked down at the brown stain near the drain. The stain looked a little like the state of Nevada. I put my head under the warm water, cupped my hand, and sloshed liquid into my mouth and over my inflated tongue. The tongue deflated slightly and, using the sink for support, I turned around.

Beyond Wayne, who looked at me with his forehead furrowed in curiosity, the Murphy bed stood open and on it lay the former Lewis Vance. He was definitely not asleep, not with that hole through his forehead.

I must have looked sick, surprised, or bewildered.

"You did that?" Wayne said pointing his gun at the corpse.

"No," I said as emphatically as I could. I even shook my head, which was one hell of a mistake. The red cotton candy inside my skull turned to liquid and threatened to come out of every available opening.

Slowly, painfully, I told my tale. The call, the offer from Vance, the drugged Pepsi. Wayne listened, nodding once in a while.

"And," I concluded, "I've got a feeling that hole in Vance's face came from a bullet in my gun, the one in your hand, the one with your fingerprints on it."

Wayne looked at the gun, shrugged and said, "Supposing I believe you. Where do we go now?"

First I asked him why he was in the room, holding my gun.

"Got a call," he said, gun still on me though he looked over at the corpse from time to time. "Man said I should get over here fast, a friend of mine named Dick Lang had taken an overdose of something. I came fast and walked in to find you out with the gun in your hand and your friend Vance. He's never been my stand-in. I don't owe anyone any money and no one is looking for me. I was planning on going to a party at C. B. DeMille's to celebrate the finish of *Reap the Wild Wind* when the call came. I don't think old C.B. is going to be too happy that I didn't come. Won't surprise me if I've worked for him for the last time."

The rain got louder and the day darker.

"Why should I believe you, Peters?"

"When you were a kid you used to go in the driveway of Pevsner's grocery store in Glendale," I said making my way back to the chair and dropping into it. "About two blocks from your dad's drug store. You used to go to that driveway and throw a ball against the wooden wall. You did that for about two weeks till Pevsner's son came out and hit you in the head."

Wayne's mouth opened slightly and his hand went up to his head, a spot right behind the ear.

"That was you?" he said.

"My brother Phil," I said. "He's a Los Angeles cop now."

I figured Wayne was about thirty-five or thirty-six now, but there was still a little of that kid in him.

"I thought you said your name was Peters?" Wayne said suspiciously.

"Professional change," I said. "I thought your name was Marion Morrison?"

"You made your point," he agreed. "But knowing your brother beat me up when I was a kid doesn't exactly prove you didn't shoot that fella over there."

I got out of the chair again and started to stagger around the room in the hope of clearing my head and returning my agonized body to its former, familiar level of constant ache.

"Let's go over it," I said, looking at Vance. "Someone wanted me here. Vance or someone else. Let's figure the idea was to set me up for Vance's murder. Vance thought it was for something else. Who knows what? He put me out with the drink and our killer steps in, takes my gun, and punctuates Vance."

"And then," Wayne interrupted, "the killer calls me and I come over and step into it. Publicity could ruin the DeMille picture and maybe my career. Could be we're dealing with an old enemy of mine."

"Could be we're dealing with an old enemy of both of us," I said. "The only one I can think of is my brother Phil and I doubt if he'd go this far to get either one of us. Maybe it's a blackmail deal. The phone will ring and we'll get . . . No. It would have happened by now. It's a frame-up, simple and dirty."

"Let's try it another way," Wayne said furrowing his brow. "Fella over there puts something in your drink. You feel you're going out, get out the gun, put some holes in him, and pass out. I come in, find the gun in your hand and . . ."

"Who called you?" I said. My mind was starting to work again, not as well as I would have liked, but that's what I feel even if I haven't had a boiled Pepsi.

"Beats me, Pilgrim," Wayne shrugged.

The knock at the door cut off our further exploration of possibilities. We looked at each other and he delegated me with a wave of the .38 to be the door opener. I opened the door. The woman standing there was more than thirty and less than fifty, but that was about the best I could do with her age. She had a body that could pass for twenty-five. Her hair was red and frilly. So was her tight dress.

She looked at me, at Wayne—whom she didn't seem to recognize—and over at Vance on the bed who had his head turned away.

"You didn't say anything about three," she said. "Three is more."

She stepped in, looked at Wayne, and added appreciatively, "Maybe not much more." He had pocketed the gun in his windbreaker and was looking at me for an explanation.

"What did I say?" I said. "On the phone."

She stepped in, put her small red handbag on the yellow table next to my lethal Pepsi, and looked at me as if I had a few beans loose, which I did.

"You said ten in the night," she said looking now at the body of Vance with the first hint of awareness. "It's ten and here I am." Then she turned to Wayne, looked at him enough to get him to look away, and added, "You really are Randolph Scott."

"John Wayne," I said.

"Right," she said with a snap of the fingers. "That's what you said, John Wayne." Her eyes stayed on Wayne who gave me a sigh of exasperation and said,

"Thanks for clearing it up for the lady, Peters. I wouldn't want her to forget who she met here."

She took a few steps of curiosity toward the Murphy bed and Vance and I eased over as fast as my retread legs would let me to cut her off.

"Are you sure it was me on the phone?" I said, putting my face in front of hers.

"You don't know if you called me?" she said trying to look over my shoulder at Vance. "Voice on the phone is all I know. You trying to back out of this? And what's with the guy on the bed?"

Wayne was leaning against the wall now, his arms folded, watching. He wasn't going to give me any help.

"We're not backing out," I said. "You'll get paid, Miss . . ."

"Olivia Fontaine," she said.

"Classy," I said.

"Thanks," she answered with a smile that faded fast. "That guy on the bed. Is he hurt or something?"

"Or something," I said.

"He's dead, lady," Wayne said pushing away from the wall. "And we're going to call the police."

"Dead?" she repeated and backed away from me. "I don't want no part of 'dead,' " she said, looking for something, spotted her red bag, and clacked her red high heels toward it.

"You're going to have to stay awhile, ma'am," Wayne said, stepping in front of the door. "I don't like this much, but you walk out of here and that's one more complication that has to be unwound."

"You didn't talk like that to Claire Trevor in *Stagecoach*," Olivia Fontaine said with her hands on her hips. "She was a hooker and you was . . . were nice to her, for Chrissake."

"That was a movie, lady," Wayne said.

"Me, other girls I know, love that movie," she said forgetting for a second the corpse on the bed. "I saw it five times. Hooker goes riding off with you at the end to a new life, ranch or something. Only thing is I thought you were Randolph Scott."

This knock at the door was louder than Olivia's. It was the one-two knock of someone who is used to knocking at hotel room doors . . .

Olivia, Wayne and I looked at each other. Then Wayne nodded at me.

"Who is it?" I asked.

"Hotel detective," came a familiar voice. "Got a call to come up here."

Wayne shrugged, Olivia looked for someplace to hide, found nothing, and sat in the chair I had recently passed out in. I opened the door and he came in. He was Merit Beeson, sixty, a massive white-haired man who had once been shot by a Singapore sailor. The shot had hit him in the neck and when it was clear he would survive, it also became clear that he would never be able to turn his neck again. Hence Merit Beeson became known as Straight-Ahead Beeson. The stiff neck lost him his job as a Los Angeles cop, but it gave him a strange dignity, which got him steady if not high-paying work in hotels. Straight-Ahead looked like a no-nonsense guy, a stand-up almost British butler in appearance with strong ham arms and a craggy face. His suit was always pressed and he always wore a tie. Straight-Ahead avoided a lot of trouble just by looking impressive, but he wasn't going to be able to avoid this one.

He took it all in fast, Olivia, me, Wayne, and the body.

"You know the guy on the bed, Merit?" I said.

He stepped into the room, closed the door behind him, and looked at me carefully.

"Before we talk," he said without turning his body to John Wayne, which would have been the only way to acknowledge the actor, "I want the cowboy to ease the radiator out of his pocket and put it nice and gentle on the dresser. You think we can arrange it?"

Wayne took the gun out and did just what Straight-Ahead wanted.

"Good start," Beeson said, though he hadn't turned to watch. In the thirty years he had looked straight ahead, he had developed great peripheral vision. "I've seen the gent staining the Murphy around the lobby now and then. Gave him a light rousting. Mean customer. Threatened to cut up Merit Beeson. Can you imagine that, Toby?"

"Can't imagine it, Merit," I said shaking my head for both of us. Something he said hit me gently and whispered back that I should remember it.

"You or the cowboy or the lady shoot him?" Merit said.

"None of us," I answered.

"Speak for yourself," Olivia said jumping up. "I didn't shoot him is all I know."

"Sal," Beeson said, his body moving toward the corpse, "I thought you agreed to stay out of the Alhambra after the unfortunate incident of the trollop and the ensign. You recall that tale?"

"I recall," she said. "I'm not Sal anymore. I'm Olivia, Olivia Fontaine."

Straight-Ahead was leaning forward over the bed in that awkward stiff-back way he had. When Merit moved, people watched.

"And I am now General Douglas MacArthur," he sighed touching the body carefully. "The former Mr. Vance has been with his maker for maybe five hours. That how you peg it, Toby?"

" 'Bout that, Merit," I agreed.

He stood up, pushing his bulk from the bed with dignity. The springs squealed and the body of Lewis Vance bounced slightly.

"And what do we do now?" he said.

"We call the police," said Wayne.

"That the way you want it?" Beeson said.

"No," Wayne admitted, stepping forward. "It's not the way I want it, but it's the way it has to be, isn't it?" He pointed at the bed and said, "We've got a murdered man here."

"Not the first in the Alhambra," Straight-Ahead said. He now had his hands folded over his belly like a satisfied Sunday School teacher. "You even had one the last time you filled in for me if my memory serves me, right, Toby?"

"You've got it, Merit," I agreed. "Salesman in 512, but it was suicide, not murder."

"Not that time," he agreed. "not that time." Then to Wayne, "No, you see Mr. Wayne, hotels usually don't like to promote the number of people who get killed within them. It's not like they keep charts and compete with each other because it will bring in new trade. No, we usually do our best to keep such things from the attention of the populace."

I explained, "It is not unheard of for a corpse to be carted off to some alley by a house dick."

Wayne shook his head and looked at us as if he had been trapped in a room with the incurably insane.

"You mean you're suggesting that we just take . . ."

"Vance," I supplied, "Lewis Vance."

"Right, Vance," Wayne said. "That we take Vance and dump him in some alley and walk away?"

"No," I said emphatically.

"Of course not," Straight-Ahead concurred. "Too many people involved now and you're too big a name. Sal . . ."

"Olivia," she corrected from her chair as she reached for my unfinished Pepsi.

"Olivia," Merit said, "would be happy to walk away and forget it. Toby knows the routine. He'd walk in a twinkling."

I nodded agreement and reached Olivia just as she was bringing the glass to her mouth. I took it from her. She gave me a dirty look, but I weathered it and put the flat, warm drink on the dresser near the gun.

"So," Wayne said. "What now?"

"We get the killer in here and try to work something out," I said.

"That's the way of it," Straight-Ahead agreed.

"But we don't know who killed him," Wayne said, running his hand through his hair.

"Sure we do," said Straight-Ahead looking straight ahead at Wayne.

"We do now," I agreed. Olivia didn't give a damn.

I moved to the telephone, picked it up, and dialed a number.

"The who of it is easy," said Merit, unfolding his hands and scratching his white mane. It didn't do his image much good, but his head clearly itched. "It's the why we have to figure. Then we'll know what to do."

The killer answered the phone on the third ring and I said, "Get up to 303 fast." I hung up.

The rain took this pause in the conversation to get really mad and start rocking the window in its loose fitting. It rocked and rattled and said bad things while we waited.

"Can I go?" Sally Olivia asked Merit.

"Let's all just stay cosy till we wind it up," Merit said. "That's how you put it in the movies, right?"

"Wrap it up," Wayne volunteered with a sigh. "Call it a wrap."

Straight-Ahead nodded and filed that information for future use.

"You think he might skip?" I asked.

"Human nature is a fickle thing, Toby," Straight-Ahead said now facing the door, "a fickle thing. He might skip, it's true, but where's he to go? And going will be a confession. No, he'll bluff it out or try. Besides, he doesn't yet know that we know."

"That's the way I see it," I agreed.

Wayne and Olivia looked at each other for an answer, got none, and joined Straight-Ahead in looking at the door and listening to the rain and the rattling window. I glanced at Lewis Vance's body, trying not to be angry about what he had done to my head and gotten me into. Then the knock came, almost unheard under the noise of the rain.

"Come right in," Merit shouted.

A key turned in the lock and the door opened to reveal Theodore Longretti. He stepped in, eyes darting around, and closed the door behind him.

"What is this all about?" he said, his eyes finding John Wayne and fixing on him.

"Murder," I said. "Over on the bed."

Teddy Spaghetti turned his long, yellow face to the bed and registered fake surprise.

"He's dead?" he said.

"You ought to know," I said. "You put the bullet in him with my gun." I nodded toward the dresser and Teddy's eyes followed me.

"Me?" he said, pointing to his thin chest and looking around at each of us for a touch of support, a sign of realization that it was too absurd to consider the possibility of his having killed anyone.

"You," I said.

"I'm calling the police," Teddy said stepping toward the phone. I stepped in front of him.

"Let's just work it through," Straight-Ahead said, turning slowly to look at us. "Then we'll decide what to do about it. Give it to him, Toby."

I stepped away from Teddy knowing I had his attention and that of everyone else in the room. I eased back to the metal railing of the Murphy bed.

"Number one, Vance has been seen hanging around the lobby," I began. "Which means you knew him. But you told me you'd never seen him before."

"I knew him, but . . ." Teddy began looking around the group for support. All he got was distant curiosity.

"I get a call on a Sunday to come to a room in this hotel, your hotel, while you are on the desk. You know me. You know Vance. Nothing tight here yet, but it's adding up. You following me?"

"Toby . . ." Teddy started, but he was stopped by Straight-Ahead who put his finger to his ample lips and said, "Shhhhhh."

"Then Sal . . . Pardon me, Olivia shows up. Someone called her. Someone who knows she is for rent. You know Olivia, don't you Teddy?"

He looked at her and she looked back at him.

"I've seen her," he said. "I've seen lots of whores."

"Seen is right," she said disdainfully. "Just seen."

"I've done plenty," Teddy said standing straight and thin.

"We're not questioning your manhood," Merit said. "We're trying to clean a dirty room. Hush it now."

"Then John Wayne gets a call," I said.

Teddy looked at John Wayne, who nodded.

"And finally, Merit gets a call to come up here," I went on. "Seems to me whoever did the dialing knew a lot about who was coming and going not just to the Alhambra but Room 303. You follow my reasoning?"

"No," Teddy said stubbornly.

"We could be wrong," Straight-Ahead said.

"We could be," I agreed.

"But we're not," Straight-Ahead added.

"We're not," I agreed again.

"Hold it just a minute here," John Wayne said, shaking his head. "You mean this fella here set this all up, killed that fella on the bed, fixed it so it would look like you did it, and fixed it so I'd be found here with the corpse, you and . . . the lady."

"Looks that way to me," I said.

"What in the name of God for?" Wayne asked reasonably.

"You want to answer that one, Teddy?" I asked as if I knew the answer but was willing to give up the stage to let the supporting cast take over. I had tried to set it up this way with Merit's help and the moment of truth or lies had come. All Teddy had to do was keep his mouth shut and we'd be stuck with having to make a decision. There was about enough evidence to nail him on a murder charge as there was to get Tojo to give up by midnight. A little digging might put him in the bag, but a little digging would mean enough time for the newspapers to make John Wayne and the Alhambra big news. That gave me an idea.

"Publicity," I prompted. "You want to talk about publicity, Teddy?"

Teddy didn't want to talk about anything. He looked as if he were in a voodoo trance, his face almost orange as the thunder cracked outside.

"Teddy," Merit prompted. "I've got work to do and no one is on the desk downstairs."

Teddy shook himself or rather a wave or chill went through him.

"It got all crazy," he said. "I'll tell you it got all crazy."

Olivia sighed loudly to let us know she had no interest in hearing Teddy tell it, but she had no choice.

"I didn't plan on killing him, you see," Teddy said, playing with his shirt front and looking down. "Idea of it was to get you here, Toby, put you out or something, get Wayne in, and then Sally, and have Merit walk in on it. Idea was to give the *Times* a tip about a love nest thing at the Alhambra, have a photographer and reporter maybe right behind. You'd confirm the whole thing and . . ."

"That was one hell of a stupid idea," Olivia said angrily from the chair.

Teddy shrugged. It hadn't worked out the way he planned.

"Idea was publicity," he whispered to his shirt.

"That John Wayne was making it with a prostitute in your hotel?"

"You think the Alhambra is such a hot-shot address?" Teddy came back defensively with a little animation. "Kind of people we got coming it could be a real attraction, you know what I mean? Idea was to set something up like this with a whole bunch of movie people, you know, real he-man types, Wild Bill Elliott, Alan Ladd, you know."

"And then the girls would be kicking back a few bucks to you just to work the rooms," Straight-Ahead said.

"Never thought of that," said Teddy, who had evidently considered just that. "But it was the publicity. Rooms aren't going as good as they should. Management needs it at seventy-eight percent or they'll sell and I'll lose my job."

"Hold it," John Wayne pitched in. He walked over to Teddy who shrank back, almost flopping like a dry noodle over the coffee table. "This is one hell of a harebrained scheme, Pilgrim, and I've got a mind to snap a few pieces off of you, but I want to know why you shot that man."

Teddy was still backing away from Wayne toward the wall. He almost stumbled over Olivia's stretched-out legs, but she pulled them in just in time.

"An accident," Teddy said. "An accident. Vance called me, said Toby had passed out. I had already made the calls to Sally and Wayne, got his phone number from a friend at Republic. Vance called me up, said he wanted more than the ten bucks I promised him, wanted in on whatever I was doing. I told him I didn't have more than ten bucks to give him, that there might be more money later, but he wouldn't listen. It was not a good situation."

"Not a good situation at all," Straight-Ahead agreed, turning toward him. "So you took Toby's gun and shot Lewis Vance between the eyes.

"He threatened to beat me up, kill me," Teddy whined. "It was self-defense."

"That's the story I'd tell," I agreed.

"It's the truth," Teddy squealed, bumping into the wall with Wayne advancing. I realized what was coming but I couldn't stop it. It should have been plain to a room in which half the living people were detectives, but it wasn't. Teddy reached up in the dresser at his elbow and came down with my .38 in his right hand. It reached out at the end of his spindly arm and pointed at the stomach of John Wayne who stopped abruptly and put up his hands.

"You are making me mad, mister," Wayne said through his teeth, but he took a step backward.

"Teddy, Teddy, Teddy," I said shaking my head. "You are not going to shoot all four of us. Put the gun down and let's talk."

I could see no good reason why he wouldn't shoot all four of us, but I hoped that the prospect of mowing down citizens would not appeal to the shaking desk clerk whose experience in mayhem, as far as I knew, had been limited to one unfortunate scrape a few hours earlier with an apparently unpleasant third-rate bully. "Think of the publicity."

He thought of the publicity and his mouth went dry. He reached over and took a sip of the flat Pepsi to moisten it. I didn't stop him. No one moved. We just watched him and hoped he would down the whole thing.

"Five bodies in one room, one a famous actor," Straight-Ahead chimed in. "The Alhambra might have a hell of a time surviving that."

"I can shoot you and get away," Teddy reasoned. He took another drink.

"Never get away with it," I said. People always said that in situations like this. My experience was that they very often did get away with it, but you don't tell things like that to killers holding guns. You just hoped they saw the same movies and listened to the same radio shows you did. The room suddenly went quiet. The rain had stopped.

Teddy blinked his eyes and looked at us. I couldn't tell whether he was considering who to shoot first or was realizing that he couldn't pull the trigger. I never got the chance to ask him.

"I've had just about enough," Wayne said and took a step, the final step, forward. Teddy, already a little drowsy from the drink, moved his gun-holding hand and fired. It missed Wayne, breezed past me, and shattered the window, letting in a rush of rain-smelling air. Wayne's punch slammed Teddy against the wall. The gun fell, hit the floor, bounced a few times, and rested.

Olivia screamed and Straight-Ahead walked slowly straight ahead toward the slumped figure. Wayne, fists still clenched, stepped back to let the house detective take over. It was a show and a half to see Merit get to his knee, lift the now silent desk clerk up, and deposit him on the chair near the desk.

"Let's go," I said exchanging a look of understanding with Merit when he turned around.

"Go?" asked Wayne, his dark hair over his forehead. "What are you talking about? This man killed that man and we . . ."

"Can go," I said.

Olivia didn't need persuading. She grabbed her red bag and headed for the door.

"You've never been in this room," Straight-Ahead said to her.

"I've never been in this hotel," she answered. "Nice to meet you, John." And out she went.

"Merit will work a deal with Teddy," I explained to the bewildered Wayne. "Teddy says he shot Vance in self-defense and no one else was around. Merit backs him up. Story's over. Teddy doesn't want it that way, Merit calls him a liar trying to save his skin, but that won't happen. Teddy will back it up and you're out of it."

"With some embellishments, that's the way it really was," Merit said looking at Teddy.

"It's. . . ." John Wayne began.

"Not like the movies," I finished. "Not this time, anyway. The rain's stopped. You want to stop for a cup of coffee?"

"I guess," said Wayne, shaking his head. "It's too late for DeMille's party." He took a last look at the corpse on the bed and the scrawny killer in the chair. The Ringo Kid wouldn't have handled it like this, but what the hell. He looked at Straight-Ahead who said, "Go on. It's my job."

Wayne nodded and went into the hall after I said, "I'll be right there."

Teddy was showing no signs of waking up.

"The gun," I said.

"The gun," Merit repeated giving up on a revival of Teddy Spaghetti in the near future. "We say you left it here for Teddy. Protection. He was threatened by all kinds. That sort of thing. It'll hold up."

"It'll shake a lot," I said, "but it'll hold. Take care."

A breeze from the broken window swirled around the room as Straight-Ahead waved his arm at me and sat slowly in the overstuffed chair to wait for Teddy to wake up. I closed the door quietly and joined John Wayne in the hall.

"This happen to you a lot?" he said as we got onto the elevator.

"When things are going well," I said. "Only when things are going well."

My head began to ache again and I longed for a plate of tacos from Manny's a few blocks away. I wondered if I could talk Wayne into a trip to Manny's.

The Granny Woman

•

Dorothy B. Hughes

Three superb novels of psychological suspense by Dorothy B. Hughes were made into major films in the forties: The Fallen Sparrow *(1942),* Ride the Pink Horse *(1946), and* In a Lonely Place *(1947). She has published only a few short stories during her long career, but each is as meticulously crafted as her novels, and each is quite different from the others. In "The Granny Woman" the departure is considerable in setting and style as well as in content. The scene here is the Ozark Mountains rather than her usual milieus of New York, New Mexico, and California, and she utilizes the folksy patois of the region to tell her memorable tale.*

They was waiting for him, the three of them, setting there on the stoop of Aunt Miney's cabin. I remember like it was yesterday. Old Cephus wasn't rightly on the stoop, he was on the gallery in Uncle Dauncy's rocking chair. He wa'nt rocking. He was setting tall and upright as the silver-mounted Old Betsey he was holding aside him. Ol Cephus must of been eighty year then, gaunt and gray as an old goose, but strong not weak in his age.

Orville was setting on the top of the stoop. He wasn't doing anything, just setting there chawing, looking mean and sloppy and dirty like always. You'd find it hard to believe Orville was Old Cephus' son. There wa'nt nothing like in them.

Down on the low step was Toll, Cousin Tolliver Sorkin, another mean one, though he wa'nt no more than twenty year to Orville's fifty. Toll was whittling nothing like he'd do when he was waiting. Some men whittle something, a dog or a bird, or maybe a doll poppet, but Toll never whittled nothing.

I knowed the man wasn't coming friendly because none of them was fixed for company. They was wearing their working pants and shirts, dusty boots, and their old sweaty-stained hats. None of them appeared to be looking down the road, but they was seeing without looking. They didn't know I was there, hiding up in the old crab-apple tree aslant of the house. I'd sneaked up in the tree afore they come out on the stoop. If'n they'd knowed, they'd of sent me packing. They wa'nt meaning no good to the man.

You could see him coming over the hill afore he was in sight. You could see him when he wa'nt no more than a twig of a man, down there below. It could of been that Toll, when he took his maw and paw down to Middle Piney that morning, heerd about him coming. But I think they'd knowed it afore then, the way a body does know things in these hills. Knowing don't come from smoke signals like the Indians made when they lived here afore the war, leastways the Granny Woman used to claim she'd seed smoke signals when first she come to the Ozarks. Knowing is just knowing something afore you been told. It whispers out of the town and up into the hills some way or tuther.

I could hear everything the menfolks was saying, not that it was much. The man was big enough to reckanize as a man when Cephus asked for about the hundredth time, "Is he still a-coming?"

"He's a-coming all right," Orville grunted.

"Purty nigh here." Toll had that sly mouth on him, like he was itching for trouble.

"What-all's he coming up here for anyway?" Cephus complained.

"You know what for," Toll said.

"You best keep your mouth shet, Toll." When Orville had that real ugly look, it'd fair give you the shivers.

"Sure, Orville. You don't need to worry none about me."

Cephus' voice sounded again. "Where's he at now?"

"Cain't you see for yourself, Paw?"

"The sun gits in my eyes. How nigh is he?"

Toll said real quiet, "Not more'n six or seven paces."

I'd been watching my kin for a time, not the road, so I'd missed him approaching that night. Now I looked down at him, a nice clean-appearing man, older'n Toll, not so old as Orville. He was wearing jeans and a blue shirt, too, but they wasn't all begaumed, the shirt had been clean afore he sweated it out clumbing up the hill. A woman can tell these things. He stopped there out in the road, keeping his distance until he was invited in, like was the custom. When he commenced talking, he talked somewhat like he was a native. Young as I was then, I figgered out he was Ozark born but had been gone long enough to be a furriner.

"Howdy," he said.

None of the menfolks said anything for what seemed an awful long time. Finally Toll spoke up. "Howdy."

"Mighty hot day."

"Yeh." Toll took his time responding. "Hotter'n the cinders of hell." He gave a sidelong look at the stranger. "You come far?"

"From Middle Piney."

"A far piece," Toll allowed. "Mighty hot day to clumb all the way up here." Middle Piney was about seven mile uphill to Tall Piney.

"I found that out," the man said rueful-like.

Toll throwed away his whittling stick. "Light down and set a spell," he said like he was natural neighborly. "You must be plumb tuckered out."

"Thanks." The man walked over towards the stoop. "Could I trouble you first for a drink of water?"

"Help yourself." Toll pointed with his knife. "Bucket's around yander."

I didn't dast move a muscle when the man walked under the tree to the water bucket. First he drunk a full dipper of water, then he took off his hat and poured a little water onto his head. I didn't blame him none. No place in the world hotter'n Missouri in August. He shook off the water and took another drink from the dipper afore going back to the stoop. He set hisself down at the far end of the second step. This way he could be looking at all three menfolks while he visited, and them at him.

Orville said, "You must of had some extry special purpose to clumb all the way up here today."

The stranger seemed to think about it. Before he had a chanct to answer, Toll cut him off like as if he was suddenly reckanizing him.

"Ain't you the Perfessor been stopping down to Little Piney?"

You could tell by the Perfessor's face that he'd knowed all along the three of them knowed who he was. But he feigned he didn't know. He said, "That's right. I'm Professor James. From the University up at Columbia."

"Pleased to make your acquaintance, Perfessor." Toll put out his hand and shook the Perfessor's. If I hadn't seed how they was waiting for him, I'd of thought Toll was right friendly. "I'm Tolliver Sorkin, mostly known as Toll. This here's my cousin, Orville. That's old Cephus up there on the gallery. He's my cousin also.'' That's the way the kinship was. Toll wasn't a close cousin to us, he was removed.

The Perfessor reared up and shook hands with Orville. He stretched for to shake old Cephus' hand, but Cephus wa'nt letting go of Old Betsey. That meant plain that the Perfessor was no friend so far as Cephus was concerned. Cephus wasn't no sly one like Toll nor a bully like Orville. He was straight out what he was.

''Pleased to meet you all,'' the Perfessor said, setting again.

Toll took up another stick to whittle. He went on talking, reasonable, if you hadn't knowed he was up to something. ''I thought I reckanized you. You're the ballut man.''

''That's what folks call me down at Little Piney.'' Little Piney was ten mile downhill from Middle Piney. It was the County Seat.

''This is the second summer I've been around, looking for old ballads.''

''We'n got no ballut singers at Tall Piney,'' Orville said, real hostile.

''Down at Little Piney I heard different.''

''Like to hear anything down Little Piney.'' Orville spat through the railing slats.

Toll said, sort of cautious, ''What might they been telling you down there?''

''They said if I was to go up to Tall Piney, I might get some real good ballads off the Granny Woman.''

''Reckon you won't.''

''Why not?''

Orville said it blunt. ''She's dead.''

''She's dead?'' He was just pretending to be surprised. I knowed it and I'm sure the menfolks knowed it, too. But they went on feigning they didn't.

''Deader'n a doornail,'' Toll said.

''Been dead nigh on two weeks now,'' Orville went on. ''Kind of peculiar they wouldn't know bout that down to Little Piney. Who all you been visiting with there?''

''I've been stopping with the Preacher,'' the Perfessor said. ''He didn't say he'd done any preaching over the Granny Woman.''

''She didn't hold with preaching.'' Orville spat again.

And Toll asked, ''Didn't the Reverint tell you that?''

When the Perfessor answered, it was almost like hearing preaching about her. It was like he'd been fond of her the same as I,

105

although he hadn't ever knowed her. "He told me if anyone would know the old, old ballads, she would. He told me she was the oldest woman in the Pineys. She could remember coming by wagon from Virginny when she was a young maid, before the war. Folks say she might be a hundred years old."

Suddenly Cephus shouted out in his loud old voice, "She's dead!"

Orville acted like nobody had heerd his paw. "We give her a proper burial."

Toll elaborated, "We didn't have no preachment because she didn't hold with preaching, but we buried her proper."

"That her cabin up yonder?" the Perfessor asked, looking up to where it stood on the tiptop of the hill.

"Now, how'd you know that?" Toll asked him.

"The Preacher told me she lived on top of Tall Piney. Is that hers?"

"It's hern," Orville admitted.

"Might be her ballad book is still there."

"There ain't no ballut books there," Orville said flatly.

"What did you do about her belongings?"

Toll was quick to defend himself just in case. "We didn't touch nothing of hern."

"There wa'nt no ballut book," Orville repeated ugly. "There never was none."

Toll of a sudden looked right up into the tree I was in. I was so still I twinged but even so I was scairt he might of seen me. Sometimes it 'pears he has eyes like a chicken hawk. He didn't say nothing, he just turned hisself round to the Perfessor.

"Orville's right, Perfessor." He snapped his knife shut and put it in his pocket. "Now, if it's a ballut you're hankering for, reckon I can give you one myself." He began to sing in that scrawny voice of his:

"There onct was a mountain girl, Bonnie Bluebell,
She lived on Tall Piney or so I've heerd tell,
She didn't know naught cause she'd never been taught,
Oh, hark to my story . . ."

I didn't let him finish his silly old song. I didn't care that I was discovered. I yelled at him, "You stop that, Tolliver," and I jumped down out of that tree and run over to him.

He grinned, singing up high like a woman, "Oh, hark to my story of Bonnie Bluebell."

He was twict as tall as I, and though he looked skinny enough for the wind to blow away, he was strong. I didn't care. I pounded on him. "You stop that right this minute. If'n you don't, I'll fix you so's you . . ."

He held me off. "Youl'll do what?" He begun louder:

"She run with the hounds and she run with the hare . . ."

All at onct I realized what I must appear like to the stranger man, my face and hands all gaumed from climbing the tree, and my feet even dirtier, and my old house dress ripped in the arms. I pushed Toll away and said dignified, "That ain't no ballut-song. You're just making that up."

Orville yelled at me, "Git home, Bluebell."

"You make him stop that fool singing."

"Git home." Orville got on his feet and started down the step towards me.

I didn't move far, I just backed up a bit. "I come over to fetch Grampaw. When I seed you had company—"

"Git home and git the supper."

"Supper's ready." The stew pot had been on all afternoon and I'd mixed the johnnycake afore I sneaked over to see what they was up to.

"Dish it up," Orville said. "I'll fetch Paw. Git now."

From the look in his eyes I decided might be I'd better git afore he whaled at me. But I knew I wasn't going to have a chanct to warn the perfessor man about them unless I made sure right now that he'd be invited to sup. Orville was too mean and stingy to invite anyone in on his own. "You ast the stranger to supper, Paw?" I said real innocent like. I was still calling him Paw then.

He scowled at me, but he had to make the invitation being as I'd brought it up. "You kin sup with us," he told the Perfessor.

"I'd appreciate that."

"I'm a-coming, too, Bluebell," Toll said.

I'd knowed he'd invite hisself. "Won't your Maw and Paw feed you no more?" I put my head up high and walked away.

He hollered after me, "You know dern well Maw and Paw are down to Middle Piney—"

I didn't linger to hear no more from him. Onct I was across the road I scatted down to our cabin. I wanted time to wash up and comb out the tangles of my hair and put on a fresh dress afore the Perfessor arrived. We didn't have company often. First I slammed the johnnycake into the oven and I opened a big jar of my best plum sass. I washed quick, but I used soap and I went behind the curtain to pull off that old dress and put on my sprigged blue, the one I wore to wedding frolics and buryings. When Orville and Cephus come in, I was trying to get a comb through my hair, standing out in front of the looking glass I'd hung over the wash bench. The Perfessor wasn't with them.

For a moment I was anxious. "Ain't he a-coming?"

Orville said, "He's follering after us. He's washing up at Toll's." He went over to the wash bench and splattered a little bit of water on his hands. "City fellers are allus hankering after soap and water. I remember when I was in the War." He wasn't talking about the real War but about when they'd fit the Kaiser four years back. "Should think they'd have the skin clean washed off afore they're old enough to spit."

"It don't seem to hurt them none," I told him.

Cephus had walked to the hearth to place Old Betsey up over the fireplace where he kept her. She was a beautiful long rifle with her silver mountings. He took better care of her than he did of himself. After he'd put her up, he set down in his rocking chair.

Orville went over to him, wiping dirt on the towel.

"What's he want to come up here for?" Cephus asked him. "What's he want anyhow?"

"It ain't no ballut book, Paw."

Cephus shook his head from side to side, trying to figger things. Finally he burst out, "The Granny Woman's dead. Ain't no call for him to come up here trying to rise the dead."

Orville said real calm, "Ain't no one's going to riz her up, Pappy. Not till the Last Judgment." He walked back with the towel and hung it on the drying rack. Like he didn't know that nobody but a pig would want to use it again until it was washed and biled. "Be careful what you say, Paw. Don't say nothing the Perfessor can carry tales about." He didn't pay no heed to what I was hearing. "One thing's for sartin, Paw. He was lying when he said he hadn't knowed the Granny Woman was dead. He knowed it all right."

I wouldn't of thought Orville was that smart. He must of been doing a deal of thinking today. Or Toll had been filling his mind up with what-for.

"How'd you figger that, Orvy?"

"Figger it yourself. When Toll was down to Middle Piney last week, he told that the Granny Woman was dead. What you tell in Middle Piney runs downhill to Little Piney afore you can blink an eye. And who gits the first word in Little Piney about deaths and so forth? The preacher man, that's who. The preacher man what the Perfessor's been a-visiting with. So he knowed."

Cephus nodded over it. "Reckon you're right, Orvy. What you aim to do about it?"

"We'll give him his vittles and after that—" He thumped his fist and rattled the table. "After that we'll see if he wants to go peaceful back down to Little Piney. If'n he don't . . ."

He didn't finish what he had to say because right then we heard Toll tittering to the Perfessor out on the path. My hair was combed out tolerably well. I was tying it back, with an old piece of blue ribbon the Granny Woman had give me, when Orville come over and put his hand on my arm.

"Don't you let me catch you talking to that there Perfessor man," he said.

"I won't."

"You keep your mouth shet, hear me?"

His hand squeezed until I couldn't help crying out. "You're hurting me!"

"I'll hurt you worse'n that if you don't keep your mouth shet."

The Perfessor and Toll was at the door by then so Orville let go of me. He went to table, set hisself down, and commenced dishing up his plate. "Fetch me some johnnycake, Bluebell," he hollered at me.

My arm hurt worse'n it had been hit by a stick, but I went right ahead tying my ribbon until I made a bow. Toll set down at the table with Orville and begun dishing his plate also. The Perfessor stood waiting.

Orville hollered again. "You hear me, fetch the johnnycake."

I opened the oven door. "Some folks wait for the company to set before they commence eating."

It was Toll who took care of the inviting. "Come on, Perfessor, set down and dig in. Bluebell ain't the best cook in the Ozarks, but there' allus a-plenty on Old Cephus' table. Come on, Cephus, you're getting left."

The Perfessor waited to set until Cephus come to the table. He must of seen by then that Ozark ladies don't eat with the gentlemen. He took the only chair left.

I dished up a big platter of johnnycake and I toted it right over to the Perfessor to make sure he got the best piece. Then I passed him the other dishes real polite, like I'd been larned by the Granny

Woman. "Try this rabbitmeat stew, Perfessor. It's real fresh." It was, too. Cephus had skun the rabbit only this morning. "Some wild sallet?" The greens had stewed just long enough, not too long to be bitter. "Have some plum sass, too, it goes good with johnnycake."

"Plum sass!" Toll exclaimed greedy-like. "You must of knowed there was company coming."

I ignored him, bringing the pitcher of milk and inquiring. "Can I help you to milk, Perfessor? Or maybe you'd prefer sweet milk?"

Orville grunted with his mouth full, "Leave the Perfessor eat his vittles, Bluebell. Stop urging him." He took another piece of johnnycake and pushed half of it into his mouth. He should have et with the pigs.

The Perfessor give me a big smile. He had the nicest smile you ever did see and he give it right at me, like I was a lady. He held up his glass. "This is just fine, Bluebell. Everything's fine. I'll bet you are the best cook in the Ozarks."

I retired to the stove, sort of flustered. I knew Toll would be mocking me and the Perfessor later on, but I just didn't care. It was worth it being treated like a lady for onct. There wasn't any talk while they was eating, Orville didn't hold with talk at table. But when he'd stuffed hisself to the busting point, he pushed back his chair and come right out with it.

"Seems a mite peculiar the preacher'd be sending you up here now the old woman's gone."

"Seems like he didn't know she was gone," the Perfessor said, filling up his pipe.

"Mighty peculiar he wouldn't know."

"Had she been ill?"

"No, sir!" Toll spoke up. "She was right as rain one day and the next she was dead." He dropped his voice. "Could have been that old screech owl what she heerd outside her door round about that time."

The Perfessor looked up, real interested. "It scared her?"

Toll peered over his shoulder. "Nobody's going to feel easy if he hears a screech owl on his doorstep. It's a sign of death for sure."

"At her age, a fright like that could cause a heart attack." The Perfessor puffed on his pipe.

"Not the Granny Woman! She come out with her old sweeping broom and shooed that owl off in a hurry." Real quick Toll added,

"I just happened to be passing by when she done it. Might be she give that old owl a heart attack." He snickered behind his hand.

"I'm sorry I came too late to meet her," the Perfessor said.

"Wouldn't of done you no good," Toll told him. "She couldn't of sung you no balluts. She was crazy as a wild mule."

I wanted to shout out that she was not, but I was afeared if I said anything Orville might tell me to git.

"She was crazy all right," Orville yawned out loud. "Reckon you'll want to be gitting back to Middle Piney. It's a far walk. Even going downhill."

"I don't think I'll go back tonight," the Perfessor said. "As long as I'm here I might as well have a look at her cabin."

Orville started to rise up, but Toll had a hold of his arm. "Seems like you won't take our word there ain't no ballut books there," Toll said.

"I'd sort of like to look around for myself." The Perfessor got up from the table then, moving slow, like the menfolks was strange dogs what might spring at him if he moved rapid. He wasn't no more than a step away when Toll was aside him.

"If'n I was you, I'd consider it real careful afore going inside her cabin. It mightn't be safe."

The Perfessor wasn't afeared. He looked straight at Toll. "Why not?"

Toll almost whispered it. "You might be witched."

This sure enough surprised the Perfessor. His mouth went open and he had to grab for his pipe. "You mean you think she was a witch?"

Cephus hadn't said a word up till then. Now he started sing-songing real loud, the way he used to do afore the Granny Woman died. Though we-uns was used to it, it always made me jump. It almost made the Perfessor jump out of his skin.

"She witched the cow out of her milk! She witched away my little girl, my little Rosebud! She witched my old hound dog! Howling into the woods he went and he never come back no more."

Orville said, "Now, Paw—"

"She won't lay no more spells on me and mine," Old Cephus declared. "She's dead. Dead and buried deep."

The Perfessor seemed sorry for Cephus. He turned away from him and he asked Toll, "Do you honestly believe she was a witch?"

Toll nodded his head solemn and slow. "She was a real Granny

Woman, Perfessor. Not the kind you hear tell of nowadays, the kind that births the babies. A *real Granny Woman*."

I was surprised that the Perfessor knew what Toll was talking about, but he did. He said kind of to hisself, "The old kind. The witch."

I couldn't keep quiet no more. I cried out, "She wa'nt no witch!"

"She was witching you," Orville hollered back at me. "You just didn't know it."

Toll reached inside his shirt and hung out the carved hickory nut on a string which he always wore. "You see that?" he said to the Perfessor. "Onct when I was a little shaver, the Granny Woman tried to take aholt of me in the woods. I skun home so fast you couldn't see my dust and my maw tied this to me. So's that old witch would never put a spell on me."

"If she's dead," the Perfessor asked him, "why do you still wear it?"

Toll stuck it back under his shirt. "It don't do no harm," he muttered.

Old Cephus burst out loud again, "There ain't but one way to kill a witch! With a silver bullet!"

Orville come quick to him, helping him up from the chair. "Now, Paw, no use gitting het up. She cain't witch you no more." He headed Cephus toward the hearth. "Git him his snuff stick, Blue-bell."

When he had his snuff stick, Old Cephus would almost always quieten down. But this time he kept right speaking. "She was the purtiest girl in the Pineys. I promised her maw I'd care for her."

Toll said offside, "He gits to wandering some, Perfessor. He was mighty partial to Rosebud. She was his youngest. She run off to the city." He snickered, "He claims it was the Granny Woman witched her away, but I don't see as how you can blame her for that."

The Perfessor picked up his hat from the bench. "I'm obliged for the supper." He looked at me and sort of made a bow. "I've never had a better one in the Ozarks, Miss Bluebell."

When he turned round to the door, Orville was in his way. "Where you going at?"

"Like I told you, I'm going to the Granny Woman's cabin. I've never been afraid of witches. And I'm not trespassing. I have permission from Deputy Clegg to visit it." He took a folded piece of paper out of his pocket and passed it to Orville.

The Granny Woman

Orville studied it when he passed it to me. "Speak it out loud, Bluebell. You've had more book larning than we-uns."

I read it oral, like he told me. I had to go slow on the big words, but I sounded them out like the teacher had larned me at the school house. "To whom it may concern: This gives permission for Professor Richard James to visit the Granny Woman's cabin at Tall Piney. Signed, Deputy Jim Clegg."

Orville and Toll never said no word. I reckon they was too overcome right then. The Perfessor took back the paper from me and said, "Good night, Miss Bluebell. Good night, Old Cephus. Good night, Orville and Toll."

With that he walked plumb out the door, Orville moving out of his way like in a daze. When he was gone, Orville sunk down in a chair. "Jim Clegg had no business writing them words on the paper. He'd no business letting a furriner rummage and root through the Granny Woman's belongings."

Old Cephus didn't appear to be listening, but he heerd. He set his mouth tight. "You aim to let him do that, Orvy?"

Orville said, "No, Paw." He walked to the corner where he kept his rifle and he took it up.

Toll run over to him. "Look here, Orvy! Scaring him out is one thing, but you got no call to take a gun after him. We don't want no trouble with the law."

"If Jim Clegg wants to let a furriner snoop around our property, I reckon it'll be his fault if trouble comes of it."

"I ain't talking about Deppity Jim's law," Toll argufied. "I'm talking about city law, Orville. This here feller's a college perfessor from the University. If you was to harm him . . ."

"Leave me be, Toll. I know what I'm at." I'd never seen Orville so mean and determined.

"Wait a minute, Orvy." Toll hung on his arm. "We got to talk this over. He ain't going to run away. He's going to snoop through that there cabin first. But he ain't going to do no harm there."

Orville didn't put down his rifle but he did set hisself down again. "How do you know he ain't?"

"There's nothing there for him to find out. So ain't it best to let him do his snooping there? Instead of certain other places?"

Orville wasn't convinced. "That property's ourn now. He's got no call to set foot on our property."

I'd been working at the dishes while they was talking. I had to warn the Perfessor man that Orville was coming after him with a load of buckshot. But I didn't know how I was going to get away to do it. Old Cephus give me my chanct. All at onct he reared up from his rocking chair and reached for his Old Betsey. His voice was like thunder. "It takes a silver bullet to kill a witch!"

Toll and Orville both hurried over to calm him. I took up the dish pan of water, just in case they should ask where I was going, and I skun on outside. I dumped the water and I run like a hare through the trees towards the special path to the cabin that only the Granny Woman and I ever used. The menfolks knowed about it, but they never set foot on it. They called it the Witch's Path.

I got the edge of the clearing before the Perfessor did. I could hear him coming, strangers cain't move soft-footed through the brush like we'ns can. And I could smell his pipe. It was dark of the moon, but I didn't want to step out into the open for fear Orville and Toll might already have set out. When the Perfessor was nearby, I whispered, "Perfessor man!"

He jumped like I was a bobcat. "Who is it?"

I stepped out where he could see me.

"What are you doing here?"

"I come to warn you. Orville's got his rifle. He means to stop you."

He sort of smiled. "I'm not afraid, Bluebell."

"But you got to be afraid!" I told him. "Orville won't let nobody up there. Not even me."

He said, meaning to be kind, "Then you better get back to the cabin before your Paw misses you. I wouldn't want any trouble to come to you from me."

"He ain't my Paw." I up and told him like I'd never told nobody before. "He states he is but he ain't. My Paw was a Joplin man."

He seemed real surprised. "Then you're Rosebud's daughter."

"What if I am? It ain't true all them lies they tell about her. She didn't run off to the city. The Granny Woman helped her to git away. She saved up her yarb money to help her. Afore she died she was saving her yarb money for me to get away, too."

"And so they killed her."

I couldn't explain it all to him then, there wasn't time. "She died natural. In her bed."

"Then what are they afraid of, Bluebell? Why don't they want me to go to her cabin?"

I told him part of the truth. "They promised Cephus. He's afeered of stirring her up. He's afeered she might come back."

"Is that it?" He puffed on his pipe and then he smiled at me again. "Well, I'm not afraid of ghosts or ghoulies or sorkinses. You scat home now, Bluebell. I don't want you following me to the cabin, just in case trouble should develop."

He set off. The only way I could of stopped him was to run after him, and I was scairt they'd be missing me if I was away longer. I run all the way home. After I'd caught my breath, I picked up the dishpan and come back in.

"Where you been?" Orvy asked right away.

"I been out back," I said. I carried the pan over to where I kept it by the stove. Then I noticed that Toll was loading a rifle, too. I rushed over to him. "What you doing with that gun, Tolliver Sorkin?"

"Orvy and me aim to do a little hunting tonight."

I could scarce believe my ears. Instead of him talking Orville around, it was the other way.

"You're going to the Granny Woman's cabin!"

"It's nary of your business where we're going." Orville got up on his feet. "You stay put and tend to your knitting. And see to it that Grampaw don't foller us."

"You cain't shoot the Perfessor! He don't know nothing about what you done." I clamped my hand over my mouth, but I'd said it.

Orville come advancing to me and I backed up fast, nigh to Old Cephus by the fire.

"You been spying on us."

"No, I ain't. Swear to God, I ain't!"

"You swear to a lie, you'll burn in hellfire."

"I ain't swearing to no lie!"

Orville didn't stop for Grampaw being there. He grabbed my wrist and pulled me out to him. "You follered us to the grave."

"I didn't!" I screamed it because he was hurting me bad. "I swear—"

"Leave her be," Toll shouted over my screaming. "We're wasting time. You can take keer of her later."

Orville give me a shove as he let go. I fell down to the floor. He stumped out the door after Toll. Every bone in my body was bruised. When I leaned on my wrist trying to get up, it felt like it was broken though it wa'nt.

Cephus asked, "Where they going? Why don't they want me to go with them?"

I was mad enough to tell him, "They're going hunting."

"Whyn't they wait for me? I can outhunt both of them." He commenced to rise up from his chair.

"It's night times, Grampaw." I managed to push myself up from the floor, favoring my bad wrist. "You cain't hunt at night no more. You don't see no good."

"I can see further than both of them together. Me and my old hound dog—" He remembered and sank back sorrowing. "My old hound dog. He never come back. She witched him away."

"She didn't have naught to do with it, Grampaw. It was Orville's meanness druv him away."

"It was her done it." He was starting to meander into the past again. "If'n I'd knowed she was a witch, she couldn't of witched me with her daughter like she done. When I first seen Amarylly, she didn't look like no witch's brat. She had yellowy hair and rosebud in her cheeks. Rosebud! That's the name she give our own little one." He come back from his meandering. "She witched Rosebud away from me."

"My maw." I don't know why I said it to him then, I never had before.

"Who's been telling you sech things?"

"The Granny Woman told me."

"What else did she tell you?"

"Nothing wrong. She said you was the strongest man in the Pineys onct. You stood so straight and tall, there wa'nt a man could match up to you."

He recollected, "I was felling a big old pine tree when she and her child come on me. They was gathering yarbs."

"After her child was dead, you took Rosebud away from the Granny Woman."

"I wa'nt going to let my little Rosebud grow up a witch's child. My old woman never knowed why I took the little one." Without any warning, he stood up, roaring mad. He towered over me. "What else did she tell you? How to dry up the old cow? How to sour the milk?"

"No!" I tried to inch away. I'd never seed him like this before.

"Did she tell you how to witchride a man all night through the brambles? Did she tell you how to set a pure young gal to lallygagging in the woods? Did she tell you how she witched Rosebud into running away from her own Paw? Did she tell you how to drive a man's faithful old hound howling into the night?"

I kept saying No and No and inching, but I couldn't get clear to make it to the door. When he reached to take down Old Betsey, I tried to stop him. But he brushed me aside, not mean like Orville, just like I was nothing, a pine branch in his path.

"She didn't know I was a witchkiller like my pappy afore me. She didn't know he larned me to kill witches same as him. You got to have a silver gun and a silver bullet to kill a witch."

"No, Grampaw, no!" I screamed it at him. He had that rifle pointed right to my heart. Somehow he'd made hisself believe she'd passed her witching on to me, that I was a witch child. And then I remembered. "You got no silver bullet," I hollered. "You used it on the Granny Woman."

Slowly he lowered the rifle. The spirit went out of him. "It takes a long time to git enough silver to make a bullet."

"Set down, Grampaw," I said to him kindly. "I swear she didn't larn me no witching. She was good to me."

He stood there holding fast to the long rifle. "Nigh on to fifteen years it took me to git enough silver. Pure silver it's got to be."

I freshened up his snuff stick and held it out to him. "Just rest yourself, Grampaw. Rock a bit."

Instead of setting down, he started to the door. I run after him. "No, Grampaw. Orvy don't want you to foller him. It's dark of the moon." You see, I knowed his intent. He was going after his silver bullet.

He paid me no heed. He kept right on walking. I didn't hardly wait until he was out of sight. I tore out of there and over to the Witch's Path. The only chanct I had was to get the Perfessor to protect me. I knew what Old Cephus meant to do. And Orville and Toll wouldn't stop him if'n they could. They'd be a-feared he was right.

I didn't reckon Orville and Toll would be at the Granny Woman's cabin yet. First they'd have gone down to the stump, where their mountain dew was hid out, to get some courage in them. They was shy of her cabin even in daylight.

I run like I never run before and when I come to the cabin I didn't knock on the door, I busted right in. The Perfessor man looked up real surprised to see me. He'd lit her table lamp and he was rummaging through her old horsehair trunk. He'd already took out the face fan she'd carried back in Virginny when she was a girl. And the silk and satin baby bonnet, so tiny you wouldn't think it would fit a poppet, but it had been my maw's. He was holding her

117

papers, the ones she kept tied with a blue ribbon, when I busted in.

He said, "I told you not to come here, Bluebell."

"I had to. Old Cephus is out gitting him a silver bullet to kill me with."

"To kill you?" His eyes most popped out of his head. "Why would he want to kill you?"

"Because . . ." I didn't want to tell him. "Because he thinks she made me into a witch."

Just then I heerd someone outside the door and I run over and crouched down behind the Perfessor. Maybe I was daft thinking he could protect me without no gun nor nothing, but I did think so. I reckon it was because he wa'nt afraid. He didn't even put down the papers.

I closed my eyes when the door started to open. And I heered him say, "Come in, Jim." So I opened up my eyes and there was Deputy Jim Clegg closing the door.

Deputy Jim said, "Looks like you got you some company, Rick." Deputy Jim was as big as Orville, but he wa'nt nothing like him otherwise. He was clean and strong and I never in my life seed him do a mean thing to man or beast. He was born and raised right here in the Ozarks, but he'd gone to school up at Columbia and knowed how to talk good. He said to me, "What you doing here, Bluebell?"

I told him, "Orville and Toll are hunting the Perfessor man and Old Cephus is hunting me. He's got in his mind that the Granny Woman made a witch of me."

"So he's going to kill you like he killed the Granny Woman?"

The Perfessor spoke up. "Bluebell says she died natural, in her bed."

Deputy Jim said, "A witch killer doesn't have to kill you to make you die, Rick."

Because he understood, I told him, "Orvy stuck the pins in the dishrag and burnt it. Toll trapped the screech owl to set outside her door. Old Cephus molded the silver bullet and feathered it into the tree. And she died."

The Perfessor looked across at Deputy Jim. Deputy Jim put his hand in his pocket and brought out what looked like a ball of silver. He said, "I found the silver bullet. In the tree, not in her heart."

"You don't have to put the bullet in a witch's heart," I told them.

"You can peel the bark off the tree and sketch her shape there. Then you can feather the bullet into her on the tree."

Deputy Jim put the bullet back into his pocket. "Thanks to you keeping them busy, Rick, we found the grave, down by Piney Run. And we didn't have any interruptions at the exhumation. Doc's taking her down to Little Piney for an autopsy, but it looks like she died what you'd call natural. So I was wrong. I'm going down to their cabin now. Want to come?"

I didn't know much what he was talking about, but I knowed I didn't want to go back to the cabin again. Not even with Deputy Jim and the Perfessor for protection. I was readying to say so when we heard Orville roaring outside, "Come out of there Perfessor. If'n you don't . . ." He shot off his gun for a warning.

Deputy Jim walked over and swung open the door wide. When Orville and Toll saw who it was, they let their rifles down. Deputy Jim asked them, "Could it be you're hunting witches?"

Orville said, "We come to protect our property."

"It's not your property," Deputy Jim said. "It's Bluebell's. By direct descent from the Granny Woman." He shook his head and sighed. "Seems like there ought to be something I could arrest you for, Orvy, but blamed if I know what it could be this time. You might better watch your Paw closer, however, before he gets in some trouble I might have to arrest him for."

You mightn't think Orville set store by anything, but he did by his Paw. "I will," he vowed. Then he noticed me and he hollered, "Where is Paw? You was supposed to be caring for him, Bluebell."

"I couldn't hold him," I said. "He took old Betsey and he—"

They didn't wait for me to finish. Orville and Toll both set out running down the hill, hollering, "Paw" and "Old Cephus."

Deputy Jim said, "Come on."

I hung back until the Perfessor took me by the hand. "You needn't be afraid, Bluebell. Jim and I will take care of you."

By my path we got the cabin almost as soon as Orville and Toll. Old Cephus was already back inside. He was tearing up the almanac and scattering the writing around on the floor. He already had the feathers spread around in the fireplace and under the windows and on the doorsill. When he saw us all standing there, he thundered, "She's riz up! There ain't no time to make a fire ring, we got to git her shet out of here afore she comes trying to sneak in. Help me, Orvy." He pushed the book into Orville's hands. "Git the dishrag,

Tolliver, and stick them pins in it for the burning. They's up on Bluebell's shelf in the matchbox."

"Them pins been burnt onct, Cephus," Toll said. "The time the dog run off."

"They's all we have, we'll have to make use of them again."

Toll was about to do like Cephus said when Deputy Jim spoke up. "By the time that old witch picks up all these feathers and reads all that writing, it'll be cockcrow and she can't do you no harm tonight, Cephus." He dipped his hand in his pockets like he had afore and brought out the silver bullet on his palm.

Cephus picked it out of his hand, looked at the markings and he shook his head like he couldn't believe it. "No wonder she riz up," he whispered. "The silver bullet come out of her heart." He set down heavy in the rocking chair. "I'm too old. I've lost my powers to kill witches."

Deputy Jim said, "You feather it back into the tree tomorrow, Old Cephus. Maybe it'll go deep enough this time." He turned round to me. "Get your things together, Bluebell."

"What for?" Toll spoke up though it wasn't his business.

"She's coming down to Little Piney with us," Deputy Jim told him. "I'll find a place for her to board and maybe fix it up for her to go back to school. It's better she stays off of Tall Piney for a time."

Orville asked, "And who's going to cook for me and Paw while she's gone away?"

"If you weren't so mean, Orvy," Deputy Jim answered him, "you could find a wife to cook for you."

That was how it come about I went down to Little Piney for my education, not that it took on me much. I didn't go back to Tall Piney until after Toll and me was married. Onct Toll got away from Orville's influence, he stopped being so mean. Fact is, Orville wasn't so dirty and mean hisself after the Widder Claggett married up with him. She wouldn't put up with a pig in her cabin.

Old Cephus was dead by then, peaceful. He fell asleep in his rocking chair one afternoon and never woke up. The Perfessor bought his Old Betsey off'n Orville and give it to the Historical Society. You can see it up at their museum.

The Granny Woman was buried again, this time on the hill nearby her cabin, where Toll and me live. The Perfessor put up a headstone for her: Mary Virginia Piper, born in Roanoke, Virginia, 1823; died on Tall Piney, Missouri, 1924.

The Granny Woman

The silver bullet is still in the tree by Piney Run where Old Cephus feathered it twict. Nobody in the Pineys would dast prize it out.

The Siren and the Shill

•

John Jakes

The realistic crime stories of John Jakes have appeared in two previous volumes in this series, Prime Suspects *and* Fatal Attractions. *In "The Siren and the Shill" he once again provides a gripping and hard-edged tale, this time with a small traveling carnival as its setting. Jakes, whose most recent best-selling historical book is* Heaven and Hell *(1987), the final volume in his North-South trilogy, is also the author of a number of mystery novels, among them* The Imposter *(1959) and* Johnny Havoc and the Doll Who Had "It" *(1963).*

Dan Wilde scratched his head for the second time. He reached across the table for a cigarette, shoved it into his determined mouth and got it lit without taking his eyes off the piece of paper. Angie's handwriting, all right. *I want to get something settled,* she wrote. *And this time, no dodging me. I'll meet you at the truck.* No signature. He was supposed to know who sent it. Well, damn it, he did. Angrily, he reached out, crumpled the note with a savage gesture, and flung it into the wastebasket. He glanced at his watch. Fifteen minutes to twelve. He grabbed his leather jacket off the chair, flipped out the lights, and went out of the trailer, down the steps to the south end of the midway.

Clay Brothers' Carnival lay like a Christmas tree on its side. A quarter mile of spangled lights and color. A ceaseless hum of voices, a constant thud of feet on sawdust that rose to a minor roar. The ferris wheel went plunging down, and a girl's pleasured scream cut the night. The calliope wheezed away with *The Eyes of Texas.* Dan moved past the frame structure where a long gasp arose like a gust of wind, in accompaniment to the grinding clamor of the motorcycles. Hell's Motordrome. The bells on the shooting gallery were clanging away as some amateur marksman demonstrated his skill. Hawkers peddled their cotton candy, their red hots, their plaster dolls spangled with mica dust. Dan kept moving, a big heavy-set man of around thirty. People glanced at his ruggedly-cut face and instinctively moved out of his way. This was his, Dan Wilde's show. He ran it, he kept it bringing in the money. One more season like this, and he'd have the desk job he wanted so badly. General Manager of Underwood's United Shows, of which the carnival was only one part. Dan thought of the job now as he walked. He liked the idea, but he didn't smile.

Angie was kicking up some kind of a fuss. Clay Brothers' was a business, nothing else. Everybody did their jobs like robots, at Dan's command. When people stopped acting like robots and started getting human, getting personal affairs tangled up with business, Dan clamped down.

He wondered how much he would have to clamp down on Angie. They had a more or less binding agreement that they would be married. But they never talked of it. Dan refused to consider a wedding until he got the desk job, and the security it brought. He managed to keep himself going, just another efficient robot, without getting his affair with Angie all mixed up with business matters. But her note disturbed him. Maybe the personal element was rearing its head once more. He didn't want to think about that.

He walked on through the crowds of the midway. Emmanuel Fedderson, the barker for the Hawaiian Nights pitch, caught Dan's eye over the heads of the mostly male audience, raised his cane, and nodded slightly. But the round button mouth in the center of Fedderson's chubby face kept right on working, emitting its stream of nasal talk, promising delights on the inside for only a quarter, rhapsodizing over those hula honeys, those lovely ladies from the sunlit sands of Waikiki. Dan waved back and stopped, standing at the rear of the crowd, hands thrust in his pockets.

". . . and now," Manny exclaimed, "as just a sample of what you're going to see on the inside, I'm going to bring three of the little ladies out here. Three beautiful belles from the enchanted islands, featuring our own Miss Mawani Ba'ya, an authentic Hawaiian princess doing her celebrated Love Hula. Come on out, girls." The phono needle scraped and an electric guitar recording boomed out over the crowd. The curtains behind the platform parted and the girls came dancing onto the platform, bumping their hips generously. Bubbles on the left, Harriet on the right. And Angie in the middle.

2.

Dan allowed himself a grin. She really put it over. With a dark wig and dark makeup and her trim little body sunburned a deep nut-brown under the imitation grass skirt and halter, she looked authentic enough. Her maternal grandfather, he knew, had been an exporter and importer in Hong Kong and had married a Chinese woman, which may or may not have accounted for the slight teasing tilt of her dark eyes.

Under the wig, though, was ash blond hair. As the girls went into their routine, Dan caught himself noticing her figure. The shapely legs and pert sturdy breasts. She was a refined broad. Wouldn't work in a smutty show at all. But she had the assets, and she took a kind of impish pleasure in holding herself aloof from male admirers. Tonight, though, Dan saw a new seriousness in her face. Her lips were parted in a smile, but her eyes stared out over the bald heads, full of a faraway emptiness.

Dan grew conscious of someone standing at his elbow. He turned. Chick Morrison stood there, in his usual flowered sport shirt and dark slacks. He, too, was deeply tanned, well built. Hot-tempered blue eyes stared up at Angie's undulating figure. Chick had crew-cut blond hair and thickly-muscled limbs. He didn't take his eyes off Angie. "Cool tonight," he said to Dan. "Wish I had a jacket."

"Relax, Chick," Dan said. "You don't have to make small talk."

"If she was my girl," Chick replied, "I'd be damned if I'd let her get up there where all these old duffers could eye her." He said it grimly.

"It's business," Dan shot back. But he saw that Chick's attention was riveted more firmly than ever on Angie, or Princess Mawani Ba'ya, as Manny had named her in his far from authentic knowledge of Hawaiian names.

This Chick was a funny kid, Dan thought. Ex-college boy, ex-Marine, ex-everything. He'd picked up some capital somewhere and signed with Old Man Underwood to run the concessions in the carnival, under the name *Independent Amusement Enterprises*. A fancy name for a hard-headed kid who ran clean games and got a good rake-off and guarded his property with all the jealousy of his fiery nature. Chick had replaced a more crooked outfit of concessionaries, and brought a certain degree of peace to the midway.

He was a shill, Dan admitted, but a damned good one. He egged the customers on. He banged away at the shooting gallery and

124

knocked over all the clay rabbits through his experience with fire-arms in the marines. He always spilled the milk because he was once a farm team southpaw with a good chance at the majors. He could come up with right guesses on the wheels and horse race games nearly ninety percent of the time because he'd been a math major before he got restless and quit college. A clean honest shill, who liked to talk, liked his work, and had a personality marred only by an intense, hot-tempered jealousy of what was his own. He liked Angie. He'd told Dan that. If he ever got her on his team, he'd be just as jealous of her as he was of his concessions.

Manny wound up his spiel, the girls danced back into the tent, and the crowd started its expectant surge forward toward the ticket booth. Saturday night. They'd be working for a long time yet.

Dan started to say something to Chick when he noticed a flurry of movement just in front of him. A skinny rat-faced guy in a dirty, threadbare suit bumped against a bald-headed man and apologized loudly. Dan went forward and grabbed the skinny man's shoulder, spinning him around. He snatched the wallet from the guy's hand and tossed it to the spluttering bald man.

"Get off the lot," Dan said quietly.

3.

The skinny man's mouth curled nastily. He kicked Dan in the shins and twisted. Someone shouted hoarsely. A knife blade gleamed suddenly in the man's hand, throwing off the glare of colored lights. "Son . . ." the man hissed, lunging. Dan grabbed the man's arm and snapped it across his knee. The man howled. Dan belted him in the stomach and he went reeling backwards. Chick Morrison grabbed him and ripped into his jaw with a ham-mering uppercut, every bit as powerful as Dan's blow. The pick-pocket seemed to sprout wings, rising upward until he slammed back down onto the midway. He picked himself up hastily and scuttled off through the crowd. Dan retrieved the knife from the sawdust, closed it, and put it in his jacket pocket.

"Guys like that are a pain," Chick said, wiping his hands on his pants.

"It's a hell of a job, trying to run a clean midway," Dan agreed.

"Hey," Chick said, "how about having a dog with me? I'd like to talk."

"Okay," Dan said as they began to walk. Chick seemed very

formal now, very businesslike. Dan sensed that something spelled trouble was on its way. Trouble that would be a lot harder to handle than ordinary two-bit grifters and pickpockets, who seemed to sprout only in sawdust.

Chick said nothing until they got their dogs from the nearest stand. Dan ladled on the mustard and took a bite. He winced at the sharp taste, letting his eyes bore into Chick. He swallowed the bite and said, "Well, what's the topic for tonight?"

Chick didn't look away. "Angie."

"She knows how to hula, all right," Dan said.

"Quit kidding around, Wilde. You know what I mean. I want to know the score. Are you two going to get married?"

"Someday, yes," Dan replied. "But I don't see where that concerns you."

"It concerns me because I like Angie," Chick answered. His eyes got that funny, glazed look, and Dan sensed that he was getting angry. Well, let him. Better to squelch the trouble before it got really bad. "You don't say boo to Angie half of the time," Chick went on, "and it doesn't seem to me that a guy who treats a girl like that has any right to put his brand on her. What I mean to say is, either say it one way or another. You're either going to get married for sure, and I don't mean just talk about it, or she's up for grabs." He grimaced. "That's not such a good word, I guess, but you get the meaning."

"Yeah," Dan said evenly, "I do. I also think you'd better keep your nose out of my business, Chick. What I do is my own affair."

Chick nodded. "Suit yourself. You run the show around here. You're nothing but a big adding machine, Wilde. So you'll have to get ready to move over. I'm taking Angie."

"Like hell you are," Dan blazed back.

Chick grinned. "Try and stop me. You've got so much to do figuring out percentages and cutting corners, you haven't got time for anything else. You haven't got a chance, buster."

Filled with quick sudden anger, Dan tried to shift the dog awkwardly from his right to his left hand. He wanted to throw a punch at Chick, but while he still fumbled clumsily with the bun, Chick brought his left hand down sharply, slapping the dog away. Mustard splattered on Dan's hands. He felt like a fool. "And don't try any rough stuff," Chick snorted, "or you'll get it right back." Before Dan could bring his fist up, Chick was gone, disappearing into the sluggishly moving crowd.

Dan stood there for a moment, angry and confused. A pair of high school girls and their dates snickered as they went by. Shamefaced, Dan got out his handkerchief and wiped the mustard away. He cursed softly. Not only did Angie have to bother him tonight, but Chick Morrison, too. That boy could be real trouble. The way he acted, quickly, intemperately, could blot out every bit of good sense he might otherwise have. If Chick got hold of an idea, if he once got a purpose fixed in his mind, Dan knew that all hell couldn't blast him loose from it. Dan slapped his fist restlessly into his palm and started to walk, not noticing the crowds and the lights any more. He felt a cold sweat of fear, because the finely oiled mechanism named Dan Wilde was no longer running efficiently. He found himself angry and swearing, and that wasn't good. The whole structural efficiency of the carnival could slide right out from under him if he didn't watch himself. He could lose Angie, he could lose Old Man Underwood's faith, and he could lose every chance he'd ever had for that desk job.

He moved in a kind of haze as the night wore on. He gave orders, took care of minor matters with thoughtless, instinctive action. By the time most of the marks had drifted off to their beds in town, minus a good deal of their money, he thought he knew what he must do.

4.

About two-thirty the work gangs began to strike canvas. The lights went out and the tinseled wonderland fell apart at the seams. The big trucks ground their gears and spewed out their loading platforms. The performers and concessionaries packed up. Under the dark cover of night, the carnival stirred like a living organism, getting ready to move.

Dan was in the trailer, counting the receipts and making a record of them, when Manny Fedderson came in, shuffling his little stubby legs rapidly. He poured himself a cup of coffee from the pot bubbling on the hot plate, and gulped it down. "Had some more trouble with the cats tonight, I hear. Dorman almost got himself killed."

Dan finished his work, put the cash box and the ledger in the squat black safe, and slammed the door. "I didn't hear anything about it."

Manny peered at him curiously. "Dorman and his wife are going at it worse than ever. You know how mad he gets at her, and he takes it out on the cats. Rajah got tired of having the blanks go off in his face and tried to take a hunk out of Dorman. He just got out of the cage in time.''

Dorman was a stocky, foreign-born man who handled two lions and a Bengal tiger named Rajah in a show at the other end of the midway. His wife, an acid-tongued slut, told fortunes. They fought constantly. Dan couldn't remember having been down that far this evening. It bothered him. After the incident with Chick, things remained pretty much a blank. He was thankful when Manny changed the subject, but he knew by the look on the older man's face that Manny had sensed something out of place in Dan's behavior. Everyone in the show knew that Dan was all places at all times, nightly. Tonight he had slipped. It wouldn't be good if word got around. He had to be careful. It made his determination to stick to his decision about Angie stronger than ever, even though a part of him rebelled.

''You got the jumps, boy,'' Manny said abruptly.

''What?'' Dan said absently. Manny pointed. Dan looked down and saw that his hand which held a cigarette was trembling.

''I said you got the jumps.''

Dan stood up abruptly. ''So I got the jumps. What the hell difference should it make to you?'' He stalked quickly toward the trailer door, aware of the puzzled, half-pained look on Manny's face. He slammed the door behind him and inhaled a deep breath of the cool night air. Get hold of yourself, Wilde. You can't crack. It's not that bad. Nothing ever happened to make you crack. Just hold on. After a minute, he stopped trembling.

The rigs came down and the trucks finished loading. They lined up at the edge of the grounds in a long column, headlights glaring yellow through the black night. Reluctantly Dan headed toward the front truck. He went around to the left side, opened the cab door, and climbed up. Manny usually rode with him. Tonight Manny wasn't around. Manny must have gotten the word.

A cigarette glowed orange. Dan turned on the ignition. The motor roared to life under his control. All along the line, he could hear the other motors starting. Finally he turned toward her. ''Hello, kid,'' he said softly. He kept all feeling out of his voice.

5.

He saw her face in the cigarette glow, breathtakingly pretty. Blond hair now, the phony wig gone. A firm honest face that belonged around kids and a bright kitchen. He knew it, but he couldn't bring himself to give it to her. Not now, not this way. The machine had to keep running at all costs, or everything he had ever worked for, dreamed of, would be gone down the drain.

She said nothing. He leaned out the window and waved. The big truck started forward, bumping over the field until it hit the highway. The caravan headed west, through the small town and into the dark rolling country beyond. The headlight pierced yellow shafts into lonely blackness. Dan fumbled around and got a cigarette lit for himself.

"I got your note," he said. "You've got something important to talk about, I guess." He kept his eyes rigidly staring ahead.

"I want to talk about us, Dan." Her voice was soft, a trifle sorrowful.

"Well." He tried to laugh. It was no good. "Let's have it."

Her hand touched his arm. "Dan, I've been thinking a lot lately. An awful lot. We just seem to drift along from day to day, getting older. I know we've got an agreement, but . . ."

"We agreed to get married when I got the desk job," he said sharply.

"But why do we have to wait, Dan? Why?"

"Because, damn it," he said loudly, "I want to quit this business. It's a second-rate way to live at best. I like it, but I don't want my kids to grow up inhaling sawdust and getting a diet of pop and hot dogs."

"But we wouldn't have to wait . . ." she insisted.

"Look." He twisted the wheel, swinging the great truck around a curve. "We've hashed this all out before. Have you got anything else to say?" He hated himself, hated himself with a part of his mind that spat out curses, all directed at that stupid methodical machine that ran a carnival, Dan Wilde.

"Yes," she said. Her voice was pitched low, held in tight, but it trembled. "Yes, Dan. Either we do it now or we don't ever do it." He knew what she was waiting for. Knew she waited for him to break because he loved her. Knew that she trembled on the brink of something dark, with all her faith held in her hand. Knew, and somehow forced himself not to care.

"All right," he said. "I guess that's the way it is. I want that desk job."

No hysterics. She was too good for that, he thought. Nothing but a faint muffled sob and her head averted so that he could not see her face in the green glow of the dash. "I'm going to sleep, Dan," she said. "We open in Crystal City Monday and . . ." Her voice quavered, broke, but she got control after an instant. ". . . and it's a long way."

6.

The long concrete ribbon stretched out ahead of them, swallowing up towns and sleeping people and peaceful houses. Dan tried to keep from thinking about her, about the good times they had had together since he took over the carnival after the war. They had seemed right then. She hadn't been a stopgap for the machine. His mouth twisted bitterly.

He turned to her suddenly. "Angie." She mumbled in her sleep. He repeated her name and she finally opened her eyes. Just up from the depths of sleep, her eyes were raw, tormented. "Have you been talking to Chick Morrison?" he asked levelly. She didn't understand, through the haze of sleepiness. He repeated his question and she seemed surprised, the way people do when your momentous statement means nothing to them at all. She said she hadn't and Dan felt foolish. "Okay," he said. "Sorry." But she would be talking to him before long. Word would get around.

When a gray dawn spread itself over the east, the caravan pulled in to an all-night truck stop. Dan felt self-conscious, sitting by himself at the counter while the crew jammed the booths and tables, talking loudly and laughing much. Manny slid onto a stood beside him. "You look tired," Manny said.

"Now listen . . ." Dan began.

Manny raised one hand. "Don't start on me, Dan. I'm just making an observation. Crystal City's a big town and we'll have a tough run. Lots of marks. You ought to sleep." He stirred his coffee, staring into space with studied carelessness. "Now Wiskolski could take over the trailer and I could drive lead and you could sack in. Just a suggestion, of course."

Dan smiled thinly. "Sorry I snapped like that. You're right. Thanks." He got up and walked out of the restaurant, aware that the people watched him. He risked a quick glance toward the corner where Angie sat. She was bent over her coffee, in earnest conversation with Chick Morrison. Neither one noticed him.

Dan stepped outside into the gray morning. He felt cold, hollow. He lit a cigarette and tossed it away after the first drag, the flat taste heavy in his mouth. He walked rapidly down the line of trucks parked by the building, opened the door of the trailer, and walked over to the bunk. He took off his jacket and flopped on his face. Forget it, Dan, he told himself. A kootch dancer and a high-class shill. They'll make a good pair. But somehow, it was no good. He was asleep before the trucks began to roll.

7.

They hit Crystal City midafternoon Sunday. Dan, feeling rested after a long sleep, though no more satisfied with things as they were than he had been the the night before, was driving the lead truck. They rolled through the broad main street, largely deserted except for a rash of bicycles in front of the movie houses. Turning left, they passed through a residential section. The streets dozed in sun-dappled shade, the big elms arching their branches to form a curtain of green. Comfortable looking houses sat well back on spacious lawns. Dan saw men and women on the porches eyeing the trucks. No doubt disturbed by the sight of a carnival clattering down their street on Sunday, Dan thought.

Bitterness gnawed his thoughts again when he realized that in all probability Angie was watching, too, seeing those houses with their respectable owners sipping lemonade or scotch on their porches, and wishing that she, Angie, could do the same. Maybe she'd get what she wanted from Chick Morrison. A kid on a bicycle came down the street toward them and Dan blatted the truck horn loudly, taking pleasure in the jarring noise that split the respectable Sunday afternoon air.

The Crystal City fairgrounds lay dusty in the heat. Banners and placards welcomed you to the County Fair, to begin Monday. A few people had already arrived, setting up the stands for the live-stock and foods displays. The trucks pulled up on the huge open lot beyond the grandstand. Shedding his T-shirt, Dan began to bawl orders, and within minutes the canvas was rising and the wonder-land was being put together out of poles and canvas and lights, for a week's engagement.

Dan worked the men hard, and the pitches were in place by

seven. He got his supper in the cook wagon, but he ate alone. Most of the kids had gone off to see the big city, investigating the liquor situation. Crystal City ran wide open, Dan knew. They'd find the bars open on Sunday night. He mentally made a note to check for violent drunkenness the next morning. Once again, his cigarettes were tasteless, as was the food. He pushed the plate away, his meal only half-finished and stalked out along the midway. The sun sat on the horizon like a pale red ball and the breeze lifted eddies of sawdust. A canvas flap whipped noisily in the wind. Dan walked along, hands thrust deep in his pockets. The tent poles stood out like gaunt accusing fingers against the paling sky.

Manny was playing solitaire in the trailer. He looked up as Dan came in. "Hi. Place is like a tomb, ain't it?"

Dan sat down glumly. "It sure is. I don't think there's a person left on the lot."

Manny chuckled. "Even Dorman and his wife made a night of it. We still got the cats on our hands. Drives me nuts." Dan listened and heard the wild vicious tiger-scream, floating up along the midway. "That baby's gonna kill somebody someday," Manny commented. "Want to play some euchre, or should we go hit the bars, too?"

Dan wanted to say no, we might run into Angie and Chick. Instead he said, "Let's play cards."

8.

About eight-forty a knock sounded on the trailer door. Before Dan could say anything, a short warty-skinned man with muddy dark eyes sauntered in. He wore cheap clothes, a silk shirt, and a loud purple tie. His blue suede shoes squeaked faintly. Dan didn't like the insolent sneering curve of his mouth. Dan put down his cards and stood up. "Something?"

The man fished out a grimy white card with one corner missing. "I want to see the boss. Or the guy who runs your concessions." His lips split in a grin, revealing uneven horsy teeth. His eyes remained muddy, snake-hard in their shine. "That is, if it's one and the same. Otherwise, the guy handling the concessions."

"I run the show," Dan said. "Chick Morrison handles the concessions."

"Where can I find him?" the man asked.

"Depends on what you want him for. Let's see that card." Dan

132

stuck out his hand. The man's eyes met his for an instant, hard and insolent, and then the false grin reappeared. He handed over the square of cardboard. On it were the words, *Mumford Mightier Midways*. And in smaller type, *Crystal City*. Dan handed the card back.

"My name's de Packh. Lester de Packh. I represent Mumford," the man said.

"I've heard about you. We haven't got any business for you. We run a clean midway."

De Packh guffawed nastily. "Jesus, don't tell me you're one of *those*. Listen, mister, Mumford can make a profit for you while you're here. For a forty percent cut, we'll guarantee to double your volume of concession business. Triple it." He stabbed a squat finger at Dan for emphasis. Manny watched, frowning.

"No thanks," Dan said evenly. "I don't need that kind of profit. Rigged wheels and floating crap games and armed hoods to take care of any suckers who might object to being fleeced. I'm not buying." Dan turned his back on the man.

"Listen here . . ." de Packh said sharply. Dan whirled, glaring at him. De Packh didn't scare. Dan searched for the bulge under his suit jacket and found it.

"Leave," Dan said. "Right now."

"I can give you plenty of trouble," de Packh said. "I just tried to make a little money for you. I don't like it when somebody refuses a little friendly help."

Dan took a step forward. He kept his voice pitched low. "Are you going out, or do I have to break your neck for you?"

De Packh hesitated. Dan noticed that the man's right hand flexed almost automatically. Gun itch, Dan thought. He was getting mad. De Packh finally shrugged and headed for the door. Before he went out, he turned. His voice was quiet, but loaded with sarcastic venom. "So long, sport. I'm not going to forget about you." He slammed the door hard behind him, making the glass vibrate.

Dan went back to the table. Manny shook his head. "Boys like that I don't like. If you get on the wrong side of them, they can put the kibosh on things overnight. A few boys with axes and clubs, and bang . . ." He snapped his fingers. "No more carnival."

Dan glowered at him. "What the hell was I supposed to do? Write him a ticket to bring all his crooks in here? No dice."

Manny's eyes seemed apologetic. "It's what they call the horns of a dilemma."

Dan scarcely heard. He thought again of the warty face of Lester de Packh, and remembered that he had mentioned Chick Morrison's name. That bothered him. He had no specific reason, and yet he was uneasy about it.

He finally tumbled into bed in a black, angry mood. He heard some of the kids come onto the lot about one, laughing and singing. He turned over restlessly and slammed his fist into the pillow. It didn't do one bit of good. He kept thinking of Angie and Chick Morrison and Dorman and his kill-crazy cat and Lester de Packh and Mumford Mightier Midways. The more he thought, the worse it became. At last, around four, he managed to go to sleep. But then he dreamed—of riding the rods, as he'd done when he was a kid, wandering, without a job, and he woke up in a cold sweat.

9.

At nine A.M. Monday morning, the gates of the fair grounds opened and the crowd poured in. Monday was usually an off day, but by noon Dan could see that they were drawing crowds comparable to Saturday nights in smaller towns. The shows, the rides ran full tilt. The sun blazed down, the smell of sweat and tobacco and popcorn rose like a tangible haze toward the sky. Hogs trumpeted in the stock barns. Women gabbled about their quilts and preserves. Cows made long mournful foghorn sounds. The barkers screamed. Manny was hoarse by two in the afternoon, but the crowds kept coming. Dan lounged in the shade of the root beer stand, a cold mug in his hand, realizing that it would be a capacity week. Which meant more opportunities for things to go wrong. Nerves grew frazzled. Arguments sprouted into full-scale brawls. This would be a week to remember.

He saw Angie on the platform at Hawaiian Nights. She didn't notice him. They were through, Dan knew. He had hardly any occasion to see her now. Like being in another world. He turned away, determined to put his mind on other things. He saw Chick Morrison approaching. Chick threw a flip, "Hi, boss," at Dan and hurried on by. Dan turned to see him standing in the crowd, watching Angie avidly. She had her eyes on him, a grin a mile wide on her lips. He had already moved in, and he was guarding the new treasure.

Dan caught Dorman between shows and dressed him down for fooling with the cats. The stocky foreigner was half-drunk, and Zelda, his fortune-telling wife, chipped away at them both in her purple native dialect. Dorman cursed, too, yelling at her one minute, pleading with Dan in his thickly accented syllables the next. Dorman loudly promised to reform. But Dan determined to keep an eye on him.

Rajah, the Bengal, prowled the small cage restlessly. The two mangy lions slept, but Rajah prowled. The cat had the death-look in his great yellow eyes. His flanks were lean, and he needed a good meal. Dan stopped by the cook wagon and put in an order for Freddie to get some extra rations over to Dorman's tent right away.

Despite Crazy Chad Chapman and his stunt drivers, who were crashing their Fords head on and ramming them through flaming walls in front of the grandstand, the midway was packed to overflowing that night. Before nine o'clock rolled around, Dan had picked up three pickpockets, one shifty-eyed old man selling lewd pictures, and a woman who insisted on taking off her clothes in public, laughing like a drunken hyena all the while. Dan had promptly booted them off the lot. Minor troubles at best. He hoped fervently that nothing worse would develop during the week. Things like this he could handle.

Ten o'clock came and went. Dan loitered in the trailer, drinking coffee. At ten-thirty the Hawaiian Nights girls came out again. Dan knew the time by heart. Angrily, he swore at himself even as he left the trailer and headed down the midway. The crowd was bigger than usual. Sheepishly he slipped into the outer fringes. Here he was, skulking around like a sentimental kid, waiting for a look at her.

Manny went into his spiel, obviously worn out. The girls were listless in their dance, but that didn't seem to bother the customers. Chick was in the crowd, on the right down front. He gazed raptly up at Angie and she smiled wearily back at him. Dan wondered if the smile was sincere.

10.

The trouble started with a fat man in the front row of the crowd. His beefy face was flushed, his words clogged with the fumble-footed effects of too much liquor. He began talking loudly, pointing at Angie and making boisterous and ungentlemanly remarks. Dan flung a quick glance at Chick. Chick's face was rigid, angry. His blue eyes blazed. The fat man kept on talking. Manny leaned over and said, ''All right, friend, if you make a disturbance you'll have to . . ." With a roar of laughter, the drunk seized the ticket booth, pulled himself up on the platform with a loud *ooof*ing noise, and lunged for Angie, giggling. Harriet screamed shrilly. The crowd stirred like an awakened rattlesnake. The drunk lurched back and forth, crooking his finger and saying, "C'mere, sugar, c'mere," in a ridiculously small voice.

Before Dan knew it, Chick had vaulted onto the platform. The whirring flash of a fist, and the drunk dropped over the side of the platform. Someone shouted angry words at Chick, and Chick leaped down off the platform, too, swinging. Dan shouldered his way through the crowd hastily. Damn him, he thought, damn that smart punk. He had his hooks in Angie and he thought he owned her now. That temper of his . . . But it didn't help matters to think of Chick. The brawl was on full force. Chick swung at the fat man's friends. Others charged into the fray, until the crowd became a heaving mass of angry men, slugging at each other, shouting and yelling at guys they had never seen before as if they were life-long enemies. The girls had fled the platform, all except Angie. She stood watching the spectacle, her eyes fastened on Chick.

Dan dodged a punch and jabbed a man in the stomach with his elbow. He kicked his way through the mob, aware that boys had left the concession stands and were already quieting the rowdies on the outer edges of the crowd. But up by the platform, Chick and his adversaries, unknown and unnamed, brutally continued to slug it out. Dan shoved the last man out of the way, placing himself in front of Chick's rocketing fist. He rolled his head with the punch, standing his ground. Chick lowered his fists, glaring. He was breathing heavily.

Almost at once, men stopped fighting. Conversation lowered to an angry rumble, then died altogether. Dan faced Chick Morrison, angry now. "Chick," he said, "I can't have you wrecking the show because of personal feelings. Manny could have handled that guy."

"Lay off me, Wilde," Chick shouted hoarsely.

"Dammit, you're not going to mouth off around here!"

"I said lay off!" Chick's voice rose to a harsh yell as he belted Dan in the stomach. Dan doubled over, side-stepping to miss the sizzling uppercut. He straightened up, regaining his breath. Talking wouldn't do any good now. He waded into Chick. Chick was strong, and fast. But the men didn't move around. They stood firmly, feet planted wide apart, facing each other, pounding blows home, ripping piledriver blows into the face and stomach. They hammered

at each other, shaking like great trees under the bite of the axe each time a blow landed, but neither one gave ground. Dan's face was laced with dull pain. But he kept slugging. He put all his strength into it. Chick faltered for an instant. Dan pressed his advantage, smashing home one thundering blow after another. Chick's nose dissolved into a red smear. Dan could see him gritting his teeth. Stubborn. He wouldn't give. Dan kept pounding. At last, Chick dropped to one knee, shaking his head dazedly. It was all over.

11.

Dan stepped back and wiped his raw knuckles on his trousers. Most of the crowd had been herded away by Manny and some of the concession boys. A few passing marks gawked. But Dan didn't pay any attention. He looked up at Angie. Her face showed a mixture of shock and contempt. Chick raised his eyes and looked at her, too, his cut lower lip stuck out petulantly. He seemed to be demanding something.

Nervously, Angie came down off the platform and helped Chick to his feet. He mumbled, "Thanks," rubbing blood out of his eyes. He looked at Dan and his face went hard.

"Morrison," Dan said, "you're through. You can stay till we finish our run here. By then I'll have someone to replace you."

Chick's chest was heaving. "You fire me," he gasped, "and you'll really have trouble, Wilde. I can be pushed around just so long. This isn't the last time we'll tangle." Dan could see that he meant every word of it, meant it from the deep pit of his wounded pride.

Angie stepped in front of Dan, the hurt look still in her eyes. "Why, Dan? You didn't have to beat him like that."

Dan pushed his hair back off of his forehead. "We can't have disturbances like that on the midway." He tried to sound calm.

"You made a worse disturbance," she said hotly. "And you did it because of me, no matter what you say." She bit her lip. Discouraged, Dan realized that she was right. She was hurt, and angry at him. Angrier than he had ever seen her.

"Well, honey," Chick said to her. "You heard the big boss. I'm through. How about you?"

"I . . ." She glanced at Dan, and quickly away. "I'm coming with you, Chick. Saturday will be my last day with the show. Come on. You've got to get cleaned up.'' She took Chick's arm and led him away. But not before he faced Dan once more, fiery mad.

"Today's Monday, Wilde. I'm here till Saturday. So watch yourself.''

They disappeared around the tent. Dan hunted for a cigarette and got it going after a minute. Not until then did he feel that he was calm enough to walk away. Damned little broad, he thought. Still fighting me. Great times she'll have with Chick. On the rebound all the way. *But are you any better?* No, he had to admit, he wasn't. The fight with Chick had been more out of personal jealousy than anything else. He bumped into Lester de Packh before he recognized him.

De Packh munched on popcorn from the bag in his hand. His greasy smile looked pasted on his unpleasant face. "Get the hell out of my way,'' Dan said. De Packh didn't move.

"I'm just wandering around having some fun,'' de Packh said jovially. "That was some brawl. You having trouble around here, Wilde?''

Unthinking, Dan brought his fist up. De Packh dropped the popcorn bag quickly. One hand slapped down hard on Dan's fist, the other dropped into his jacket pocket. De Packh's eyes glittered in the glare of the colored lights. "Easy, tough guy,'' he hissed. "This isn't a stick of chewing gum in my pocket.''

Dan shoved him roughly out of the way and walked on. De Packh's laugh floated in the air behind him, sharp and contemptuous. Dan looked around once, but the man was gone.

He sat for a long time in the trailer, brooding over the untasted cup of coffee. The calliope music dinned in his ears. Finally Manny arrived, whistling. He stopped after a moment, aware that he wasn't getting through to Dan. He pulled down the shades of the trailer windows and poured himself a cup of coffee. "Dan, I've got something to say.''

"What is it?''

"The kids are talking. They're saying big tough Dan Wilde is going to pieces. Letting a broad twist him around her finger. Letting his feelings run him. Things'll loosen up around here if you let that happen, Dan. They'll be a lot tougher than they already are.'' Dan stared at him, hollow-eyed, a crust of blood still smearing his cheek, his left eye turning mottled brown. He didn't say a thing. "End of sermon,'' Manny breathed. "Want me to help you go over the receipts?''

Dan nodded slowly. "Sure, I'd appreciate it."

Later, he lay in bed staring at the dark ceiling. Dan Wilde, the smooth-running machine, was breaking apart. That's what they were saying. And why not? Trouble piling on trouble, creating a maze he couldn't get out of. Angie leaving on Saturday with Chick, hurt and angry. Chick hotheaded and potentially dangerous. That wart-faced de Packh hanging around. And the finely precise machinery that kept Clay Bros. in the black—disintegrating piece by piece under him, while he stood by like a fool and watched it wreck itself. He'd have to take hold. Really take hold. No more kidding around, Wilde. Clamp down on the exhaust valves. Even if you blow up in six months, you've got to last the season. You've got to do that, or you'll be back riding the rods. Clamp down, Wilde. *Clamp down.* In his dreams, he was caught in a giant vise, with Angie and Chick twisting the lever tighter, tighter. He was being clamped, smaller and smaller, tighter and tighter. At the end of the dream, he exploded, just like a balloon.

12.

Tuesday came, Wednesday, Thursday, and the crowds grew larger. By Friday night, you could hardly move on the packed midway. The shows turned people away, the vendors ran out of food, and the men and women with bills in their fists stood three-deep at the wheels and the games, waiting their turn. The week had passed with agonizing slowness for Dan. There had been no big troubles, just the usual stuff. Drunks, and an attempted stick-up on Wednesday afternoon. Petty-thief business. It seemed as if the week had mounted in a rising crescendo of nerves, of being stretched taut like a rubber band, farther and farther, all the time knowing that sometime, something had to break.

Dan saw Chick Morrison occasionally. Chick kept to his job, playing the shill for his own stands. On two occasions, he looked thoroughly drunk, and thoroughly angry when he saw Dan. Lester de Packh had disappeared, but Dan couldn't escape the uneasy feeling that the warty man was somewhere around. Dan went about his job keeping himself clamped together tightly, not giving in an inch to the emotions that battered at him.

Friday, hot and humid. Stale air like an oven. By midafternoon the sky was a mass of angry gray cloud fronts. But still the crowds came. Night darkened the world and the lights went on. In the grandstand, a vaudeville show featuring a singer from Hollywood was scheduled, but still the midway was jammed beyond capacity. Biggest crowd they'd ever pulled in, Dan thought. The air remained hot, heavy, like a paper bag threatening to burst. But the water inside the bag didn't show up. There was only an ominous rumbling in the distance, and pale flashes of lightning over the rooftops of Crystal City. The crowd yammered away, pushing, laughing, shouting, howling, plunging up and down the sawdust avenue in search of pleasure. Dan had trouble making his way through the clogging press of humanity.

He frowned as he walked. The air smelled of trouble. Trouble that ran like an electric current along the midway. One spark of trouble and that mob of people would erupt into a frantic stampede of fear. It made clammy sweat break out on Dan's skin, just to think about it.

He moved past the Hawaiian Nights pitch, noticing with startled surprise that Angie was missing from her center spot. Another girl filled in between Harriet and Bubbles. Dan caught Manny's eye. Manny jerked his head in the direction of the rear of the tent. His eyes bored into Dan's for an instant. He meant business.

Dan pushed through the crowd and moved down the shadowy aisle between the walls of canvas. In the girlie tent, he heard a feminine voice exclaim, "Aw, knock it off, sweetie," followed by a chorus of piping giggles. Dan rounded the corner of the tent. A cigarette glowed orange for a moment. Angie rose to meet him. He could see lines of tension around her mouth.

"Dan . . ." She put her hand out instinctively, then drew it back.

"Manny sent me back here. I didn't know he was sending me to see you."

She nodded her blond head quickly. He noticed that she hadn't even changed into her costume. "I couldn't do this show, Dan," she explained. "I had to talk to you. I told Manny to keep an eye on the midway, in case you . . ."

He cut her off sharply. "All right. I haven't got a lot of time to waste. If it's anything personal, I'd rather not talk about it. We settled things between us last week."

In the cigarette glow, he saw the hurt look flare in her eyes. "Oh, Dan . . ." She shook her head, as if confused. "It's Chick . . . I . . ."

Dan started to turn away. "If you've gotten me back here to give me a sob story about your troubles, forget it, Angie. I'm busy."

She seized his arm, desperately. "Dan, I can't kid myself. I don't love Chick. I couldn't. He's too . . . I don't know . . . too conceited, maybe. But that isn't it!" He stared at her accusingly. "Dan, believe me, it *isn't*. There's going to be trouble. Chick's been drunk almost all week, and he's told me he was going to get you for beating him like you did. Tonight . . ."

Dan could see that she wasn't faking. Not at all. "What about tonight?"

"Well, after the eight-thirty show, he came around and we sat out here, having a cigarette. He had a bottle with him. He was swearing a lot, and . . . and this man came from somewhere and Chick laughed when he saw him. Dan, it was terrible, that laugh. Cruel. He knew the man. He said he had business with him. He and the man walked off a few feet and stood talking. I heard the man say everything was all set. And he had a gun. He gave it to Chick."

Dan frowned. The pattern clicked into place in his mind. He shot a quick description of Lester de Packh at Angie. She nodded. "Yes, that's the one. I'm sure of it."

Dan gripped her arms tightly. "Angie . . . Angie, I appreciate your telling me this. I'm sorry if I was rough with you. You know how I feel about you."

She smiled. But he saw a faint tear gleam in the corner of her eye. She shook her head doggedly, sniffing. "I tried to forget about it, Dan. I . . . I couldn't." Dan patted her shoulder and started to say something else. Then he heard the commotion out on the midway. Voices pitched high, frenzied. A woman's siren scream. Someone came running around the tent. Dan whirled. "Manny . . ."

"Holy Christ!" Manny shouted. "This is it, Dan. *Rajah's loose* . . ."

13.

The woman's scream sounded again, hellishly shrill. Dan's stomach turned to ice. Manny kept on babbling until Dan slapped him across the cheek.

"Listen to me! Have you got your thirty-eight?"

"In the tent," Manny wheezed.

"Get it," Dan ordered. Manny disappeared. He returned an instant later, pressing the gun into Dan's hand. Without another word, Dan bolted down the line of tents. He could hear the panic out on the midway. Wild confused voices. Didn't know what was the matter, rumors, rumors. Rumors could start a stampede. He came to Dorman's tent. A huge gap had been torn out of the canvas. On the sawdust, Dan saw prints of animal pads. Impressed in reddish-brown blood. Dan rushed into the tent, jamming the gun into his pants pocket.

Joe Knox, one of the roustabouts, stood at the front of the tent. The flap had been closed. Knox shouted, "Christ, Dan, am I glad to see *you*." Dan looked down. He choked. He recognized Dorman's uniform, but the man's head was a featureless mass of blood and gray gore. Zelda stood over him, head buried in her hands, sobbing brokenly.

Dan grabbed her hands and pulled them down. "What happened, Zel?" he said. She gazed at him dumbly and went on crying. He seized her shoulders and shook her violently, until the sobs subsided. "What happened?" he repeated.

"The bastard," she whimpered. "Said he'd kill me. We . . . we had another argument. He hit me. Threatened me. I didn't know what I was doing. I opened the cage and let Rajah out. Right before the nine-thirty show. He tried to fight the tiger with his blank cartridge pistol. Oh, God . . ." Fresh sobs broke forth.

Dan motioned to Knox. "Get a dozen men and try to round the cat up. I've got two rifles in the trailer. Take them and kill the cat if you have to. Find Manny Fedderson and get some of the other boys circulating along the midway, stopping the rumors. Tell them somebody had an appendicitis attack, any damn thing." He whirled on Zelda. "Nobody saw the cat get loose, did they?"

She shook her head blindly. "They . . . they must have heard Boris scream."

Joe Knox disappeared at the back of the tent. Dan made sure that the cage door was locked. The two lions were inside, prowling restlessly. They smelled blood. Well, they'd smell a lot more blood if things got much worse. Dan raged out of the tent, jamming himself into the crowd on the midway. "Nothing's wrong," he yelled at the milling crowd, "somebody just got sick, that's all." People turned to stare at him. Somebody shouted, "You're a damned liar, I heard real screams!" "Somebody got sick," Dan shouted, hurrying on.

There was new commotion up by Hawaiian Nights. Manny was out on the midway, with a dozen of the men around him. He was gesturing wildly when Dan came up. Dan grabbed Manny's shoulder. "What's wrong now? Did they corner the cat?"

Manny shook his head frantically. He pointed to the opposite end of the midway. His mouth moved spasmodically for a second before words came out. "He's . . . he's up there . . . with . . . with a whole army of goons . . . they're wrecking the midway . . . clubs . . . axes . . ."

"Who?" Dan shouted above the din. "Who's up there?"

"De Packh," came the frightened reply.

"Come on!" Dan gathered the carney hands around him and they went plunging down the midway, an angry wedge of men. Most of them had clubs of some sort. Manny had found a butcher knife. The crowd drew back fearfully as the phalanx shoved its way along. Dan could see the pandemonium up ahead. His ears caught the *chunk* of axes in wood, the sound of ripping canvas. His hands tightened into angry balled fists. Savagely now, he pushed people out of his way.

The crowd had cleared away somewhat down here. The hoods, tough-looking bruisers in levis and work shirts, swung their axes and clubs on Hell's Motordrome. The tents and stands below the motorcycle show were a shambles. Dan's men waded in, swinging. One of the thugs caught a club behind the ear and went down. Dan shoved through the angry mob, hunting for two men. A hairy arm seized his neck and jerked him back. Dan sent a series of triphammer blows at the man's belly, doubling him over, then rabbit-punched him to the ground. Dan saw one of the men he wanted. Chick Morrison, swinging an axe into the plank sides of the Motordrome, a flushed drunken look on his face.

Dan swung Chick around. Chick's face knotted up savagely as he swung the axe. Dan ducked and felt the blade swish past his head, and heard the ugly sound as it thudded into the wooden wall. Chick had his arm back, ready to throw a punch, when a voice said sharply, "Hold it." A gun barrel jammed into Dan's spine.

14.

Dan stood quietly. "All right," the voice of Lester de Packh said, "let's go. Around the back." Dan started walking. Chick grinned recklessly and walked a few steps behind. They rounded the tent into relative darkness. Lightning flickered on the horizon and a muffled rumble filled the night. Searchlights blazed in the grandstand and Dan heard a ripple of applause as the band finished a number. That all seemed very far away. "Turn around," de Packh said.

Dan turned. Chick stood beside the warty crook, hands on his hips. "Well, Wilde," he said thickly, "I guess you got yourself into something you couldn't handle. All you'll have left when de Packh's boys get through is a mess of wood and canvas that even a junkdealer won't buy."

"So you were in on this," Dan said grimly.

"Yeah, I was in on this! De Packh here thought I might like to join up with him. He was only going to wreck one or two shows. I persuaded him to knock the hell out of the whole midway." Chick laughed. "And right now, I'm going to have the pleasure of knocking the hell out of *you*." Chick's eyes blazed half with anger, half with drunken humor as he stepped forward.

De Packh waved his pistol. "You shut up. We're going to handle Wilde my way."

"What do you mean?" Chick asked.

"I mean I don't like guys like this. I told you I'd fix you, Wilde. If something happens to you, Old Man Underwood and all the other carnies will sign with Mumford. And that'll make me happy. I'm going to be a lot happier killing you, though."

"Killing . . ." Chick exploded.

"Yeah, killing," de Packh snarled. "We aren't in kindergarten, buster. Mr. Wilde here is going to get a nice neat bullet through his skull. And then we'll take a club and beat his brains out so they'll never know he got shot. Just a casualty of the brawl." He laughed, a sound like wind rattling dry leaves.

"I didn't deal myself in for any shooting," Chick said uncertainly.

"Well, you're in now. Stand back."

Chick wavered uncertainly. Dan watched him, aware that he was debating with himself. The drunken stupor had vanished. He was stone sober, and he knew that this was murder. Suddenly, Dan started. He heard a savage purring sound, somewhere in the darkness, and the pit of his stomach went cold. The other two men didn't notice.

Chick finally shook his head. "No. I'm not going to kill him."

"Get out of my way, you dumb . . ." De Packh threw Chick's restraining arm off. Chick's hand dove into his pants pocket and came up with the gun Angie had spoken of. De Packh pushed him, firing at the same time. A lance of red fire cut the darkness and Chick shouted hoarsely, clutching the left side of his body just above the belt. He reeled a few steps backward and collapsed weakly on the ground.

Dan had already moved forward. Before de Packh could swing his gun around, Dan twisted it out of his hands and tossed it away. De Packh raised his fists to fend off the blow. Dan belted him in the stomach and then on the jaw. Lester de Packh sagged, his eyes going closed. Dan rubbed his knuckles, starting forward toward Chick. Suddenly, he froze.

Baleful yellow eyes gleamed out of the darkness, two feet behind where Chick lay. A rough hissing sound. "What's wrong?" Chick groaned. He heard the growl. "My God! That sounds like . . ."

Dan nodded. "Keep quiet," he whispered. The cat was crouching into a spring. It would be on Chick in one leap. Dan calculated swiftly. If he moved suddenly, Rajah would come for him instead. He felt the thirty-eight Manny had given him weighing heavily in his pocket. He moved his hand slowly and pulled it out, watching the cat. The hissing rose to a hoarse wild growl. Dan bolted abruptly and ran to the left.

Rajah hesitated, and then sprang for Dan. Dan brought the thirty-eight up, just as he frantically remembered to check the safety. The cat's body was a black shape arching across the sky, coming for him. Dan's fingers fumbled wildly, cursing Manny for not checking the safety. He got it off and tried to turn. The huge, reeking animal body struck him and bore him to the ground. Blades of fire cut down into his arm, grinding on the bone. The yellow eyes shone like giant moons in front of his face, the fangs dripped, the breath roared like a blast out of a stinking oven.

With a savage twist of his head, Rajah pulled free of Dan's arm, his jaws gaping. Desperately Dan raised the gun and pulled the trigger. He kept on firing, hearing the cat's scream as the bullets blasted up through the roof of the cat's mouth into its brain. Dan rolled over wildly, escaping the last frantic clamp of the jaws as Rajah rolled in his death agonies. Cat screams cut the night air, and Dan heard a siren somewhere. He staggered to his feet, and only then did he feel the intense pain. He looked down at the ripped skin and flesh of his bloody arm. He shook his head, dazed. Chick said something he could not hear. Rajah whimpered, his body still quivering. Dan felt his legs sagging out from under him, and he tried to hold himself up, but it was impossible. He slammed into the dirt and lay still, his mind floating down into a deep dark well that swallowed him completely after a moment.

15.

He awoke in his bunk in the trailer. Morning sunlight poured in through the windows. He groaned and rolled over. Manny and Angie were bending over him anxiously. His arm was in a sling. He groaned again. "I fell like I went through a meat grinder."

Manny laughed weakly. "You practically did, boy. One more minute and Rajah would have made hamburger out of you."

Questions flooded into Dan's mind. He poured out a babble of words until Angie said, "Hold on, Dan. One at a time and we'll answer them."

"How badly did they wreck us?"

Manny said, "I'll take that question, Doctor. Nothing much beyond the Motordrome. The boys stopped them. The Sheriff arrived with a party of local lawmen and finished off the rowdies. Chick charged that de Packh with attempted murder before they took him to the hospital. The Mumford outfit is through. With Chick's evidence, they've got enough on them to close down the business for good."

"How is Chick?"

Angie spoke up. "The bullet went in and came right out again. He'll be up in a week or so."

"Good," Dan said. He listened a minute. "Hey, that sounds like the calliope. Are we still in business?"

"Why not?" Manny grinned broadly. "You're not the only guy that can run a midway. They dragged Zelda Dorman off to the local jail, so that cuts out the cat show, but we've still got enough to kill 'em with. Today's Saturday, boy. Carneys can't pass up a day like Saturday."

Dan grinned tiredly. "No, I guess they can't." He yawned.

Angie leaned over and patted his hand. "You'd better sleep some more." He started to protest. She bent down further and pressed her lips on his, warmly. "No more talk," she whispered. "Sleep."

"Aye aye sir," he said hazily, already drowsy.

He got up Sunday morning, ate a giant breakfast in town with Angie, and the two of them went over to the Crystal City Hospital to see Chick. He was sitting up when they came in, and he grinned. But sheepishly.

"How you feeling?" Dan asked.

"Swell," Chick replied. "The nurses here are classy."

Dan grinned. "You'd better hurry up and get well. The concessions will go to pieces without you."

Chick stared at him, puzzled. "You . . . mean . . . I'm still working for you?"

"If you want to."

"Hell," Chick said, "wild horses won't stop me. Dan . . ." His eyes grew serious. "After what I did . . . de Packh and all . . . you could have left me there for Rajah. No one would have blamed you."

Dan shook his head. "No, Chick. We lost our heads over a broad. This one right here. Men don't think straight when that happens. We'll forget about it."

"I sure was off my head," Chick said. His smile was forced. "Angie, you'll just have to persuade this lug that you and I just weren't made for each other. I'll have to wait until some doll comes along who can stand my being jealous of her. Now maybe one of the nurses around here . . ."

"You'll find her, Chick," Angie said softly.

"Well, in the meantime . . ." He looked at Dan. "Thanks," he said.

The afternoon was cool, a relief after the heat of the preceeding week. Angie put her arm through Dan's as they left the hospital. When they reached the edge of the fairgrounds, he stopped, stood looking out over the deserted midway, bare of tents, strewn with pop bottles and paper sacks and cigarette butts. Angie tugged his sleeve. "Hey. You're not saying much."

"Thinking," he said. "No matter how well I tell it, Old Man Underwood isn't going to hand me that desk job for a couple of years. So there's only one thing for me to do." He looked down at her.

"What's that?"

"Marry you. That is, if you think you can wait for the house and the new car that'll go along with the desk."

She squeezed his arm. "You're crazy, Dan Wilde. But I love you for it. You can run yourself, and the carnival, like a machine. But when you're with me, strictly personal. And I'll even resign my title as a Hawaiian princess."

They walked on across the fairgrounds, watching the wind lift sawdust, seeing the trucks loading. Dan felt good. In an hour, two, they would be rolling again. The highway waited for them, the towns waited for the laughter and the lights of their wonderland. And beyond, the future waited.

A very fine future indeed, Dan thought.

Time and Time Again

•

Harry Kemelman

The debut appearance of Harry Kemelman's Rabbi David Small,
Friday the Rabbi Slept Late, *won an MWA Edgar as Best First Novel
of 1964. Several subsequent entries in the series have been best-
sellers. Rabbi Small was not the first series detective created by
Kemelman, however; that honor belongs to professor of English
language and literature Nicky Welt, whose cerebral approach to
crime-solving is the focus of several short stories published in* Ellery
Queen's Mystery Magazine *and collected in* The Nine Mile Walk
*(1967). "Time and Time Again" is among the most entertaining of
Nicky Welt's investigations.*

Although it was more than two years since I had left the Law
Faculty to become County Attorney, I still maintained some connection with the university. I still had the privileges of the gymna-
sium and the library and I still kept up my membership in the
Faculty Club. I dropped in there occasionally for a game of billiards, and about once a month I dined there, usually with Nicholas
Welt.

We had finished dinner, Nicky and I, and had repaired to the
Commons Room for a game of chess, only to find that all the tables
were in use. So we joined the group in front of the fire where there
was always interminable talk about such highly scholarly matters
as to whether there was any likelihood of favorable action by the
trustees on an increase in salary schedules—there wasn't—or
whether you got more miles per gallon with a Chevrolet than you
got with a Ford.

This evening as we joined the group, the talk was about Professor
Rollins' paper in the *Quarterly Journal of Psychic Research*, which
no one had read but on which everyone had an opinion. The title
of the paper was something like "Modifications in the Sprague

Method of Analysis of Extra-Sensory Experimentation Data,'' but the academic mind with its faculty for generalization had quickly gone beyond the paper and Rollins' theories to a discussion on whether there was anything in ''this business of the supernatural,'' with burly professor Lionel Graham, Associate in Physics, asserting that ''of course, there couldn't be when you considered the type of people who went in for it, gypsies and whatnot.'' And gentle, absentminded Roscoe Summers, Professor of Archaeology, maintaining doggedly that you couldn't always tell by that and that he had heard stories from people whose judgment he respected that made you pause and think a bit.

To which Professor Graham retorted, ''That's just the trouble. It's always something that happened to somebody else. Or better still, something that somebody told you that happened to somebody *he* knew.'' Then catching sight of us, he said, ''Isn't that right, Nicky? Did you ever hear about anything supernatural as having happened to somebody you yourself knew well and whose word and opinion you could rely on?''

Nicky's lined, gnomelike face relaxed in a frosty little smile. ''I'm afraid that's how I get most of my information,'' he said. ''I mean through hearing about it at third or fourth hand.''

Dr. Chisholm, the young instructor in English Composition, had been trying to get a word in and now he succeeded. ''I had a case last summer. I mean I was there and witnessed something that was either supernatural or was a most remarkable coincidence.''

''Something on the stage, or was it a seance in a dark room?'' asked Graham with a sneer.

''Neither,'' said Chisholm defiantly. ''I saw a man cursed and he died of it.'' He caught sight of a pompous little man with a shining bald head and he called out, ''Professor Rollins, won't you join us? I'm sure you'd be interested in a little incident I was about to tell.''

Professor Rollins, the author of the paper in the *Quarterly*, approached and the men sitting on the red leather divan moved over respectfully to make room for him. But he seemed to sense that he was being asked to listen as an expert and he selected a straight-backed chair as being more in keeping with the judicial role he was to play.

I spent my summer vacation (Chisholm began) in a little village on the Maine coast. It was not a regular summer resort and there was little to do all day long except sit on the rocks and watch the gulls as they swooped above the water. But I had worked hard all year and it was precisely what I wanted.

The center of the town was inland, clustered about the little railroad depot, and I was fortunate in getting a room way out at the end of town near the water. My host was a man named Doble, a widower in his forties, a decent quiet man who was good company when I wanted company and who did not obtrude when I just wanted to sit and daydream. He did a little farming and had some chickens; he had a boat and some lobster pots; and for the rest, he'd make a little money at various odd jobs. He didn't work by the day but would contract for the whole job, which put him a cut above the ordinary odd jobman, I suppose.

Ours was the last house on the road and our nearest neighbor was about a hundred yards away. It was a large nineteenth-century mansion, set back from the road, and decorated with the traditional fretsaw trim and numerous turrets and gables. It was owned and occupied by Cyrus Cartwright, the president of the local bank and the richest man in town.

He was a brisk, eager sort of man, like the advertisement for a correspondence course in salesmanship, the type of man who carries two watches and is always glancing at his wristwatch and then checking it against his pocket watch.

(Chisholm warmed as he described Cyrus Cartwright, the result of the natural antipathy of a man who spends his summer watching sea gulls for the type of man who weighs out his life in small minutes. Now he smiled disarmingly and shrugged his shoulders.)

I saw him only once. I had come in town with Doble and before going home, he stopped in at the bank to see if Cartwright was still interested in making some change in the electric wiring system in his house, which they had talked about some months ago. It was typical of Doble that he should only now be coming around to make further inquiry about it.

Cartwright glanced at the radium dial of his wristwatch and then tugged at his watch chain and drew out his pocket watch, squeezing it out of its protective chamois covering. He mistook my interest in the ritual for interest in the watch itself and held it out so that I could see it, explaining with some condescension that it was a repeater, a five-minute repeater he was at some pains to point out, and then proceeded to demonstrate it by pressing a catch so that I could hear it tinkle the hour and then in a different key tinkle once for every five-minute interval after the hour.

I made some comparison between the man who carries two watches and the man who wears both a belt and suspenders. But though he realized I was joking, he said with some severity, "Time is money, sir, and I like to know just where I am with both. So I keep accurate books and accurate watches."

Having put me in my place, he turned to Doble and said crisply, "I don't think I'll bother with it, Doble. It was Jack's idea having the extra light and switch in the hallway and now that he's gone into the service, I don't think I'll need it. When it gets dark, I go to bed."

Once again he glanced at his wristwatch, checked its accuracy against his pocket watch as before, and then he smiled at us, a short, meaningless, businessman's smile of dismissal.

As I say, I saw him only that once, but I heard a great deal about him. You know how it is, you hear a man's name mentioned for the first time and then it seems to pop up again and again in the next few days.

According to Doble, Cartwright was a tight-fisted old skinflint who had remained a bachelor, probably to save the expense of supporting a wife.

When I pointed out that paying a housekeeper to come in every day was almost as expensive as keeping a wife, and that in addition he had brought up his nephew Jack, Doble retorted that nobody but Mrs. Knox would take the job of Cartwright's housekeeper and that she took it only because no one else would take her. She was almost stone deaf and general opinion was that her wages were small indeed.

"As for Jack," he went on, "the old man never let him see a penny more than he actually needed. He never had a dime in his pocket, and when he'd go into town of an evening, he'd just have to hang around—usually didn't even have the price of a movie. Nice young fellow, too," he added reflectively.

"He could have got a job and left," I suggested.

"I suppose he could've," Doble said slowly, "but he's the old man's heir, you see, and I guess he figured it was kind of politic, as you might say, to hang around doing any little jobs at the bank that the old man might ask of him."

I was not too favorably impressed with the young man's character from Doble's description, but I changed my mind when he came down a few days later on furlough.

He turned out to be a decent chap, quiet and reserved, but with a quick and imaginative mind. We grew quite close in those few days and saw a great deal of each other. We went fishing off the rocks, or lazed around in the sun a good deal talking of all sorts of things, or shot at chips in the water with an old rifle that he had.

He kept his gun and fishing rod over at our house. And that gives some indication of the character of Cyrus Cartwright and of Jack's relations with him. He explained that his uncle knew that he wasn't doing anything during this week of furlough and didn't really expect him to, but if he saw him with the fishing rod, that traditional symbol of idleness, it would seem as though he were flaunting his indolence in his face. As for the gun, Cyrus Cartwright considered shooting at any target that could not subsequently be eaten as an extravagant waste of money for shells.

Jack came over every evening to play cribbage or perhaps to sit on the porch and sip at a glass of beer and argue about some book he had read at my suggestion. Sometimes he spoke about his uncle and in discussing him, he was not bitter—ironic, rather.

On one occasion he explained, "My uncle is a good man according to his lights. He likes money because it gives him a sense of accomplishment to have more than anyone else in town. But that alone doesn't make him a hard person to live with. What does make him difficult is that everything is set in a rigid routine, a senseless routine, and his household has to conform to it. After dinner, he sits and reads his paper until it gets dark. Then he looks at his wristwatch and shakes his head a little as though he didn't believe it was that late. Then he takes his pocket watch out and checks the wristwatch against it. But, of course, even that doesn't satisfy him. So he goes into the dining room where he has an electric clock and he sets both watches by that.

"When he's got all timepieces perfectly synchronized, he says, 'Well, it's getting late,' and he goes upstairs to his room. In about fifteen minutes he calls to me and I go up to find him already in bed.

" 'I forgot to fix the windows,' he says. So I open them an inch at the top and an inch at the bottom. It takes a bit of doing because if I should open them a quarter of an inch too wide, he says he'll catch his death of cold, and if it is short of an inch, he's sure he'll smother. But finally I get them adjusted just right and he says, 'My watch, would you mind, Jack?' So I get his pocket watch that he had put on the bureau while undressing and I put it on the night table near his bed.

"As far back as I can remember, I've had to do that little chore. I am sure he insists on it so as to fix our relations in my mind. While I was away, he must have remembered to do it for himself, but the first day I got back I had to do it."

(Chisholm looked from one to the other of us as if to make sure that we all understood the characters and their relations with each other. I nodded encouragingly and he continued.)

Jack was scheduled to leave Sunday morning and naturally we expected to see him Saturday, but he did not show up during the day. He came over in the evening after dinner, however, and he was hot and angry.

"The hottest day of the summer," he exclaimed, "and today of all days my uncle suddenly finds a bunch of errands for me to do. I've been all over the county and I couldn't even take the car. I'll bet you fellows were lying out on the beach all day. How about going in for a dip right now?"

Well, of course, we had been in and out of the water all day long, but it was still hot and muggy, and besides we could see that he wanted very much to go, so we agreed. We took some beer down and we didn't bother with bathing suits since it was already quite dark. After a while, however, it began to get chilly. It had clouded up and the air was oppressive as though a storm were impending. So we got dressed again and went back to our house.

The atmosphere had a charged, electric quality about it, and whether it was that or because he was leaving the following day, Jack was unusually quiet and conversation lagged. Around half past eleven, he rose and stretched and said he thought he ought to be going.

"It's been good meeting you," he said. "I don't look forward to this furlough particularly, but now I'm sure I'm going to look back on it."

We shook hands and he started for the door. Then he remembered about his fishing rod and his rifle and came back for them. He seemed reluctant to leave us, and Doble, understanding, said, "We might as well walk down with you, Jack."

He nodded gratefully and all three of us strolled out into the darkness. We walked along slowly, Jack with his fishing rod over one shoulder and his gun over the other.

I offered to carry the gun, but he shook his head and handed me the rod instead. I took it and walked on in silence until we reached the gate of his uncle's house. Perhaps he misinterpreted my silence and felt that he had been ungracious, for he said, "I'm a lot more used to carrying a rifle than you are." And then lest I take his remark as a reflection on my not being in the service, he hurried on with, "I'm kind of fond of this gun. I've had it a long time and had a lot of fun with it."

He patted the stock affectionately like a boy with a dog and then he nestled the butt against his shoulder and sighted along the barrel.

"Better not, Jack," said Doble with a grin. "You'll wake your uncle."

"Damn my uncle," he retorted lightly, and before we could stop him, he pulled the trigger.

In that silence, the crack of the rifle was like a thunderclap. I suppose we all expected one of the windows to fly up and the irate voice of old Cartwright to demand what was going on. In any case, instinctively, like three small boys, we all ducked down behind the fence where we could not be seen. We waited several minutes, afraid to talk lest we be overheard. But when nothing happened, we straightened up slowly and Doble said, "You better get to bed, Jack. I think maybe you've had a little too much beer."

"Maybe I ought at that," Jack answered and eased the gate open.

Then he turned and whispered, "Say, do you fellows mind waiting a minute? I think I may have locked the door and I haven't a key."

We nodded and watched as he hurried down the path to the house. Just before he reached the door, however, he hesitated, stopped, and then turned and came hurrying back to us.

"Could you put me up for the night, Doble?" he asked in a whisper.

"Why sure, Jack. Was the door locked?"

He didn't answer immediately and we started down the road to our house. We had gone about halfway when he said, "I didn't check to see if the door was locked or not."

"I noticed that," I remarked.

There was another silence and then as we mounted the porch steps, the moon, which had been hidden by clouds, suddenly broke through and I saw that he was deathly pale.

"What's the matter, Jack?" I asked quickly.

He shook his head and did not answer. I put my hand on his arm and asked again, "Are you all right?"

He nodded and tried to smile.

"I've—I've— Something funny happened to me," he said. "Did you mean what you said the other day about believing in spirits?"

At first I could not think what he was referring to, and then I remembered having argued—not too seriously—for belief in the supernatural during a discussion of William Blake's *Marriage of Heaven and Hell*, which I had lent him.

I shrugged my shoulders noncommittally, wondering what he was getting at.

He smiled wanly. "I didn't really have too much beer," he said and looked at me for confirmation.

"No, I don't think you did," I said quietly.

"Look," he went on, "I'm cold sober. And I was sober a few minutes ago when I started for my uncle's house. But as I came near the door, I felt something like a cushion of air building up against me to block my progress. And then, just before I reached the door, it became so strong that I could not go on. It was like a wall in front of me. But it was something more than an inanimate wall. It did not merely block me, but seemed to be pushing me back as though it had a will and intelligence like a strong man. It frightened me and I turned back. I'm still frightened."

"Your uncle—" I began.

"Damn my uncle!" he said vehemently. "I hope he falls and breaks his neck."

Just then Doble's kitchen clock chimed twelve. The brassy ring, coming just as he finished, seemed to stamp the curse with fateful approval.

It made us all a little uncomfortable. We didn't seem to feel like talking, and after a while we went to bed.

We were awakened the next morning early by someone pounding on the door. Doble slipped his trousers on and I managed to get into my bathrobe. We reached the front door about the same time. It was Mrs. Knox, Cartwright's housekeeper, and she was in a state of considerable excitement.

"Mister Cartwright's dead!" she shouted to us. "There's been an accident."

Since she was deaf, it was no use to question her. We motioned her to wait while we put on our shoes. Then we followed her back to the house. The front door was open as she had left it when she

156

had hurried over to us. And from the doorway we could see the figure of Cyrus Cartwright in an old-fashioned nightgown, lying at the foot of the stairs, his head in a sticky pool of blood.

He was dead all right, and looking up we could see the bit of rumpled carpeting at the head of the stairs which had probably tripped him up and catapulted him down the long staircase.

He had died as he had lived, for in his right hand he still clutched his precious pocket watch. The watch he was wearing on his wrist, however, had smashed when he fell and it gave us the time of his death. The hands pointed to just before twelve, the exact time as near as I could judge, that Jack had uttered his curse!

There was a minute of appreciative silence after Chisholm finished. I could see that no one's opinion had been changed materially by the story. Those who had been skeptical were scornful now and those who were inclined to believe were triumphant, but we all turned to Professor Rollins to see what he thought and he was nodding his head portentously.

Nicky, however, was the first to speak. "And the pocket watch," he said, "had that stopped, too?"

"No, that was ticking away merrily," Chisholm replied. "I guess his hand must have cushioned it when he fell. It had probably been badly jarred though, because it was running almost an hour ahead."

Nicky nodded grimly.

"What about Jack? How did he take it?" I asked.

Chisholm considered for a moment. "He was upset naturally, not so much over his uncle's death, I fancy, since he did not care for him very much, but because of the fact that it confirmed his fears of the night before that some supernatural influence was present." He smiled sadly. "I did not see him much after that. He had got his leave extended, but he was busy with his uncle's affairs. When finally he went back to the army, he promised to write, but he never did. Just last week, however, I got a letter from Doble. He writes me occasionally—just the usual gossip of the town. In his letter he mentions that Jack Cartwright crashed in his first solo flight."

"Ah." Professor Rollins showed interest. "I don't mind admitting that I rather expected something like that."

"You expected Jack to die?" Chisholm asked in amazement.

Rollins nodded vigorously. "This was truly a supernatural manifestation. I haven't the slightest doubt about it. For one thing, Jack felt the supernatural forces. And the curse, followed almost immediately by its fulfillment even to the manner of death, that is most significant. Now, of course, we know very little of these things, but we suspect that they follow a definite pattern. Certain types of supernatural forces have what might be called an ironic bent, a sort of perverted sense of humor. To be sure, when Jack uttered his fervent wish that his uncle fall and break his neck, he was speaking as a result of a momentary exasperation, but it is the nature of evil or mischievous forces to grant just such wishes. We meet with it again and again in folklore and fairy tales, which are probably the cryptic or symbolic expression of the wisdom of the folk. The pattern is familiar to you all, I am sure, from the stories of your childhood. The wicked character is granted three wishes by a fairy, only to waste them through wishes that are just such common expressions of exasperation as Jack used. You see, when supernatural forces are present, a mere wish, fervently expressed, may serve to focus them, as it were. And that is what happened at the Cartwright house that fateful evening.''

He held up a forefinger to ward off the questions that leaped to our minds.

"There is another element in the pattern," he went on soberly, "And that is that whenever a person does profit materially through the use of evil supernatural forces, even though unintentionally on his part, sooner or later, they turn on him and destroy him. I have no doubt that Jack's death was just as much the result of supernatural forces as was the death of his uncle.''

Professor Graham muttered something that sounded like "rubbish.''

Dana Rollins, who could have gone on indefinitely I suppose, stopped abruptly and glared.

But Professor Graham was not one to be silenced by a look. "The young man died as a result of a plane crash. Well, so did thousands of others. Had they all been granted three wishes by a wicked fairy? Poppycock! The young man died because he went up in a plane. That's reason enough. As for the old man, he tumbled down the stairs and cracked his skull or broke his neck, whichever it was. You say his nephew's curse must have been uttered about the same time. Well, even granting that by some miracle Doble's kitchen clock was synchronized to Cartwright's watches, that would still be nothing more than a coincidence. The chances are that the young man uttered that same wish hundreds of times. It was only natural: he was his heir and besides, he didn't like him. Now on one of those hundreds of times, it actually happened. There's nothing supernatural in that—not even anything out of the ordinary. It makes a good story, young man, but it doesn't prove anything.''

"And Jack's sensing of a supernatural force," asked Chisholm icily, "is that just another coincidence?"

Graham shrugged his massive shoulders. "That was probably just an excuse not to go home. He was probably afraid he'd get a dressing down from his uncle for shooting off his rifle in the middle of the night. What do you think, Nicky?"

Nicky's little blue eyes glittered. "I rather think," he said, "that the young man was not so much afraid of his uncle asking him about the rifle as he was that he would ask him what time it was."

We all laughed at Nicky's joke. But Professor Graham was not to be put off.

"Seriously, Nicky," he urged.

"Well, then, seriously," said Nicky with a smile as though he were indulging a bright but impetuous freshman, "I think you're quite right in calling the young man's death an accident. Parenthetically, I might point out that Dr. Chisholm did not suggest that it was anything else. As for the uncle's death, I cannot agree with you that it was merely coincidence."

Professor Rollins pursed his lips and appeared to be considering Nicky's cavalier dismissal of half his theory, but it was obvious that he was pleased at his support for the other half. I could not help reflecting how Nicky automatically assumed control over any group that he found himself in. He had a way of treating people, even his colleagues on the faculty, as though they were immature schoolboys. And curiously, people fell into this role that he assigned to them.

Professor Graham, however, was not yet satisfied. "But dammit all, Nicky," he insisted, "a man trips on a bit of carpet and falls downstairs. What is there unusual about that?"

"In the first place, I think it is unusual that he should go downstairs at all," said Nicky. "Why do you suppose he did?"

Professor Graham looked at him in aggrieved surprise like a student who has just been asked what he considers an unfair question.

"How should I know why he went downstairs?" he said. "I suppose he couldn't sleep and wanted a snack, or maybe a book to read."

"And took his pocket watch with him?"

"Well, according to Chisholm he was always checking his wristwatch against it."

Nicky shook his head. "When you're wearing two watches, it's almost impossible not to check the other after you've glanced at the one, just as we automatically glance at our watches when we pass the clock in the jeweler's window even though we might have set it by the radio only a minute or two before. But for Cyrus Cartwright to take his pocket watch downstairs with him when he had a watch on his wrist is something else again. I can think of only one reason for it."

"And what's that?" asked Chisholm curiously.

"To see what time it was on the electric clock."

I could understand something of Graham's exasperation as he exclaimed, "But dammit, Nicky, the man had two watches. Why would he want to go downstairs to see the time?"

"Because in this case, two watches were not as good as one," said Nicky quietly.

I tried to understand. Did he mean that the supernatural force that had manifested itself to Jack Cartwright that night and had prevented him from entering the house had somehow tampered with the watches?

"What was wrong with them?" I asked.

"They disagreed."

Then he leaned back in his chair and looked about him with an air of having explained everything. There was a short silence and as he scanned our faces, his expression of satisfaction changed to one of annoyance.

"Don't you see yet what happened?" he demanded. "When you wake up in the middle of the night, the first thing you do is look at the clock on the mantelpiece or your watch on the night table in order to orient yourself. That's precisely what Cyrus Cartwright did. He woke up and glancing at his wristwatch he saw that it was quarter to twelve, say. Then quite automatically he reached for his pocket watch on the night table. He pressed the catch and the chiming mechanism tinkled twelve and then went on to tinkle half or three quarters past. He had set the watches only a few hours before and both of them were going, and yet one was about an hour faster than the other. Which was right? What time was it? I fancy he tried the repeater again and again and then tried to dismiss the problem from his mind until morning. But after tossing about for a few minutes, he realized that if he hoped to get back to sleep that night, he would have to go downstairs to see what time it really was.'' Nicky turned to Chisholm. ''You see, the jar from the fall would not have moved the watch ahead. A blow will either stop the movement or it might speed up or slow down the escapement for a few seconds. But a watch with hands so loose that a jar will move them would be useless as a timepiece. Hence, the watch must have been moved ahead sometime before the fall. Cyrus Cartwright would not do it, which means that his nephew must have, probably while transferring the watch from the bureau to the night table.''

''You mean accidentally?'' asked Chisholm. ''Or to annoy his uncle?''

Nicky's little blue eyes glittered. ''Not to annoy him,'' he said, ''to murder him!''

He smiled pleasantly at our stupefaction. ''Oh yes, no doubt about it,'' he assured us. ''After arranging the windows to his uncle's satisfaction and placing the watch on the night table, Jack bade his uncle a courteous good night. And on his way out, he stopped just long enough to rumple or double over the bit of carpet at the head of the stairs. There was no light in the hallway remember.''

''But—but I don't understand. I don't see—I mean, how did he know that his uncle was going to wake up in the middle of the night?'' Chisholm finally managed.

''Firing off his rifle under his uncle's windows insured that, I fancy,'' Nicky replied. He smiled. ''And now you can understand, I trust, why he could not enter his uncle's house that night. He was afraid that his uncle, awake now, would hear him come in and instead of venturing downstairs, would simply call down to him to ask what time it was.''

This time we did not laugh.

The silence that followed was suddenly broken by the chiming of the chapel clock. Subconsciously, we glanced at our watches, and then realizing what we were doing, we all laughed.

''Quite,'' said Nicky.

Deceptions

•

Marcia Muller

Sharon McCone, Marcia Muller's compassionate San Francisco sleuth, is one of the most popular and acclaimed of the modern fictional private eyes. McCone has appeared in nine novels to date, among them Edwin of the Iron Shoes *(1977),* Leave a Message for Willie *(1984),* Eye of the Storm *(1988), and* There's Something in a Sunday *(1989). "Deceptions" is McCone—and Muller—at her best, in a harrowing and suspenseful tale set literally in the shadow of San Francisco's Golden Gate Bridge.*

San Francisco's Golden Gate Bridge is deceptively fragile-looking, especially when fog swirls across its high span. But from where I was standing, almost underneath it at the south end, even the mist couldn't disguise the massiveness of its concrete piers and the taut strength of its cables. I tipped my head back and looked up the tower to where it disappeared into the drifting grayness, thinking about the other ways the bridge is deceptive.

For one thing, its color isn't gold, but rust red, reminiscent of dried blood. And though the bridge is a marvel of engineering, it is also plagued by maintenance problems that keep the Bridge District in constant danger of financial collapse. For a reputedly romantic structure, it has seen more than its fair share of tragedy: Some 800-odd lost souls have jumped to their deaths from its deck.

Today I was there to try to find out if that figure should be raised by one. So far I'd met with little success.

I was standing next to my car in the parking lot of Fort Point, a historic fortification at the mouth of San Francisco Bay. Where the pavement stopped, the land fell away to jagged black rocks; waves smashed against them, sending up geysers of salty spray. Beyond the rocks the water was choppy, and Angel Island and Alcatraz were mere humpbacked shapes in the mist. I shivered, wishing I'd

162

worn something heavier than my poplin jacket, and started toward the fort.

This was the last stop on a journey that had taken me from the toll booths and Bridge District offices to Vista Point at the Marin County end of the span, and back to the National Parks Services headquarters down the road from the fort. None of the Parks Service or bridge personnel—including a group of maintenance workers near the north tower—had seen the slender dark-haired woman in the picture I'd shown them, walking south on the pedestrian sidewalk at about four yesterday afternoon. None of them had seen her jump.

It was for that reason—plus the facts that her parents had revealed about twenty-two-year-old Vanessa DiCesare— that made me tend to doubt she actually had committed suicide, in spite of the note she'd left taped to the dashboard of the Honda she'd abandoned at Vista Point. Surely at four o'clock on a Monday afternoon *someone* would have noticed her. Still, I had to follow up every possibility, and the people at the Parks Service station had suggested I check with the rangers at Fort Point.

I entered the dark-brick structure through a long, low tunnel— called a sally port, the sign said—which was flanked at either end by massive wooden doors with iron studding. Years before I'd visited the fort, and now I recalled that it was more or less typical of harbor fortifications built in the Civil War era: a ground floor topped by two tiers of working and living quarters, encircling a central courtyard.

I emerged into the court and looked up at the west side; the tiers were a series of brick archways, their openings as black as empty eyesockets, each roped off by a narrow strip of yellow plastic strung across it at waist level. There was construction gear in the courtyard; the entire west side was under renovation and probably off limits to the public.

As I stood there trying to remember the layout of the place and wondering which way to go, I became aware of a hollow metallic clanking that echoed in the circular enclosure. The noise drew my eyes upward to the wooden watchtower atop the west tiers, and then to the red arch of the bridge's girders directly above it. The clanking seemed to have something to do with cars passing over the roadbed, and it was underlaid by a constant grumbling rush of tires on pavement. The sounds, coupled with the soaring height of the fog-laced girders, made me feel very small and insignificant. I shivered again and turned to my left, looking for one of the rangers.

The man who came out of a nearby doorway startled me, more because of his costume than the suddenness of his appearance. Instead of the Parks Service uniform I remembered the rangers wearing on my previous visit, he was clad in what looked like an old Union Army uniform: a dark blue frock coat, lighter blue trousers, and a wide-brimmed hat with a red plume. The long saber in a scabbard that was strapped to his waist made him look thoroughly authentic.

He smiled at my obvious surprise and came over to me, bushy eyebrows lifted inquiringly. "Can I help you, ma'am?"

I reached into my bag and took out my private investigator's license and showed it to him. "I'm Sharon McCone, from All Souls Legal Cooperative. Do you have a minute to answer some questions?"

He frowned, the way people often do when confronted by a private detective, probably trying to remember whether he'd done anything lately that would warrant investigation. Then he said, "Sure," and motioned for me to step into the shelter of the sally port.

"I'm investigating a disappearance, a possible suicide from the bridge," I said. "It would have happened about four yesterday afternoon. Were you on duty then?"

He shook his head. "Monday's my day off."

"Is there anyone else here who might have been working then?"

"You could check with Lee—Lee Gottschalk, the other ranger on this shift."

"Where can I find him?"

He moved back into the courtyard and looked around. "I saw him start taking a couple of tourists around just a few minutes ago. People are crazy; they'll come out in any kind of weather."

"Can you tell me which way he went?"

The ranger gestured to our right. "Along this side. When he's done down here, he'll take them up that iron stairway to the first tier, but I can't say how far he's gotten yet."

I thanked him and started off in the direction he'd indicated.

There were open doors in the cement wall between the sally port and the iron staircase. I glanced through the first and saw no one. The second led into a narrow dark hallway; when I was halfway down it, I saw that this was the fort's jail. One cell was set up as a display, complete with a mannequin prisoner; the other, beyond an archway that was not much taller than my own five-foot-six, was unrestored. Its waterstained walls were covered with graffiti, and a metal railing protected a two-foot-square iron grid on the floor in one corner. A sign said that it was a cistern with a forty-thousand-gallon capacity.

Well, I thought, that's interesting, but playing tourist isn't helping me catch up with Lee Gottschalk. Quickly I left the jail and hurried up the iron staircase the first ranger had indicated. At its top, I turned to my left and bumped into a chain link fence that blocked access to the area under renovation. Warning myself to watch where I was going, I went the other way, toward the east tier. The archways there were fenced off with similar chain link so no one could fall, and doors opened off the gallery into what I supposed had been the soldiers' living quarters. I pushed through the first one and stepped into a small museum.

The room was high-ceilinged, with tall, narrow windows in the outside wall. No ranger or tourists were in sight. I looked toward an interior door that led to the next room and saw a series of mirror images: one door within another leading off into the distance, each diminishing in size until the last seemed very tiny. I had the unpleasant sensation that if I walked along there, I would become progressively smaller and eventually disappear.

From somewhere down there came the sound of voices. I followed it, passing through more museum displays until I came to a room containing an old-fashioned bedstead and footlocker. A ranger, dressed the same as the man downstairs except that he was bearded and wore granny glasses, stood beyond the bedstead lecturing to a man and a woman who were bundled to their chins in bulky sweaters.

"You'll notice that the fireplaces are very small," he was saying, motioning to the one on the wall next to the bed, "and you can imagine how cold it could get for the soldiers garrisoned here. They didn't have a heated employees' lounge like we do." Smiling at his own little joke, he glanced at me. "Do you want to join the tour?"

I shook my head and stepped over by the footlocker. "Are you Lee Gottschalk?"

"Yes." He spoke the word a shade warily.

"I have a few questions I'd like to ask you. How long will the rest of the tour take?"

"At least half an hour. These folks want to see the unrestored rooms on the third floor."

I didn't want to wait around that long, so I said, "Could you take a couple of minutes and talk with me now?"

He moved his head so the light from the windows caught his granny glasses and I couldn't see the expression in his eyes, but his mouth tightened in a way that might have been annoyance. After a moment he said, "Well, the rest of the tour on this floor is pretty much self-guided." To the tourists, he added, "Why don't you go on ahead and I'll catch up after I talk with this lady."

They nodded agreeably and moved on into the next room. Lee Gottschalk folded his arms across his chest and leaned against the small fireplace. "Now what can I do for you?"

I introduced myself and showed him my license. His mouth twitched briefly in surprise, but he didn't comment. I said, "At about four yesterday afternoon, a young woman left her car at Vista Point with a suicide note in it. I'm trying to locate a witness who saw her jump." I took out the photograph I'd been showing to people and handed it to him. By now I had Vanessa DiCesare's features memorized: high forehead, straight nose, full lips, glossy wings of dark-brown hair curling inward at the jawbone. It was a strong face, not beautiful but striking—and a face I'd recognize anywhere.

Gottschalk studied the photo, then handed it back to me. "I read about her in the morning paper. Why are you trying to find a witness?"

"Her parents have hired me to look into it."

"The paper said her father is some big politician here in the city."

I didn't see any harm in discussing what had already appeared in print. "Yes, Ernest DiCesare—he's on the Board of Supes and likely to be our next mayor."

"And she was a law student, engaged to some hotshot lawyer who ran her father's last political campaign."

"Right again."

He shook his head, lips pushing out in bewilderment. "Sounds like she had a lot going for her. Why would she kill herself? Did that note taped inside her car explain it?"

I'd seen the note, but its contents were confidential. "No. Did you happen to see anything unusual yesterday afternoon?"

"No. But if I'd seen anyone jump, I'd have reported it to the

Coast Guard station so they could try to recover the body before the current carried it out to sea.''

"What about someone standing by the bridge railing, acting strangely, perhaps?''

"If I'd noticed anyone like that, I'd have reported it to the bridge offices so they could send out a suicide prevention team.'' He stared almost combatively at me, as if I'd accused him of some kind of wrongdoing, then seemed to relent a little. "Come outside,'' he said, "and I'll show you something.''

We went through the door to the gallery, and he guided me to the chain link barrier in the archway and pointed up. "Look at the angle of the bridge, and the distance we are from it. You couldn't spot anyone standing at the rail from here, at least not well enough to tell if they were acting upset. And a jumper would have to hurl herself way out before she'd be noticeable.''

"And there's nowhere else in the fort from where a jumper would be clearly visible?''

"Maybe from one of the watchtowers or the extreme west side. But they're off limits to the public, and we only give them one routine check at closing.''

Satisfied now, I said, "Well, that about does it. I appreciate your taking the time.''

He nodded and we started along the gallery. When we reached the other end, where an enclosed staircase spiraled up and down, I thanked him again and we parted company.

The way the facts looked to me now, Vanessa DiCesare had faked this suicide and just walked away—away from her wealthy old-line Italian family, from her up-and-coming liberal lawyer, from a life that either had become too much or just hadn't been enough. Vanessa was over twenty-one; she had a legal right to disappear if she wanted to. But her parents and her fiancé loved her, and they also had a right to know she was alive and well. If I could locate her and reassure them without ruining whatever new life she planned to create for herself, I would feel I'd performed the job I'd been hired to do. But right now I was weary, chilled to the bone, and out of leads. I decided to go back to All Souls and consider my next moves in warmth and comfort.

All Souls Legal Cooperative is housed in a ramshackle Victorian on one of the steeply sloping sidestreets of Bernal Heights, a working-class district in the southern part of the city. The co-op caters mainly to clients who live in the area: people with low to middle incomes who don't have much extra money for expensive lawyers. The sliding fee scale allows them to obtain quality legal assistance at reasonable prices—a concept that is probably outdated in the self-centered 1980s, but is kept alive by the people who staff All Souls. It's a place where the lawyers care about their clients, and a good place to work.

I left my MG at the curb and hurried up the front steps through the blowing fog. The warmth inside was almost a shock after the chilliness at Fort Point; I unbuttoned my jacket and went down the long deserted hallway to the big country kitchen at the rear. There I found my boss, Hank Zahn, stirring up a mug of the Navy grog he often concocts on cold November nights like this one.

He looked at me, pointed to the rum bottle, and said, "Shall I make you one?" When I nodded, he reached for another mug.

I went to the round oak table under the windows, moved a pile of newspapers from one of the chairs, and sat down. Hank added lemon juice, hot water, and sugar syrup to the rum; dusted it artistically with nutmeg; and set it in front of me with a flourish. I sampled it as he sat down across from me, then nodded my approval.

He said, "How's it going with the DiCesare investigation?"

Hank had a personal interest in the case; Vanessa's fiancé, Gary Stornetta, was a long-time friend of his, which was why I, rather than one of the large investigative firms her father normally favored, had been asked to look into it. I said, "Everything I've come up with points to it being a disappearance, not a suicide."

"Just as Gary and her parents suspected."

"Yes. I've covered the entire area around the bridge. There are absolutely no witnesses, except for the tour bus driver who saw her park her car at four and got suspicious when it was still there at seven and reported it. But even he didn't see her walk off toward the bridge." I drank some more grog, felt its warmth, and began to relax.

Behind his thick horn-rimmed glasses, Hank's eyes became concerned. "Did the DiCesares or Gary give you any idea why she would have done such a thing?"

"When I talked with Ernest and Sylvia this morning, they said Vanessa had changed her mind about marrying Gary. He's not admitting to that, but he doesn't speak of Vanessa the way a happy husband-to-be would. And it seems an unlikely match to me—he's close to twenty years older than she."

"More like fifteen," Hank said. "Gary's father was Ernest's best friend, and after Ron Stornetta died, Ernest more or less took him on as a protégé. Ernest was delighted that their families were finally going to be joined."

"Oh, he was delighted all right. He admitted to me that he'd practically arranged the marriage. 'Girl didn't know what was good for her,' he said. 'Needed a strong older man to guide her.' " I snorted.

Hank smiled faintly. He's a feminist, but over the years his sense of outrage has mellowed; mine still has a hair trigger.

"Anyway," I said, "when Vanessa first announced she was backing out of the engagement, Ernest told her he would cut off her funds for law school if she didn't go through with the wedding."

"Jesus, I had no idea he was capable of such . . . Neanderthal tactics."

"Well, he is. After that Vanessa went ahead and set the wedding date. But Sylvia said she suspected she wouldn't go through with it. Vanessa talked of quitting law school and moving out of their home. And she'd been seeing other men; she and her father had a bad quarrel about it just last week. Anyway, all of that, plus the fact that one of her suitcases and some clothing are missing, made them highly suspicious of the suicide."

Hank reached for my mug and went to get us more grog. I began thumbing through the copy of the morning paper that I'd moved off the chair, looking for the story on Vanessa. I found it on page three.

The daughter of Supervisor Ernest DiCesare apparently committed suicide by jumping from the Golden Gate Bridge late yesterday afternoon.

Vanessa DiCesare, twenty-two, abandoned her 1985 Honda Civic at Vista Point at approximately four P.M., police said. There were no witnesses to her jump, and the body has not been recovered. The contents of a suicide note found in her car have not been disclosed.

Ms. DiCesare, a first-year student at Hastings College of Law, is the only child of the supervisor and his wife, Sylvia. She planned to be married next month to San Francisco attorney Gary R. Stornetta, a political associate of her father. . . .

Strange how routine it all sounded when reduced to journalistic language. And yet how mysterious—the "undisclosed contents" of the suicide note, for instance.

"You know," I said as Hank came back to the table and set down the fresh mugs of grog, "that note is another factor that makes me believe she staged this whole thing. It was so formal and controlled. If they had samples of suicide notes in etiquette books, I'd say she looked one up and copied it."

He ran his fingers through his wiry brown hair. "What I don't understand is why she didn't just break off the engagement and move out of the house. So what if her father cut off her money? There are lots worse things than working your way through law school."

"Oh, but this way she gets back at everyone, and has the advantage of actually being alive to gloat over it. Imagine her parents' and Gary's grief and guilt—it's the ultimate way of getting even."

"She must be a very angry young woman."

"Yes. After I talked with Ernest and Sylvia and Gary, I spoke briefly with Vanessa's best friend, a law student named Kathy Graves. Kathy told me that Vanessa was furious with her father for making her go through with the marriage. And she'd come to hate Gary because she'd decided he was only marrying her for her family's money and political power."

"Oh, come on. Gary's ambitious, sure. But you can't tell me he doesn't genuinely care for Vanessa."

"I'm only giving you her side of the story."

"So now what do you plan to do?"

"Talk with Gary and the DiCesares again. See if I can't come up with some bit of information that will help me find her."

"And then?"

"Then it's up to them to work it out."

The DiCesare home was mock-Tudor, brick and half-timber, set on a corner knoll in the exclusive area of St. Francis Wood. When I'd first come there that morning, I'd been slightly awed; now the house had lost its power to impress me. After delving into the lives of the family who lived there, I knew that it was merely a pile of brick and mortar and wood that contained more than the usual amount of misery.

The DiCesares and Gary Stornetta were waiting for me in the living room, a strangely formal place with several groupings of furniture and expensive-looking knicknacks laid out in precise patterns on the tables. Vanessa's parents and fiancé—like the house—seemed diminished since my previous visit: Sylvia huddled in an armchair by the fireplace, her gray-blonde hair straggling from its elegant coiffure; Ernest stood behind her, haggard-faced, one hand protectively on her shoulder. Gary paced, smoking and clawing at his hair with his other hand. Occasionally he dropped ashes on the thick wall-to-wall carpeting, but no one called it to his attention.

They listened to what I had to report without interruption. When I finished, there was a long silence. Then Sylvia put a hand over her eyes and said, "How she must hate us to do a thing like this!"

Ernest tightened his grip on his wife's shoulder. His face was a conflict of anger, bewilderment, and sorrow.

There was no question of which emotion had hold of Gary; he smashed out his cigarette in an ashtray, lit another, and resumed pacing. But while his movements before had merely been nervous, now his tall, lean body was rigid with thinly controlled fury. "Damn her!" he said. "Damn her anyway!"

"Gary." There was a warning note in Ernest's voice.

Gary glanced at him, then at Sylvia. "Sorry."

I said, "The question now is, do you want me to continue looking for her?"

In shocked tones, Sylvia said, "Of course we do!" Then she tipped her head back and looked at her husband.

Ernest was silent, his fingers pressing hard against the black wool of her dress.

"Ernest?" Now Sylvia's voice held a note of panic.

"Of course we do," he said. But the words somehow lacked conviction.

I took out my notebook and pencil, glancing at Gary. He had stopped pacing and was watching the DiCesares. His craggy face was still mottled with anger, and I sensed he shared Ernest's uncertainty.

Opening the notebook, I said, "I need more details about Vanessa, what her life was like the past month or so. Perhaps something will occur to one of you that didn't this morning."

"Ms. McCone," Ernest said, "I don't think Sylvia's up to this right now. Why don't you and Gary talk, and then if there's anything else, I'll be glad to help you."

"Fine." Gary was the one I was primarily interested in questioning, anyway. I waited until Ernest and Sylvia had left the room, then turned to him.

When the door shut behind them, he hurled his cigarette into the empty fireplace. "Goddamn little bitch!" he said.

I said, "Why don't you sit down."

He looked at me for a few seconds, obviously wanting to keep on pacing, but then he flopped into the chair Sylvia had vacated. When I'd first met with Gary this morning, he'd been controlled and immaculately groomed, and he had seemed more solicitous of the DiCesares than concerned with his own feelings. Now his clothing was disheveled, his graying hair tousled, and he looked to be on the brink of a rage that would flatten anyone in its path.

Unfortunately, what I had to ask him would probably fan that rage. I braced myself and said, "Now tell me about Vanessa. And not all the stuff about her being a lovely young woman and a brilliant student. I heard all that this morning—but now we both know it isn't the whole truth, don't we?"

Surprisingly he reached for a cigarette and lit it slowly, using the time to calm himself. When he spoke, his voice was as level as my own. "All right, it's not the whole truth. Vanessa *is* lovely and brilliant. She'll make a top-notch lawyer. There's a hardness in her; she gets it from Ernest. It took guts to fake this suicide . . ."

"What do you think she hopes to gain from it?"

"Freedom. From me. From Ernest's domination. She's probably taken off somewhere for a good time. When she's ready she'll come back and make her demands."

"And what will they be?"

"Enough money to move into a place of her own and finish law school. And she'll get it, too. She's all her parents have."

"You don't think she's set out to make a new life for herself?"

"Hell, no. That would mean giving up all this." The sweep of his arm encompassed the house and all of the DiCesares's privileged world.

But there was one factor that made me doubt his assessment. I said, "What about the other men in her life?"

He tried to look surprised, but an angry muscle twitched in his jaw.

"Come on, Gary," I said, "you know there were other men. Even Ernest and Sylvia were aware of that."

"Ah, Christ!" He popped out of the chair and began pacing again. "All right, there were other men. It started a few months ago. I didn't understand it; things had been good with us; they still *were* good physically. But I thought, okay, she's young; this is only natural. So I decided to give her some rope, let her get it out of her system. She didn't throw it in my face, didn't embarrass me in front of my friends. Why shouldn't she have a last fling?''

''And then?''

''She began making noises about breaking off the engagement. And Ernest started that shit about not footing the bill for law school. Like a fool I went along with it, and she seemed to cave in from the pressure. But a few weeks later, it all started up again—only this time it was purposeful, cruel.''

''In what way?''

''She'd know I was meeting political associates for lunch or dinner, and she'd show up at the restaurant with a date. Later she'd claim he was just a friend, but you couldn't prove it from the way they acted. We'd go to a party and she'd flirt with every man there. She got sly and secretive about where she'd been, what she'd been doing.''

I had pictured Vanessa as a very angry young woman; now I realized she was not a particularly nice one, either.

Gary was saying, ''. . . the last straw was on Halloween. We went to a costume party given by one of her friends from Hastings. I didn't want to go—costumes, a young crowd, not my kind of thing—and so she was angry with me to begin with. Anyway, she walked out with another man, some jerk in a soldier outfit. They were dancing . . .''

I sat up straighter. ''Describe the costume.''

''An old-fashioned soldier outfit. Wide-brimmed hat with a plume, frock coat, sword.''

''What did the man look like?''

''Youngish. He had a full beard and wore granny glasses.''

Lee Gottschalk.

The address I got from the phone directory for Lee Gottschalk was on California Street not far from Twenty-fifth Avenue and only a couple of miles from where I'd first met the ranger at Fort Point. When I arrived there and parked at the opposite curb, I didn't need to check the mailboxes to see which apartment was his; the corner windows on the second floor were ablaze with light, and inside I could see Gottschalk, sitting in an armchair in what appeared to be his living room. He seemed to be alone but expecting company, because frequently he looked up from the book he was reading and checked his watch.

In case the company was Vanessa DiCesare, I didn't want to go barging in there. Gottschalk might find a way to warn her off, or simply not answer the door when she arrived. Besides, I didn't yet have a definite connection between the two of them; the "jerk in a soldier outfit" *could* have been someone else, someone in a rented costume that just happened to resemble the working uniform at the fort. But my suspicions were strong enough to keep me watching Gottschalk for well over an hour. The ranger *had* lied to me that afternoon.

The lies had been casual and convincing, except for two mistakes—such small mistakes that I hadn't caught them even when I'd read the newspaper account of Vanessa's purported suicide later. But now I recognized them for what they were: The paper had called Gary Stornetta a "political associate" of Vanessa's father, rather than his former campaign manager, as Lee had termed him. And while the paper mentioned the suicide note, it had not said it was *taped* inside the car. While Gottschalk conceivably could know about Gary managing Ernest's campaign for the Board of Supes from other newspaper accounts, there was no way he could have known how the note was secured—except from Vanessa herself.

Because of those mistakes, I continued watching Gottschalk, straining my eyes as the mist grew heavier, hoping Vanessa would show up or that he'd eventually lead me to her. The ranger appeared to be nervous: He got up a couple of times and turned on a TV, flipped through the channels, and turned it off again. For about ten minutes, he paced back and forth. Finally, around twelve-thirty, he checked his watch again, then got up and drew the draperies shut. The lights went out behind them.

I tensed, staring through the blowing mist at the door of the apartment building. Somehow Gottschalk hadn't looked like a man who was going to bed. And my impression was correct: In a few minutes he came through the door onto the sidewalk carrying a suitcase—pale leather like the one of Vanessa's Sylvia had described to me—and got into a dark-colored Mustang parked on his side of the street. The car started up and he made a U-turn, then went right on Twenty-fifth Avenue. I followed. After a few minutes, it became apparent that he was heading for Fort Point.

When Gottschalk turned into the road to the fort, I kept going until I could pull over on the shoulder. The brake lights of the

Mustang flared, and then Gottschalk got out and unlocked the low iron bar that blocked the road from sunset to sunrise; after he'd driven through he closed it again, and the car's lights disappeared down the road.

Had Vanessa been hiding at drafty, cold Fort Point? It seemed a strange choice of place, since she could have used a motel or Gottschalk's apartment. But perhaps she'd been afraid someone would recognize her in a public place, or connect her with Gottschalk and come looking, as I had. And while the fort would be a miserable place to hide during the hours it was open to the public—she'd have had to keep to one of the off-limits areas, such as the west side—at night she could probably avail herself of the heated employees' lounge.

Now I could reconstruct most of the scenario of what had gone on: Vanessa meets Lee; they talk about his work; she decides he is the person to help her fake her suicide. Maybe there's a romantic entanglement, maybe not; but for whatever reason, he agrees to go along with the plan. She leaves her car at Vista Point, walks across the bridge, and later he drives over there and picks up the suitcase. . . .

But then why hadn't he delivered it to her at the fort? And to go after the suitcase after she'd abandoned the car was too much of a risk; he might have been seen, or the people at the fort might have noticed him leaving for too long a break. Also, if she'd walked across the bridge, surely at least one of the people I'd talked with would have seen her—the maintenance crew near the north tower, for instance.

There was no point in speculating on it now, I decided. The thing to do was to follow Gottschalk down there and confront Vanessa before she disappeared again. For a moment I debated taking my gun out of the glovebox, but then decided against it. I don't like to carry it unless I'm going into a dangerous situation, and neither Gottschalk nor Vanessa posed any particular threat to me. I was merely here to deliver a message from Vanessa's parents asking her to come home. If she didn't care to respond to it, that was not my business—or my problem.

I got out of my car and locked it, then hurried across the road and down the narrow lane to the gate, ducking under it and continuing along toward the ranger station. On either side of me were tall, thick groves of eucalyptus; I could smell their acrid fragrance and hear the fog-laden wind rustle their brittle leaves. Their shadows turned the lane into a black winding alley, and the only sound besides distant traffic noises was my tennis shoes slapping on the broken pavement. The ranger station was dark, but ahead I could see Gottschalk's car parked next to the fort. The area was illuminated only by small security lights set at intervals on the walls of the structure. Above it the bridge arched, washed in fog-muted yellowish light; as I drew closer I became aware of the grumble and clank of traffic up there.

I ran across the parking area and checked Gottschalk's car. It was empty, but the suitcase rested on the passenger seat. I turned and started toward the sally port, noticing that its heavily studded door stood open a few inches. The low tunnel was completely dark. I felt my way along it toward the courtyard, one hand on its icy stone wall.

The doors to the courtyard also stood open. I peered through them into the gloom beyond. What light there was came from the bridge and more security beacons high up on the wooden watchtowers; I could barely make out the shapes of the construction equipment that stood near the west side. The clanking from the bridge was oppressive and eerie in the still night.

As I was about to step into the courtyard, there was a movement to my right. I drew back into the sally port as Lee Gottschalk came out of one of the ground-floor doorways. My first impulse was to confront him, but then I decided against it. He might shout, warn Vanessa, and she might escape before I could deliver her parents' message.

After a few seconds I looked out again, meaning to follow Gottschalk, but he was nowhere in sight. A faint shaft of light fell through the door from which he had emerged and rippled over the cobblestone floor. I went that way, through the door and along a narrow corridor to where an archway was illuminated. Then, realizing the archway led to the unrestored cell of the jail I'd seen earlier, I paused. Surely Vanessa wasn't hiding in there. . . .

I crept forward and looked through the arch. The light came from a heavy-duty flashlight that sat on the floor. It threw macabre shadows on the water-stained walls, showing their streaked paint and graffiti. My gaze followed its beams upward and then down, to where the grating of the cistern lay out of place on the floor beside the hole. Then I moved over to the railing, leaned across it, and trained the flashlight down into the well.

I saw, with a rush of shock and horror, the dark hair and once-handsome features of Vanessa DiCesare.

She had been hacked to death. Stabbed and slashed, as if in a frenzy. Her clothing was ripped; there were gashes on her face and hands; she was covered with dark smears of blood. Her eyes were open, staring with that horrible flatness of death.

I came back on my heels, clutching the railing for support. A wave of dizziness swept over me, followed by an icy coldness. I thought: He killed her. And then I pictured Gottschalk in his Union Army uniform, the saber hanging from his belt, and I knew what the weapon had been.

"God!" I said aloud.

Why had he murdered her? I had no way of knowing yet. But the answer to why he'd thrown her into the cistern, instead of just putting her into the bay, was clear: She was supposed to have committed suicide; and while bodies that fall from the Golden Gate Bridge sustain a great many injuries, slash and stab wounds aren't among them. Gottschalk could not count on the body being swept out to sea on the current; if she washed up somewhere along the coast, it would be obvious she had been murdered—and eventually an investigation might have led back to him. To him and his soldier's saber.

It also seemed clear that he'd come to the fort tonight to move the body. But why not last night, why leave her in the cistern all day? Probably he'd needed to plan, to secure keys to the gate and fort, to check the schedule of the night patrols for the best time to remove her. Whatever his reason, I realized now that I'd walked into a very dangerous situation. Walked right in without bringing my gun. I turned quickly to get out of there . . .

And came face-to-face with Lee Gottschalk.

His eyes were wide, his mouth drawn back in a snarl of surprise. In one hand he held a bundle of heavy canvas. "You!" he said. "What the hell are you doing here?"

I jerked back from him, bumped into the railing, and dropped the flashlight. It clattered on the floor and began rolling toward the mouth of the cistern. Gottschalk lunged toward me, and as I dodged, the light fell into the hole and the cell went dark. I managed to push past him and ran down the hallway to the courtyard.

Stumbling on the cobblestones, I ran blindly for the sally port. Its doors were shut now—he'd probably taken that precaution when he'd returned from getting the tarp to wrap her body in. I grabbed the iron hasp and tugged, but couldn't get it open. Gottschalk's footsteps were coming through the courtyard after me now. I let go of the hasp and ran again.

When I came to the enclosed staircase at the other end of the court, I started up. The steps were wide at the outside wall, narrow at the inside. My toes banged into the risers of the steps; a couple of times I teetered and almost fell backwards. At the first tier I paused, then kept going. Gottschalk had said something about unrestored rooms on the second tier; they'd be a better place to hide than in the museum.

Down below I could hear him climbing after me. The sound of his feet—clattering and stumbling—echoed in the close space. I could hear him grunt and mumble: low, ugly sounds that I knew were curses.

I had absolutely no doubt that if he caught me, he would kill me. Maybe do to me what he had done to Vanessa. . . .

I rounded the spiral once again and came out on the top floor gallery, my heart beating wildly, my breath coming in pants. To my left were archways, black outlines filled with dark-gray sky. To my right was blackness. I went that way, hands out, feeling my way.

My hands touched the rough wood of a door. I pushed, and it opened. As I passed through it, my shoulder bag caught on something; I yanked it loose and kept going. Beyond the door I heard Gottschalk curse loudly, the sound filled with surprise and pain; he must have fallen on the stairway. And that gave me a little more time.

The tug at my shoulder bag had reminded me of the small flashlight I keep there. Flattening myself against the wall next to the door, I rummaged through the bag and brought out the flash. Its beam showed high walls and arching ceilings, plaster and lath pulled away to expose dark brick. I saw cubicles and cubbyholes opening into dead ends, but to my right was an arch. I made a small involuntary sound of relief, then thought *Quiet!* Gottschalk's footsteps started up the stairway again as I moved through the archway.

The crumbling plaster walls beyond the archway were set at odd angles—an interlocking funhouse maze connected by small doors. I slipped through one and found an irregularly shaped room heaped with debris. There didn't seem to be an exit, so I ducked back into the first room and moved toward the outside wall, where gray outlines indicated small high-placed windows. I couldn't hear Gottschalk any more—couldn't hear anything but the roar and clank from the bridge directly overhead.

The front wall was brick and stone, and the windows had wide waist-high sills. I leaned across one, looked through the salt-caked glass, and saw the open sea. I was at the front of the fort, the part that faced beyond the Golden Gate; to my immediate right would be the unrestored portion. If I could slip over into that area, I might be able to hide until the other rangers came to work in the morning.

But Gottschalk could be anywhere. I couldn't hear his footsteps above the infernal noise from the bridge. He could be right there in the room with me, pinpointing me by the beam of my flashlight. . . .

Fighting down panic, I switched the light off and continued along the wall, my hands recoiling from its clammy stone surface. It was icy cold in the vast, echoing space, but my own flesh felt colder still. The air had a salt tang, underlaid by odors of rot and mildew. For a couple of minutes the darkness was unalleviated, but then I saw a lighter rectangular shape ahead of me.

When I reached it I found it was some sort of embrasure, about four feet tall, but only a little over a foot wide. Beyond it I could see the edge of the gallery where it curved and stopped at the chain link fence that barred entrance to the other side of the fort. The fence wasn't very high—only five feet or so. If I could get through this narrow opening, I could climb it and find refuge . . .

The sudden noise behind me was like a firecracker popping. I whirled, and saw a tall figure silhouetted against one of the seaward windows. He lurched forward, tripping over whatever he'd stepped on. Forcing back a cry, I hoisted myself up and began squeezing through the embrasure.

Its sides were rough brick. They scraped my flesh clear through my clothing. Behind me I heard the slap of Gottschalk's shoes on the wooden floor.

My hips wouldn't fit through the opening. I gasped, grunted, pulling with my arms on the outside wall. Then I turned on my side, sucking in my stomach. My bag caught again, and I let go of the wall long enough to rip its strap off my elbow. As my hips squeezed through the embrasure, I felt Gottschalk grab at my feet. I kicked out frantically, breaking his hold, and fell off the sill to the floor of the gallery.

Fighting for breath, I pushed off the floor, threw myself at the fence, and began climbing. The metal bit into my fingers, rattled and clashed with my weight. At the top, the leg of my jeans got hung up on the spiky wires. I tore it loose and jumped down the other side.

The door to the gallery burst open and Gottschalk came through it. I got up from a crouch and ran into the darkness ahead of me. The fence began to rattle as he started up it. I raced, half-stumbling, along the gallery, the open archways to my right. To my left was probably a warren of rooms similar to those on the east side. I could lose him in there . . .

Only I couldn't. The door I tried was locked. I ran to the next one and hurled my body against its wooden panels. It didn't give. I heard myself sob in fear and frustration.

Gottschalk was over the fence now, coming toward me, limping. His breath came in erratic gasps, loud enough to hear over the noise from the bridge. I twisted around, looking for shelter, and saw a pile of lumber lying across one of the open archways.

I dashed toward it and slipped behind, wedged between it and the pillar of the arch. The courtyard lay two dizzying stories below me. I grasped the end of the top two-by-four. It moved easily, as if on a fulcrum.

Gottschalk had seen me. He came on steadily, his right leg dragging behind him. When he reached the pile of lumber and started over it toward me, I yanked on the two-by-four. The other end moved and struck him on the knee.

He screamed and stumbled back. Then he came forward again, hands outstretched toward me. I pulled back further against the pillar. His clutching hands missed me, and when they did he lost his balance and toppled onto the pile of lumber. And then the boards began to slide toward the open archway.

He grabbed at the boards, yelling and flailing his arms. I tried to reach for him, but the lumber was moving like an avalanche now, pitching over the side and crashing down into the courtyard two stories below. It carried Gottschalk's thrashing body with it, and his screams echoed in its wake. For an awful few seconds the boards continued to crash down on him, and then everything was terribly still. Even the thrumming of the bridge traffic seemed muted.

I straightened slowly and looked down into the courtyard. Gottschalk lay unmoving among the scattered pieces of lumber. For a moment I breathed deeply to control my vertigo; then I ran back to the chain link fence, climbed it, and rushed down the spiral staircase to the courtyard.

When I got to the ranger's body, I could hear him moaning. I said, "Lie still. I'll call an ambulance."

He moaned louder as I ran across the courtyard and found a phone in the gift shop, but by the time I returned, he was silent. His breathing was so shallow that I thought he'd passed out, but then I heard mumbled words coming from his lips. I bent closer to listen.

"Vanessa," he said. "Wouldn't take me with her. . . ."

I said. "Take you where?"

"Going away together. Left my car . . . over there so she could drive across the bridge. But when she . . . brought it here she said she was going alone. . . ."

So you argued, I thought. And you lost your head and slashed her to death.

"Vanessa," he said again. "Never planned to take me . . . tricked me. . . ."

I started to put a hand on his arm, but found I couldn't touch him. "Don't talk any more. The ambulance'll be here soon."

"Vanessa," he said. "Oh God, what did you do to me?"

I looked up at the bridge, rust red through the darkness and the mist. In the distance, I could hear the wail of a siren.

Deceptions, I thought.

Deceptions. . . .

All the Heroes Are Dead

•

Clark Howard

Clark Howard is one of the three or four best writers of the contemporary mystery short story, as evidenced by this unusual "antidetective" tale set among bootleggers in rural Georgia, and by his 1980 MWA Best Short Story Edgar for "Horn Man." Howard also writes evocative true crime (Brothers in Blood) *and suspense novels; among the best of the latter are* The Doomsday Squad *(1970) and* Mark the Sparrow *(1976).*

The district director finished perusing the personnel file and shook his head dubiously. "Are you sure you've selected the right man for this assignment?" he asked his chief investigator. "We need someone to infiltrate a very close-knit bootlegging operation in Lasher County, Georgia. That's redneck country. This agent David Berry somehow doesn't seem the type for it. His background, I mean: political-science major at Yale, midwestern upbringing, interests in soccer and the theater—"

"His interest in the theater is precisely one of the reasons I selected Berry," the chief investigator said. "He's an amateur actor, belongs to a little-theater group in Alexandria. It's going to take someone who can put on a very good performance to fool those people in Lasher County."

"Maybe a better performance than you think," the director said. "The state authorities put an undercover man down there last year. He dropped out of sight and hasn't been heard from since. There are lots of deep woods and swamps in that part of Georgia. Good places to dispose of a body."

"I still feel Berry's the man for the job," the chief insisted.

"All right," the director said with a quiet sigh. "Have him come in."

The chief rose and summoned David Berry from an outer office.

When the director saw him, his doubts were by no means assuaged. Berry's hair was styled, he wore a three-piece Brooks Brothers suit, and carried an attaché case. He belonged, the director thought, in the bank examiners section, not in illegal whiskey.

"Berry, you've been with Treasury for three years now," the director said. "According to your file, all of your assignments up until now have been desk work. Do you think you can handle an undercover job?"

"Yes sir, I do," Berry replied. "I've been eager for field work for quite some time now." His voice was precise, educated.

"You've read the Lasher County file," the director said, "so you know what the case is all about. An estimated 100,000 gallons of liquor are being manufactured illegally somewhere down there every year. That's not what we consider a huge operation, by any means. The government loses tax revenue on about two-and-a-half-million dollars annually based on their selling price, which is around one-third the cost of legal liquor, so we wouldn't go broke if we let them operate indefinitely. But that's not the point. The issue here is a violation of the law—manufacturing liquor without a license and distributing liquor without a tax stamp."

"Most of their sales, as you know from the file," the chief said, "are to rural residents in south Georgia and Alabama, and northern Florida. People that are commonly known as 'rednecks.' They live in and around places like the Apalachicola Forest, the Osceola Forest, and the Okefenokee Swamp. That's where we think they've got their manufacturing plant—their whiskey still: in the Okefenokee."

David Berry nodded. "Yes, sir, I noticed in the file that at one point there was nearly a 600-percent increase in the sale of Mason jars in the swamp communities."

The chief smiled. "That's how we pinpointed the manufacturing site. Normally they make runs about a hundred miles away for their Mason jars, but apparently they ran out of them from their regular suppliers and had to buy locally. It was a sure tipoff—you can't bootleg hooch without Mason jars."

The director, still looking worried, sat forward and folded his hands on the desk. "Berry, I want to emphasize to you the potential peril of an assignment like this. You'll be going into a completely foreign environment, among people who are totally different from the kind you're accustomed to associating with."

"I know that, sir," Berry said. "I plan to spend a few weeks

183

traveling around small towns in northern Georgia to learn how to act the part. I fully intend to prepare for the role.''

"Your dress, your mannerisms, your speech—you'll have to change everything.''

"Well, Ah don't think Ah'll have too much trouble with the speech, suh,'' Berry said, suddenly falling into a very good southern drawl. ''Ah been listenin' to some dialect records over at that there linguistic department at the university an' Ah spects Ah'll have the talkin' down pat pretty quick like.'' Smiling, Berry reverted to his own speech pattern. "As for the clothes, visits to a couple of thrift shops and surplus stores will take care of that. And the mannerisms—well, just opening the beer can and drinking out of it ought to do for a start.''

The chief flashed an I-told-you-so-smile at the director. "We've established a complete new identity for him,'' he said. "His name will be Dale Barber. We chose that surname because Barber is very common in the southeastern U.S. He'll have an Alabama driver's license, army discharge, social security card, and two membership cards to private after-hours clubs in Tuscaloosa. We picked that city because it's far enough away from where he'll be operating to make it difficult for anybody to check up on him, and it's large enough—about 150,000—to throw them off if they do. I think we've got all the bases covered, sir.''

"It certainly seems like it.'' But there was still a trace of doubt in the director's voice, a gut feeling of reluctance inside him, some instinct—perhaps based on his thirty years of law enforcement experience—that told him not to give David Berry the Lasher County assignment. It was nothing he could put his finger on and he knew if he tried to explain it to his chief investigator he would sound as if he were procrastinating. Based on the chief's recommendation and Berry's apparent ability to discharge the assignment, he was left with no choice. "All right, Berry, the job's yours,'' he said.

He had a feeling that he would never see the young agent again.

Three weeks later, David Berry was cruising down Highway 441, which ran parallel to the Okefenokee Swamp. He was driving a '78 Chevy pickup with a roll-bar he'd bought with agency money in Tuscaloosa. A battered suitcase and a cardboard box containing his extra clothes rode in the rear bed along with a nearly bald spare tire, a lug wrench, an empty gas can, and a six-pack of Miller's beer. In one corner of the pickup's back window was a decal of a

Confederate flag. Inside the cab was a rifle rack with a .22 pump on it. A Slim Whitman tape was playing in the dashboard deck.

When David got to DeSota, the little town that was halfway down on the edge of the swamp, he circled the tiny town square once and pulled up in front of Luther's Café.

Getting out of the truck, he stretched and twisted some of the stiffness out of his back and shoulders. He knew that several people sitting by the window in the café had already noticed him, his truck, the Alabama plates. His appearance, he knew, fit the picture—old faded Levis, an inexpensive plaid cotton shirt, a blue denim vest, and a soiled yellow visor cap with an STP patch on it. The cap was pushed to the back of his now unstyled hair. On his feet he wore low-heel Frye boots.

Going inside, David sat at the counter and looked at the hand-written menu. A waitress came over to him—redheaded, well built, a sexy wide mouth, too much mascara. She wore a white uniform that had "Tommy Sue" embroidered above her left breast.

"Hi," she said, setting a glass of water in front of him.

"Hi, Tommy Sue," he said, reading her uniform. "Ah'll have three chicken wings, some coleslaw, an' fried okra. An' iced tea."

Their eyes met just long enough for them to realize it. Then David reached down the counter and retrieved the sports section of the Tallahassee *Democrat*. He pretended to read, but he was actually thinking about Eileen, his girl friend. She was working on her master's in history at Georgetown. Eileen was tall, slim, chic, and proper—almost too proper sometimes. She had not been at all pleased about this field assignment.

"Georgia!" she had said. "Really, David. Can't you get out of it somehow? The Clarys' lawn party is coming up."

"I don't want to get out of it," he had told her. "This is my first opportunity in three years to get away from a desk."

"But *Georgia*! Couldn't you get an assignment someplace close?"

"There aren't many illegal whiskey stills in Bethesda or Arlington or Alexandria," he pointed out. "We have to go where the violation is. I'm sorry about the Clarys' party."

Tommy Sue brought his food and David put the paper aside. He began to eat the chicken wings with his fingers. Out of the corner of his eye he saw the fry cook come out of the kitchen, wiping his hands on a greasy apron. "That your pickup with the 'Bama plates?" he asked.

185

"Tha's me," David said with his mouth full.

"Where'bouts in 'Bama you from?"

"Tuscaloosa. Ax'ly Ah'm from Coker, a little piece north. But ain't nobody ever heard of Coker, so Ah say Tuscaloosa."

The fry cook nodded. "Jus' passin' through?"

David shook his head. "Lookin' for work. Heard up in Waycross that ya'll had a canning factory down here that might be hirin' on."

"Cannin' factory shut down last week. Soybeans done poorly this year. Nothin' to can."

David shook his head in disappointment and kept on eating. In a booth near the window sat three men he could sense listening with interest to his conversation with the fry cook.

"Know of anything else around?" he asked.

"Such as?"

David shrugged. "Ah ain't particular. Fillin' station, farm work, construction."

"Things is real slow right now. Maybe fu'ther south. Florida maybe."

David grunted. "Ah'm runnin' low on lookin' money. There a poolroom in town?"

"Right across the square. Leon's Pool Hall."

"Maybe Ah can pick up a couple dollars."

"Don't count on it," the fry cook said.

There was a motel called Harley's Motor Inn a mile out the highway: twelve units that usually filled up only during the legal fishing season. The season was past now and the alligators were breeding in the swamp waters, so there was no one at Harley's except a notions salesman who worked the territory between Macon and Orlando. The salesman was in Unit One, so Harley put David in Unit Two when David drove out after lunch and checked in.

"How long you be staying?" Harley asked.

"Couple days maybe. Lookin' for work."

"Things is real slow around here. Be twelve-fifty a night, first night in advance. No playin' the television after midnight."

David carried his old suitcase and cardboard box into the room and unpacked. Then he pulled off his boots to stretch out on the bed for a while. It was funny about those boots. He had expected to hate them. His taste ran to Carranos: glove-leather, Italian-made. But these Frye boots, after a week of breaking in, were as comfortable as anything he'd ever put on his feet. It was the same with the Chevy pickup. In Washington he drove a low-slung Datsun 280-Z and rode close to the pavement. The cab of the pickup was up high, above everything except motor homes and tractor rigs. You saw a lot more in a pickup cab than in a sportscar.

David spent the afternoon resting, then at sunset he showered, put on clean jeans and a striped shirt, and drove back uptown. He found a phonebooth next to the post office and called the chief on a blind telephone number with a memorized credit card number. "I'm settled," he said when the chief answered. "I should be able to spot the delivery truck tonight. Unless you hear from me to the contrary, I'm ready for stage two."

"I understand," the chief said. "Good luck."

David left the booth and walked across the street to Luther's Café again. Tommy Sue was still on duty. "You work all the time?" he asked when she handed him the supper menu.

"Girl's got to make a living," she answered. While he studied the menu she said, "I saw you in the phonebooth. Calling your wife like a good little boy?"

"Don't have no wife. Let me have the fried catfish and hush puppies. Iced tea. Pecan pie for dessert."

"Calling your girl friend then?" she asked as she wrote down his order.

"Calling my mama. Your curiosity satisfied now?"

"Well, 'scuse me for livin'," she said huffily.

Throughout his meal David occasionally caught her glancing at him. Whenever he did, he threw her a smile or a wink. She turned her nose up at him. When he paid his supper check he said, "Next time Ah talk to Mama, Ah'll tell her you said hello."

"Don't bother."

"No trouble. Ah'll tell her Ah met this here little Georgia peach who's too pretty to even describe."

"You might's well save it, Alabama. You got off on the wrong foot with me with that curiosity crack. I was only makin' small talk."

Outside the window David saw a Buick drive up to Leon's Pool Hall followed closely by a Dodge pickup. One man got out of the Buick, two out of the pickup, and they all went inside. They were the same three who had listened so intently to David's conversation with the fry cook at noon.

"Let's you and me start all over," David said, turning his attention back to Tommy Sue. "At breakfast."

187

"I don't work breakfast," she told him. "I come on at eleven-thirty."

"What time do you get off?"

"Nine-thirty—when we close. I work ten hours a day, four days a week. That way I get to spend three days a week with Lonnie."

"Lonnie?"

"My little boy. He's four. My mama keeps him for me, over in Talbot."

"Oh." David glanced out the window again and his thoughts went momentarily to the Dodge pickup. It looked like the right truck, he thought. The one the department had come so close to catching several times.

Tommy Sue, taking his silence for disinterest, handed him his change, shrugged, and started to walk away.

"Hey, wait a minute. What time did you say?"

"What's it matter? You turned awful cold soon's you found out I had a kid. But don't feel bad, it's happened before."

"I didn't turn cold, I simply became distracted," David said, lapsing into his normal speech before he realized it. Tommy Sue frowned, staring curiously at him. David locked eyes with her for a moment, then forced a smile. "That was Tony Randall. Ah can do Johnny Carson, too." His awkward smile faded. "Can Ah come back at nine-thirty? Take you for a beer?"

She shrugged. "I guess," she said. But there was now a trace of reluctance in her voice.

David went back to his pickup and drove out of town. Cursing himself for his momentary lapse of cover, he drove up and down the back roads for an hour, until twilight came and a grayness began to settle over the red dirt fields. Then he headed back uptown. It was fully dark when he parked in front of Leon's Pool Hall. Walking toward the door, he stopped at the Dodge, put his foot up on the back bumper, and pretended to pull a pebble out of his heel. While he was doing it, he palmed a miniature electronic transmitter with a magnet on the back of it, and attached it to the inside of the bumper. Then he went on into the pool hall.

Leon's was a prototype of every poolroom in every small town in the South. Six Brunswick tables so old their cushions could barely reject a ball. Drop pockets with net catchers. A shelf near each table holding a can of talcum for the cuestick shaft and blue chalk for its tip. A few rickety raised wooden benches for tobacco-chewing spectators. Half a dozen spittoons. Two pinball machines that paid off in free games that could be cashed in for money. A wooden bar with an illuminated beer-logo clock over the cash register behind it. And on the bar two large jars—one of pickled eggs, one of pigs' feet. All under a cloud of gray smoke that hung at the ceiling because it had noplace else to go.

David went to the bar and got a bottle of Bud. The three men who had driven up earlier were shooting nine-ball on a middle table. David stepped up on one of the benches and sat down to watch. Two of the men shooting were either twins or brothers very close in age. They wore jeans with leather belts that had their names tooled on the back of them—Merle and Earl. The latter, David noticed, also had E-A-R-L tattooed on the top joint of each finger on his right hand. The work didn't look professional. It was a jailhouse tattoo, David guessed. The third man was the oldest, probably fifty, with a pot-belly hanging over the waist of a pair of self-belted polyester trousers. He wore a shirt that had a western scene embroidered across the yoke. David sensed that he was studying him from under a pair of tinted lenses between shots.

David watched the progress of the game, waiting for an opportunity to interject a comment. To come right out with a remark would have been poor form and would have marked him at once as a total outsider, an "up-North" type. He had to be subtle about it. He waited until Earl, the one with the tattoos, missed a fairly easy straight-in corner shot, then he rolled his eyes toward the ceiling and groaned quietly. But not so quietly that Earl couldn't hear him.

"What's your problem, boy?" Earl said antagonistically. "Don't nobody ever miss a shot where you come from?"

"Not that kind," David said. Then he raised his hands, palms out. "Hey, Ah'm sorry, hear? Ah didn't have no call to remark. It just slipped out."

"You a pool player?" asked the older man, smiling across the table.

David shrugged. "Ah shoot a game ever' now and then." Which was a gross understatement. David had been president of the billiards club at college for five semesters.

The older man came around the table. He had a chaw of tobacco in one cheek, but instead of using a spittoon he kept a Dixie cup handy. "We heard you say at Luther's today that you hoped to win a little money over here. You care to shoot a game of rotation with Earl here? Say for twenty-five dollars?"

David pursed his lips. "That's mighty temptin'."

The man in the polyester trousers smiled. "What's your name, boy?"

"Dale Barber. From Tuscaloosa, Alabama."

"I didn't ask where you was from. My name's Billy Roy Latham. My friends call me Billy Roy. You can call me Mr. Latham." He peeled twenty-five dollars off a roll and stuck it in one of the corner pockets. "Anytime you're ready."

David covered the bet and beat Earl 67 to 53. He could have run the balls and blanked him, but he didn't want to look like a slicker trying to skin the locals. Neither did he want his thumbs broken. So he laid back and just won by two balls, the six and the eight. As he was fishing his winnings out of the pocket, Earl's brother Merle said, "Lemme have a crack at him, Billy Roy."

Latham nodded and put another twenty-five in the pocket. Merle was about in the same league as Earl. David beat him a little more badly, 71 to 49, winning with the two, three, seven, and ten balls.

After the game with Merle, Latham removed his tinted glasses and smiled an artificial smile at David. "Ah cain't decide if you're good or jus' lucky. How 'bout you and me shoot a game for the fifty you've won?"

David glanced around. A dozen men had idled up from the other tables and were gathered around watching. They were somber, leathery men, their eyes squinty from years in the bright sun of the fields. Maybe they worked for Latham, maybe they didn't. But David knew instinctively that even if he had wanted to there was no way he'd be allowed to walk out with the fifty he had won.

"How 'bout it, boy?" Latham pressed. "You an' me for fifty each."

"Whatever you say, Mr. Latham."

The balls were racked and Latham won the break. He made the six on the break, then ran the one, two, and three, and dropped the twelve off the three-ball. David saw at once that Latham was a much better pool shooter than Merle and Earl.

On his first shot, David ran the four, five, seven, and eight, tying it up with twenty-four points each. Latham made the nine and ten, but scratched on the ten and had to spot it back on the table. David then made it in the side pocket but missed the eleven-ball. Latham made the eleven. David made the thirteen, to go three points ahead, 47 to 44. Latham made the fourteen, to move up to forty-eight. Then he missed the fifteen and it was David's turn.

The fifteen was the game-winning ball. It was dead on the side rail, midway down from the end pocket. Its position did not present a difficult shot, merely a tricky one—the cueball had to hit the rail and the fifteen-ball at the same time in order to run the fifteen straight along the cushion into the pocket. If the cueball hit the fifteen first, the fifteen would be brought out from the rail and go nowhere, leaving the opponent a good shot. If the cueball hit the rail first, the fifteen would roll straight along the rail but wouldn't have enough momentum to go all the way to the pocket.

David chalked his cue-tip and bent low over the far end of the table. Wetting his lips, he took dead-perfect aim and let go a slow shot that hit the fifteen and the cushion at the same time. The fifteen rolled along the rail—and stopped four inches from the pocket.

There was a general murmur of approval from the onlookers: the stranger had lost. David shook his head and stepped back. Billy Roy Latham leaned casually over the side rail and eased the ball on in to win the game. He got more than a few pats on the back as he dug the fifty dollars out of the end pocket.

In the men's room, David and Latham stood side by side washing the talcum off their hands at a tin sink. "You could've made that last shot," Latham said quietly.

"Can't win 'em all," David said.

"You could've won that one. Why didn't you?"

David shrugged. "Your town, your people. No call to beat a man in his own town. 'Sides, Ah broke even."

Latham studied him for a long moment as he dried his hands. Then he made up his mind about David and nodded to himself. "There's a place called Joe's Pit out on the highway that's got good barbecued ribs and ice-cold beer. How 'bout havin' a bite?"

"No offense," David said, "but Ah got other plans." He winked at Latham. "Tommy Sue over at the café."

Latham grinned. "You Alabama rednecks is all the same. After the sun goes down you only got one thing on your mind."

"Yep. Jus' like you Georgia rednecks." David bobbed his chin. "See you around."

He bought a cold six-pack at Luther's and drove away from the square with Tommy Sue. "Where do ya'll park around here?" he asked.

"Out by the cemetery. It's quiet there."

191

"Ah reckon it would be."

She showed him the way. When they were parked, David opened both doors of the pickup and two cans of the beer. They sat holding hands and sipping the beer. Someone had burned a stump during the day and there was still a smell of scorched wood in the air. It mixed with the fragrance of hackberry plants that grew wild along the side of the road. The result was an odd, almost sensual night scent. After they finished a can of beer each, David guided Tommy Sue onto the seat and put his lips on her throat. He found himself whispering things to her that he would never have dared say to Eileen. Things that made Tommy Sue draw in her breath and entwine her fingers in his hair.

It was later, when they were having their second beer, that she asked, "Who are you anyway?"

"Jus' plain ol' Dale Barber from Tuscaloosa, honey."

"You're not 'just plain old' anybody from anywhere," she said. "And that wasn't no Tony Randall imitation you were doing earlier. That was the real you."

David looked out at the moonlight and thought it over. "Suppose it was the real me? What would you do about it?"

"Depends on who you came here to hurt. I'm not from DeSota, I'm from Talbot, but the people here been good to me. I wouldn't stick nobody in the back."

"I wouldn't ask you to. Let's get to know each other a little better first. Then we can decide what's right and what's wrong." He kissed the tips of her fingers as he talked.

"You're so gentle," she said softly. "I can't imagine you hurting nobody." She turned her hand around. "Do that to the palm."

"Tell me about your little boy."

"I already told you. His name is Lonnie and he's four and my mama keeps him for me over in Talbot. He's just like any other little boy. Likes cowboys and trucks and beaches. I keep tellin' him we'll go down to the Florida beaches some weekend but, Lord, I never seem to find the time."

"Where's his daddy?"

"Run off with another woman. Last I heard he was on welfare out in California. He left we with Lonnie to raise. I couldn't find no work in Talbot so I come over here to DeSota. A friend of Mama's sent me to see Mr. Latham. He gave me the job at Luther's and fixed the hours so I could spend three days a week back home."

"Billy Roy Latham? He owns Luther's?"

"Sure. Luther's. Leon's Pool Hall. DeSota Market. The filling station, the canning factory, even the undertaker's parlor. He owns just about everything in Lasher County."

"When he helped you out, did he make any moves on you?"

"Not one. He's been a perfect gentleman. He's good to lots of people, and most times he don't ask nothin' in return."

A Georgia godfather, David thought. He had guessed as much from the demeanor of the men in the poolroom. But he had not imagined that Latham owned the entire county. It would be interesting to see how he reacted the following day when his illegal whiskey operation began to fall apart.

But that was tomorrow and tonight was still tonight. David slipped his hand up Tommy Sue's back under her blouse. He felt nothing except flesh.

"Where do you stay the four nights you're in DeSota?" he asked.

"Out at Harley's Motor Inn. I rent Number Twelve by the week."

"I'm in Number Two," he told her.

She put her lips on his ear. "Small world," she said.

David started the pickup.

The next day when David drove up to Luther's for breakfast, Billy Roy Latham and one of the brothers, Merle, were drinking coffee in a booth and looking worried. David nodded a greeting and sat at the counter. The fry cook was in the kitchen doorway, moving a toothpick back and forth in his mouth. "Somethin' wrong?" David asked, bobbing his chin toward the somber men in the booth.

"Revenue agents caught that fellow's brother Earl with a load of bootleg last night. Got him just after he crossed the Florida line."

David nodded. "Oh." The fry cook's wife, who worked mornings until Tommy Sue came on, handed him a menu. "Just grits and sausage," David said.

While David was eating, Merle got up and left the booth. After he was gone, Latham waved David over to join him. "Bring your plate on over," he said hospitably. David carried his coffee and the rest of his meal over.

"How'd you make out with Tommy Sue last night?" Latham asked.

"Struck out," David lied. "She's a right proper girl."

"You got that right," Latham said. "Gonna make a fine little

193

wife for some man someday." Latham sighed wearily and took a sip of coffee.

"Fry cook tells me you got problems this morning." David said.

Latham shot an irritated look over at the counter. "Fry cook's got a big mouth." Then he studied David for a moment. "But he's right. One of them boys you whipped at pool last night got caught in a revenue-agent trap." Latham narrowed his eyes. "You know anything about bootlegging?"

"A little," David admitted.

Latham tossed down his last swallow of coffee. "Come on, take a ride with me. Somethin' I want to show you."

They rode in Latham's Buick down Route 441 to a narrow country road that cut east into Okefenokee Swamp. Five miles along, Latham turned into a rutted dirt path barely wide enough for the car to negotiate. The farther they drove, the more the morning sunlight was shut out by the entangled treetops overhead and the more eerie the great swamp became. A bit of fog still clung to the ground on both sides of the car, looking wet and cold, making David think of the warmth he had left behind in Tommy Sue's bed. He shivered slightly and wished he was still there.

Before the road ended, Latham turned into a bog path and guided the car with a sure, practiced eye onto a log raft ringed with empty fifty-five gallon drums to keep it afloat. Sticking his head out the window, he whistled three times. Presently the raft began to float across the marsh to an island, being pulled along by an unseen rope under the murky water. The trip took only three or four minutes, then Latham, who had not even shut off the engire, drove the car onto the island and into a stand of tall pines. David saw the rope and pulley that were used to bring the raft over. A black man with enormous muscles was standing next to the pulley crank. "That's Mose," said Latham. "He can crush a man's skull between his hands." David didn't doubt it for a moment.

The car drove through the shade of the pines, and up ahead David could see the whiskey still. It consisted of several large wooden tubs and a couple of cast-iron vats with kerosene burners under them. Everything was connected by wires and tubes, and with the escaping steam and the bubbling surface in two of the vats it reminded David of the mad doctors' laboratories he used to see in the movies as a kid. Latham parked and they got out. "Come on," he said, "I'll give you the ten-cent tour."

He led David to the layout of tubs, where several lean sweating white men were pouring industrial alcohol from ten-gallon cans into the first tub, then straining it through a water-and-charcoal filter into a second one. "That's how we wash the noxious chemicals out of the alky," Latham said. "Over here in this here tub is where we mix water with the alky, then we run it into that iron vat and cook it some, put some caramel or butterscotch coloring in it to make it look good, then run it into the last tub there to simmer and cool." He grinned sheepishly. "I usually pour a fifth of bonded rye into the final batch to give it a little extra flavor. Like a taste?"

"Why not?" David said.

Behind the last vat were several young boys filling Mason jars with the freshly cooled liquor. Latham opened one of the jars and handed it to David. Although his taste ran to very dry martinis and good brandy, David knew he had to take a convincing drink of the bootleg stuff, as if he'd been drinking it all his life. He took a respectable swallow, prepared to forcibly hold back both cough and tears if necessary, but to his surprise the drink went down not only smoothly but with a tart good taste. He saw that Latham was smiling at him.

"Smooth, ain't it?"

"Sure is, man," David admitted. "And good, too."

"Ah don't make nothin' but the best for my customers," Latham bragged. He nodded toward a picnic table and benches under a low weeping willow at the edge of the clearing. "Let's set a spell." As he spoke, Latham pulled back one side of his coat and for the first time David saw that he had a pistol stuck in his belt. Glancing around, he also now saw two men armed with rifles, one at each end of the compound. "Sure 'nuff, Mr. Latham," David said easily and followed him over to the table.

"You know," Latham said, sitting down and shaking a Camel out of a soft pack, "I sometimes wonder what the ol' world's comin' to. I read in the papers and see on the evenin' news all the stories about crime in the streets, violence in the schools, poverty in the slums, crooks in gub'ment, all that sort of thing. Makes me realize more ever' day that things is changin' too fast to keep up with— and not necessarily for the better neither. Hell, even all the heroes are dead. Harry Truman's dead. Audie Murphy's dead. John Steinbeck's dead. Ain't nobody around to admire no more. Nowadays all's a man can do is hope to keep his own little part of the world protected from outside influences that might corrupt it. You take Lasher County now. It's my own little corner of the earth and I try to look after it as best I can. I own nearly all there is to own from one end of it to the other, and ever'body except the postmaster and a couple of bankers works for me.''

Latham leaned forward on the table and locked eyes with David.

''I run this county like the whole country ought to be run. We don't have no welfare recipients or food stamps down here 'cause we don't need 'em. Ever'body that *can* work *does* work. An' the ones that can't, why the others take care of 'em. Our old people and our sick people don't want for nothin'. Nobody sleeps cold in the wintertime, nobody goes hungry at suppertime, and nobody has to be afraid *any*time. We ain't got no real crime in Lasher County—no robberies, burglaries, that sort of thing. People here *work* for what they want. They work for me—in my café, my pool hall, my grocery market, my filling station, my farms, my canning factory, and ever'thing else I own. My farms and canning factory are the economic backbone of this county. And when the economy don't stay up, when crops are bad or inflation keeps me from making enough to go around for ever'body, why then this whiskey bi'ness takes up the slack. It's this right here—'' he waved an arm around ''—that keeps the people of Lasher County free and independent of the rest of our dyin' and decayin' society.'' Now Latham's expression seemed to turn hard as stone. ''And I'm here to tell you I'll do anythin' I have to do to keep it that way. Do you take my meanin'?''

David, his mouth as dry as old wood, managed to speak. ''Yessir, Mr. Latham, I take your meanin'.''

''Good,'' Latham said quietly. He sat back and seemed to relax a little, toying with the burnt-out stick match he had used to light his cigarette. ''I don't know,'' he said matter-of-factly, ''if it was just a coincidence you comin' to town one day and Earl gettin' caught with a load that same night. I don't know if you're really Dale Barber from Tuscaloosa or if you're a revenue agent from Washington. I know that Tommy Sue is crazy about you—I talked to her on the phone after Harley called to tell me you'd left the motel. Incidentally, I admire the fact that you said you struck out with her instead of braggin' the other way; that's the mark of a good man. Anyway, Tommy Sue says she thinks you're who you say you are.''

She lied for me, David thought.

''But I'd like to hear it from you,'' Latham said. ''For some funny reason I kind of like you. And I kind of trust you. Enough to give you the benefit of the doubt anyhow. I think I'll know if you lie to me. So I'll just ask you outright: who are you, boy?"

A montage of his own world saturated David's mind. Washington. Eileen. The Clarys' lawn party. Dry martinis. Sportscars. Italian shoes. Styled hair. A career in government.

Then the montage dissolved into another world. Lasher County. Frye boots and Levis. A Chevy pickup. Catfish and hush puppies. Tommy Sue's warm neck and the things he could whisper against it.

David met Billy Roy Latham's fixed stare with a calm sureness. "I'm Dale Barber, Mr. Latham. From Tuscaloosa."

The letter he wrote to the district director was brief and polite. He was sorry to resign so abruptly in the middle of a field assignment, but he had been offered a job in private industry that he couldn't turn down. He wished the department luck in its pursuit of further leads in Lasher County even though based on his own investigation he didn't believe it would be possible to find an illegal whiskey still in the vast Okefenokee Swamp.

The letter to Eileen was also brief, and apologetic. He was leaving government service for private employment and he had to be honest and tell her he had become interested in another woman. He would always remember her fondly, he said, and was certain that, attractive educated woman that she was, she would find someone who deserved her much more than he did.

He mailed the letters in the box outside the DeSota post office, then pulled up in front of Luther's just as Tommy Sue was leaving for the night. She was carrying a small suitcase.

"Hop in," he said. "I'll give you a lift."

"I'm fixin' to catch the ten o'clock bus to Talbot," she told him. "My three days off starts tomorrow."

"I'll give you a lift to Talbot," he said.

"You mean it?"

"Sure I mean it. Get in."

She put her suitcase in the back and climbed into the cab.

"I start work for Mr. Latham on Monday," he told her.

Tommy Sue's eyebrows went up. "Doin' what?"

"Helping him run Lasher County, honey. He said a good ol' boy like me from Tuscaloosa would fit right in. Said that someday I might even take over and run it for him. How's that for a future?"

"Sounds like you've got the future all worked out. What about the past?"

"There isn't any past," David replied quietly. "There's just today. And tomorrow. Listen, let's pick up your little boy and drive down to Florida to the beach. Would you like that?"

"I'd like it just fine." Tommy Sue slid over close and curled up to him. "You're wrong about there bein' just today and tomorrow," she said.

"Am I? What else is there?"

"There's tonight."

The pickup drove out of town and into the Georgia night.

Failed Prayers

•

Edward Gorman

---

*How do private investigators get to be private investigators? This is
just one of the themes Edward Gorman explores in "Failed Pray-
ers," the intense and powerful story of "a very bitter winter" in
the life of his series detective, Jack Dwyer. Gorman has, in a short
time, risen to the front rank among contemporary writers of crime
fiction with such stories as this one and such Dwyer novels as* New,
Improved Murder *(1985),* Murder Straight Up *(1986), and* The
Autumn Dead *(1987). He also writes accomplished Westerns and
creepy fantasy/horror novels under a pseudonym.*

In my days as a police officer I mostly laughed at the few private
investigators I knew. For some reason, they were usually small men
with fierce little eyes and sour little mouths and enough comic-
opera swagger to do an entire rodeo of cowboys proud. They carried weapons of unimaginable size—Magnums seemed coin of the
realm—which was especially curious when you considered that their
prime job was installing electronic bugs.

But that wasn't why I disliked them so much. I mean, we're all
foolish in our way, and each of us whores to survive.

No, what I disliked about them was the fact that they traded on
human misery for their money. Here, sir, are the pictures of your
wife you wanted; I even got her smiling midorgasm. (Here, ma'am,
is your husband. A pitiful figure, isn't he, his fat ass bucking up
and down?)

Living is a matter of choices, and private investigators have made
the worst choice of all.

I say this with no little hypocrisy. There is the matter of my
present employer, the American Security Agency. There is the matter of my own private investigator's license. There is the matter two
weeks ago, of my following a married woman to an assignation so

that I could snap several 35 mm. shots of her. (I did not go up to the motel room; I did not slide a bug beneath the mattress. Even hypocrites have some scruples.)

So how did I get from reasonably honest cop to reasonably dishonest private investigator?

It was winter, a very bitter winter. . . .

When she slapped him, everybody turned around and looked, including me. I'm just as addicted to the spectacle of human misery as anybody else.

This was six years ago, back when I was still married. Ostensibly, anyway. I had just discovered acting and my wife had just discovered her husband-to-be. It was a trade, of sorts.

Anyway, that's how I came to be in Belmondo's that snowy Friday night. Belmondo's is a singles bar where cops hang out. I had already passed on the all available cop groupies and was hoping that the door was going to open up and somebody female was going to come in with sunshine in her smile.

Which is when the woman, seated at a small cuddling table near the middle of the place, leaned over and slapped the man she was with very hard.

My partner Ryan said, "Jesus." Ryan had a mournful way of cursing that was more a failed prayer than blasphemy. As if he wanted to appeal to God but had learned through bitter experience that the Big Guy didn't always come through for you.

Everybody tried to look away after it was all over, but you couldn't help but let your eyes drift back to them, to see what they were doing.

And what they were doing, of course, was suffering.

They were my age, early thirties, a spawn of good colleges and good taste. He was probably an investment banker or something very much like it—preppy blond hair, pin-striped shirt with collar pin, slightly condescending smile for waitresses and anybody else who wasn't a member of whatever Club these guys are always members of—and she was the prize upper middle-class men always fight for, one of those gentle dark women with the glistening impenetrable gaze of a Spanish Madonna and a presence that was both dignified and erotic. In their college days they'd probably made love in the back seat of any number of Volvos. But they were long past their college days now, so long past that she'd done the unthinkable. Created a scene in a public place.

Ryan said "Jesus" again and I looked up from my drink.

"Yeah," I said.

Ryan so happened to be going through the same kind of divorce I was. He'd done what I'd proposed doing but couldn't get my wife to agree to—gone to a counselor. Whom he told all the things he'd told me and presumably other things, too. Ryan, or so Ryan told me anyway one drunken blistering night in a parking lot when we'd both beat the hell out of our cars in useless and adolescent rage, Ryan hadn't had a decent hard-on in a year and every time he thought about his wife leaving him, he started crying. You don't expect this from a guy who looks like a middleweight fighter, including the tattoos, gone slightly to flesh.

"Wonder who's dumping who," Ryan said, nodding in their direction. "I mean, between them?"

"Does it matter? The result is the same."

"Yeah."

So we spent more time watching the door. Frank Ryan was waiting for a sweetheart bearing sunshine, too. You meet the right woman suddenly it's no longer gray November. It's spring. But even above the juke box I could hear the winter wind whip and feel the night abandon me.

Some other cops came and we talked cop stuff, or I did anyway. Ryan, who's never had a reliable bladder, went several times to the john and when he wasn't peeing, he stared openly at the couple in the center of the place. They still looked miserable.

Nothing else of note happened that night. I did find a woman finally and we went to her place and she asked me a lot of questions about herpes with the lights still on and then in the darkness she told me about a kid she'd lost in a custody battle and a second husband who'd turned out to be gay. I managed a forlorn little erection and got out of there as soon as I could. I was really looking forward to being single again. You meet such a lot of happy people.

Six months went by, during which time my wife told me about her lover and our two kids went through the pain of deciding which parent to hate most, me for being a Dad *in absentia*, Mom for being at least a bit of a tart. Both of us deserved to be put in the same bag and tossed in the same river. You never forget how your kids sound just then, sobbing over how you've betrayed them. Their sobbing goes down the timelines. Forever.

I saw Ryan from time to time of course, usually in a singles bar.

By then his wife had been through a few more affairs and he was spending all his money on a shrink. He had pretty much given up looking for women. Instead he was spending most of his time being both father and mother to his daughter. It's amazing how the pain of betrayal turns normally insensitive men like Ryan into real people. For a couple of weeks we did what most dumped lovers do—took up racquetball. We had big hopes for racquetball. We were going to pound that frigging ball so hard it was going to be a creative act in and of itself, and our human sweat was going to cleanse us of our griefs. We paid something like a $200 fee to join the club and I think we went maybe seven times in all. I found an excuse not to go one night and then he found an excuse, then the next time we both found excuses and right then we decided, without words of course, to blow off our $200 per initiation fee. What the hell, I was rich.

Then it was spring again and the Cubs were sending hopeful messages from training camp (sort of like the message General Custer sent from Little Big Horn) and along the river you saw women strolling whom God put on the planet just so you'd have somebody to dream about.

Then one night I saw the man's picture on the six o'clock news. At first I didn't recognize him. Instead of the investment banker suit, they had him here in a mug shot. He looked out of sleep and out of luck. Amazing how a single bad night can transform you into a derelict.

The reason he was on TV was simple enough. The fellows at one of the downtown precincts were accusing him of murder. The next shot was of his Madonna-like wife. Her you didn't forget. I remembered them then. The night in the singles bar. The slap. The slow grinding misery in their eyes afterward. Now she was dead, murdered, and he was accused. Was it really a surprise? Doubtful.

I can't say I followed the trial, not at first anyway, with more than perfunctory interest. I had my own work at the precinct and my own life. Anyway there were a lot of murder trials on the tube and this one didn't have as much inherent interest as the one, say, that involved the guy who drove around chopping people in half, then trying to sell their carcasses to slaughterhouses. He now resides downstate in a room with only one window but many bars.

But the singles bar guy came back to my attention when he tore up the courtroom. Just went berserk one day. All the while shouting his innocence.

The TV boys and girls got a shot of him leaving the courtroom. He had the look of somebody who is no longer quite human—rage or sorrow had turned him into a man without grace notes. All he could do was scream one thing, over and over again, till he died, "I AM INNOCENT." Not that this meant he was innocent. He might well have killed her and was now simply in the process of denying it to himself. Or he might be a great, or at least flamboyant, actor.

Then Ryan showed up at my apartment one night with a six-pack of Miller's Lite and said, "He didn't kill her."

"Who?"

"Dobbs."

"Hell, Frank, you were there that night. You saw the slap. You know what it's like when you're in a state like that." The press had detailed how this perfect Yuppie couple had gone gradually to hell. Neighbors testified to the violence of their arguments. Lovers, a blonde lady for him, a swarthy man for her, attested to how much Dobbs hated his wife falling in love with somebody else, and how much his wife hated Dobbs for not letting her go.

"He didn't kill her," Ryan said.

"How do you know?"

"I've just got a feeling."

"You know how far that'll take you in court?"

"He didn't kill her. It's that god damn simple."

"Let's watch the Cubs."

"Who they playing?"

"Dodgers."

For the first time that night, he grinned. "Let's just go down and watch them make sausage instead. It's the same thing."

Three days later, over sub sandwiches, Ryan convinced me to help him check out the dead woman's boyfriend.

So that afternoon we went to the health club where Carlos Sanchez worked.

He had hot brown eyes, hotter still when we identified ourselves as detectives. We sat in a sunny room, his office, and watched him pat aftershave onto his cheeks. He had biceps that did little dances each time he asked them to.

"Damn," he said. Here he'd been looking perfect, a magazine doll, but the dirty word spoiled the effect.

"Meaning what?" I said.

"Meaning Dobbs' lawyer hired three different private investigators to check me out. To prove that I killed Melissa."

"And they didn't get anywhere?" Ryan said.

"They got right here." And he jammed his arm up in bitter salute.

"Maybe we're smarter than private cops," I said.

"If you were smart, you wouldn't be any kind of cops at all."

"Right," Ryan said. "We'd work in health clubs so we could be around big muscular guys and smell their sweat all day."

"I don't have to take this shit. I can call my lawyer."

"Call him," Ryan said.

"You have an alibi for that night?" I said.

He laughed. "You haven't been reading the papers, have you? I've got the best alibi of all."

"What's that?"

"I was out of town."

"And you can prove it?"

He rubbed brown hands on his clean white T-shirt. "I have a witness who says that I was with her all night. In Detroit."

"If you were so hot for Melissa, what were you doing with another woman?" I asked.

"Who said I was hot for Melissa?"

"The papers seem to give that impression."

"You know what the papers can do."

"So you weren't hot for Melissa?"

"She was messed up, man. Totally messed up. Tranks. Booze. Crying jags. Jesus."

"So why did you have an affair with her?"

"She came out to the club here. Often. I have affairs with lots of the ladies."

I could see Ryan's blood anger working up. He wasn't the kind of guy who could sit in the presence of a gigolo for long. Especially not a gigolo as callous as this one.

"So if you wanted rid of her why didn't you send her back to her husband?" I said.

"Hey, man, what the hell you think I tried to do? But she wouldn't go. She blew this whole thing out of all proportion."

"What's the name of your witness?" Ryan said.

"Angie Swanson."

"Where do we find her?" I asked.

"Towel room."

"She works here?"

He grinned again, as if he were about to impart some pleasingly shocking secret. "Sure, man. Sometimes I have affairs with the staff, too."

I got Ryan out of there while there was still time.

Over the next few days we interviewed Angie Swanson twice, but it didn't work at all (Carlos seemed to inspire the sort of desperate loyalty brought out frequently by lust and only rarely by love) and then we interviewed Dobbs' girl friend who turned out to be a beautiful but somewhat hysterical interior designer with expensive clothes and nails bitten into blood. She was like a prom queen with stigmata. She was no help at all.

In the car, I said, "You know what?"

"What?"

"I think he did it."

"Dobbs?"

"Yeah."

"Why?"

"Because it's starting to be obvious."

"He's like us, Dwyer." His voice was somber.

"What?"

"He's like us. Went through the number. Bad wife."

"Hey, Frank, Christ. I'm past the stage now."

"What stage?"

"Blaming my wife for everything. Hell, I was a bad father and an even worse husband. It was at least a fifty-fifty failure."

"That's what the shrinks all try to convince you of, anyway. You think it was my fault that my wife liked to go out with every strange jerk that came her way?"

He said it with such heat and hatred that I knew it was a good time to be still. To just look at the traffic.

A couple blocks later, he said, "Sorry."

"It's all right."

"We're buddies, Dwyer, you and me."

"I know."

"Went through the same stuff together. '

"Right."

"Just like Dobbs."

"So you want to keep on?"

"I'll keep on alone if I have to—soon as I get back, I mean."

"Where you going?"

"This friend of mine's got a cabin downstate. Fishing for a few days."

"It'll be good for you."

"Yeah, I started calling her again. My ex-wife, I mean."

He said it sadly, the way he said "Jesus" sometimes. "She's still a bitch."

Next day was my day off. I went to an audition for a stage play and watched all the parts go to other actors and then I went out and had a few beers and then I decided to go home and study for another commercial part my agent felt I had a shot at. Thus far I'd done three spots—public safety things about being a good driver. They had led to promises of work that, for now, remained only that. Promises.

There was a call on my machine and I imagined it was the director back at the dinner theater saying he'd made a big mistake and why didn't I come back and take the lead in the play they were doing.

It turned out to be Dobbs' girl friend, the one with the bitten nails. She said she wanted to see me as soon as she could.

I started watching a Cubs game, but there were two wild pitches in the first inning so I thought I might as well spare myself some grief and go over and talk to Rita Tavers.

She was showing carpet samples and handling them with the care one would a newborn infant. A young couple returned her reverence by gazing on the samples as if they were precious stones.

I listened to Rita work—she had a certain nervous verve and I liked her sad edge despite myself—and when the couple was gone and she came over, I said, "You've really got it down."

She bit at her nails. "I wish I had my life down as well."

I smiled. "I know the feeling."

She surprised me by smiling back. "Yes, for some reason I think you do."

"You want a drink? There's a nice bar around the corner."

She bit at her nails again. I wanted to buy her a pair of insulated gloves. "Yes. Why not?"

* * *

"I don't think he's ever realized how much I love him," Rita Tavers said.

She was about to cry. We were sitting in a restaurant built of redwood and ferns.

"Don't you tell him that?"

"Yes, but—well, he's almost in a trance these days. Since the verdict I mean."

"He'll be out in six years."

"He didn't do it."

I sighed. "I've spent some time on this. I've got a friend who doesn't think he did it, either. But I think you're both wrong. His wife betrayed him and he couldn't take it and he killed her. It's not a new story."

"She was seeing someone else."

"Carlos."

"Other than him."

"What?"

From her purse she took a small bound book. "This is her diary."

"Melissa Dobbs'?"

"Yes."

"Where did you get it?"

She flushed. She had green eyes and very white skin and a wry little mouth. I liked the hell out of her. "I broke in. To their home I mean."

"When?"

"This was just before she died."

"Why?"

"Why did I break in you mean?"

"Right."

"I was—insane sort of. He didn't want me around him anymore. He said that he was going to figure out a way that she'd take him back. He was insane, too. So I broke in—I didn't know what I was looking for, but I wanted some evidence of just how much he needed me instead of her. I found—this. I wasn't sure it was important till now." She nodded to the book. Then she glanced at her watch. "I've really got to get back. But take the diary. Read it carefully. Then you'll see what I mean."

I walked her back to her office in the bright summer day and then I went home and read the diary and then I made my plans.

* * *

Frank Ryan said, "How did you figure it out?"

"This." I handed him the diary.

We were riding down the street. I'd called as soon as he'd gotten back from fishing, told him I needed to see him. For the first time—obviously sensing something—he seemed nervous.

"What does it say?"

"Just about how this guy stopped her one day—this guy she'd never seen before—and seemed to know all about her life. And told her to go back to her husband."

We sat at a stoplight.

"All I really wanted to do was help them," he said.

"The weird thing is, Frank, I believe you."

"I mean, that night in the bar, when she slapped him, I got their names. I wasn't even sure why, then. But then I started following them around, trying to find out everything I could about them. I found out a lot. I followed them for months. I didn't make any contact with either of them. I just followed them. It was like I was—monitoring them, or something. They were both decent people—they really were—but they were a little spoiled, especially her. She needed more excitement than Dobbs so she took up with that fucking Carlos asshole. She really thought it was love. All I wanted her to do was stop seeing him for a couple of weeks. Give Dobbs another chance."

"So you strangled her?"

"I just—got carried away. Jesus."

"You thought you could throw any suspicion off yourself—if it ever came up—by investigating the murder yourself."

He sighed. "You're not giving me anything, Dwyer."

"I want to give you something, Frank. Help me."

"It wasn't that I wanted to throw suspicion off *me*. I didn't want him to do time. I figured if we investigated we could nail Carlos for it in some way."

I laughed. "I almost wish it would have worked, Frank. Because you're a friend of mine, and this is all crazy."

"You know what my wife's gonna say?" he said.

I didn't say anything for a time. Then, "What's she gonna say?"

"She's gonna say—I always knew he was a killer. Then she'll completely absolve herself of all the crap she did to me and everybody will feel real sorry for her."

Now it was my turn. "Jesus," I said.

I said it just the way Frank always did.

As a prayer.
A failed prayer.

I went to see him a couple of times upstate in prison. Both times he tried looking jaunty—a lot of grinning and diddly-bopping—but he couldn't do anything about his eyes. They hurt me to look at.

He'd done three years when they got him that night just after dinner and put a spoon fashioned into a knife straight up deep into his chest. There were three of them and they must have got all caught up in the frenzy of it because they didn't stop with stabbing him once—they stabbed him thirty-four times. "Savages," the warden said for the sake of the press.

So I left the force and started picking up bits as an actor and meanwhile I supported myself as a part-time security guard and private investigator.

Ryan wouldn't have been able to handle it, of course, my job. Listening to tapes of laughter and betrayal. Watching that particular type of smirk only adultery seems to produce.

No, Ryan wouldn't have been able to handle it at all.

The Phantom Pistol

•

Jack Adrian

*Britisher Jack Adrian wears many literary hats: essayist, book re-
viewer, archivist, bibliophile, editor, anthologist, writer of comic
strips, science fiction, war, horror, and mystery stories. His first
book, published in 1975, was a Sexton Blake thriller; and one of
his best anthologies,* Sexton Blake Wins *(1986), likewise features
the adventures of that long-lived British pulp sleuth. Adrian is an
authority on the works of Edgar Wallace, Sapper, and E. F. Benson,
and on the impossible-crime story. He puts his "impossible" knowledge to good use in "The Phantom Pistol," an atmospheric and
good-humored tale of the baffling murder of a 1912 stage magician
that is solved by a detective of rather more impressive credentials
than even Sexton Blake.*

On this chill November night fog rolled up from the River
Thames, a shifting, eddying blanket that insinuated itself inexora-
bly through the grimy streets of central London. It pulsed like a
living thing, moved by its own remorseless momentum—for there
was no wind—great banks of it surging across the metropolis, soot
and smoke from a hundred thousand chimneys adding to its murk.
Within an hour from the moment the faint tendrils of a river mist
had heralded its approach, the fog, like a dirty-ochre shroud, had
entombed the city.

Here, in the heart of the metropolis, in High Holborn, the rattle of hansom cab wheels, the raucous coughs of the newfangled
petrol-driven taxis, were muffled, the rumble of the crawling traffic
stifled as it edged and lurched its way along, the dim yellow light
of street lamps serving to obscure rather than illuminate. On the
pavements, slick with a slimy dew, hunched figures, only dimly
discerned, almost wraithlike, groped and shuffled along through

the gloom, an army of the newly blind, snuffling and hawking at the harsh, choking reek of soot and coalsmoke.

Yet only fifty yards away from the main thoroughfare, down a narrow side street that had not changed appreciably since Dr. Johnson's day, sodium flares fizzed and roared, powerful electric globes thrust back the muddy haze. For only a few feet, to be sure, yet enough to reveal the tarnished gilt portico of the Empire Palace of Varieties, a large poster outside announcing in bold scarlet lettering, two inches high, that here, and only here, were to be witnessed the dazzling deeds of the Great Golconda—illusionist *extraordinaire*!

Inside the theatre the atmosphere was just as miasmal, but here the fog was a blend of pungent penny cigars and the richer reeks of Larangas, Partagas, Corona-Coronas, and Hoyos de Monterrey, for the astonishing variety and ingenuity of the Great Golconda's baffling feats of prestidigitation fascinated the rich as well as the poor.

The Great Golconda was something of a democrat. He had consistently refused to perform in the gilded palaces that lined the Haymarket and Shaftesbury Avenue, preferring the smaller halls of the outer circuit. Thus whenever and wherever he appeared, rich men, dukes, earls, high-born ladies, and even (it was whispered) members of the Royal Family were forced to make the unaccustomed trek away from the gilt and glitter of London's West End to less salubrious haunts, there to mix with the lower orders—not to mention enjoy the unusual experience of paying half the price for twice the amount of entertainment. For certainly the Great Golconda was a magician and illusionist of quite extraordinary ability. It was even rumored that emissaries of Maskelyne and Devant—whose fame as illusionists was spread worldwide—had endeavored to lure his secrets away with fabulous amounts of money and, when these offers were spurned, had even gone so far as to try for them by less scrupulous methods.

Whether or not this was true, the Great Golconda stubbornly performed on the stages of the tattier music halls, and all kinds and conditions and classes of men and women flocked to see him, and to cheer him.

But tonight was a special night. The Great Golconda was retiring from the stage. This was to be positively his final performance.

Unusually, the act started the show. Normally, the Great Golconda and his assistant Mephisto came on for the last half hour of the first house and the last half hour of the second. As an act, nothing could follow it.

Tonight, however, the audience—restless at the thought of having to sit through the somewhat dubious hors d'oeuvres of jugglers, low comedians, soubrettes, and "Come-into-the-garden-Maud" baritones before getting down to the main course—sat up in eager anticipation as the curtain rose at last to reveal a totally bare stage with a black backcloth, from the center of which stared two enormous eyes woven in green and gold.

For several seconds there was utter silence, a total absence of movement—on the stage and off. Then the lights dimmed and the glowing figure of the Great Golconda himself could be seen—in black silk hat, long flowing cloak, arms folded across his chest—descending slowly from the darkness above the stage, apparently floating on air. Simultaneously, two more Golcondas, dressed exactly alike, marched towards the center of the stage from both left and right wings. Just before they met, there was a flash of white light, a loud bang, a puff of red smoke, and all three figures seemed to merge.

And there, standing alone, smiling a bit maliciously, stood the Great Golconda. The audience roared.

From then on, for the next twenty minutes, wonders did not cease.

White horses cantered across the boards, to disappear in a dazzling firework display; doves, peacocks, birds-of-paradise soared and strutted, all, seemingly, appearing from a small Chinese lacquered cabinet on a rostrum; a girl in sequinned tights pirouetted in midair, had her head sawn off by the Great Golconda's assistant Mephisto, then, carrying her head beneath her arm, climbed a length of rope and slowly vanished, like the smile of the Cheshire Cat, about thirty feet above the ground.

Part of the performance was what appeared to be a running battle between the Great Golconda and his assistant Mephisto. Mephisto made it plain he wanted to do things his way but invariably, like the sorcerer's apprentice, failed, the Great Golconda smoothly but sensationally saving the trick—whatever trick it happened to be—at the very last moment. Penultimately, Mephisto became so incensed at the Great Golconda's successes that he knocked him down, crammed and locked him into a four-foot-high oak sherry cask, and then proceeded to batter and smash it to pieces with a long-handled axe.

Triumphantly, he turned to the audience, his chalk-white, clown-like face (its pallor accentuated by the skin-tight black costume he wore, leaving only his face, neck, and arms below the elbows bare) leering malevolently—to be greeted by gales of laughter as the Great Golconda himself suddenly appeared from the wings behind him to tap him on the shoulder.

At last the stage was cleared for the final act. Mephisto was to fire a revolver at the Great Golconda, who would catch the bullet between his teeth.

Members of the audience were invited up to the front of the stage to examine the .45 service revolver and six bullets and vouch for their authenticity. Among them was a stocky, moustachioed man in his late forties, in frock coat and bowler hat, who clearly, from the professional way he handled the gun—flicking open the chamber, extracting the bullets, testing them between his teeth—had more than a little knowledge of firearms. The Great Golconda noticed this.

"You, sir!"

The stocky figure acknowledged this with an abrupt nod.

"You seem to know your way about a pistol, sir."

"I should do," admitted the man.

"May I enquire of your profession, sir?"

"You may. I'm a superintendent at Scotland Yard."

The Great Golconda was clearly delighted. Seen close up he was younger than the Scotland Yard man had supposed—perhaps in his midthirties. Something else he noted was the distinct resemblance between the Great Golconda and his assistant Mephisto, now standing to one side, his pasty white face impassive.

"And your name, sir?"

"Hopkins. Stanley Hopkins."

The Great Golconda bowed.

"A name that is not unknown to me from the newssheets, sir. Indeed, a name to be—ha-ha!—*conjured* with! And what is your professional opinion of the revolver, Superintendent?"

Still holding the bullets, Hopkins dry-fired the gun. The hammer fell with a loud 'click,' the chamber snapped round.

"Perfectly genuine."

"Preee-*cisely*!"

With a flourish of his cape, the Great Golconda handed the revolver to his assistant Mephisto and ushered the half dozen or so members of the audience off the stage.

213

The lights dimmed. Twin spots bathed the two men in two separate cones of light. They stood at the rear of the stage, against the black backcloth, about ten yards apart. All around them was utter darkness. From his seat Hopkins watched intently.

Mephisto, wearing black gloves now and holding the gun two-handed, raised his arms slowly into the air, high above his head. Hopkins, following the movement, could only just see the revolver, which was now above the circle of radiance surrounding Mephisto—then light glittered along the barrel as the assistant brought his hands back into the spotlight's glare and down, his arms held straight out. The revolver pointed directly at the Great Golconda.

It seemed to Hopkins that the Great Golconda's expression—up until then one of supercilious amusement—suddenly slipped. A look of mild puzzlement appeared on his face.

Hopkins glanced at the right-hand side of the stage but could see nothing but darkness. At that moment there was the oddly muted crack of a shot, and Hopkins, his eyes already turning back to the Great Golconda, saw the illusionist cry out and throw up his arms, then fall to the floor.

There was a stunned silence.

Even from where he was sitting, the Scotland Yard man could see plainly that around the Great Golconda's mouth were scarlet splashes, where none had been before.

Then the screaming started.

Mr. Robert Adey, the manager of the Empire Music Hall, looked as though he was on the verge of an apoplexy. His face was red, his mouth gaped, his mutton-chop whiskers quivered with emotion.

He stuttered, "It . . . it *couldn't* have happened!"

"But it did," Superintendent Stanley Hopkins said bluntly.

They were on the stage of the now-empty theatre. Even with all the stagelights up and the crystal chandeliers blazing over the auditorium, there was a desolate air about the place; shadows still gathered thickly in the wings, and above, beams and struts and spars could only just be glimpsed.

Since the shocking death of the Great Golconda—whose body now lay under a rug where it had fallen—nearly an hour had elapsed. During that time an extraordinary fact had emerged: although the Great Golconda had been shot, his assistant Mephisto (now detained in his dressing room) could not have shot him. Of that, there seemed not a doubt.

And yet neither could anyone else.

Adey—with a slight West Midlands twang to his voice—gabbled, "It . . . it's utterly inexplicable!"

"This is 1912," said a sharp voice behind him. "*Nothing* is inexplicable."

Adey turned. The man who had spoken—a tall, thin, almost gaunt individual of sixty or so, with a high forehead, dark hair shot with gray, an aquiline nose, and eyes that seemed to pierce and probe and dissect all that they looked upon—had accompanied Hopkins up to the stage when the theatre had been cleared. Adey had no idea who he was.

"A colleague?" he muttered to the Scotland Yard man.

"Just a friend," said Hopkins, "a very old friend. We're both interested in the impossible—why we're here tonight. The Great Golconda's illusions had certain . . ." he glanced at his friend ". . . points of interest."

"Although many, I fancy, were accomplished with the aid of certain kinematic devices," said the older man. "The girl in the sequinned tights, for example—a lifelike image only, I take it."

Adey nodded uneasily.

"Of course, I know very little about how he managed his tricks. Magicians are a close-mouthed bunch. This one in particular. He was adamant that during his act both wings should be blocked off, so no one—not even the stagehands—could see what he was doing. Always worried people were trying to pinch his tricks. Of course, he had to have some assistance in erecting certain items on stage, but all the preliminary construction work was done by him and his brother."

"Mephisto," said Hopkins.

"Yes. Their real name was Forbes-Sempill. Golconda was Rupert, Mephisto Ernest. They were twins—not identical. Rupert was the elder by fifteen minutes . . ." Adey's voice sank to a worried mumble. "That was half the trouble."

"The reason why the Great Golconda was retiring from the stage?" said the gaunt man. "The baronetcy, and the 200,000 pounds?"

Adey stared at him, open-mouthed.

"How the devil did you know that?"

"Ah," Hopkins said waggishly, "my friend here keeps his finger on the pulse of great events—don't you, Mr. H?"

The older man permitted himself a thin smile.

"Now *you* tell us about the baronetcy, and all them sovs," said the Scotland Yard detective.

Adey shrugged his shoulders.

"Both Rupert and Ernest had a row with their family years ago. Left the ancestral home—somewhere in Scotland, I believe—never," he smiled faintly, "to darken its doors again. But their father's recently died, and Rupert succeeded to the title, estates, and money. It's as simple as that, although it wasn't generally known."

"I take it," said the gaunt old man, "that Ernest disliked his brother?"

"Ernest *hated* Rupert. Made no secret of the fact. One of the reasons their act went down so well—Ernest communicated that hatred to the audience. Rupert didn't object. Said it added spice to the performance. I don't see it myself, but it seemed to work."

"Doubtless the new Viennese school of mind analysis could explain that," said the older man dryly, "but for the time being I am far more interested in why Mephisto should for no apparent reason have donned black gloves to fire his revolver tonight."

"So he did," said Adey, in a surprised tone. "But how . . . ?"

"This is not the first time we have seen the Great Golconda perform. As Mr. Hopkins implied, his act was an unusual one, and I have always had an interest in the more sensational aspects of popular culture." The gaunt old man's eyes took on a faraway, introspective look. "On previous occasions Mephisto fired his revolver bare-handed. That he did not this time seems to me to be a matter of some significance."

"But the *weapon*, Mr. H!" said Hopkins, almost violently. "We now know what ought to have happened. The real revolver is shown to the audience. It's stone-cold genuine. But when Golconda hands the gun to Mephisto—flourishing his cloak and all—he's already substituted it for another gun—one that only fires blank shots. The real gun is now hidden in his cloak. Mephisto fires the fake gun at him and he pretends to catch the bullet, which is already in his mouth, between his teeth. Simple!"

"Except that this time he falls dead with a bullet in his head."

"*From a phantom pistol!*" exploded Hopkins. "The gun Mephisto held in his hands didn't fire that bullet—*couldn't* fire that bullet! The real gun was still in the folds of the Great Golconda's cloak—so that's out, too! He wasn't killed by someone firing from the wings, because the wings were blocked off! Nor through the backcloth, because there ain't no hole! Nor from above or from the audience, because the bullet went into his head in a straight line through his mouth!"

Here Adey broke in excitedly.

"It's as I said—inexplicable! Indeed, downright *impossible*!"

The gaunt old man shot him a darkly amused look.

"In my experience, Mr. Adey, the more bizarre and impossible the occurrence, the less mysterious it will in the end prove to be."

"That's all very well, sir," said the manager a bit snappishly, "but facts are facts! The entire audience was watching Mephisto. When Golconda fell dead, all Mephisto did was drop the revolver he was holding and stand there gaping. Let's say for the sake of argument he had another weapon. What did he do with it? Damn it, sir, he didn't move an inch from where he was standing, nor did he make any violent gesture, as though to throw it away from him. We've searched the entire stage. We've even searched him—not that that was at all necessary because his costume's so skin-tight you couldn't hide a button on him without it bulging."

"Perhaps," said the older man slowly, "he didn't need to throw it away."

"Didn't need?" Adey's voice rose to an outraged squeak. "You'll be telling me next he popped it into his mouth and ate it!"

"By no means as outrageous a suggestion as you might imagine," said the gaunt old man sternly. He turned to the Scotland Yard detective. "You will recall, Hopkins, the case of the abominable Italian vendettist, Pronzini, who did just that."

Hopkins nodded sagely. The older man began to pace up and down the stage, gazing at the sable backcloth.

"Notice how black it is," he murmured, gesturing at the curtain. "How very black . . ." He swung around on Adey again. "Apart from the incident of the gloves, is there anything else to which you might wish to draw our attention?"

"Anything else?"

"Anything unusual."

Adey's honest face assumed a perplexed expression.

"Well . . . no, I don't believe so."

"The placing of the Great Golconda's act, for example?"

"Oh. Why, yes! Right at the beginning, you mean? That was unusual. They did have a bit of a barney about that. It was Mephisto's idea—begin the show and end it, he said. Golconda finally agreed."

"Nothing else?"

"Not that I can . . ."

"I noticed that tonight they both stood at the rear of the stage. Did they not normally stand at the front?"

"Well, yes. Now you come to . . ."

"You will forgive my saying so, Mr. Adey," there was a touch of asperity in the old man's voice, "but your powers of observation are somewhat limited."

"You believe Mephisto killed Golconda?" said Hopkins.

"I am convinced of it."

"Then we'd better have a chat with him."

The older man smiled frostily.

"That will not be necessary. You have a stepladder?" he enquired of Adey. "Bring it on."

"Stepladder?" muttered Hopkins. "You think there's something up top?"

"Of course. There has to be. A second gun. Golconda was killed by a bullet. Bullets, for the most part, are shot from guns. Golconda's revolver was incapable of shooting anything, only of making a noise. Thus . . ."

The Scotland Yard man interrupted. "Ah. But. Wait on, Mr. H. These two were masters of illusion, am I correct?"

"Certainly."

"But when you get right down to it, their illusions, like all illusions, are fake. Created. Constructed."

"To be sure."

"So this here Mephisto needn't have used a gun at all. He was a clever fellow. Could've built some kind of weapon that fired a bullet, and . . ." He stopped as a thought struck him. "Here, remember the to-do you once had with that tiger-potting colonel. Now *he* had a special shooter."

"Indeed, an air-gun constructed by a German mechanic who, though blind, had a genius for invention." The old man smiled a skeletal smile. "But you miss the point entirely, my dear Hopkins. It matters not *what* the weapon is, but *where* it is. That is the nub of the problem. We have searched everywhere, eliminated everything, on this level. As we must inevitably strike out from our enquiry any suggestion of magic, the inexorable conclusion we must come to is that the weapon—whatever it is—must be above us."

Hopkins struck the palm of his hand with a clenched fist. "But it can't be! Mephisto stood stock-still the whole time. We *know* he didn't chuck anything into the air."

"As I remarked before, perhaps he did not need to . . ."

By this time the heavy wheeled ladder had been trundled on and heaved to the center of the stage. A stagehand climbed into the darkness above.

"Merely look for anything that seems out of the ordinary," the old man directed.

In less than a minute the stagehand was calling out excitedly. "Something here . . . wound round one of the spars on—why, it's elasticated cord!"

"Unwind it. Let it drop."

Seconds later a small object fell through the air, then bounced upwards again as the cord reached its nadir. The old man stretched up and caught it before it could fly out of reach. He turned to the watchers.

"What do you see?"

Hopkins frowned.

"Not a thing."

The old man opened his fingers.

"Come closer."

The Scotland Yard detective stepped forward, his expression turning to one of amazement. Gripped in the gaunt old man's hand—clearly seen against the white of his skin—was a miniature chamberless pistol, perhaps five inches long from grip to muzzle, painted entirely matt-black. The old man pressed at the bottom of the stock and the barrel slid forward, revealing a two-inch cavity.

"A Williamson derringer pistol, capable of firing one shot only—quite enough to kill a man," said the old man dryly. "Hand me the false pistol."

He held the blank-firing pistol in his left hand with the derringer gripped in his right, leveling both at an imaginary target. From the side all that could be seen was the massive bulk of the service revolver. Then he clicked the triggers of both guns and opened his right hand. The derringer, at the end of the taut elasticated cord—totally invisible against the black backcloth—flew upwards into the darkness above, whipping round and round the high spar to which it was attached.

Adey looked utterly at sea.

"But how did you . . . what made you . . . ?" he babbled.

"When three singular variations in a set routine—the black

gloves, the change of position not only of the act itself but of the two principals on the stage in that act—take place," said the old man a trifle testily, "one is tempted, to use the vernacular, to smell a rat. After that, it is a matter of simple deduction. The gift of observation—sadly lacking in the general populace—allied to intuition. Believe me, there is really no combination of events—however inexplicable on the surface—for which the wit of man cannot conceive an elucidation."

He began to pace up and down the stage again, his hands clasped firmly behind his back.

"Mephisto tied the derringer to the spar, letting it hang down just within reach of his outstretched arm. It could not be seen because he had painted it black and hung it close to the black curtain. In any case, the lighting was subdued. Even so, there was the risk of someone spotting it, so he persuaded his brother that their act should start the show. Came the climax of the performance. The two spotlights only lit up the area within their twin beams. Mephisto raised his arms, holding the false revolver, until his hands were just above the spotlight's glare. He had positioned himself perfectly—no doubt he rehearsed the entire sequence thoroughly—and the hanging derringer was now within inches of his right hand. If his hands had been bare, one might possibly have noticed that he was holding something else, but he took the precaution of wearing black gloves, thereby making assurance double sure. Grasping the derringer, he pulled it down on its elasticated thread, pressing it to the side of the much larger weapon, as his arms dropped to the leveled-off position. He was now holding not one, but *two* guns—one hidden from the audience's view and in any case virtually invisible. Except to the man at whom he was pointing them."

"Yes!" snapped Hopkins. "That's what made Golconda look surprised. I thought he'd seen something *behind* Mephisto."

"Mephisto then fired the derringer, releasing his grip on the gun, which shot up into the air. All eyes were on Golconda falling to the floor. The derringer wound itself round the spar to which its cord was attached. In the confusion afterwards, doubtless, Mephisto meant to get rid of the evidence. What he did not reckon on was the presence of a Scotland Yard detective who would immediately take charge of the proceedings and confine him to his dressing room. But in the meantime there was absolutely nothing to show that he had just murdered his brother in cold blood. It was as though," the old man finished, shrugging, "the Great Golconda had indeed been shot with a phantom pistol."

"And being next in line," said Hopkins, "Mephisto would've stepped into the baronetcy and all them lovely golden sovs. Nice work, Mr. H. Nice work, indeed!"

Storm

•

Ed McBain

Acclaimed worldwide for the authenticity of the police work they depict, the 87th Precinct novels of Ed McBain (Evan Hunter) now number more than forty. The first, Cop Hater, *appeared in 1956; outstanding among those that have followed are* Killer's Wedge *(1959),* He Who Hesitates *(1965),* Fuzz *(1968),* Sadie When She Died *(1972), and* Ghosts *(1980). One of the familiar names among the cops of the 87th Squad is Cotton Hawes, and it is Hawes who does the detecting in the suspenseful novelette that follows. The scene, however, is not the crowded urban streets that are his usual bailiwick, but the snowy mountains of New England where a double murder spoils what was to have a been a romantic ski weekend.*

The girl with Cotton Hawes had cold feet.

He didn't know what to do about her feet because he'd already tried everything he could think of, and they were still cold. He had to admit that driving in subzero temperatures with a storm some fifteen minutes behind him wasn't exactly conducive to warm pedal extremities. But he had turned the car heater up full, supplied the girl with a blanket, taken off his overcoat and wrapped that around her—and she still had cold feet.

The girl's name was Blanche Colby, a very nice euphonic name, which she had adopted the moment she entered show business. That had been a long time ago. Blanche's real name was Bertha Cooley, but a press agent those many years back told her that Bertha Cooley sounded like a mentholated Pullman, and not a dancer. Blanche Colby had class, he told her, and if there was one thing Bertha Cooley wanted, it was class. She had taken the new name and gone into the chorus of a hit musical twenty-two years ago, when she was only fifteen. She was now thirty-seven, but all those years of prancing the boards had left her with a youthful body, lithe

222

and long-legged. She was still, with a slight assist from Clairol, a soft honey-blonde. Her green eyes were intelligent and alert. Her feet, unfortunately, *ahhhh*, her feet.

"How are they now?" he asked her.

"Freezing," she said.

"We're almost there," Hawes told her. "You'll like this place. One of the guys on the squad—Hal Willis—comes up here almost every weekend he's off. He says the skiing is great."

"I know a dancer who broke her leg in Switzerland," Blanche said.

"Skiing?"

"Sure, skiing."

"You've never skied before?"

"Never."

"Well . . . ." Hawes shrugged. "Well, I don't think you'll break any legs."

"That's reassuring," Blanche said. She glanced through the window on her side of the car. "I think that storm is catching up to us."

"Just a few flurries."

"I wonder how serious it'll be. I have a rehearsal Monday night."

"Four to six inches, they said. That's not very much."

"Will the roads be open?"

"Sure. Don't worry."

"I know a dancer who got snowed in for six days in Vermont," Blanche said. "It wouldn't have been so bad, but she was with a Method actor."

"Well, I'm a cop," Hawes said.

"Yeah," Blanche answered noncommittally.

They were silent for several moments. The light snow flurries drifted across the road, turning it into a dreamlike, white, flowing stream. The headlights illuminated the shifting macadam. Sitting behind the wheel, Hawes had the peculiar feeling that the road was melting. He was glad to see the sign for Rawson Mountain Inn. He stopped the car, picking out the sign from the tangle of other signs announcing accommodations in the area. He set the car in motion again, turning left over an old wooden bridge, the timbers creaking as the convertible passed over them. A new sign, blatant red and white, shouted the features of the area—a 1,600-foot mountain, two chair lifts, a T-Bar, a rope tow, and, definitely not needed with a storm on the way, a snow-making machine.

FELONIOUS ASSAULTS

The inn lay nestled in the foothills at the base of the mountain. The trees around the inn were bare, standing in gaunt silhouette against the snow-threatening sky. Snow-nuzzled lights beckoned warmly. He helped Blanche out of the car, put on his overcoat, and walked with her over old packed snow to the entrance. They stamped their feet in the doorway and entered the huge room. A fire was going at one end of the room. Someone was playing the piano. A handful of tired weekday skiers were sprawled around the fireplace, wearing very fashionable afterski boots and sweaters, drinking from bottles onto which they'd hand-lettered their names. Blanche went directly to the fire, found a place on one of the couches, and stretched her long legs to the blaze. Hawes found the desk, tapped a bell on it, and waited. No one appeared. He tapped the bell again. A skier passing the desk said, "He's in the office. Over there on your left."

Hawes nodded, found the door marked OFFICE, and knocked on it. A voice inside called, "Yes, come in," and Hawes twisted the knob and entered.

The office was larger than he'd expected, a good fifteen feet separating the entrance door from the desk at the opposite end of the room. A man in his late twenties sat behind the desk. He had dark hair and dark brows pulled low over deep brown eyes. He was wearing a white shirt open at the throat, a bold reindeer-imprinted sweater over it. He was also wearing a plaster cast on his right leg. The leg was stretched out stiffly in front of him, the foot resting on a low ottoman. A pair of crutches leaned against the desk, within easy reach of his hands. Hawes was suddenly glad he'd left Blanche by the fire.

"You're not a new skier, I hope," the man said.

"No, I'm not."

"Good. Some of them get scared by the cast and crutches."

"Was it a skiing accident?" Hawes asked.

The man nodded. "Spiral break of the tibia and fibula. Someone forgot to fill in a sitzmark. I was going pretty fast, and when I hit the hole . . ." He shrugged. "I won't be able to walk without the crutches for at least another month."

"That's too bad," Hawes said. He paused, and then figured he might as well get down to business. "I have a reservation," he said. "Adjoining rooms with bath."

"Yes, sir. What was the name on that?"

"Cotton Hawes and Blanche Colby."

224

Storm

The man opened a drawer in his desk and consulted a typewritten sheet. "Yes, sir," he said. "Two rooms in the annex."

"The annex?" Hawes said. "Where's that?"

"Oh, just a hundred yards or so from the main building, sir."

"Oh. Well, I guess that'll be . . ."

"And that's *one* bath, you understand."

"What do you mean?"

"They're adjoining rooms, but the bathroom is in 104. 105 doesn't have a bath."

"Oh. Well, I'd like two rooms that *do* have baths," Hawes said, smiling.

"I'm sorry, sir. 104 and 105 are the only available rooms in the house."

"The fellow I spoke to on the phone . . ."

"Yes, sir, that's me. Elmer Wollender."

"How do you do?" Hawes said. "You told me both rooms had baths."

"No, sir. You said you wanted adjoining rooms with bath, and I said I could give you adjoining rooms with bath. And that's what I've given you. Bath. Singular."

"Are you a lawyer, Mr. Wollender?" Hawes asked, no longer smiling.

"No, sir. Out of season, I'm a locksmith."

"What are you in season?"

"Why, a hotel-keeper, sir," Wollender said.

"Don't test the theory," Hawes answered. "Let me have my deposit back, Mr. Wollender. We'll find another place to stay."

"Well, sir, to begin with, we can't make any cash refunds, but we'll be happy to keep your deposit here against another time when you may wish . . ."

"Look, Mr. Wollender," Hawes said menacingly, "I don't know what kind of a . . ."

"And of course, sir, there *are* lots of places to stay here in town, but none of them, sir, *none* of them have any private baths at all. Now if you don't mind walking down the hall . . ."

"All I know is . . ."

". . . and sharing the john with a hundred other skiers, why then . . ."

"You told me on the phone . . ."

"I'm sure you can find other accommodations. The *lady*, how-

225

ever, might enjoy a little privacy.'' Wollender waited while Hawes considered.

"If I give her 104 . . .'' Hawes started and then paused. "Is that the room with the bath?''

"Yes, sir, 104.''

"If I give her that room, where's the bath for 105?''

"Down at the end of the hall, sir. And we *are* right at the base of the mountain, sir, and the skiing *has* been excellent, and we're expecting at least twelve inches of fresh powder.''

"The radio said four to six.''

"That's in the city, sir. We normally get a lot more snow.''

"Like what I got on the phone?'' Hawes asked. "Where do I sign?''

2.

Cotton Hawes was a detective, and as a member of the 87th Squad he had flopped down in a great many desirable and undesirable rooms throughout the city and its suburbs. Once, while posing as a dock walloper, he had taken a furnished room overlooking the River Harb, and had been surprised during the night by what sounded like a band of midgets marching at the foot of his bed. The midgets turned out to be giants, or at least giants of the species *Rattus muridae*—or as they say in English, rats. He had turned on the light and picked up a broom, but those brazen rat bastards had reared back on their hind legs like boxers and bared their teeth, and he was certain the pack of them would leap for his throat. He had checked out immediately.

There were no rats in rooms 104 and 105 of the annex to Rawson Mountain Inn. Nor was there very much of anything else, either. Whoever had designed the accommodations was undoubtedly steeped in Spartan philosophy. The walls were white and bare, save for a single skiing poster over each bed. There was a single bed in each room, and a wooden dresser painted white. A portable cardboard clothes closet nestled in the corner of each room. The room Hawes hoped to occupy, the one without the bath, was excruciatingly hot, the vents sending in great waves of heated air. The room with the bath, Blanche's room, was unbearably cold. The single window was rimmed with frost, the floor was cold, the bed was cold, the heating ducts and vents were either clogged or blocked, but certainly inoperative.

"And *I'm* the one with the cold feet," Blanche said.

"I'd let you have the heated room," Hawes said gallantly, "but this is the one with the bath."

"Well, we'll manage," Blanche said. "Shall we go down for the bags?"

"I'll get them," Hawes answered. "Stay in my room for now, will you? There's no sense freezing in here."

"I may get to like your room," Blanche said archly, and then turned and walked past him through the connecting door.

He went down the long flight of steps to the front porch, and then beyond to where the car was parked. The rooms were over the ski shop, which was closed for the night now, silent and dark. He took the two valises out of the trunk, and then pulled his skis from the rack on top of the car. He was not a particularly distrustful man, but a pair of Head skis had been stolen from him the season before, and he'd been a cop long enough to know that lightning sometimes *did* strike twice in the same place. In his right hand, and under his right arm, he carried the two bags. In his left hand, and under his left arm, he carried his skis and his boots. He struggled through the deepening snow and onto the front porch. He was about to put down the bags in order to open the door when he heard the heavy thud of ski boots on the steps inside. Someone was coming down those steps in a hell of a hurry.

The door opened suddenly, and a tall thin man wearing black ski pants and a black-hooded parka came onto the porch, almost colliding with Hawes. His face was narrow, handsome in a fine-honed way, the sharply hooked nose giving it the edged striking appearance of an ax. Even in the pale light filtering from the hallway, Hawes saw that the man was deeply tanned, and automatically assumed he was an instructor. The guess was corroborated by the Rawson Mountain insignia on the man's right sleeve, an interlocking R and M in bright red letters. Incongruously, the man was carrying a pair of white figure skates in his left hand.

"Oh, I'm sorry," he said. His face broke into a grin. He had spoken with an accent, German or Swedish, Hawes couldn't tell which.

"That's all right," Hawes said.

"May I help you?"

"No, I think I can manage. If you'd just hold the door open for me . . ."

"It will be my pleasure," the man said, and he almost clicked his heels together.

"Has the skiing been good?" Hawes asked as he struggled through the narrow doorway.

"Fairly good," the man answered. "It will be better tomorrow."

"Well, thanks," Hawes said.

"My pleasure."

"See you on the mountain," Hawes said cheerfully and continued up the steps. There was something slightly ridiculous about the entire situation, the adjoining rooms with only one bath, the pristine cells the rooms had turned out to be, the heat in one, the cold in the other, the fact that they were over the ski shop, the fact that it had begun snowing very heavily, even the hurried ski instructor with his polite Teutonic manners and his guttural voice and his figure skates, there was something faintly reminiscent of farce about the whole setup. He began chuckling as he climbed the steps. When he came into his room, Blanche was stretched out on his bed. He put down the bags.

"What's so funny?" she asked.

"I've decided this is a comic-opera hotel," Hawes said. "I'll bet the mountain out there is only a backdrop. We'll go out there tomorrow morning and discover it's painted on canvas."

"This room is nice and warm," Blanche said.

"Yes, it is," Hawes answered. He slid his skis under the bed, and she watched him silently.

"Are you expecting burglars?"

"You never can tell." He took off his jacket and pulled his holstered service revolver from his back hip pocket.

"You going to wear that on the slopes tomorrow?" Blanche asked.

"No. You can't get a gun into those zippered pockets."

"I think I'll stay in *this* room tonight," Blanche said suddenly.

"Whatever you like," Hawes said. "I'll take the icebox next door."

"Well, actually," she said, "that wasn't exactly what I had in mind."

"Huh?"

"Don't detectives kiss people?"

"Huh?"

"We've been out twice together in the city, and we've just driven

228

three hours alone together in a car, and you've never once tried to kiss me.''

"Well, I . . ."

"I wish you would," Blanche said thoughtfully. "Unless, of course, there's a department regulation against it."

"None that I can think of," Hawes said.

Blanche, her hands behind her head, her legs stretched luxuriously, suddenly took a deep breath and said, "I think I'm going to like this place."

3.

There were sounds in the night.

Huddled together in the single bed, the first sound of which they were aware was the noise of the oil burner. At regularly spaced intervals, the thermostat would click, and there would be a thirty-second pause, and then a 707 jet aircraft would take off from the basement of the old wooden building. Hawes had never heard a noisier oil burner in his life. The aluminum ducts and vents provided a symphony all their own, too, expanding, contracting, banging, clanking, sighing, exhaling, whooshing. Down the hall, the toilet would be flushed every now and again, the noise sounding with cataract sharpness on the still mountain air.

There was another noise. A rasping sound, the narrow shrill squeak of metal upon metal. He got out of bed and went to the window. A light was burning in the ski shop below, casting a yellow rectangle onto the snow. Sighing, he went back to bed and tried to sleep.

Down the corridor, there was the constant thud of ski boots as guests returned to their rooms, the slamming of doors, the occasional high giggle of a girl skier intoxicated by the mountain air.

Voices.

". . . will mean a slower track for the slalom . . ."

"Sure, but everyone'll have the same handicap . . ."

Fading.

More voices.

". . . don't even think they'll open the upper trails."

"They have to, don't they?"

"Not Dead Man's Fall. They won't even be able to get up there with all this snow. Seventeen inches already, and no end in sight."

The 707 taking off again from the basement. The vents beginning their orchestral suite, the ducts supplying counterpoint. And more voices, raised in anger.

". . . because he thinks he's God almighty!"

"I tell you you're imagining things."

"I'm warning you! Stay away from him!"

A young girl's laughter.

"I'm warning you. If I see him . . ."

Fading.

At two o'clock in the morning, the Cats started up the mountain. They sounded like Rommel's mechanized cavalry. Hawes was certain they would knock down the outside walls and come lumbering into the room. Blanche began giggling.

"This is the noisiest hotel I've ever slept in," she said.

"How are your feet?"

"Nice and warm. You're a very warm man."

"You're a very warm girl."

"Do you mind my sleeping in long johns?"

"I thought they were leotards."

"Leotard is singular," Blanche said.

"Singular or plural, those are the sexiest long johns I've ever seen."

"It's only the girl in them," Blanche said modestly. "Why don't you kiss me again?"

"I will. In a minute."

"What are you listening for?"

"I thought I heard an unscheduled flight a moment ago."

"What?"

"Didn't you hear it? A funny buzzing sound?"

"There are so many noises . . ."

"Shhhh."

They were silent for several moments. They could hear the Cats grinding their way up the mountain. Someone down the hall flushed the toilet. More boots in the corridor outside.

"Hey!" Blanche said.

"What?"

"You asleep?"

"No," Hawes answered.

"That buzzing sound you heard?"

"Yes?"

"It was my blood," she told him, and she kissed him on the mouth.

4.

It was still snowing on Saturday morning. The promised storm had turned into a full-fledged blizzard. They dressed in the warm comfort of the room, Blanche putting on thermal underwear, and then two sweaters and stretch pants, the extra clothing padding out her slender figure. Hawes, standing six feet two inches tall in his double-stockinged feet, black pants and black sweater, presented a one-hundred-and-ninety pound V-shaped silhouette to the window and the gray day outside.

"Do you think I'll get back in time for Monday night's rehearsal?" Blanche asked.

"I don't know. I'm supposed to be back at the squad by six tomorrow night. I wonder if the roads are open."

They learned during breakfast that a state of emergency had been declared in the city and in most of the towns lining the upstate route. Blanche seemed blithely indifferent to the concept of being snowbound. "If there's that much snow," she said, "they'll cancel the rehearsal, anyway."

"They won't cancel the police department," Hawes said.

"The hell with it," Blanche said happily. "We're here now, and there's marvelous snow, and if the skiing is good it'll be a wonderful weekend."

"Even if the skiing is *lousy*," Hawes said, "it'll be a wonderful weekend."

They rented boots and skis for her in the ski rental shop, and then took to the mountain. Both chair lifts were in operation, but as one of the midnight voices had prophesied, the upper trails were not yet opened. A strong wind had arisen, and it blew the snow in driving white sheets across the slopes. Hawes took Blanche to the rope tow first, had her practice climbing for a while, teaching her to edge and to herringbone, and then illustrated the use of the tow—left hand clamped around the rope, right hand and arm behind the back and gripping the rope. The beginner's slope was a gentle one, but Blanche seemed immediately capable of more difficult skiing. She was a trained dancer, and she automatically thought of the skis as part of a difficult stage costume, encumbering movement, but simply something to overcome. With remarkable co-ordination, she learned how to snowplow on the beginner's slope. By mid-morning, she had graduated to the T-Bar, and was beginning to learn the rudiments of the stem christie. Hawes patiently stayed with her all morning, restricting his own skiing to the elementary slopes. He was becoming more and more grateful for the snow-clogged roads. With the roads impassable, the number of weekend skiers was limited; he and Blanche were enjoying weekday skiing on a Saturday, and the fresh snow made everything a delight.

After lunch, she suggested that he leave her alone to practice for a while. Hawes, who was itching to get at the chair lift and the real trails, nonetheless protested that he was perfectly content to ski with her on the baby slopes. But Blanche insisted, and he finally left her on the slope serviced by the T-Bar, and went to the longest of the chair lifts, Lift A.

He grinned unconsciously as he approached the lift. Eight or ten skiers were waiting to use the chairs, as compared to the long lines one usually encountered on weekends. As he approached the loading area, he caught a blur of black movement from the corner of his eye, turned and saw his German or Swedish ski instructor from the night before *wedeln* down the mountain, and then turning, parallel in a snow-spraying stop near the lift. He did not seem to recognize Hawes, but Hawes was not at all surprised. Every skier on the line was wearing a hooded parka, the hoods covering their heads and tied securely beneath their chins. In addition, all the skiers were wearing goggles, most with tinted yellow lenses in defense against the grayness of the day, some with darker lenses in spite of the grayness. The result, in any case, was almost total anonymity. Male and female, they all looked very much alike. They could have been a band of Martians waiting to be taken to a leader. Instead, they were waiting for chairs. They did not have to wait very long.

The chairs on their cable kept rounding the bend, came past the grinding machinery. Hawes moved into position, watched the girl ahead of him sit abruptly as the chair came up under her behind. He noticed that the chair gave a decided lurch as it cleared the platform, and he braced himself for the expected force, glanced back over his shoulder as another chair rounded the turn. Ski poles clutched in his left hand, his right hand behind him to grip the edge of the chair as it approached, he waited. The chair was faster and had a stronger lurch than he'd anticipated. For a moment, he thought it would knock him down. He gripped the edge of the seat with his mittened right hand, felt himself sliding off the seat, and automatically grabbed for the upright supporting rod with his left hand, dropping his poles.

"Dropped your poles!" one of the loaders shouted behind him. "We'll send them up!" the other loader called.

He turned slightly in the chair and looked back. He could see one of the loaders scrambling to pick up his poles. There were two empty chairs behind him, and then a skier got into the third chair, and the loader handed him the poles Hawes had dropped. Behind that chair, two other skiers shared a chair. The wind and the snow made it difficult to see. Hawes turned his head abruptly, but the wind was even stronger coming down the mountain. The chair ahead of him was perhaps thirty feet away, but he could barely make out the shadowy figure of the person sitting in it. All he saw was a dim silhouette obscured by blinding snow and keening wind. He could feel snow seeping under the edges of his hood. He took off his mittens and tightened the string. Quickly, before the biting cold numbed his fingers, he put the mittens on again.

The lift was a new one, and it pulled the chairs silently up the mountain. On his right, Hawes could see the skiers descending, a damn fool snowplowing out of control down a steep embankment pocked with moguls, an excellent skier navigating turns in parallel precision. The wind keened around and under his hood, the only sound on the mountain. The ride was a pleasant one, except for the wind and the cold. In some spots, the chair was suspended some thirty feet above the snow below. In other places, the chair came as close as six feet to the ground. He was beginning to anticipate the descent. He saw the unloading station ahead, saw the sign advising him to keep the tips of his skis up, and prepared to disembark. The skier ahead of him met with difficulty as he tried to get off his chair. The snow had been falling too heavily to clear, and there was no natural downgrade at the top of the lift; the chair followed its occupant, rather than rising overhead at the unloading point. The girl ahead of Hawes was almost knocked off her feet by her own chair. She managed to free herself as the chair gave a sharp lurch around the bend to begin its trip down the mountain again. Hawes concentrated on getting off the chair. Surprisingly, he did so with a minimum of effort and without poles, and then waited while the two empty chairs passed by. The third following chair approached the station. A man clambered off the chair, handed Hawes his poles with a "These yours?" and skied to the crest of the slope. Hawes stood just outside the station booth, hanging his poles over his wrists. He was certain that the fourth chair behind his had contained *two* skiers at the bottom of the lift, and yet it seemed to be approaching now with only a single person in it. Hawes squinted through the snow, puzzled. Something seemed odd about the person in the fourth chair, something was jutting into the air at a curious angle—a ski? a leg? a . . . ?

The chair approached rapidly.

The skier made no move to disembark.

Hawes opened his eyes wide behind his yellow-tinted goggles as the chair swept past the station.

Through the driving snow, he had seen a skier slumped back into the passing chair, gloved hands dangling limply. And sticking out of the skier's chest at a malicious angle over the heart, buffeted by the wind and snow so that it trembled as if it were alive, thrust deep through the parka and the clothing beneath it like an over-sized, slender aluminum sword, was a ski pole.

5.

The chair gave its sharp lurch as it rounded the bend.

The skier slid from the seat as the chair made its abrupt turn. Skis touched snow, the body fell forward, there was a terrible snapping sound over the keening of the wind, and Hawes knew instantly that a leg had been broken as bone yielded to the unresisting laminated wood and the viselike binding. The skier fell face downward, the ski pole bending as the body struck the snow, one leg twisted at an impossible angle, the boot still held firmly in its binding.

For a moment, there was only confusion compounded.

The wind and the snow filled the air, the body lay motionless, face down in the snow as the chair whipped around the turn and started its descent. An empty chair swept past, another, a third, and then a chair came into view with a man poised to disembark, and Hawes shouted to the booth attendant, "Stop the lift!"

"What?"

"Stop the goddamn lift!"

"What? What?"

Hawes moved toward the body lying in the snow just as the man on the chair decided to get off. They collided in a tangle of poles and skis, the relentless chair pushing them along like a bulldozer, sending them sprawling onto the body in the snow, before it snapped around for its downward passage. The booth attendant finally got the message. He ran into the small wooden shack and threw the control switch. The lift stopped. There was a deeper silence on the mountain.

"You okay?" he called.

"I'm fine," Hawes said. He got to his feet and quickly unsnapped his bindings. The man who'd knocked him down was apologizing profusely, but Hawes wasn't listening. There was a bright red stain spreading into the snow where the impaled skier had fallen. He turned the body over and saw the ashen face and sightless eyes, saw the blood-soaked parka where the pole had been pushed through the soft and curving breast into the heart.

The dead skier was a young girl, no more than nineteen years old.

On the right sleeve of her black parka was the insignia of a Rawson Mountain ski instructor, the interlocking R and M in red as bright as the blood which seeped into the thirsty snow.

"What is it?" the booth attendant shouted. "Shall I get the ski patrol? Is it an accident?"

"It's no accident," Hawes said, but his voice was so low that no one heard him.

6.

As befitted this farcical hotel in this comic-opera town, the police were a band of Keystone cops led by an inept sheriff who worked on the premise that a thing worth doing was a thing worth doing badly. Hawes stood by helplessly as he watched these crackerbarrel cops violate each and every rule of investigation, watched as they mishandled evidence, watched as they made it hopelessly impossible to gain any information at all from whatever slender clues were available.

The sheriff was a gangling oaf named Theodore Watt who, instead of putting Lift A out of commission instantly while his men tried to locate the victim's chair, instead rode that very lift to the top of the mountain, followed by at least three dozen skiers, hotel officials, reporters, and local cretins who undoubtedly smeared any latent prints lingering on *any* of the chairs, and made the task of reconstructing the crime almost impossible. One girl, wearing bright lavender stretch pants and a white parka, climbed off the chair near the booth and was promptly informed there was blood all over the seat of her pants. The girl craned her neck to examine her shapely behind, touched the smear of blood, decided it was sticky and obscene, and almost fainted dead away. The chair, meantime, was happily whisking its way down the mountain again to the loading station where, presumably, another skier would again sit into a puddle of the dead girl's blood.

The dead girl's name, as it turned out, was Helga Nilson. She was nineteen years old and had learned to ski before she'd learned to walk, as the old Swedish saying goes. She had come to America when she was fifteen, had taught in the ski school at Stowe, Vermont, for two years before moving down to Mt. Snow in that same fair state, and then abandoning Vermont and moving to Rawson Mountain, farther south. She had joined the Rawson ski school at the beginning of the season, and seemed to be well liked by all the instructors and especially by many beginning skiers who, after one lesson with her, repeatedly asked for "Helga, the little Swedish girl."

The little Swedish girl had had a ski pole driven into her heart with such force that it had almost exited through her back. The pole, bent out of shape when Helga fell from the chair, was the first piece of real evidence the Keystone cops mishandled. Hawes saw one of the deputies kneel down beside the dead girl, grasp the pole with both hands, and attempt to pull it out of her body.

"Hey, what are you doing?" he shouted, and he shoved the man away from the body."

The man glanced up at him with a baleful upstate eye. "And just who in hell're *you*?" he asked.

"My name's Cotton Hawes," Hawes said. "I'm a detective. From the city." He unzipped the left hip pocket of his ski pants, pulled out his wallet, and flashed the tin. The deputy seemed singularly unimpressed.

"You're a little bit aways from your jurisdiction, ain't you?" he said.

"Who taught you how to handle evidence?" Hawes asked heatedly.

Sheriff Watt sauntered over to where the pair were arguing. He grinned amiably and said, "What seems to be the trouble here, hmmm?" He sang out the "hmmm," his voice rising pleasantly and cheerfully. A nineteen-year-old girl lay dead at his feet, but Sheriff Watt thought he was an old alumnus at Dartmouth's Winter Carnival.

"Feller here's a city detective," the deputy said.

"That's good," Watt said. "Pleased to have you with us."

"Thanks," Hawes said. "Your man here was just smearing any latent prints there may be on that weapon."

"What weapon?"

"The ski pole," Hawes said. "What weapon do you think I . . . ?"

"Oh, won't be no fingerprints on that, anyway," Watt said.

"How do you know?"

"No damn fool's gonna grab a piece of metal with his bare hands, is he? Not when the temperature's ten below zero, now is he?"

"He might have," Hawes said. "And while we're at it, don't you think it'd be a good idea to stop that lift? You've already had one person smearing up whatever stuff you can have found in the . . ."

"I got to get my men up here before I order the lift stopped," Watt said.

"Then restrict it to the use of your men."

"I've already done that," Watt said briefly. He turned back to his deputy. "Want to let me see that pole, Fred?"

"Sheriff, you let him touch that pole again, and . . ."

"And *what*?"

". . . and you may ruin . . ."

"Mister, you just let me handle this my own which-way, hmmm? We been in this business a long time now, and we know all about skiing accidents."

"This wasn't an accident," Hawes said angrily. "Somebody shoved a ski pole into that girl's chest, and that's not . . ."

"I know it wasn't an accident," Watt said. "That was just a manner of speaking. Let me have the pole, Fred."

"Sheriff . . ."

"Mister, you better just shut up, hmmm? Else I'll have one of my men escort you down the mountain, and you can warm your feet by the fire."

Hawes shut up. Impotently, he watched while the deputy named Fred seized the ski pole in both hands and yanked it from Helga's chest. A spurt of blood followed the retreating pole, welled up into the open wound, overflowed it, was sopped up by the sodden sweater. Fred handed the bent pole to the sheriff. Watt turned it over and over in his big hands.

"Looks like the basket's been taken off this thing," he said.

The basket, Hawes saw, had indeed been removed from the bottom of the aluminum pole. The basket on a ski pole is a circular metal ring perhaps five inches in diameter, crossed by a pair of leather thongs. A smaller ring stamped into the thongs fits over the end of the pointed pole and is usually fastened by a cotter pin or a tight rubber washer. When the basket is in place on the end of a pole, it prevents the pole from sinking into the snow, thereby enabling the skier to use it in executing turns or maintaining balance. The basket had been removed from this particular pole and, in addition, someone had sharpened the normally sharp point so that it was as thin as a rapier. Hawes noticed this at once. It took the sheriff a little while longer to see that he was holding a razor-sharp weapon in his hands, and not a normally pointed pole.

"Somebody been working on the end of this thing," he said, the dawn gradually breaking.

A doctor had come up the lift and was kneeling beside the dead girl. To no one's particular surprise, he pronounced her dead. One of the sheriff's bumbling associates began marking the position of the body, tracing its outline on the snow with a blue powder he poured liberally from a can.

Hawes couldn't imagine what possible use this imitation of investigatory technique would serve. They were marking the position of the body, true, but this didn't happen to be the scene of the crime. The girl had been murdered on a chair somewhere between the base of the mountain and the top of the lift. So far, no one had made any attempt to locate and examine the chair. Instead, they were sprinkling blue powder onto the snow, and passing their big paws all over the murder weapon.

"May I make a suggestion?" he asked.

"Sure," Watt said.

"That girl got on the lift with someone else. I know because I dropped my poles down there, and when I turned for a look, there were two people in that chair. But when she reached the station here, she was alone."

"Yeah?" Watt said.

"Yeah. I suggest you talk to the loaders down below. The girl was a ski instructor, and they may have recognized her. Maybe they know who got on the chair with her."

"Provided anyone did."

"Someone did," Hawes said.

"How do you know?"

"Because . . ." Hawes took a deep breath. "I just told you. I *saw* two people in that chair."

"How far behind you?"

"Four chairs behind."

"And you could see four chairs behind you in this storm, hmmm?"

"Yes. Not clearly, but I could see."

"I'll just bet you could," Watt said.

"Look," Hawes insisted, "someone was in that chair with her. And he undoubtedly jumped from the chair right after he killed her. I suggest you start combing the ground under the lift before this snow covers any tracks that might be there."

"Yes, we'll do that," Watt said. "When we get around to it."

"You'd better get around to it soon," Hawes said. "You've got a blizzard here, and a strong wind piling up drifts. If . . ."

"Mister, I hadn't *better* do anything. You're the one who'd just better butt his nose out of what we're trying to do here."

"What is it you're trying to do?" Hawes asked. "Compound a felony? Do you think your murderer's going to sit around and wait for you to catch up to him? He's probably halfway out of the state by now."

"Ain't nobody going noplace, mister," Watt said. "Not with the condition of the roads. So don't you worry about that. I hate to see anybody worrying."

"Tell that to the dead girl," Hawes said, and he watched as the ski patrol loaded her into a basket and began taking her on her last trip down the mountain.

7.

Death is a cliché, a tired old saw.

He had been a cop for a good long time now, starting as a rookie who saw death only from the sidelines, who kept a timetable while the detectives and the photographers and the assistant M.E. and the laboratory boys swarmed around the victim like flies around a prime cut of rotten meat. Death to him, at that time, had been motion-picture death. Standing apart from death, being as it were a uniformed secretary who took the names of witnesses and jotted in a black book the arrivals and departures of those actually concerned with the investigation, he had watched the proceedings dispassionately. The person lying lifeless on the sidewalk, the person lying on blood-soaked sheets, the person hanging from a light fixture, the person eviscerated by the onrushing front grille of an automobile, these were all a trifle unreal to Hawes, representations of death, but not death itself, not that grisly son of a bitch.

When he became a detective, they really introduced him to death.

The introduction was informal, almost casual. He was working with the 30th Squad at the time, a very nice respectable squad in a nice respectable precinct where death by violence hardly ever came. The introduction was made in a rooming house. The patrolman who had answered the initial squeal was waiting for the detectives when they arrived. The detective with Hawes asked, "Where's the stiff?" and the patrolman answered, "He's in there," and the other detective turned to Hawes and said, "Come on, let's take a look."

That was the introduction.

They had gone into the bedroom where the man was lying at the foot of the dresser. The man was fifty-three years old. He lay in his undershorts on the floor in the sticky coagulation of his own blood. He was a small man with a pinched chest. His hair was black and thinning, and bald patches showed his flaking scalp. He had probably never been handsome, even when he was a youth. Some men do not improve with age, and time and alcohol had squeezed everything out of this man, and drained him dry until all he possessed was sagging flesh and, of course, life. The flesh was still there. The life had been taken from him. He lay at the foot of the dresser in his undershorts, ludicrously piled into a heap of inert flesh, so relaxed, so impossibly relaxed. Someone had worked him over with a hatchet. The hatchet was still in the room, blood-flecked, entangled with thin black hair. The killer had viciously attacked him around the head and the throat and the chest. He had stopped bleeding by the time they arrived, but the wounds were still there to see, open and raw.

Hawes vomited.

He went into the bathroom and vomited. That was his introduction to death.

He had seen a lot of death since, had come close to being dead himself. The closest, perhaps, was the time he'd been stabbed while investigating a burglary. The woman who'd been burglarized was still pretty hysterical when he got there. He asked his questions and tried to comfort her, and then started downstairs to get a patrolman. The woman, terrified, began screaming when he left. He could hear her screams as he went down the stair well. The superintendent of

the building caught him on the second floor landing. He was carrying a bread knife, and he thought that Hawes was the burglar
returned, and he stabbed repeatedly at his head, ripping a wound
over his left temple before Hawes finally subdued him. They let the
super go; the poor guy had actually thought Hawes was the thief.
And then they'd shaved Hawes' red hair to get to the wound, which
time of course healed as it does all wounds, leaving however a
reminder of death, of the closeness of death. The red hair had
grown in white. He still carried the streak over his temple. Sometimes, particularly when it rained, death sent little signals of pain
to accompany the new hair.

He had seen a lot of death, especially since he'd joined the 87th,
and a lot of dying. He no longer vomited. The vomiting had happened to a very young Cotton Hawes, a very young and innocent
cop who suddenly awoke to the knowledge that he was in a dirty
business where the facts of life were the facts of violence, where
he dealt daily with the sordid and grotesque. He no longer vomited.
But he still got angry.

He had felt anger on the mountain when the young girl fell out
of the chair and struck the snow, the ski pole bending as she dropped
into that ludicrously ridiculous posture of the dead, that totally
relaxed and utterly frightening posture. He had felt anger by jux-
taposition, the reconstruction of a vibrant and life-bursting athlete
against the very real image of the same girl, no longer a girl, only
a worthless heap of flesh and bones, only a body now, a corpse,
"Where's the stiff?"

He had felt anger when Theodore Watt and his witless assistants
muddied the residue of sudden death, allowing the killer a precious
edge, presenting him with the opportunity for escape—escape from
the law and from the outrage of humanity. He felt anger now as he
walked back to the building which housed the ski shop and the
rooms overhead.

The anger seemed out of place on the silent mountain. The snow
still fell, still and gentle. The wind had died, and now the flakes
drifted aimlessly from overhead, large and wet and white, and there
was a stillness and a peace to Rawson Mountain and the countryside
beyond, a lazy white quiet which denied the presence of death.

He kicked the packed snow from his boots and went up the steps.

He was starting down the corridor toward his room when he
noticed the door was slightly ajar. He hesitated. Perhaps Blanche
had come back to the room, perhaps . . .

But there was silence in the corridor, a silence as large as noise. He stooped and untied the laces on his boots. Gently, he slipped them from his feet. Walking as softly as he could—he was a big man and the floor boards in the old building creaked beneath his weight—he approached the room. He did not like the idea of being in his stockinged feet. He had had to kick men too often, and he knew the value of shoes. He hesitated just outside the door. There was no sound in the room. The door was open no more than three inches. He put his hand against the wood. Somewhere in the basement, the oil burner clicked and then *whoooomed* into action. He shoved open the door.

Elmer Wollender, his crutches under his arms, whirled to face him. His head had been bent in an attitude of . . . prayer, was it? No. Not prayer. He had been listening, that was it, listening *to* something, or *for* something.

"Oh, hello, Mr. Hawes," he said. He was wearing a red ski parka over his white shirt. He leaned on his crutches and grinned a boyish, disarming grin.

"Hello, Mr. Wollender," Hawes said. "Would you mind telling me, Mr. Wollender, just what the hell you're doing in my room?"

Wollender seemed surprised. His eyebrows arched. He tilted his head to one side, almost in admiration, almost as if he too would have behaved in much the same way had he come back to *his* room and found a stranger in it. But the admiration was also tinged with surprise. This was obviously a mistake. Head cocked to one side, eyebrows arched, the boyish smile on his mouth, Wollender leaned on his crutches and prepared to explain. Hawes waited.

"You said the heat wasn't working, didn't you?" Wollender said. "I was just checking it."

"The heat's working fine in this room," Hawes said. "It's the room next door."

"Oh." Wollender nodded. "Oh, is that it?"

"That's it, yes."

"No wonder. I stuck my head up there to check the vent, and it seemed fine to me."

"Yes, it would be fine," Hawes said, "since there was never anything wrong with it. I told you at the desk this morning that the heat wasn't working in 104. This is 105. Are you new here, Mr. Wollender?"

"I guess I misunderstood you."

"Yes, I guess so. Misunderstanding isn't a wise practice, Mr.

Wollender, especially with your local cops crawling all over the mountain.''

"What are you talking about?''

"I'm talking about the girl. When those imitation cops begin asking questions, I suggest . . .''

"What girl?''

Hawes looked at Wollender for a long time. The question on Wollender's face and in his eyes looked genuine enough, but could there possibly be someone on the mountain who still had not heard of the murder? Was it possible that Wollender, who ran the inn, the center of all activity and gossip, did not know Helga Nilson was dead?

"The girl,'' Hawes said. "Helga Nilson.''

"What about her?''

Hawes knew enough about baseball to realize you didn't throw your fast ball until you'd tried to few curves. "Do you know her?'' he asked.

"Of course, I know her. I know all the ski instructors. She rooms right here, down the hall.''

"Who else rooms here?''

"Why?''

"I want to know.''

"Just her and Maria,'' Wollender said. "Maria Fiers. She's an instructor, too. And, oh yes, the new man. Larry Davidson.''

"Is he an instructor?'' Hawes asked. "About this tall?''

"Yes.''

"Hooked nose? German accent.''

"No, no. You're thinking of Helmut Kurtz. And that's an Austrian accent.'' Wollender paused. "Why? Why do you want to . . . ?''

"Anything between him and Helga?''

"Why, no. Not that I know of. They teach together, but . . .''

"What about Davidson?''

"Larry Davidson?''

"Yes.''

"Do you mean, is he dating Helga, or . . .''

"Yes, that's right.''

"Larry's married,'' Wollender said, "I would hardly think . . .''

"What about you?''

"I don't understand.''

"You and Helga. Anything?''

"Helga's a good friend of mine," Wollender said.

"Was," Hawes corrected.

"Huh?"

"She's dead. She was killed on the mountain this afternoon."

There was the fast ball, and it took Wollender smack between the eyes. "Dea—" he started, and then his jaw fell slack, and his eyes went blank. He staggered back a pace, colliding with the white dresser. The crutches dropped from his hands. He struggled to maintain his balance, the leg with the cast stiff and unwieldy; he seemed about to fall. Hawes grabbed at his elbow and pulled him erect. He stooped down for Wollender's crutches and handed them to him. Wollender was still dazed. He groped for the crutches, fumbled, dropped them again. Hawes picked them up a second time, and forced them under Wollender's arms. Wollender leaned back against the dresser. He kept staring at the wall opposite, where a poster advertising the pleasures of Kitzbühel was hanging.

"She . . . she took too many chances," he said. "She always went too fast. I told her . . ."

"This wasn't a skiing accident," Hawes said. "She was murdered."

"No." Wollender shook his head. "No."

"Yes."

"No. Everyone liked Helga. No one would . . ." He kept shaking his head. His eyes stayed riveted to the Kitzbühel poster.

"There are going to be cops here, Mr. Wollender," Hawes said. "You seem like a nice kid. When they start asking questions, you'd better have a more plausible story than the one you invented about being in my room. They're not going to fool around. They're looking for a killer."

"Why . . . why do you *think* I came here?" Wollender asked.

"I don't know. Maybe you were looking for some pocket money. Skiers often leave their wallets and their valu—"

"I'm not a thief, Mr. Hawes," Wollender said with dignity. "I only came here to give you some heat."

"That makes it even," Hawes answered. "The cops'll be coming here to give *you* some."

244

8.

He found the two loaders in the lodge cafeteria. The lifts had been closed at four-thirty, the area management having reached the conclusion that most skiing accidents took place in the waning hours of the afternoon, when poor visibility and physical exhaustion combined to create gentle havoc. They were both burly, grizzled men wearing Mackinaws, their thick hands curled around coffee mugs. They had been loading skiers onto chairs ever since the area was opened, and they worked well together as a team. Even their dialogue seemed concocted in one mind, though it issued from two mouths.

"My name's Jake," the first loader said. "This here is Obey, short for Obadiah."

"Only I ain't so short," Obadiah said.

"He's short on brains," Jake said and grinned. Obadiah returned the grin. "You're a cop, huh?"

"Yes," Hawes said. He had shown them his buzzer the moment he approached them. He had also told an outright lie, saying he was helping with the investigation of the case, having been sent up from the city because there was the possibility a known and wanted criminal had perpetrated the crime, confusing his own doubletalk as he wove a fantastic monologue, which Jake and Obadiah seemed to accept.

"And you want to know who we loaded on them chairs, right? Same as Teddy wanted to know."

"Teddy?"

"Teddy Watt. The sheriff."

"Oh. Yes," Hawes said. "That's right."

"Whyn't you just ask *him*?" Obadiah said.

"Well, I have," Hawes lied. "But sometimes a fresh angle will come up if witnesses can be questioned directly, do you see?"

"Well, we ain't exactly witnesses," Jake said. "We didn't see her get killed, you know."

"Yes, but you did load her on the chair, didn't you?"

"That's right. We did, all right."

"And someone was in the chair with her, is that right?"

"That's right," Jake said.

"Who?" Hawes asked.

"Seems like everybody wants to know *who*," Jake said.

245

"Ain't it the damnedest thing?" Obadiah said.

"Do you remember?" Hawes asked.

"We remember it was snowing, that's for sure."

"Couldn't hardly see the chairs, it was snowing that hard."

"Pretty tough to reckernize one skier from another with all that wind and snow, wouldn't you say, Obey?"

"Next to impossible," Obadiah answered.

"But you did recognize Helga," Hawes suggested.

"Oh, sure. But she said hello to us, you see. She said, 'Hello, Jake. Hello, Obey.' And also, she took the chair closest to the loading platform, the inside chair. The guy took the other chair."

"Guy?" Hawes asked. "It was a man then? The person who took the chair next to her was a man?"

"Well, can't say for sure," Jake said. "Was a time when men's ski clothes was different from the ladies', but that don't hold true no more."

"Not by a long shot," Obadiah said.

"Nowadays, you find yourself following some pretty girl in purple pants, she turns out to be a man. It ain't so easy to tell them apart no more."

"Then you don't know whether the person who sat next to her was a man or a woman, is that right?" Hawes asked.

"That's right."

"Coulda been either."

"Did this person say anything?"

"Not a word."

"What was he wearing?"

"Well, we ain't established it was a *he*," Jake reminded him.

"Yes, I know. I meant the . . . the person who took the chair. It'll be easier if we give him a gender."

"Give him a *what*?"

"A gen—if we assume for the moment that the person was a man."

"Oh." Jake thought this over. "Okay, if you say so. Seems like pretty sloppy deduction to me, though."

"Well, I'm not actually making a deduction. I'm simply trying to facilitate . . ."

"Sure, I understand," Jake said. "But it's sure pretty sloppy."

Hawes sighed. "Well . . . what *was* he wearing?"

"Black," Jake said.

"Black ski pants, black parka," Obadiah said.

"Any hat?" Hawes asked.

"Nope. Hood on the parka was pulled clear up over the head. Sunglasses over the eyes."

"Gloves or mittens?" Hawes asked.

"Gloves. Black gloves."

"Did you notice whether or not there was an insignia on the man's parka?"

"What kind of insignia?"

"An R-M interlocked," Hawes said.

"Like the instructors wear?" Jake asked.

"Exactly."

"They wear it on their *right* sleeves," Obadiah said. "We told you this person took the outside chair. We couldn'ta seen the right sleeve, even if there *was* anything on it."

Hawes suddenly had a wild idea. He hesitated before he asked, and then thought *What the hell, try it.*

"This person," he said, "was he . . . was he carrying crutches?"

"Carrying *what*?" Jake asked incredulously.

"Crutches. Was his leg in a cast?"

"Now how in hell . . . of *course* not," Jake said. "He was wearing skis, and he was carrying ski poles. Crutches and a cast! My God! It's hard enough getting on that damn lift as it is. Can you just picture . . ."

"Never mind," Hawes said. "Forget it. Did this person say anything to Helga?"

"Not a word."

"Did she say anything to him?"

"Nothing we could hear. The wind was blowing pretty fierce."

"But you heard her when she said hello to you."

"That's right."

"Then if she'd said anything to this person, you might have heard that, too."

"That's right. We didn't hear nothing."

"You said he was carrying poles. Did you notice anything un- usual about the poles?"

"Seemed like ordinary poles to me," Jake said.

"Did both poles have baskets?"

Jake shrugged. "I didn't notice. Did you notice, Obey?"

"Both seemed to have baskets," Obadiah said. "Who'd notice a thing like that?"

"Well, you might have," Hawes said. "If there'd been anything unusual, you might have noticed."

"I didn't notice nothing unusual," Obadiah said. "Except I thought to myself this feller must be pretty cold."

"Why?"

"Well, the hood pulled up over his head, and the scarf wrapped almost clear around his face."

"What scarf? You didn't mention that before."

"Sure. He was wearing a red scarf. Covered his mouth and his nose, reached right up to the sunglasses."

"Hmmm," Hawes said, and the table went still.

"You're the fellow dropped his poles on the way up, ain't you?" Jake asked.

"Yes."

"Thought I remembered you."

"If you remember *me*, how come you can't remember the person who took that chair alongside Helga's?"

"You saying I *should*, mister?"

"I'm only asking."

"Well, like maybe if I seen a guy wearing black pants and a black hood, and sunglasses, and a scarf wrapped clear around his face, why maybe then I would recognize him. But, the way I figure it, he ain't likely to be wearing the same clothes right now, is he?"

"I don't suppose so," Hawes said, sighing.

"Yeah, neither do I," Jake answered. "And I ain't even a cop."

9.

Dusk was settling upon the mountain.

It spread into the sky and stained the snow a purple-red. The storm was beginning to taper off, the clouds vanishing before the final triumphant breakthrough of the setting sun. There was an unimaginable hush to the mountain, and the town, and the valley beyond, a hush broken only by the sound of gently jingling skid-chains on hard-packed snow.

He had found Blanche and taken her to the fireplace in the inn, settling her there with a brace of double Scotches and a half-dozen copies of a skiing magazine. Now, with the moun-

tain and the town still, the lifts inoperative, the distant snow
brushed with dying color, he started climbing the mountain.
He worked through the deep snow directly under the lift, the
chairs hanging motionless over his head. He was wearing ski
pants and afterski boots designed for lounging beside a fire.
He had forsaken his light parka for two sweaters. Before he'd
left the room, he had unholstered the .38 and slipped it into
the elastic-reinforced waistband of his trousers. He could feel
it digging into his abdomen now as he climbed.

The climb was not an easy one.

The snow under the lift had not been packed, and he struggled against it as he climbed, encountering drifts which were
impassable, working his way in a zigzagging manner across
the lift line, sometimes being forced to leave the high snow for
the Cat-packed trail to the right of the lift. The light was waning. He did not know how much longer it would last. He had
taken a flashlight from the glove compartment of his car, but
he began to wonder whether its glow would illuminate very
much once the sun had set. He began to wonder, too, exactly
what he hoped to find. He was almost certain that any tracks
the killer had left would already have been covered by the drifting snow. Again, he cursed Theodore Watt and his inefficient
slobs. Someone should have made this climb immediately after
they discovered the dead girl, while there was still a possibility
of finding a trail.

He continued climbing. After a day of skiing, he was physically and mentally exhausted, his muscles protesting, his eyes
burning. He thumbed on the flashlight as darkness claimed the
mountain, and pushed his way through knee-deep snow. He
stumbled and got to his feet again. The snow had tapered almost completely, but the wind had returned with early evening,
a high keening wind that rushed through the trees on either
side of the lift line, pushing the clouds from the sky. There
was a thin sliver of moon and a scattering of stars. The clouds
raced past them like silent dark horsemen, and everywhere on
the mountain was the piercing shriek of the wind, a thin scream
that penetrated to the marrow.

He fell again.

Loose snow caught under the neck of his sweater, slid down his
back. He shivered and tried to brush it away, got to his feet, and
doggedly began climbing again. His afterski boots had not been

designed for deep snow. The tops ended just above his ankles, offering no protection whatever. He realized abruptly that the boots were already packed with snow, that his feet were literally encased in snow. He was beginning to regret this whole foolhardy mission, when he saw it.

He had come perhaps a third of the way up the lift line, the mountain in absolute darkness now, still except for the maiden scream of the wind. The flashlight played a small circle of light on the snow ahead of him as he stumbled upward, the climb more difficult now, the clouds rushing by overhead, skirting the thin moon. The light touched something that glinted momentarily, passed on as he continued climbing, stopped. He swung the flashlight back. Whatever had glinted was no longer there. Swearing, he swung the flashlight in a slow steady arc. The glint again. He swung the light back.

The basket was half-covered by the snow. Only one edge of its metallic ring showed in the beam of his light. It had probably been covered completely earlier in the day, but the strong fresh wind had exposed it to view again, and he stooped quickly to pick it up, almost as if he were afraid it would vanish. He was still bending, studying the basket in the light of the flash, when the man jumped onto his back.

The attack came suddenly and swiftly. He had heard nothing but the wind. He had been so occupied with his find, so intent on studying the basket, which, he was certain, had come from the end of the ski-pole weapon, that when he felt the sudden weight on his back he did not connect it immediately with an attack. He was simply surprised, and his first thought was that one of the pines had dropped a heavy load of snow from its laden branches, and then he realized this was no heavy load of snow, but by that time he was flat on his belly.

He rolled over instantly. He held the ski pole basket in his left hand, refusing to let go of it. In his right hand, he held the flashlight, and he swung that instantly at the man's head, felt it hitting the man's forearm instead. Something solid struck Hawes' shoulder; a wrench? a hammer? and he realized at once that the man was armed, and suddenly the situation became serious. He threw away the flashlight and groped for the .38 in his waistband.

The clouds cleared the moon. The figure kneeling over him, straddling him, was wearing a black parka, the hood pulled up over his head. A red scarf was wrapped over his chin and his mouth and his nose. He was holding a hammer in his right hand, and he raised the hammer over his head just as the moon disappeared again. Hawes' fingers closed on the butt of the .38. The hammer descended.

It descended in darkness, striking Hawes on his cheek, ripping the flesh, glancing downward and catching his shoulder. Hawes swore violently, drew the .38 in a ridiculously clumsy draw, brought it into firing position, and felt again the driving blow of the other man's weapon, the hammer lashing out of the darkness, slamming with brute force against his wrist, almost cracking the bone. His fingers opened involuntarily. The gun dropped into the snow. He bellowed in pain and tried to kick out at his attacker, but the man moved away quickly, gained his feet, and braced himself in the deep snow for the final assault. The moon appeared again. A thin silvery light put the man in silhouette against the sky, the black hooded head, the face masked by the scarf. The hammer went up over his head.

Hawes kicked out at his groin.

The blow did nothing to stop the man's attack. It glanced off his thigh, missing target as the hammer came down, but throwing him off balance slightly so that the hammer struck without real force. Hawes threw a fist at him, and the man grunted and again the hammer came out of the new darkness. The man fought desperately and silently, frightening Hawes with the fury of his animal strength. They rolled over in the snow, and Hawes grasped at the hood, tried to pull it from the man's head, found it was securely tied in place, and reached for the scarf. The scarf began to unravel. The man lashed out with the hammer, felt the scarf coming free, pulled back to avoid exposing his face, and suddenly staggered as Hawes' fist struck home. He fell into the snow, and all at once, he panicked. Instead of attacking again, he pulled the scarf around his face and began to half run, half stumble through the deep snow. Hawes leaped at him, missing, his hands grabbing air. The man scrambled over the snow, heading for the pines lining the lift. By the time Hawes was on his feet again, the man had gone into the trees. Hawes went after him. It was dark under the trees. The world went black and silent under the pines.

He hesitated for a moment. He could see nothing, could hear

nothing. He fully expected the hammer to come lashing out of the darkness.

Instead, there came the voice.

"Hold it right there."

The voice startled him, but he reacted intuitively, whirling, his fist pulling back reflexively, and then firing into the darkness. He felt it connecting with solid flesh, heard someone swearing in the dark, and then—surprisingly, shockingly—Hawes heard the sound of a pistol shot. It rang on the mountain air, reverberated under the pines. Hawes opened his eyes wide. A pistol? But the man had only a hammer. Why hadn't . . . ?

"Next time, I go for your heart," the voice said.

Hawes stared into the darkness. He could no longer locate the voice. He did not know where to jump, and the man was holding a pistol.

"You finished?" the man asked.

The beam of a flashlight suddenly stabbed through the darkness. Hawes blinked his eyes against it, tried to shield his face.

"Well, well," the man said. "You never can tell, can you? Stick out your hands."

"What?" Hawes said.

"Stick out your goddamn hands."

Hesitantly, he held out his hands. He was the most surprised human being in the world when he felt the handcuffs being snapped onto his wrists.

10.

The office from which Theodore Watt, sheriff of the town of Rawson, operated was on the main street alongside an Italian restaurant whose neon sign advertised LASAGNA * SPAGHETTI * RAVIOLI. Now that the snow had stopped, the plows had come through and banked snow on either side of the road so that the door of the office was partially hidden by a natural fortress of white. Inside the office, Theodore Watt was partially hidden by the fortress of his desk, the top of which was covered with Wanted circulars, FBI flyers, carbon copies of police reports, a pair of manacles, a cardboard container of coffee, a half-dozen chewed pencil stubs, and a framed picture of his wife and three children. Theodore Watt was not in a very friendly mood. He sat behind his desk-fortress, a frown on his face. Cotton Hawes stood before the desk, still wearing the handcuffs that had been clamped onto his wrists on the mountain. The deputy who'd made the collar, the self-same Fred who had earlier pulled the ski pole from Helga Nilson's chest, stood alongside Hawes, wearing the sheriff's frown, and also wearing a mouse under his left eye, where Hawes had hit him.

"I could lock you up, you know," Watt said, frowning. "You hit one of my deputies."

"You ought to lock *him* up," Hawes said angrily. "If he hadn't come along, I might have had our man."

"You might have, huh?"

"Yes."

"You had no right being on that damn mountain," Watt said. "What were you doing up there?"

"Looking."

"For what?"

"Anything. He gave you the basket I found. Apparently it was important enough for the killer to have wanted it, too. He fought hard enough for it. Look at my cheek."

"Well now, that's a shame," Watt said drily.

"There may be fingerprints on that basket," Hawes said. "I suggest . . ."

"I doubt it. Weren't none on the ski pole, and none on the chair, neither. We talked to the two loaders, and they told us the one riding up with Helga Nilson was wearing gloves. I doubt if there's any fingerprints on that basket at all."

"Well . . ." Hawes said, and he shrugged.

"What it amounts to, hmmmm," Watt said, "is that you figured we wasn't handling this case to your satisfaction, ain't that it? So you figured you'd give us local hicks a little big-time help, hmmmm? Ain't that about it?"

"I thought I could possibly assist in some . . ."

"Then you shoulda come to me," Watt said, "and *asked* if you could help. This way, you only fouled up what we was trying to do."

"I don't understand."

"I've got six men on that mountain," Watt said, "waiting for whoever killed that girl to come back and cover his mistakes. This basket here was one of the mistakes. But did our killer find it? No. Our helpful big-city detective found it. You're a lot of help, mister, you sure are. With all that ruckus on the mountain, that damn killer won't go anywhere near it for a month!"

"I almost had him," Hawes said. "I was going after him when your man stopped me."

"Stopped you, hell! *You're* the one who was stopping *him* from doing his job. Maybe I *ought* to lock you up. There's a thing known as impeding the progress of an investigation. But, of course, you know all about that, don't you? Being a big-city detective. Hmmm?"

"I'm sorry if I. . ."

"And, of course, we're just a bunch of local hicks who don't know nothing at all about police work. Why, we wouldn't even know enough to have a autopsy performed on that little girl, now would we? Or to have tests made of the blood on that chair, now would we? We wouldn't have no crime lab in the next biggest town to Rawson, would we?"

"The way you were handling the investigation . . ." Hawes started.

". . . was none of your damn business," Watt concluded. "Maybe we like to make our own mistakes, Hawes! But naturally, you city cops never make mistakes. That's why there ain't no crime at all where you come from."

"Look," Hawes said, "you were mishandling evidence. I don't give a damn what you . . ."

"As it turns out, it don't matter because there wasn't no fingerprints on that pole, anyway. And we had to get our men up the mountain, so we had to use the lift. There was a hell of a lot of confusion there today, mister. But I don't suppose big-city cops ever get confused, hmmmm?" Watt looked at him sourly. "Take the cuffs off him, Fred," he said.

Fred looked surprised, but he unlocked the handcuffs. "He hit me right in the eye," he said to Watt.

"Well, you still got the other eye," Watt said drily. "Go to bed, Hawes. We had enough of you for one night."

"What did the autopsy report say?" Hawes asked.

Watt looked at him in something close to astonishment. "You still sticking your nose in this?"

"I'd still like to help, yes."

"Maybe we don't need your help."

"Maybe you can use it. No one here knows . . ."

"There we go with the damn big-city attitu—"

"I was going to say," Hawes said, overriding Watt's voice, "that no one in the area knows I'm a cop. That could be helpful to you."

Watt was silent. "Maybe," he said at last.

"*May* I hear the autopsy report?"

Watt was silent again. Then he nodded. He picked up a sheet of paper from his desk and said, "Death caused by fatal stab wound of the heart, penetration of the auricles and pulmonary artery. That's where all the blood came from, Hawes. Wounds of the ventricles don't usually bleed that much. Coroner figures the girl died in maybe two or three minutes, there was that much loss of blood."

"Anything else?"

"Broke her ankle when she fell out of that chair. Oblique fracture of the lateral malleolus. Examiner also found traces of human skin under the girl's fingernails. Seems like she clawed out at whoever stabbed her, and took a goodly part of him away with her."

"What did the skin tell you?"

"Not a hell of a lot. Our killer is white and adult."

"That's all?"

"That's all. At least, that's all from the skin, except the possibility of using it later for comparison tests—if we ever get anybody to compare it with. We found traces of blood on her fingers and nails, too, not her own."

"How do you know?"

"Blood on the chair, the girl's blood, was in the AB grouping. Blood we found on her hands was in the O grouping, most likely the killer's."

"Then she scratched him enough to cause bleeding."

"She took a big chunk of skin from him, Hawes."

"From the face?"

"Now how in hell would I know?"

"I thought maybe . . ."

"Couldn't tell from the skin sample whether it came from the neck or the face or wherever. She coulda scratched him anyplace."

"Anything else?"

"We found a trail of the girl's blood in the snow under the lift. Plenty of it, believe me, she bled like a stuck pig. The trail started about four minutes from the top. Took her two or three minutes to die. So, assuming the killer jumped from the chair right soon's he stabbed her, then the girl . . ."

". . . was still alive when he jumped."

"That's right."

"Find any tracks in the snow?"

"Nothing. Too many drifts. We don't know whether he jumped with his skis on or not. Have to have been a pretty good skier to attempt that, we figure."

"Well, anyway, he's got a scratch," Hawes said. "That's *something* to look for."

"You gonna start looking tonight?" Watt asked sarcastically.

11.

Blanche Colby was waiting for him when he got back to the room. She was sitting up in his bed propped against the pillows, wearing a shapeless flannel nightgown that covered her from her throat to her ankles. She was holding an apple in her hand, and she bit into it angrily as he entered the room, and then went back to reading the open book in her lap.

"Hi," he said.

She did not answer him, nor did she even look up at him. She continued destroying the apple, continued her pretense of reading.

"Good book?"

"*Excellent* book," she answered.

"Miss me?"

"Drop dead," Blanche said.

"I'm sorry. I . . ."

"Don't be. I enjoyed myself immensely in your absence."

"I got arrested, you see."

"You got *what*?"

"Arrested. Pinched. Pulled in. Collared. Apprehen—"

"I understood you the first time. Who arrested you?"

"The cops," Hawes said, and he shrugged.

"Serves you right." She put down the book. "Wasn't it you who told me a girl was killed on this mountain today? Murdered? And you run off and leave me when a killer . . ."

"I told you where I was going. I told you . . ."

"You said you'd be back in an hour!"

"Yes, but I didn't know I was going to be arrested."

"What happened to your cheek?"

"I got hit with a hammer."

"Good," Blanche said, and she nodded emphatically.

256

"Aren't you going to kiss my wound?" Hawes asked.

"*You* can kiss my . . ."

"Ah-ah," he cautioned.

"I sat by that damn fireplace until eleven o'clock. Then I came up here and . . . what time is it, anyway?"

"After midnight."

Blanche nodded again. "I would have packed up and gone home, believe me, if the roads were open."

"Yes, but they're closed."

"Yes, damn it!"

"Aren't you glad I'm back?"

Blanche shrugged. "I couldn't care less. I was just about to go to sleep."

"In here?"

"In the other room, naturally."

"Honey, honey . . ."

"Yes, honey-honey?" she mimicked. "*What*, honey-honey baby?"

Hawes grinned. "That's a very lovely nightgown. My grand-mother used to wear a nightgown like that."

"I thought you'd like it," Blanche said sourly. "I put it on especially for you."

"I always liked the touch of flannel," he said.

"Get your big hands . . ." she started, and moved away from him swiftly. Folding her arms across the front of her gown, she sat in the center of the bed and stared at the opposite wall. Hawes studied her for a moment, took off his sweaters, and then began unbuttoning his shirt.

"If you're going to undress," Blanche said evenly, "you could at least have the modesty to go into the . . ."

"Shhh!" Hawes said sharply. His hands had stopped on the buttons of his shirt. He cocked his head to one side now and listened. Blanche, watching him, frowned.

"What . . . ?"

"Shhh!" he said again, and again he listened attentively. The room was silent. Into the silence came the sound.

"Do you hear it?" he asked.

"Do I hear what?"

"Listen."

They listened together. The sound was unmistakable, faint and faraway, but unmistakable.

"It's the same buzzing I heard last night," Hawes said. "I'll be right back."

"Where are you going?"

"Downstairs. To the ski shop," he answered, and swiftly left the room. As he went down the corridor toward the steps, a door at the opposite end of the hall opened. A young girl wearing a quilted robe over her pajamas, her hair done in curlers, came into the hallway carrying a towel and a toothbrush. She smiled at Hawes and then walked past him. He heard the bathroom door locking behind her as he went down the steps.

The lights were on in the ski shop. The buzzing sound came from somewhere in the shop, intermittent, hanging on the silent night air, ceasing abruptly, beginning again. He walked silently over the snow, stopping just outside the door to the shop. He put his ear to the wood and listened, but the only sound he heard was the buzzing. He debated kicking in the door. Instead, he knocked gently.

"Yes?" a voice from inside called.

"Could you open up, please?" Hawes said.

He waited. He could hear the heavy sound of ski boots approaching the locked door. The door opened a crack. A sun-tanned face appeared in the opening. He recognized the face at once—Helmut Kurtz, the ski instructor who had helped him the night before, the man he'd seen today on the mountain just before he'd got on the chair lift.

"Oh, hello there," Hawes said.

"Yes? What is it?" Kurtz asked.

"Mind if I come in?"

"I'm sorry, no one is allowed in the shop. The shop is closed."

"Yes, but *you're* in it, aren't you?"

"I'm an instructor," Kurtz said. "We are permitted . . ."

"I just saw a light," Hawes said, "and I felt like talking to someone."

"Well . . ."

"What are you doing, anyway?" Hawes asked casually, and casually he wedged one shoulder against the door and gently eased it open, casually pushing it into the room, casually squeezing his way into the opening, casually shouldering his way past Kurtz, and then squinting past the naked hanging light bulb to the work bench

258

at the far end of the room, trying to locate the source of the buzzing sound that filled the shop.

"You are really not allowed . . ." Kurtz started, but Hawes was already halfway across the room, moving toward the other small area of light where a green-shaded bulb hung over the work bench. The buzzing sound was louder, the sound of an old machine, the sound of . . .

He located it almost at once. A grinding wheel was set up on one end of the bench. The wheel was still spinning. He looked at it, nodded and then flicked the switch to turn it off. Turning to Kurtz, he smiled and said, "Were you sharpening something?"

"Yes, those skates," Kurtz said. He pointed to a pair of white figure skates on the bench.

"Yours?" Hawes asked.

Kurtz smiled. "No. Those are women's skates."

"Whose?"

"Well, I don't think that is any of your business, do you?" Kurtz asked politely.

"I suppose not," Hawes answered gently, still smiling. "Were you in here sharpening something last night, too, Mr. Kurtz?"

"I beg your pardon?"

"I said, were you . . ."

"No, I was not." Kurtz walked up to the bench and studied Hawes slowly and deliberately. "Who *are* you?" he asked.

"My name's Cotton Hawes."

"How do you do? Mr. Hawes, I'm sorry to have to be so abrupt, but you are really not allowed . . ."

"Yes, I know. Only instructors are allowed in here, isn't that right, Mr. Kurtz?"

"After closing, yes. We sometimes come in to make minor repairs on our skis or . . ."

"Or sharpen up some things, huh, Mr. Kurtz?"

"Yes. Like the skates."

"Yes," Hawes repeated. "Like the skates. But you weren't in here last night, were you, Mr. Kurtz?"

"No, I was not."

"Because, you see, I heard what could have been the sound of a file or a rasp or something, and then the sound of this grinding wheel. So you're sure you weren't in here sharpening something? Like skates? Or . . ." Hawes shrugged. "A ski pole?"

"A ski pole? Why would anyone . . . ?" Kurtz fell suddenly silent. He studied Hawes again. "What are you?" he asked. "A policeman?"

"Why? Don't you like policemen?"

"I had nothing to do with Helga's death," Kurtz said immediately.

"No one said you did."

"You implied it."

"I implied nothing, Mr. Kurtz."

"You asked if I were sharpening a ski pole last night. The implication is . . ."

"But you weren't."

"No, I was *not*!" Kurtz said angrily.

"What *were* you sharpening last night?"

"Nothing. I was nowhere near this shop last night."

"Ahh, but you were, Mr. Kurtz. I met you outside, remember? You were coming down the steps. Very fast. Don't you remember?"

"That was earlier in the evening."

"But I didn't say anything about time, Mr. Kurtz. I didn't ask you *when* you were in this shop."

"I was *not* in this shop! Not at any time!"

"But you just said 'That was earlier in the evening.' Earlier than what, Mr. Kurtz?"

Kurtz was silent for a moment. Then he said, "Earlier than . . . than whoever was here."

"You saw someone here?"

"I . . . I saw a light burning."

"When? What time?"

"I don't remember. I went to the bar after I met you . . . and I had a few drinks, and then I went for a walk. That was when I saw the light."

"Where do you room, Mr. Kurtz?"

"In the main building."

"Did you see Helga at any time last night?"

"No."

"Not at any time?"

"No."

"Then what were you doing upstairs?"

"I came to get Maria's skates. Those." He pointed to the figure skates on the bench.

260

"Maria who?"

"Maria Fiers."

"Is she a small girl with dark hair?"

"Yes. Do you know her?"

"I think I just saw her in the hallway," Hawes said. "So you came to get her skates, and then you went for a drink, and then you went for a walk. What time was that?"

"It must have been after midnight."

"And a light was burning in the ski shop?"

"Yes."

"But you didn't see who was in here?"

"No, I did not."

"How well did you know Helga?"

"Very well. We taught together."

"How well is very well?"

"We were good friends."

"How good, Mr. Kurtz?"

"I *told* you!"

"Were you sleeping with her?"

"How dare you . . ."

"Okay, okay." Hawes pointed to the skates. "These are Maria's, you said?"

"Yes. She's an instructor here, too. But she skates well, almost as well as she skis."

"Are you good friends with her, too, Mr. Kurtz?"

"I am good friends with *everyone*!" Kurtz said angrily. "I am normally a friendly person." He paused. "*Are* you a policeman?"

"Yes. I am."

"I don't like policemen," Kurtz said, his voice low. "I didn't like them in Vienna, where they wore swastikas on their arms, and I don't like them here, either. I had nothing to do with Helga's death."

"Do you have a key to this shop, Mr. Kurtz?"

"Yes. We *all* do. We make our own minor repairs. During the day, there are too many people here. At night, we can . . ."

"What do you mean by *all*? The instructors?"

"Yes."

"I see. Then any of the instructors could have . . ."

The scream was a sentient thing which invaded the room suddenly and startlingly. It came from somewhere upstairs, ripping down through the ancient floor boards and the ancient ceiling timbers. It struck the room with its blunt force, and both men looked up toward the ceiling, speechless, waiting. The scream came again. Hawes got to his feet and ran for the door. *"Blanche,"* he whispered, and slammed the door behind him.

She was standing in the corridor outside the hall bathroom, not really standing, but leaning limply against the wall, her supporting dancer's legs robbed of stance, robbed of control. She wore the long flannel nightgown with a robe over it, and she leaned against the wall with her eyes shut tight, her blond hair disarrayed, the scream unvoiced now, but frozen in the set of her face and the trembling openness of her mouth. Hawes came stamping up the steps and turned abruptly right, and stopped stock still when he saw her, an interruption of movement for only a fraction of a second, the turn, the stop, and then a forward motion again, which carried him to her in four headlong strides.

"What is it?" he said.

She could not answer. She clung to the wall with the flat palms of her hands, her eyes still squeezed shut tightly, the scream frozen in her throat and blocking articulation. She shook her head.

"Blanche, what is it?"

She shook her head again, and then pulled one hand from the wall, as if afraid that by doing so she would lose her grip and tumble to the floor. The hand rose limply. It did not point, it only indicated, and that in the vaguest manner, as if it, too, were dazed.

"The bathroom?" he asked.

She nodded. He turned from her. The bathroom door was partly open. He opened it the rest of the way, rushing into the room, and then stopping instantly, as if he had run into a stone wall.

Maria Fiers was inside her clothing and outside of it. The killer had caught her either dressing or undressing, had caught her in what she supposed was privacy, so that one leg was in the trousers of her pajamas and the other lay twisted beneath her body, naked. Her pajama top had ridden up over one delicately curved breast, perhaps as she fell, perhaps as she struggled. Even her hair seemed in a state of uncertain transition, some of it held firmly in place by curlers, the rest hanging in haphazard abandon, the loose curlers scattered on the bathroom floor. The hook latch on the inside of the door had been ripped from the jamb when the door was forced. The water in the sink was still running. The girl lay still and dead in her invaded privacy, partially clothed, partially disrobed, surprise and terror wedded in the death mask of her face. A towel was twisted about her throat. It had been twisted there with tremendous force, biting into the skin with such power that it remained twisted there now, the flesh torn and overlapping it in places, the coarse cloth almost embedded into her neck and throat. Her tongue protruded from her mouth. She was bleeding from her nose where her face had struck the bathroom tile in falling.

He backed out of the room.

He found a pay telephone in the main building, and from there he called Theodore Watt.

12.

Blanche sat on the edge of the bed in room 105, shivering inside her gown, her robe, and a blanket, which had been thrown over her shoulders. Theodore Watt leaned disjointedly against the dresser, puffed on his cigar, and said, "Now you want to tell me exactly what happened, Miss Colby?"

Blanche sat shivering and hunched, her face pale. She searched for her voice, seemed unable to find it, shook her head, nodded, cleared her throat, and seemed surprised that she could speak. "I . . . I was alone. Cotton had gone down to see what . . . what the noise was."

"What noise, Hawes?" Watt asked.

"A grinding wheel," he answered. "Downstairs in the ski shop. I heard it last night, too."

"Did you find who was running the wheel?"

"Tonight, it was a guy named Helmut Kurtz. He's an instructor here, too. Claims he was nowhere near the shop last night. But he did see a light burning after midnight."

"Where's he now?"

"I don't know. Sheriff, he was with me when the girl was killed. He couldn't possibly have . . ."

Watt ignored him and walked to the door. He opened it, and leaned into the corridor. "Fred," he said, "find me Helmut Kurtz, an instructor here."

"I got that other guy from down the hall," Fred answered.

"I'll be right with him. Tell him to wait."

"What other guy?" Hawes asked.

"Instructor in 102. Larry Davidson." Watt shook his head. "Place is crawling with goddamn instructors, excuse me, miss. Wonder there's any room for guests." He shook his head again. "You said you were alone, Miss Colby."

"Yes. And I . . . I thought I heard something down the hall . . . like . . . I didn't know what. A loud sudden noise."

"Probably the bathroom door being kicked in," Watt said. "Go on."

"And then I . . . I heard a girl's voice saying, 'Get out of here! Do you hear me? Get out of here!' And . . . and then it was quiet, and I heard someone running down the hall and down the steps, so I . . . I thought I ought to . . . to look."

"Yes, go on."

"I went down the . . . the hallway and looked down the steps, but I didn't see anyone. And then, when I . . . when I was starting back for the room, I . . . I heard the water running in the bathroom. The . . . the door was open, so I . . . Oh Jesus, do I *have* to?"

"You found the girl, is that right?"

"Yes," Blanche said, her voice very low.

"And then you screamed."

"Yes."

"And then Hawes came upstairs, is that right?"

"Yes," Hawes said. "And I called you from the main building."

"Um-huh," Watt said. He went to the door and opened it. "Want to come in here, Mr. Davidson?" he asked.

Larry Davidson came into the room hesitantly. He was a tall man, and he stooped as he came through the doorway, giving an impression of even greater height, as if he had to stoop to avoid the top of the door frame. He was wearing dark trousers and a plaid woolen sports shirt. His hair was clipped close to his scalp. His blue eyes were alert, if not wary.

"Guess you know what this is all about, huh, Mr. Davidson?" Watt asked.

"Yes, I think so," Davidson answered.

"You don't mind answering a few questions, do you?"

"No. I'll . . . I'll answer anything you . . ."

"Fine. Were you in your room all night, Mr. Davidson?"

"Not all night, no. I was up at the main building part of the time."

"Doing what?"

"Well, I . . ."

"Yes, Mr. Davidson, what were you doing?"

"I . . . I was fencing. Look, I didn't have anything to do with this."

"You were *what*, Mr. Davidson?"

"Fencing. We've got some foils and masks up there, and I . . . I was just fooling around. Look, I *know* Helga was stabbed, but . . ."

"What time did you get back here, Mr. Davidson?"

"About . . . about ten-thirty, eleven."

"And you've been in your room since then?"

"Yes."

"What did you do when you got back here?"

"I wrote a letter to my wife, and then I went to sleep."

"What time did you go to sleep?"

"About midnight."

"Did you hear any loud noise in the hall?"

"No."

"Did you hear any voices?"

"No."

"Did you hear Miss Colby when she screamed?"

"No."

"Why not?"

"I guess I was asleep."

"You sleep in your clothes, Mr. Davidson?"

"What? Oh. Oh, no. Your fellow . . . your deputy said I could put on some clothes."

"What *were* you sleeping in?"

"My pajamas. Listen, I barely knew those girls. I only joined the school here two weeks ago. I mean, I knew them to talk to, but that's all. And the fencing is just a coincidence. I mean, we always fool around with the foils. I mean, ever since I came here, somebody's been up there fooling around with . . ."

"How many times did you scream, Miss Colby?" Watt asked.

"I don't remember," Blanche said.

"She screamed twice," Hawes said.

"Where were you when you heard the screams, Hawes?"

"Downstairs. In the ski shop."

"But you were in your room, right down the hall, Mr. Davidson,

265

and you didn't hear anything, hmmm? Maybe you were too busy . . ."

And suddenly Davidson began crying. His face twisted into a grimace, and the tears began flowing, and he said, "I didn't have anything to do with this, I swear. Please, I didn't have anything to do with it. Please, I'm married, my wife's in the city expecting a baby, I *need* this job, I didn't even *look* at those girls, I swear to God, what do you want me to do? Please, please."

The room was silent except for his sobbing.

"I swear to God," he said softly. "I swear to God. I'm a heavy sleeper. I'm very tired at night. I swear. Please. I didn't do it. I only knew them to say hello. I didn't hear anything. Please. Believe me. Please. I *have* to keep this job. It's the only thing I know, skiing. I can't get involved in this. Please."

He lowered his head, trying to hide the tears that streamed down his face, his shoulders heaving, the deep sobs starting deep inside him and reverberating through his entire body.

"Please," he said.

For the first time since the whole thing had started, Watt turned to Hawes and asked his advice.

"What do you think?" he said.

"I'm a heavy sleeper, too," Hawes said. "You could blow up the building, and I wouldn't hear it."

13.

On Sunday morning, the church bells rang out over the valley.

They started in the town of Rawson, and they rang sharp and clear on the mountain air, drifting over the snow and down the valley. He went to the window and pulled up the shade, and listened to the sound of the bells, and remembered his own youth and the Reverend Jeremiah Hawes who had been his father, and the sound of Sunday church bells, and the rolling, sonorous voice of his father delivering the sermon. There had always been logic in his father's sermons. Hawes had not come away from his childhood background with any abiding religious fervor—but he had come away with a great respect for logic. "To be believed," his father had told him, "it must be reasonable. And to be reasonable, it must be logical. You could do worse than remembering that, Cotton."

There did not seem to be much logic in the killing of Helga Nilson and Maria Fiers, unless there was logic in wanton brutality. He tried to piece together the facts as he looked out over the peaceful valley and listened to the steady tolling of the bells. Behind him, Blanche was curled in sleep, gently breathing, her arms wrapped around the pillow. He did not want to wake her yet, not after what she'd been through last night. So far as he was concerned, the weekend was over; he could not ski with pleasure anymore, not this weekend. He wanted nothing more than to get away from Rawson Mountain, no, that wasn't quite true. He wanted to find the killer. That was what he wanted more than anything else. Not because he was being paid for the job, not because he wanted to prove to Theodore Watt that maybe big-city detectives *did* have a little something on the ball—but only because the double murders filled him with a sense of outrage. He could still remember the animal strength of the man who'd attacked him on the mountain, and the thought of that power directed against two helpless young girls angered Hawes beyond all reason.

Why? he asked himself.

Where is the logic?

There was none. No logic in the choice of the victims, and no logic in the choice of the scene. Why would anyone have chosen to kill Helga in broad daylight, on a chair suspended anywhere from six to thirty feet above the ground, using a ski pole as a weapon? A ski pole sharpened to a deadly point, Hawes reminded himself, don't forget that. This thing didn't just happen, this was no spur-of-the-moment impulse, this was planned and premeditated, a pure and simple Murder One. Somebody had been in that ski shop the night before the first murder, using a file and then a grinding wheel, sharpening that damn pole, making certain its end could penetrate a heavy ski parka, *and* a ski sweater, *and* a heart.

Then there must have been logic to the choice of locale, Hawes thought. Whoever killed Helga had at least planned far enough ahead to have prepared a weapon the night before. And admitting the existence of a plan, then logic could be presupposed, and it could further be assumed that killing her on the chair lift was a *part* of the plan—perhaps a very necessary part of it.

Yes, that's logic, he thought—*except that it's illogical.*

Behind him, Blanche stirred. He turned to look at her briefly, remembering the horror on her face last night, contrasting it now with her features relaxed in sleep. She had told the story to Watt three times, had told him again and again how she'd found the dead girl.

Maria Fiers, twenty-one years old, brunette, a native of Montpelier, Vermont. She had begun skiing when she was six years old, had won the woman's slalom four times running, had been an instructor since she was seventeen. She skated, too, and had been on her high school swimming team, an all-around athlete, a nice girl with a gentle manner and a pleasant smile—dead.

Why?

She lived in the room next door to Helga's, had known Helga for close to a year. She had been nowhere near the chair lift on the day Helga was killed. In fact, she had been teaching a beginner's class near the T-Bar, a good distance from the chair lift. She could not have seen Helga's murder, nor Helga's murderer.

But someone had killed her nonetheless.

And if there were a plan, and if there were supposed logic to the plan, and if killing Helga on a chair halfway up the mountain was part of that logic, then the death of Maria Fiers was also a part of it.

But how?

The hell with it, Hawes thought. I can't think straight anymore. I want to crack this so badly that I can't think straight, and that makes me worse than useless. So the thing to do is to get out of here, wake Blanche and tell her to dress and pack, and then pay my bill and get out, back to the city, back to the 87th where death comes more frequently perhaps, and just as brutally—but not as a surprise. I'll leave this to Theodore Watt, the sheriff who wants to make his own mistakes. I'll leave it to him and his nimble-fingered deputies, and maybe they'll bust it wide open, or maybe they won't, but it's too much for me, I can't think straight anymore.

He went to the bed and woke Blanche, and then he walked over to the main building, anxious to pay his bill and get on his way. Someone was at the piano, practicing scales. Hawes walked past the piano and the fireplace and around the corner to Wollender's office. He knocked on the door, and waited. There was a slight hesitation on the other side of the door, and then Wollender said, "Yes, come in," and Hawes turned the knob.

Everything looked exactly the way it had looked when Hawes

checked in on Friday night, an eternity ago. Wollender was sitting behind his desk, a man in his late twenties with dark hair and dark brows pulled low over deep brown eyes. He was wearing a white shirt open at the throat, a bold reindeer-imprinted sweater over it. The plaster cast was still on his right leg, the leg stretched out stiffly in front of him, the foot resting on a low ottoman. Everything looked exactly the same.

"I want to pay my bill," Hawes said. "We're checking out."

He stood just inside the door, some fifteen feet from the desk. Wollender's crutches leaned against the wall near the door. There was a smile on Wollender's face as he said, "Certainly," and then opened the bottom drawer of the desk and took out his register and carefully made out a bill. Hawes walked to the desk, added the bill, and then wrote a check. As he waved it in the air to dry the ink, he said, "What *were* you doing in my room yesterday, Mr. Wollender?"

"Checking the heat," Wollender said.

Hawes nodded. "Here's your check. Will you mark this bill 'Paid,' please?"

"Be happy to," Wollender said. He stamped the bill and handed it back to Hawes. For a moment, Hawes had the oddest feeling that something was wrong. The knowledge pushed itself into his mind in the form of an absurd caption: WHAT'S WRONG WITH THIS PICTURE? He looked at Wollender, at his hair, and his eyes, and his white shirt, and his reindeer sweater, and his extended leg, and the cast on it, and the ottoman. Something was different. This was not the room, not the picture as it had been on Friday night. WHAT'S WRONG WITH THIS PICTURE? he thought, and he did not know.

He took the bill. "Thanks," he said. "Have you heard any news about the roads?"

"They're open all the way to the Thruway. You shouldn't have any trouble."

"Thanks," Hawes said. He hesitated, staring at Wollender. "My room's right over the ski shop, you know," he said.

"Yes, I know that."

"Do you have a key to the shop, Mr. Wollender?"

Wollender shook his head. "No. The shop is privately owned. It doesn't belong to the hotel. I believe the proprietor allows the ski instructors to . . ."

"But then, you're a locksmith, aren't you?"

269

"What?"

"Isn't that what you told me when I checked in? You said you were a locksmith out of season, didn't you?"

"Oh. Oh, yes. Yes, I did." Wollender shifted uneasily in the chair, trying to make his leg comfortable. Hawes looked at the leg again, and then he thought, Damn it, what's wrong?

"Maybe you went to my room to listen, Mr. Wollender. Is that possible?"

"Listen to what?"

"To the sounds coming from the ski shop below," Hawes said.

"Are the sounds that interesting?"

"In the middle of the night, they are. You can hear all sorts of things in the middle of the night. I'm just beginning to remember all the things I heard."

"Oh? What did you hear?"

"I heard the oil burner clicking, and the toilet flushing, and the Cats going up the mountain, and someone arguing down the hall, and somebody filing and grinding in the ski shop." He was speaking to Wollender, but not really speaking to him. He was, instead, remembering those midnight voices raised in anger, and remembering that it was only later he had heard the noises in the shop, and gone to the window, and seen the light burning below. And then a curious thing happened. Instead of calling him "Mr. Wollender," he suddenly called him "Elmer."

"Elmer," he said, "something's just occurred to me."

Elmer. And with the word, something new came into the room. With the word, he was suddenly transported back to the interrogation room at the 87th, where common thieves and criminals were called by their first names, Charlie, and Harry, and Martin, and Joe, and where this familiarity somehow put them on the defensive, somehow rattled them and made them know their questioners weren't playing games.

"Elmer," he said, leaning over the desk, "it's just occurred to me that since Maria couldn't have *seen* anything on the mountain, maybe she was killed because she *heard* something. And maybe what she heard was the same arguing I heard. Only *her* room is right next door to Helga's. And maybe she knew *who* was arguing." He hesitated. "That's pretty logical, don't you think, Elmer?"

"I suppose so," Wollender said pleasantly. "But if you know who killed Maria, why don't you go to . . ."

"I don't know, Elmer. Do *you* know?"

"I'm sorry. I don't."

"Yeah, neither do I, Elmer. All I have is a feeling."

"And what's the feeling?" Wollender asked.

"That you came to my room to listen, Elmer. To find out how much *I* had heard the night before Helga was murdered. And maybe you decided I heard too damn much, and maybe that's why I was attacked on the mountain yesterday."

"Please, Mr. Hawes," Wollender said, and a faint superior smile touched his mouth, and his hand opened limply to indicate the leg in the cast.

"Sure, sure," Hawes said. "How could I have been attacked by a man with his leg in a cast, a man who can't get around without crutches? Sure, Elmer. Don't think that hasn't been bugg—" He stopped dead. "Your crutches," he said.

"What?"

"Your crutches! Where the hell are they?"

For just an instant, the color went out of Wollender's face. Then, quite calmly, he said, "Right over there. Behind you."

Hawes turned and looked at the crutches, leaning against the wall near the door.

"Fifteen feet from your desk," he said. "I thought you couldn't walk without them."

"I . . . I used the furniture to . . . to get to the desk, I . . ."

"You're lying, Elmer," Hawes said, and he reached across the desk and pulled Wollender out of the chair.

"My leg!" Wollender shouted.

"Your leg, my ass! How long have you been walking on it, Elmer? Was that why you killed her on the mountain? So that . . ."

"I didn't kill anybody!"

". . . so that you'd have a perfect alibi? A man with his leg in a cast couldn't possibly ride a lift or jump from it, could he? Unless he'd been in and out of that cast for God knows how long!"

"My leg is broken! I can't walk!"

"Can you *kill*, Elmer?"

"I didn't kill her!"

"Did Maria hear you arguing, Elmer?"

"No. No . . ."

"Then why'd you go after her?"

"I didn't!" He tried to pull away from Hawes. "You're crazy. You're hurting my leg! Let go of . . ."

"*I'm* crazy? You son of a bitch, *I'm* crazy? You stuck a ski pole in one girl and twisted a towel around . . ."

"I didn't, I didn't!"

"We found the basket from your pole!" Hawes shouted.

"What basket? I don't know what . . ."

"Your fingerprints are all over it!" he lied.

"You're crazy," Wollender said. "How could I get on the lift? I can't walk. I broke the leg in two places. One of the bones came right through the skin. I couldn't get on a lift if I wanted . . ."

"The skin," Hawes said.

"What?"

"The skin!" There was a wild look in his eyes now. He pulled Wollender closer to him and yelled, "Where'd she scratch you?"

"What?"

He seized the front of Wollender's shirt with both hands, and then ripped it open. "Where's the cut, Elmer? On your chest? On your neck?"

Wollender struggled to get away from him, but Hawes had his head captured in both huge hands now. He twisted Wollender's face viciously, forced his head forward, pulled back the shirt collar.

"Let go of me!" Wollender screamed.

"What's this, Elmer?" His fingers grasped the adhesive bandage on the back of Wollender's neck. Angrily, he tore it loose. A healing cut, two inches long and smeared with iodine, ran diagonally from a spot just below Wollender's hairline.

"I did that myself," Wollender said. "I bumped into . . ."

"Helga did it," Hawes said. "When you stabbed her! The sheriff's got the skin, Elmer. It was under her fingernails."

"No," Wollender said. He shook his head.

The room was suddenly very still. Both men were exhausted. Hawes kept clinging to the front of Wollender's shirt, breathing hard, waiting. Wollender kept shaking his head.

"You want to tell me?"

Wollender shook his head.

"How long have you been walking?"

Wollender shook his head again.

"Why'd you keep your leg in the cast?"

Again, Wollender shook his head.

"You killed two young girls!" Hawes bellowed. He was surprised to find himself trembling. His hand tightened on the shirt front, the knuckles showing white through his skin. Perhaps Wollender felt the sudden tension, perhaps Wollender knew that in the next instant Hawes would throttle him.

"All right," he said. His voice was very low. "All right."

"Why'd you keep wearing the cast?"

"So . . . so . . . so she wouldn't know. So she would think I . . . I was . . . was unable to walk. And that way, I could . . . could watch her. Without her knowing."

"Watch who?"

"Helga. She . . . She was my girl, you see. I . . . I loved her, you see."

"Yeah, you loved her enough to kill her," Hawes said.

"That's *not* why I . . . " He shook his head. "It was because of Kurtz. She kept denying it, but I knew about them. And I warned her. You have to believe that I warned her. And I . . . I kept the cast on my leg to . . . to fool her."

"When did it come off?" Hawes asked.

"Last week. The . . . the doctor took it off right in this room. He did a bivalve, with an electric saw, cut it right down the side. And . . . and when he was gone, I . . . I figured I could put the two halves together again, and . . . and . . . hold it in place with . . . with tape. That way, I could watch her. Without her knowing I could get around."

"And what did you see?"

"You *know* what I saw!"

"Tell me."

"Friday night, she . . . I . . . I saw Kurtz leaving the annex. I knew he'd been with her."

"He was there to pick up Maria's skates," Hawes said. "To sharpen them."

"No!" Wollender shouted, and for a moment there was force in his voice, a vocal explosion, fury and power, and Hawes remembered again the brute strength of Wollender's attack on the mountain. Wollender's voice died again. "No," he said softly, "you're mistaken. He was with Helga. I know. Do you think I'd have killed her if . . . " His voice caught. His eyes suddenly misted. He turned his head, not looking at

273

Hawes, staring across the room, the tears solidifying his eyes. "When I went up to her room, I warned her," he said, his voice low. "I told her I had seen him, seen him with my own eyes, and she . . . she said I was imagining things. And she laughed." His face went suddenly tight. "She laughed, you see. She . . . she shouldn't have laughed." His eyes filled with tears, had a curiously opaque look. "She shouldn't have laughed," he said again. "It wasn't funny. I loved her. It wasn't funny."

"No," Hawes said wearily. "It wasn't funny at all."

14.

The storm was over.

The storm, which had started suddenly and filled the air with fury, was gone. The wind had died after scattering the clouds from the sky. They drove in the warm comfort of the convertible, the sky a clear blue ahead of them, the snow banked on either side of the road.

The storm was over.

There were only the remains of its fury now, the hard-packed snow beneath the automobile, and the snow lining the roads, and the snow hanging in the branches of the trees. But now it was over and done, and now there was only the damage to count, and the repairs to be made.

He sat silently behind the wheel of the car, a big redheaded man who drove effortlessly. His anger was gone, too, like the anger of the storm. There was only a vast sadness inside him.

"Cotton?" Blanche said.

"Mmmm?" He did not take his eyes from the road. He watched the winding white ribbon and listened to the crunch of snow beneath his heavy-duty tires, and over that the sound of her voice.

"Cotton," she said, "I'm very glad to be with you."

"I am, too."

"In spite of everything," she said, "I'm very very glad."

He did a curious thing then. He suddenly took his right hand from the wheel and put it on her thigh, and squeezed her gently. He thought he did it because Blanche was a very attractive girl with whom he had just shared a moment of communication.

But perhaps he touched her because death had suddenly shouldered its way into that automobile, and he had remembered again the two young girls who had been Wollender's victims.

Perhaps he touched her thigh, soft and warm, only as a reaffirmation of life.

About the Editors

MARTIN GREENBERG has compiled over two hundred anthologies, including nine in Fawcett's Best of the West series. He is a noted scholar and teaches at the University of Wisconsin in Green Bay.

BILL PRONZINI, in addition to collaborating with Martin Greenberg on several anthologies, is an award-winning mystery writer, the author of many novels and short stories. He lives in Sonoma, California.